THE WOMEN OF STORMLAND

Books by Lois Santalo

The Wind Dies at Sunrise
Oops, I Lost My Sense of Humor
The House of Music
The Women of Stormland

THE WOMEN OF STORMLAND

by Lois Wells Santalo

iUniverse, Inc.
New York Lincoln Shanghai

The Women of Stormland

iUniverse, Inc.

For information address:
iUniverse, Inc.
2021 Pine Lake Road, Suite 100
Lincoln, NE 68512
www.iuniverse.com

ISBN: 0-595-31735-9 (pbk)
ISBN: 0-595-66402-4 (cloth)

Printed in the United States of America

To Jamie, Heather and Jennifer

Acknowledgements

My thanks, as always, to the members of the Thursday Group, Marlie Moses, Izetta Segal, Howard Fisher, Ellie Fellers, and my ever-helpful writing buddy and inspirer, Evelyn Dahms. Thanks, too, to the Tuesday Group, Bob Moore, Mary Blue, Ellen Perkins, Virginia Natwick, Eleanor Simmonds, Dale and Suzanne Gega. All of their comments and critiques helped to make this a better book.

A special thanks to Nina Williamson for her help with proof-reading, and to my son-in-law, Hezkiah Thompson, for supplying information about the black experience without which this book could not have been written.

CHAPTER 1

2002
Ashley

Okay, so here I am, sitting in the Grand Rapids airport awaiting my third cousin twice removed whom I've never met, and holding before my eyes a magazine I'm not reading. Don't ask me why I'm here; I hardly know, myself. I just wish I were elsewhere.

My name is Ashley Pennington. I feel silly when I say that. Ashley Pennington—it sounds hoity toity, a name belonging to a white chick, a *southern* white chick whose daddy owns a mansion with white columns overlooking the Mississippi. I'm not in that category. Even in the spring, like now, when my face is lighter, it's never light enough for me to pass as white. By late summer my hair, which ironically is soft and brown, no kinks, is lighter than my face. And though Dad's a Naval officer, he doesn't own a mansion with pillars. He owns a suburban California house where we've had garbage put in our mailbox to tell us we're not welcome.

In short, I'm a half-and-half person, with a white mom and a black dad. I never know where I belong, except that for sure it's not in a southern mansion. In high school I sometimes got good grades and then cringed because the other black kids gave me dirty looks. Later I opted for bad grades even though I felt embarrassed when the white kids stopped wanting to associate with me.

Worrying that I won't know my cousin when I see him, I eyeball the people walking around the waiting area. Mom had no recent pictures. But no doubt Doug will know me. I'm unique, ha ha.

I *hate* having to go stay with Whitey. White people aren't *friends* with black people, not normal friends. They're polite, they don't fight with you. They take you up as a cause, rally round, make you feel popular, then drop you—or you drop them, from sheer boredom over an unreal relationship which never develops further.

In college, I've had no end of trouble because of those bad high school grades. The counselors claim I don't know the stuff. I'm forced to take courses that bore me silly. I keep wanting to say: I *do* know this, you idiot; I just can't show that I know it. I'd lose my friends. You haven't a clue what it's like in the black culture at my school. Anti-academics is obligatory; cuss-words are the norm.

White people are so two-dimensional. They don't understand the subterfuges of black survival, how we have to conform if we want to have friends. And despite my white mother, I'm considered black. By whites, anyway. Unfortunately, the blacks aren't so ready to accept me as one of them. I'm caught between two cultures, fitting nowhere. I guess that's called falling between the cracks.

Right now, in the Kent County airport where I'm waiting to be picked up, it's three-thirty in the afternoon. I left California at eight in the morning and had a four hour flight, so it should now be noon. I'm not yet hungry for lunch and it'll soon be local dinner time.

Yesterday I made some decisions. I told my boring boyfriend, Jonah, I'm not seeing him any more, and told my parents I'm dropping out of school now that I've finished two years of community college. There were explosions, Jonah protesting, Dad scolding, Mother preaching how I'd never make anything of myself without a degree, how I'd still be working at Taco Bell when I'm fifty. I let the noise wash over me. I know what to do. I have to find a way to get noticed by the man I'm *really* attracted to, a super football hero named Kevin who looks like Denzel Washington, whom I'd die for. Also, I have to explore my roots. I have to find out who Ashley Pennington is. If I'm to go on using that name, it has to mean something.

Dad said, "I don't understand why you kids these days all have to *find* yourselves. I never lost myself, not for a minute." I told him he should try being bi-racial for a while. He'd lose himself real quick.

Mom said, "If you're going to explore your roots, start with the white ones. Your Pennington grandmother lived with us; you've already heard about the black side of the family."

When I said roots, I really meant black roots, I really meant the Penningtons of the snooty name. But mom offered to finance my trip, so what could I do? I had little money and planned to hitchhike, but when she fussed about that, I let her put me on the plane. That's how I landed in Grand Rapids awaiting my third cousin, Doug Langston.

I know what will happen when he sees my face. He'll cringe, like all my white relatives do. They try to hide it, they cover up quickly—but it's there. Especially this guy will cringe, because he's *Douglas* Langston, heir to the august name of our pioneer forebear who first settled here in Michigan. There've been Doug Langstons in almost every generation since—. Oh shit, here he comes! I'd know that puss anywhere. Except for the Van Dyke beard, he's the spit and image of great-great-gramps in family photographs: handsome, with long, narrow face, wavy brown hair, seductive smile. Dark blue business suit and blue-specked tie. Taller than me, and concealing his cringe well. Hand out, the usual garbage. Pretense, of course. He's been told to meet me, it's something he has to do, so he decided to bite the bullet and do it with style. After all, my mom, Becky Pennington, still has some clout in the family, even though she married a black dude. I mean, she's the granddaughter of Millicent the Musician who grew up at Stormland; we have to be nice to her child.

Okay, Doug puts on a great act, I'll give him that. He pretends to be all warmth and welcome. He first shakes my hand, then pulls me to him and hugs me. He says, "I always hoped to meet you." I want to say, who are you kidding? Since this guy is a third cousin twice removed, in other words third cousin to my grandmother, I'm betting he never even heard of me before this morning when his mom told him to go to the airport and meet Becky Pennington's daughter.

Oh, perhaps at some point someone mentioned to him that Cousin Becky married a black man; that sort of thing does get mentioned in families; but he probably failed to ask if there were children.

Still, like I said, he puts on a good act. I suppose his mom will, too. She'll pretend like all she ever wanted in this world was to have a black relative come to visit.

He shows off about fifty teeth in a fine imitation of a smile. He touches my elbow as I stand up. He asks about my trip. I tell him, "Plane travel isn't a trip—it's transport. You sit in a waiting room in the sky, and after a while you're there. No seeing the country, no meeting the people."

He says he guesses that's true. He hadn't thought about it that way.

We get my luggage and go out to his car. He drives a Renault, of all things. Not cool. I hate to be seen in it. Thank God nobody in Michigan knows me.

When we hit the road, he asks, "So, how's your mother?"

Talk about scintillating conversation! Come on, Whitey, you can do better than that. I suppress a yawn as I answer that she's fine. How could Mom be anything but fine? She comes of this sturdy Langston stock, at least on one side. The other side's Hispanic, or rather, Catalan. In case you didn't know, Catalans, though they live in and around Barcelona, claim they're not Spanish.

Our family sure is into mixing blood lines. I'm one quarter Scottish and Swiss, one quarter Catalan, two quarters black. And I don't like the mixture. Believe me, it's not what I'd have chosen.

"I hear you're in college," Doug says.

"Yeah, that's so." I'm not about to tell him I'm dropping out. It's none of his business. He asks what I'm majoring in. I don't know, that's part of my problem. I invent. "Psychology." What the hell. Who cares what I say to a third cousin twice removed? I don't, and I doubt he does.

He tells me he graduated a year ago from a local university. When I make no comment, he changes the subject. He says, "You've never seen Stormland, have you?"

I shake my head no. "Tell me it's not a white southern mansion with pillars!"

He chuckles. "I wish!"

Well, I don't wish. That's the last thing I want.

"But it's an interesting old house," he says. "It's been the family home for more than a hundred years. Langstons have lived there since it was built."

So tilt your nose higher, Cousin Doug. You can get away with it. I can't. People would laugh if I went around with my nose in the air talking of my old family mansion. I'd be the comedian of my generation.

I say, "Holy cats." It's the only term I can think of that won't shock anyone. Why do I have to be related to these people anyway? What was my dad thinking when he married a white chick?

Oprah Winfrey claims she has no white blood in her family. Lucky Oprah.

He pulls up in front of the family mansion. It's fairly large, white clapboard, a Michigan farmhouse type with upright and wing, the wing stretching off toward the back.

"Stormland," he announces, parking at the curb and gesturing.

So now I've got to go meet Cousin What's-her-name. Bertha? Rhoda? I'm sure Mom told me.

There's a flight of steps up an embankment. As we climb, he carrying my big bag, I the small one, I confess my ignorance. "My mom mentioned your mother's name but I forgot."

"It's Laura," he says.

Mom ordered me to be polite. Otherwise she'll cut off funds and I'll have to go home. So I'll show off as many teeth as Doug did, plaster a grin onto my face and say, "So nice to meet you, Cousin Laura." I memorize my script as I cross the lawn and climb the steps to the house. After all, this beats working at Taco Bell.

I admit Cousin Doug is gallant; he holds my elbow as we cross the porch and opens the door with a sweeping gesture. "Welcome to the Langston homestead, Cousin Ashley." I feel I'm supposed to curtsey or something.

Mother calls me a drama queen, and it may be so, but I can't think up the right drama for this occasion. Before I figure it out, a slim, blonde woman rushes toward me, all smiles, arms out for an embrace. Talk about putting on an act! She must have read a book on How to be Nice to Black Relatives.

She hugs me. "Welcome to Stormland, Ashley."

Welcome to Stormland, Ashley. If you'd been born white, you'd have been the Princess Di of the Langston family. Too bad Cousin Becky went off the rails like that. Now we must make do with what we have.

Like her son, Laura is toothy. The lower half of her face is all teeth when she grins. God, this stuff seems so phony. There's a word in Spanish—*la basura*—it means trash. My grandmother's Mexican gardener uses it all the time. Well, that's what this is. *Mucho basura.* They should bag it up and carry it out before it gets smelly.

"This is the first time in many years that anyone from your branch of the family has come to Stormland," she says. "We're so glad you could make it."

"I'll take your luggage upstairs," Doug says. "Mother's giving you the front room, the one that used to be your great-grandmother's."

I hold my smile in place while offering a thank-you. Behave yourself, Ashley. After all, these folks have to be able to assure their friends they were good to their black cousin; it'll make a great story to tell at parties. "The day my black relative came from California." I should have written a theme on it for freshman English class.

I follow my planned script. "So nice to meet you, Cousin Laura."

To me the family mansion looks just like any old house. A living room, a huge dining room, evidence of a kitchen beyond. No great sweeping stairway for me to descend when I come down to meals, just a plain flight of steps. I can't make a dramatic entrance on those.

After we've done the polite-conversation bit, with the usual How was your trip; How are your mother and grandmother, Doug picks up my bag and leads the way upward. I tramp behind him and he shows me to the front bedroom. It's just a room, with bed, dresser and desk, but you'd think it was something special the way he says, "This was Millie's room. This is where she used to practice her music. You knew, of course, that she was one of the first Michigan women ever to play in an orchestra?"

"Yeah, I heard about it." Banjo and guitar. Big deal. I can name ten people who play the guitar, including my own sister. My stupid big sister Marla who hasn't yet discovered that she has a black face. What on earth, I wonder, does she see when she looks in the mirror?

"I hope you'll be comfortable here," Doug says. "The bathroom's at the end of the hall. I'll leave you to unpack. Dinner's around six, and Mother's making a roast in your honor."

"I can smell it." It's obvious these are meat-and-potatoes people. The odor of roast beef goes all through the house. In California, we're taco-and-burrito people, at least when Mom cooks. When Gran cooks, it's paella and flan. When Dad cooks, we have soul food. We're a melting pot all by ourselves.

"You're Irish, aren't you?" I look at Doug, with his blondish-brown hair falling into his eyes like a kid's, and wish he weren't so handsome. It complicates matters. I'm true to Kevin/Denzel, now and forever.

"Scottish, like all the Langstons," he says. "Our attic is full of boxes of letters and diaries of those old-time folks. There were three sisters, Vi, Millie, and Bea—and the sister-in-law, Alana. You'll have your work cut out for you if you research all that."

Research. A crashing bore. I squelch a sigh and carry on. Like I said, it beats working at Taco Bell. At least I don't have to be up for it at seven in the morning.

"We cleared out the closet as best we could," Doug says. "I hope you'll have enough space for your clothes."

I ask where his room is. He confesses he doesn't live here. "My parents took over this house when Grandpa went into a rest home, and I mind their place for them until they get it ready to sell. It's two blocks up the street." He looks around uncertainly. "I'll leave you to unpack. If you want coffee or something before dinner, come on down."

He goes. I hear him clomping down the uncarpeted stairs. I close the door and sit on the bed, a high one covered with a hand-quilted comforter. Great-grandmother Millie's bed, I suppose. I look out at a road, cars, a street light, and more houses across the way.

So here I am, at Stormland, that fabled place Gran always talked about. I'm not the little sister anymore, I'm me, an individual. A descendant, whatever that is.

I guess I'll find out in the days to come. Tomorrow I start digging around in the attic.

At dinner that night I meet the daddy, illogically called Junior, home from the family construction firm where he and my greeter, Douglas Andrew, both work. The firm, they tell me, was founded by Douglas Andrew's great-grandfather, Menno, the only male of the line who wasn't named Doug.

This is all so complicated. I wonder if I'll ever get it all straight. I'm sure I'm looking very stupid and confused as Laura gives me a capsule history of the family. Seems our forebear who came to Grand Rapids in 1902 and built this house was Douglas Langston, the same Douglas I've seen family photos of. His wife was Rebecca. They had six kids of whom Doug's forebear, Menno, was one, and my great-grandmother Millie was another. Millie helped her other brother, Rob, found an orchestra. Menno and a third brother founded the construction firm. All industrious people that I'm supposed to be inspired by.

Douglas Andrew tells me he hopes to go back to college and do graduate work in architecture. The family construction firm, he says, needs a resident architect. He tosses me a meaningful glance as if he's trying to hint that we two could go to college together. I flick him an uneasy smile.

Don't bother coming on to me, Cousin Doug. I don't date white guys, even cute ones.

Junior sits at the head of our table looking less than patriarchal. He shed cement-spotted overalls but is now in jeans, not to mention having a shadow of a black beard. His wife, Laura, chats on about the original six children, explaining that my Millie was the middle daughter. "I guess you know about Millie's descendants, since you're one of them. Millie's older sister, Vi, had a granddaughter who now lives in Boston."

Great. Just what I need. A Boston cousin. I try not to sound facetious as I ask, "One of those old Beacon Hill families?"

Junior nods and informs me, "The first Douglas came from a Maine family who knew Emerson personally."

Emerson. Who the hell? Name's familiar.—Oh, yes, a writer. He wrote an essay on self-reliance that was crammed down our throats in English class. It strikes me as crazy, hearing this hard-hat man go on about his forebears knowing Emerson. I suppose they entertained the guy in some Victorian parlor all full of gewgaws and lace doilies.

Watch out, Beacon Hill, I'm coming. Soon you'll get to meet Cousin Ashley Pennington in person. I'll shove my nose in the air and put out my hand so tentatively that only my fingertips will touch yours. I should know how to do that, I'm to the Manor born.

"Weezy married a Jewish guy," Laura says.

Oh, shit. Maybe I should go back to working at Taco Bell after all. I don't understand this snob stuff. I always thought Jews were on the outside, like us blacks.

Junior carves more slices of roast and offers me a second helping. I pass my plate. Cousin Doug passes it back and lets his hand brush against mine. Feels kind of nice but I decide to frown.

He avoids my gaze and doesn't see the frown. I plan to make sure he notices it in days to come. I know from personal experience how white guys view black girls. They love us madly—but not for marriage or even a committed relationship.

We're just for bed and just for now.

Laura goes on about how everything started with Douglas and Rebecca, who came here with their six children around the turn of the last century from the Mennonite town of Fargo in Eastern Michigan. "Their teen-age son, Menno, got a girl in trouble and had to marry her."

Wow, this is beginning to sound juicy. Stained overalls, Jewish relatives, shotgun weddings—all mixed in with entertaining Ralph Waldo in a gewgaw parlor.

The socialites of the past—where are they now? How are the mighty fallen! Maybe I should listen up after all.

Okay, it all started with Rebecca, who moved into this house when it was new. I've got that clear, anyway. I'll begin with her letters.

CHAPTER 2

1901
Rebecca

Though her daughter, Vi, came home boasting of success at finding work, saying she'd landed a job at the big downtown store, Wurzburg's, Rebecca sensed that something was wrong. The news seemed good, yet the manner of telling was not joyful. Clearly the nineteen-year-old held something back. Anger seemed to explode out of her even as she stood talking. Rebecca studied her thoughtfully.

"The job sounds wonderful." Rebecca's voice revealed her bafflement. "A fabric store! You love to sew. I'd think you'd be happy." She'd been standing with her hand on the back of the sagging overstuffed chair which looked so out of place in the brand new parlor at Stormland. Now she moved across the room to coax a lock of hair back into her daughter's hairdo.

Vi drew her smooth young brow into a frown and began listing difficulties. "I'll need a white blouse and dark skirt right away. I start work tomorrow. I have the blouse, but no skirt."

Rebecca reminded her that her sister-in-law, Annie, had a black skirt. Actually all Annie's skirts were black; her oldest son's wife never wore colorful dresses. It seemed to be part of the woman's religion. "Perhaps she'll loan it until you can make yourself one."

"Annie's clothes are dowdy and quaint," Vi snapped. "Annie knows nothing about fashion."

Rebecca suspected that Vi's visit to the drygoods store had shown her that city folk made a big deal about clothing. They'd set her to longing for high-style apparel.

"I'll need to have your black dress, Mother," Vi decided. "I'll cut off the skirt and use a wide grosgrain ribbon for a belt. In exchange, I'll give you this outfit I'm wearing."

"Fine, if that's what you want." Rebecca bit her lip; she'd have agreed to anything to improve her daughter's mood. She was baffled by this seething anger over something that should have been cause for celebration.

Vi hastened, her footsteps thunderous on the stairs and in the upper hall, to her mother's closet, brought the dress down, and laid it out on the dining table. Grabbing the shears, she snipped ruthlessly, severing top from bottom. Rebecca peered out the window and wondered why her husband wasn't yet home from work. Must have stayed late at the shop repairing someone's clock, she supposed. She wished he'd hurry; dinner was ready and keeping hot on the franklin stove. The house smelled of the onions in the bean soup.

She turned back to watch her daughter try on the skirt, holding it up with both hands. Vi declared that, given a belt, it would work.

She sewed on the band with basting stitches. Rebecca picked up the bodice to see what use she might make of it. It was too short to serve as a blouse for herself, too wide to fit Vi's little sister, Millie, who was only five.

"It'd make a vest or over-blouse." Vi's tone softened somewhat. "They're showing those now in the Butterick patterns."

"Two blouses to be worn at the same time?" It seemed excessive. Rebecca shook her head and put the severed bodice aside. Settling down to work on the plaid school dress she was making for Millie, she tried to think how to draw her older daughter out and learn what was bothering her. To avoid coming straight out with the comment, *You blew in here like a windstorm,* she opted instead for the indirect approach. She mentioned that the soup was ready, that she'd already fed the younger children. That evoked a headshake which knocked Vi's lock of hair loose again. "Not hungry," Vi said.

Rebecca tried again. "I'd like to hear about that store. Wurzburg's is well known. How did you happen to apply in such a fancy place?"

"It was accidental," Vi confessed. "I got to talking with a salesgirl. She mentioned they were short-handed. When I told her I'd worked in a store back home, she took me to meet the manager."

Vi began to describe her new workplace, its opulence, its glass cases full of quality merchandise, the salesgirls who seemed so poised, so aloof. "I'll need to practice acting like that," she said.

As she talked, the cause of her anger finally slipped out. Frowning, she confessed, "Walking home, I encountered Pa leaving a saloon. He was with the O'Brian men—drunk, singing at the top of their lungs, weaving along the street. I pretended not to know them." She flung hands on hips. "Ma, I want to be taken seriously as a salesgirl. I don't need for Pa to be acting like a clown. What if he should wander into the store smelling of liquor, asking for me?"

Rebecca flung hand to chest and stared at her daughter. "So that's why he hasn't come home! I assumed he'd stayed to finish repairing a clock he's working on."

"No such luck." Vi's voice dripped disgust.

Rebecca had sought to conceal from the children their father's new-found tendency to drink to excess. Now she realized such things couldn't be kept secret. The youngsters would encounter him; they would see for themselves. "Why didn't you tell me right away? I should send your brother to fetch him home."

"Are you kidding? He won't come. I'm sure the three of them were off to another saloon."

Rebecca put her sewing aside and drummed her fingers nervously. "This can't go on. He's spending money without earning it."

"Mother, there's no point in upbraiding him the way you do. He only gets mad and storms off."

Driven by a forlorn hope that Douglas might yet show up, Rebecca got up and again peered out the window. She saw no pedestrians on the street. "We've got to do something," she said. "I can't imagine what got into him. He never acted this way back in Fargo."

"Oh, Mother, he always went to saloons."

"He didn't drink to excess."

Vi fumbled in the sewing basket for a thimble and slid it onto her finger. She reminded her mother that Pa had a foster-sister there who'd have been shocked—not to mention Aunt Ruth and Uncle Ephraim. He wouldn't have wanted them scorning him as he staggered and swaggered around Main Street. "In this town, he doesn't know anyone and doesn't give a hoot."

"Perhaps we need to find friends who'll care about him, folks he'll want to impress."

"Sure. But how?"

"In a church?"

"Church! When did Pa ever go to church?"

"He wouldn't go to the Mennonites. Maybe he'll go to his family's—uh—Unitarians. I'll try to talk him into it."

"Good luck." Vi frowned over her sewing.

The following Sunday, wearing Vi's blue dress made over, Rebecca dragged Douglas under protest to the Unitarian Church. Her excuse to him was that they needed to find a religious home for the children in the new city.

Leaving Vi in charge of the household, the couple walked the eight or ten blocks to downtown, Rebecca on Douglas' arm, feeling proud, as always, of her handsome, dapper, curly-haired man. She'd fallen in love with Douglas the first moment she'd seen him, when he'd come into their country schoolroom as the new boy and been seated next to her because they were both eight years old. Even then he'd been handsome—and smart, a good student, a great reader.

On stepping inside the church, Rebecca stood staring around in bafflement. The place was an auditorium, no altar, no crosses, windows of plain amber glass. That would have been all right—her own Mennonite church had been plain and she was used to it—but the people seemed formal and unfriendly. No one smiled at her. Feeling out of place, she asked the usher for a seat at the back. He obligingly guided the couple to the rear row.

No prayer opened the service, no Bible reading was offered. Gramophone music started things off, followed by a hymn. Then came a long sermon, really a lecture, in which the minister described the terrible sweatshops of the Eastern seaboard where women and children were forced to work long hours at low pay. He told shocking tales of how fires broke out and trapped people in the upper stories of the buildings. Victims died jumping from high windows, or stayed inside and died of smoke inhalation. Many were no more than eight years old.

"We must fight for child labor laws, better conditions, and shorter working days for women," he concluded. "This is the most pressing social issue of our time. We freed the slaves forty years ago but there's still slavery in this country, and when we buy ready-made garments, we support it."

Never having bought a ready-made garment, Rebecca could hardly beat her breast with *mia culpas*. She agreed with the minister that those conditions were deplorable. Still, she hadn't come to church to hear a lecture. Where was God? Prayer? Bible quotes? Where was the warmth of a caring community? She sensed that this man would expect her to help solve the sweatshop problem, not bring him a new problem to be dealt with. He wouldn't want to hear about Douglas and his drinking.

Though on the doorstep after the service, the minister, Rev. Palewood, took her hand and greeted her in friendly fashion, she knew she would never be able to confess to him about the saloons, the liquor, her fears for the future. His mind was on far more important problems.

On the way home, she questioned Douglas. "Those people dress simply; I like that about them. But where's the religion?"

"It's not like our church in Maine," Douglas said. "Back there we had an altar with candles and flowers. The minister quoted Emerson. Called him Mr. Emerson."

"And the Bible?"

"I remember hearing Bible stories as a child. Daniel in the lion's den, Jonah and the whale, Jesus and that guy he raised from the dead. Also we used to recite a litany, God is a spirit, and—and—"

"—and they that worship Him must worship Him in spirit and in truth," she finished for him. "I didn't hear that today."

"Becky, I was seven the last time I attended a Unitarian church. I don't remember much. Anyway, it won't do for you; there's no Sunday school." He gave her a sharp look; his moustache twitched. "You *did* say you wanted this for the children?"

Indeed she'd said it, and she regarded it as important, though her primary motive had been to remind Douglas of his long-ago home and religious background. A child of the orphan train, Douglas had been sent out from Maine at age seven to the next-door farm in her Mennonite community. He'd refused to attend church with his foster parents, insisting he wasn't of their faith. Her one great hope, on moving to Grand Rapids, had been that he might now find a church to his liking. Disappointed, she admitted she hadn't known Unitarian churches would be so different from one another. He explained, "I understand the congregation decides. Some want to hear about God, some don't."

"That's no kind of religion," she protested.

Walking on, they passed the Congregational church, and watched elegantly dressed people come out. A few climbed into cars parked along the curb and drove off. Douglas remarked, "Why not try the Congregationalists, Becky? I believe they have those things you're looking for, Sunday school, prayer, Bible quotes."

Rebecca shook her head. She knew she could never put foot in that place and compete with all that finery. Yet on second thought she wondered if perhaps it might be just the thing for Douglas, who'd always longed to be one of the swells. But—such an expensive-looking church, beautiful colored windows with pictures of Christ, a rose window as awesome as that of a European cathedral. Could they afford it?

She decided she'd try sending young Millie. She'd make the youngster a Sunday dress with neat stitches that would appear to have been done by a professional seamstress. Then, by urging Douglas to take the child to church, she would involve him, too, in a religious community. Perhaps she could at least slow his drinking.

Before she could implement her plan, she suffered a time of terror when her sixteen-year-old son, Menno, came down with the infamous smallpox. The house was quarantined with a large red sign on the door so no one would inadvertently enter, and the boy was put to bed with a high fever and ugly pustules. Rebecca followed the doctor around the house, wringing her hands, feeling helpless, asking what she might do.

To avoid becoming captive, the working folk, Vi and Douglas, stayed with the nearby relatives, Annie and Zeke, who also offered to care for baby Bea. Rebecca's other two children, Rob and Millie, in quarantine even though belatedly vaccinated so they would not be at risk, had to remain indoors. Twelve-year-old Rob, who'd had banjo lessons and showed promise as a musician, spent his time teaching his five-year-old sister, Millie, who, like him, seemed a natural in music and, when Douglas brought her a banjo, picked it up quickly. Rebecca would look at the two of them, heads bent over their instruments, and wonder if they might have been musicians in a former life. The learning seemed effortless for them. Within days, Millie was strumming away, accompanying herself as she sang, her small fingers stretching to reach for the strings.

Rebecca's back-yard chickens laid an abundance of eggs and, unable to go out to sell them, she gave Millie the leftovers, hard-boiled, to paint faces on and make skirts for. Millie soon had an entire village of egg-babies, each with its own round house which was really a crepe-paper-covered oatmeal carton, and a bed made from a match-box softened with scraps of cloth. With contributions of cartons from neighbors, the village took up the whole parlor. Rebecca didn't complain. The family wouldn't be entertaining visitors in that room. Not with that grim smallpox sign on the front door.

Arriving each day after work to bring groceries and feed the chickens, Douglas waved to Rebecca and the children from outside the window. Toward the end of August, the tomatoes and cucumbers began to ripen. Douglas placed them on the porch for Rebecca to collect after he departed. On watching out the window while he walked away, she felt relieved he didn't stagger. Perhaps the family's current need of him kept him from drinking to excess.

Most of the time Rebecca hovered over Menno, sponging his fevered face with a wet cloth to bring the temperature down, being careful to touch lightly lest she break the pustules and cause worse scarring than the usual pockmarks. She worried that the constant banjo-strumming might bother the boy, but he seemed too sick to notice. Rob worked hard at his music and boasted that someday he would have his own orchestra, with Millie as assistant to keep track of the music.

At last the nightmare ended. The sign on the door came down, the egg-babies and their village were put away, and Vi and Douglas were re-admitted to the house, Vi carrying her baby sister. The family was together once again.

Menno, now able to stand on shaky legs, didn't seem glad to be alive. In the mirror, he studied the great pits left over from the healed pustules and asserted that his life might better have ended with the fever.

"No girl will ever look at me again," he wailed. "This face will scare them off."

Rebecca didn't admit her dismay over the devastation of his once handsome features. She tried to keep a positive attitude. "The right sort of girls aren't looking for handsome but for a good man. A girl who judges you by your face isn't worth knowing."

"I never want to see any more girls—or have them see me."

She knew he had a specific girl in mind. Her name was Alana O'Brian and her father was a drinking buddy of Douglas' who often, in the days before Menno's illness, came to the house after work to share a pint. Alana, sent here to fetch her father home to dinner, always pretended not to notice Menno, but Rebecca had seen the two of them sneaking surreptitious peeks at one another. Finally Alana had found a way to start a conversation, and though shy, Menno had managed to come up with a response. They'd ended up on the front steps, talking.

Two days later Menno had announced he was taking Alana for a soda at the drugstore on Bridge Street. The following Saturday they'd gone to Reeds Lake together to ride the carousel and the Tunnel of Love. Rebecca knew she should put a stop to this. They were so young, Alana fifteen, Menno sixteen. Alana's blue eyes held a glint of mischief, and Rebecca felt uneasy when the girl tossed her long black hair around Menno in a saucy gesture.

So now, when Alana came to visit the convalescent, bringing a bouquet of flowers, Rebecca hesitated for a long moment before taking her upstairs. At this crucial moment when he was so sensitive about his pock-marks, she didn't want Menno to feel scorned, yet she wasn't comfortable bringing him this forward young girl who had no mother to look after her, only a big sister and a father who drank.

In bed, Menno pulled up the covers and refused to let Alana see him. She stood in the doorway and coaxed. "Don't be silly, my brothers have pock-marks, too. Lots of folks have had smallpox."

Finally, he flopped over and threw back the covers enough to reveal his face. He said in a hard voice, "Take a good look, then leave."

She didn't even blink. She shrugged her shoulders. "You look like Menno to me."

After that the visit seemed to go well. Rebecca allowed them fifteen minutes together, then, knowing that Menno was still weak, sent Alana home. The girl came again next day, and every day after that. Menno's eagerness to be with her clearly facilitated his recovery. He couldn't wait to be up and about, to go to Reeds Lake with her again while the good weather lasted.

Though apprehensive, Rebecca couldn't bring herself to forbid this. It was putting color in Menno's cheeks, a sparkle to his eyes. He returned to work but wanted to be with Alana every free moment. Rebecca finally made the decision to put her foot down and insist the couple be chaperoned.

She was too late. Two days before Thanksgiving, Alana announced that she was in the family way. There would have to be a wedding.

No longer would Menno be working to save up for his education. He'd now work to support a wife and child. He would never make it to high school, Rebecca's second son to lose out on the educational opportunities she'd hoped to provide for her children. He'd follow in the footsteps of Zeke who left home young and married Annie.

And she had to write all this bad news to her sister, who awaited word of their new life in Grand Rapids!

CHAPTER 3

2002
Ashley

Okay, so my white relatives didn't turn out to be hoity toity, as I'd supposed. At least this particular family didn't. I even feel kind of sorry for Great-Great-Grandmother Rebecca.

Unfortunately, my ordeal of meeting the gang isn't yet ended. There are other Michigan cousins who promised to come on the weekend, two days away. Laura is planning a big dinner for them.

Doesn't it ever occur to anyone that I might find it scary, being flung in among all these white relatives when I haven't a clue how they really feel about me beneath their social exterior? Mom claims I should forget I'm black. How can I forget it when the people I meet don't seem to?

In mid-afternoon of the second day, I sit on my bed and thumb through an ancient, crumbling book of snapshots. Here's the crowd I've been reading about, Vi sharing a page with a picture of a Gibson Girl, no doubt to show how much she looked like her; Millie as a little girl in a pinafore, hair in braids, squatting in the midst of her egg-babies with their carton-village. The whole thing had been set out on the lawn for the snapshot. Douglas on the lawn-swing looks dapper with a Van Dyke moustache and beard. Rebecca stands behind him in a hoover dress and a big coverall apron, her hair in a bun. She was the motherly type, the matriarch of the clan.

Rob, the musician, couldn't have been more than sixteen, yet had a page all to himself, with a professional photo showing him playing his guitar. I'd heard about Rob. When I was a kid, my great-grandmother, Millie, who then lived near us in California, talked of him often. At a young age, nineteen, he'd founded, with her help, an orchestra later moved to Hollywood. The family was proud of him.

I also knew about egg-babies. When she was an old lady, Millie made egg-babies for us kids at Easter, painting faces onto hard-boiled eggs, gluing on skirts which were really scraps of bright-colored cloth. We loved them—but just to look at. We didn't play with them as she did in her childhood. Hers had names and were real people to her.

I admit I came here wanting to dislike this branch of the family, to prove to myself they were not my kind. It would have been a justification. I'd hoped to go home and say, "Mother, *really*, you can't expect me to feel a connection to that crowd. If you wanted a daughter who felt close to the Langstons, you should have married a white dude."

So I have an attitude. So sue me.

Anyhow, it looks like I won't be able to carry out those plans to the letter. This family doesn't fit the stereotype. In fact, I haven't yet psyched them out; I don't know where they fit—or where I fit with them.

It's a mystery to me what either of my parents were thinking when they entered into the bond of union that created us half-and-half freaks, my brother Michael, my sister Marla, and me. Mike claims it doesn't bother him to be bi-racial, but of course he's lying. How can it not? When he had a car accident, and the cops came, instead of checking that he was okay, they checked the stupid registration to see if the car was stolen. Can you believe it? There he is, a teen-aged kid sitting on the ground stunned, maybe injured, holding his head, and they stand there hassling him. No asking, is he okay, does he need the paramedics? All they want to know is where he got the Toyota truck. His dad was a Naval officer, his grandfather a university professor, his great-grandfa-ther the chief airplane inspector at North Island Naval Airbase, but they want to know where he got the Toyota. Duh.

When my dad complained, they said he had an attitude. Well, he better have an attitude because that stuff is dead wrong. That was no way to treat a kid who's just been in an accident.

But it's the way life is when your skin is black—or even coffee-with-cream like mine and Mike's. We learn to expect it. When people (teachers especially) say, "Take that chip off your shoulder," I say, "Sure, just as soon as you paint your face black and try living like us for a while. See how you feel when cops and teachers are your enemy instead of your friend, when they take it for granted you did something illegal."

So I'm sitting here on the bed with this crumbling old album on my lap, remembering Great-Grandmother and her egg-babies, when I hear footsteps. Soon, in comes my third cousin twice removed, all corporate-executive in dark suit and tie, hair combed smooth. That frontal cowlick, when slicked down, makes a bump at the hairline, almost a curl.

I stare at him. "I thought you were supposed to be at work." I consult my watch. "It's not yet three o'clock."

"I had a dental appointment," he says. "No sense going back to work for a mere two hours."

I fear he plans to plunk himself down on the bed and look at albums with me, but he adds, "It's a beautiful day. I wondered if you'd like to take a drive. We could go to Reeds Lake."

I can't entirely conceal my cynicism as I ask, "The Tunnel of Love?"

"The Tunnel of Love isn't there any more," he says. "Neither is the rest of the amusement park. Too bad they didn't keep it; it would now be another Cedar Point."

"Yeah, too bad." From what I'd heard from Grandmother, it sounded like fun. She used to tell of going there as a kid; it was the thrill for her that Disney-land was for us. She says her earliest memories were of the merry-go-round with its calliope music and its little figurines clashing their cymbals, the cotton candy, the hoot of the fog-horn from the excursion boat as it moved away from the pier, banners flying, for its trip around the lake. I'd looked forward to all that.

"We could even go to Lake Michigan if you like," he adds.

I'm not at all sure I do like. I suspect his motives. But what can he pull in broad daylight? After all, it'll be good to escape this "research" for a while.

I close the album and stand up. "Why not?"

If my repartee sounds less than witty, you should know I'm under strict orders from my mom not to talk black. She claims the Langstons would be shocked by the language I use with my friends. She permits *frigging* but nothing stronger. I'm like, "They never heard the word *fucking*?" She's like, "They don't use it. It isn't done in their circles."

"Bring your swim suit," Doug says.

I fumble in my drawer for it and wrap it in a towel.

We go downstairs together. I decide to go as I am, in my jeans and t-shirt, which seem okay for the beach. Let this corporate executive worry about being over-dressed. And where's his swim suit? When I ask, he admits that he has to stop by his house to get it and change into his jeans.

So I'm relieved that he plans to get more human looking, right? Wrong. I start wondering what he has up his sleeve. I get on an anxiety trip when white guys say, "Let's go to my house." It sounds highly suspicious. And I walked right into it.

"Do you always dress so fancy to go to the dentist?" I ask him.

"No, this is how I dress for work," he says. "I'm the contact man, I shop for materials and deal with lumberyards and wholesalers. I'm supposed to look prosperous and official." He grins. "I uphold the firm's image."

Oh great. And now he has to be seen with his black cousin.

He calls out to his mother that we're heading for the beach and may return late. She calls back to suggest we take a picnic. She pokes her head in through the doorway from the kitchen and says, "I can make roast-beef sandwiches with last night's leftovers."

He looks at me, quirking an eyebrow. "Shall we?"

"Why not?" I say again. It'll spare us having another formal dinner here, complete with lists of forebears.

Laura says it'll only take her a few minutes to put together a picnic supper. I offer to help. Promising to pick me up in a few minutes, Doug takes off alone for his house to change. Relieved, I go to the kitchen. Laura plunks down bread and tells me to put on butter and mayonnaise. She sets these out, along with the saran-wrapped platter of last night's roast beef.

While she slices, I slather. She points to the fridge and says there's lettuce in the vegetable drawer. I bring it out, peel off and wash leaves. She asks how I'm coming with my research.

"Okay." I'm not about to tell her I found those letters from Rebecca. She might not like to hear that our ancestors behaved shockingly and were forced into shotgun weddings. And what about the original Douglas, our great ancestor, being a drunkard? Am I destined to poke pins into people's balloons, revealing grim truths around here? Normally, I love doing that sort of thing, but here I'm a guest and I don't exactly relish the idea of getting thrown out of the house. How would I explain to my mother that they said, "Go home, Ashley, we don't like you." Mom would demand, "Ashley, what did you *do?*" If I said, "I told the truth," she'd shake her head in disbelief.

So here I am, carrying around my dirty little secret while wondering if I can ever reveal it, and Cousin Laura says, "It's so nice to have a girl to work with me in the kitchen. I never had a daughter, and I miss that kind of closeness. Sons aren't the same."

Talk about pressing the old guilt buttons! *Now* what am I supposed to do with this garbage I gleaned? Maybe I'll have to become a reporter after all so I can write down all the stuff I can't say. Mom always wanted me to major in journalism but I couldn't see myself out there trying to trick people into revealing secrets they didn't choose to tell. I've watched reporters on news broadcasts and they struck me as cold and hard-hearted.

"I just had the two boys," Laura adds. "My older son, Scott, is an exchange student in Japan, studying for the ministry."

"That so?" I slap a chunk of lettuce onto the roast beef and press a second slice of bread on top of that. Laura comes behind me and neatly halves each sandwich. She tells me where to find the saran-wrap.

Doug soon returns, wearing jeans, and we take the sack supper and start off. Now I'm alone with the guy and the secret. So maybe I can tell *him*. He's young enough so his heart can stand a few shocks.

"The patriarch of the family was a lush," I say.

Without batting an eyelash, he admits that the cops used to bring the old guy home in the paddy wagon. "I believe his wife and older daughter nearly died of embarrassment every time it happened. They sent the kids, Rob and Millie, to find him before the cops did."

I had to award him A-plus for coolness. I'd thought I was dragging the skeleton from the closet. "So you knew about it?"

"Yes, we never discuss it, but—I'd heard it somewhere."

"In spite of that, everyone wanted to preserve the name Douglas?"

He shrugs. "The guy was basically a good person. Alcoholism's a disease." Doug turns onto the freeway. I wonder, do they call them freeways in Michigan? Or beltways, or what? He adds, "In the end, he managed to conquer his addiction and support his household—not, unfortunately, until the children were grown and had suffered through painful years of poverty and humiliation."

"You're very understanding of him," I say.

"Well, he had a hard life, poor old duffer. His father died in the Civil War, his mother married again, his stepfather didn't want him. That in itself had to be devastating for a young child. But things got worse. He was put on the orphan train and sent away to strangers, to a Mennonite farm. He came from an educated family yet had to go live with folks who viewed public education as a threat to their religion, people who generally took their children out of school after fourth grade. Somehow he persisted, and stayed in school long enough to become a small-town pharmacist."

Doug tosses me a brief smile, and when I say nothing, he goes on. "So he'd only just managed a little success, bought his own drugstore, when the railroad went out, the town literally folded up, and he had to move to Grand Rapids. Here, he wasn't able to carry on as a pharmacist because the city had higher educational qualifications for the field. He had to learn to be a watchmaker."

Wow. Why am I bothering to read old letters? This guy knows all the stuff already. I comment on the fact. "I see you've been delving in the attic."

"I didn't have to. As a child I heard stories from my grandpa." He glances at me and smiles. "See what you missed, not growing up in Michigan? You didn't get to learn about these people."

"I guess I had a deprived childhood." He doesn't know the half of it. I should describe my childhood—the time I told my mother how I dreamed I had a white face and long blonde curls, and got to stand on a stage and sing a song. In those days I actually *wanted* to be white, actually played with white children, those few who'd accept me. Worse, I used to tell my father not to come and pick me up, to let me walk home, so those girls wouldn't suspect I had a black dad. Can you believe it? I must have been out of my mind. As if they wouldn't know just by looking at me.

That was many betrayals ago, before I learned that the black person in the crowd is either the oddball or the token.

I confess to Doug that it was my mother's idea to send me out here, and that personally, I don't see that it matters any more, at this late date, what great-grandfather was like. Doug argues the point.

"I think it matters," he says. "I think the children developed an inferiority complex from being known as the offspring of an alcoholic—though they weren't called alcoholics back then—and that was passed down to their descendants. We've all had to cope with it. Of course they also developed a great fighting spirit and a determination to pull the family up by its boot-straps."

"You may be right." I speak dubiously; I certainly never thought of my great grandmother as having an inferiority complex. Quite the opposite.

"Not to worry, I can straighten you out on family lore." Doug tosses me another grin. He's kind of cute now that his hair is working out of its tight combing and falling over his eyes again. We fly along on the beltway past a downtown that looks small to me compared to San Diego's. He points out a construction site and mentions it's where he currently works.

"All right—tell me why Rebecca wrote a long letter to her sister and then didn't send it," I say. "At least I assume she didn't send it since I found it in the attic at Stormland."

He frowns, baffled. "I don't remember a letter to her sister."

"I'll show you when we get back. It was at the bottom of a box. It's three pages long, describing how her daughter Vi saw Douglas downtown, staggering, singing with his drinking buddies. And how Rebecca hoped to get him to stop drinking by involving him in a church."

"I never saw that letter," Doug says, "but I can guess why she didn't send it. It might sound complaining. Those old-time people used to worry a lot about such things. It was a matter of pride for them to be thankful for everything. Rebecca probably read the letter over, decided it wouldn't do, then put it aside and wrote another saying how great things were going since the family moved to Grand Rapids."

I wonder if we'll ever know the outcome of that story. With stacks of letters and diaries yet to be gone through, I may learn more.

Abruptly, glancing at me, Doug asks, "Why psychology?"

Not knowing what he's talking about, I stare at him. He repeats himself. "Why did you choose to major in psychology?"

I recall my lie of yesterday. Why did I say that? Now I'm stuck to wiggle out of it.

"Actually, I can't decide what to major in," I confess. "My mother keeps urging me to go into journalism but I don't see myself working in that field. She says I'd be courageous about interviewing people, which isn't true. Also I'd have to write a lot. Can you imagine going on all your life having themes assigned to you? Yuck!"

"So you picked psychology so you could talk to people without writing down anything but a few notes?"

"Yeah, I guess so." I haven't a clue why I said psychology, but this seems as good a reason as any. I ask about him. He confesses he's scheduled to go to graduate school in the fall and study architecture. "Mom wanted me to do that in the first place but I balked. I needed a chance to work and earn money first. Felt I'd been in school forever."

"I know what you mean." It's my feeling exactly. The few bucks I earned at Taco Bell only paid for my clothes. I hope to work full time so I can move away from home and go out on my own for a while. Dad's a protective parent, a good thing on the whole but there does come a time.

The beltway takes us all the way to Grand Haven, the other town on the Grand River. And it *is* a grand river, well named. We cross it a couple of times and find it awesomely scenic, all tree-lined as if it were snaking through a forest. On the far side of Grand Haven I see the lake, sparkling and brilliant even through my sunglasses. It looks like ocean to me, at least until we reach the beach. Then I know it isn't ocean. No surf. Just small waves lapping at the sandy shore.

I'm like, "It's tame-looking, not dynamic like our Blue Pacific."

"Better to swim in, though. You're not fighting waves all the time." At the gate he flashes a membership card for state parks. Entering, he slots the car in a lot only partially filled on this weekday afternoon and points toward a building. "Bring your swim suit; we can change in the bathhouse."

When I step out, the air smells clean and fresh. It seems strange not to sniff the fishy odor of kelp as one does on our California beaches, nor to see those little fly-infested bundles of seaweed near the water.

We plow through tawny sand to the building, where we separate. I head for the side labeled *Ladies*. When I come out in my turquoise swim suit, white towel slung over my shoulder, hand on hip in imitation of a model, showing off a bit because I know I have a nice figure, Doug, muscular in his green trunks and so tanned you almost wouldn't know he was white, awaits me. Flash the cameras, guys, this is the latest thing, a mixed-race couple.

I see a gleam of approval in Doug's eyes as he looks me over. That's cool; I like for white guys to approve of me. Just so they don't pursue it.

"Race you to the water," he says.

We both run barefoot through warm sand, plunge into the clear water together, and swim out side by side. The water seems chilly at first, invigorating. I feel I could swim all the way across, though I have no idea how far that is. You certainly can't see the other side from here. You can't see much of anything except the wave-free blue expanse, the shoreline back there with its sand bluffs, and a long pier to our right with a red lighthouse and a little red building at the end.

Beside me, I'm aware of Doug's muscular shoulders working. I wonder if he has a girlfriend.

Of course he has a girlfriend, Ashley, I tell myself. Don't forget your resolve, don't get sucked in here. There's nothing but pain ahead for the unwary.

By now the lake is calm as glass except where we make ripples. It seems strange to be submerged in such a vast expanse of wave-free water. We swim out until the lifeguard calls through his megaphone for us to come back. Then we swim sideways along the beach, our pace more leisurely as we begin to tire. There seems to be no problem of rip currents here. After a while I flop over onto my back and let the water hold me up. Soon my third cousin does likewise. Our fingers touch as we hold our arms out in a sprawling float.

After a while, chilled, we go back to the beach and dry off. We hike out on the pier with its red lighthouse where my grandmother used to stand to watch the big boats arrive from Chicago. I've seen pictures of that pier with the boats coming in, and heard her tell about the excitement of the occasion, how the children ran out onto the pier and breakwater so they could see the ship up close as it passed. Doug says the pier is fun when the waves are crashing up almost at your feet. Right now it's peaceful, dotted with patient fishermen, all of them white.

I always feel uncomfortable walking with a white person among other white people. In the past, I've had disapproving looks thrown at me. Once I was told to go back to my own part of town where I belong. Another time, when I was young and was with my mother, some woman stared at me open-mouthed and asked Mother, "Is she *yours*?" Though Mother calmly said, "Of course," it took me weeks to get over that one. I kept asking, "Mom, am I adopted?" I didn't then understand what the woman was going on about.

Luckily, these fisherfolk seem half asleep and don't look at us.

Eventually, we get out our sandwiches and, sitting on beach towels on the sand, we eat our dinner. I level with Cousin Doug and admit I feel out of place among all these white folks. "Aren't there any black beaches?"

"Sure, south of here," he says. "Want to drive on down? Benton Harbor?"

"No, let's stay and finish eating." I particularly don't want to be out late with Doug. I'm still afraid he might try something. That would put me in a very difficult position. Mother would not like for me to make rude remarks to pushy Whitey when Whitey is her third cousin once removed. But I must confess I never learned how to fight off white guys politely. How do you speak politely to someone who's pawing you where you don't want to be pawed? Especially when you know exactly what he has in mind and it isn't commitment? I tell them off pretty sharply; I can be snappish when I choose.

I decide I have to make sure that such a thing doesn't start. I have to suggest heading home before that old sun goes down. We still have plenty of time. We might even take another swim. Sunset in Michigan, in summer, is late, as I'd learned already.

"This is a state beach, open to everyone," Doug says.

I'd love to know how he *really* feels about having a black relative, but I lack the courage to come right out and ask. Oh, well, if I did ask, he'd probably lack the courage to come right out and tell me.

I finish my sandwich, hug my knees, and inquire instead, "Do you come here often?"

"When I have someone fun to come with," he says. "Like now."

Ooh. How do I answer that?

I can't think of a way. I'd been about to say, "I need to get back to reading those diaries." This is hardly the time for that remark. Better suggest a run along the shingle and then pretend I'm exhausted afterward.

After all, I'll have all morning tomorrow to read Vi's diary.

CHAPTER 4

1901
Vi

Vi had grown weary of Pa's complaints. Over and over, Pa repeated his lament, "Alana is a temptress. She's a Jezebel."

Vi failed to understand what the fuss was about. Pregnancy seemed to her a time-honored method for a woman to get her man. Since a woman could scarcely pursue her beau and ask him to step out with her, the only viable alternative was to give herself to him when wanted, relying on father and shotgun to make things right.

Vi herself had chosen the high road and regretted it. When handsome Nat McCurdle, who claimed to know her father, came into Wurzburg's to buy gloves for a maiden aunt, she'd fallen for him and thrilled over the way he eyed her with interest. She'd sensed that he'd be back. So when, the following week, he stopped by and invited her to go buggy-riding with him, unchaperoned, she'd readily agreed. She was nineteen, after all; she could make her own decisions, didn't need to ask permission.

They circled Reeds Lake. A few days later, he showed up again to ask her out. The rides became a regular thing, twice a week. Once his hand clamped over her breast, but when she pushed it aside he reverted to gentlemanly behavior. Men, she thought, *will* try these things, but now he knows better.

She was totally unprepared when, the following week, he stopped the horse on the by-lane and slid over against her. He kissed her hard, hard enough for his tongue to invade her mouth. Ignoring her protests, his hand went to her breast, fondled it, then slid farther down. It soon reached private parts. He jammed himself tight against her and she felt a hard lump at his crotch.

Things grew scary. When she tried to remove his hand, he ignored her efforts, jerked her knees closer to him, and kept touching her between the legs. She gasped, shoved at him, then reminded herself this was Nat, her chosen one, the man she loved. That made it all right. She relaxed and stopped struggling. What he was doing felt good.

His lips again sought hers, his tongue pushed past the barrier of teeth and explored her mouth. His hand lifted her skirt and fought its way through yards of petticoats to her drawers. When it slid inside, warm against her skin, it roused excitement. She longed for closer contact, longed to open her thighs to his touch.

Afterward she could never remember why all of a sudden she battled to stop him. She recalled, but couldn't understand, her own breathless words. "Too soon, too soon!" Why had she said that? Why had she pushed him away, moved to the far side of the buggy, neatened her skirt and hair?

He'd protested, "Hey, don't go all prim and proper on me." He'd inched after her. She only squeezed farther toward her side of the buggy, and when he followed, shoved him away a second time.

Surely the most foolish thing she'd ever done! The gates of paradise had opened, and instead of rushing through, she'd turned and fled.

After that, Nat became cool and formal. He took her home, dropped her off without a kiss, and said he'd be in touch. His tone sounded dismissive. She hadn't heard from him again. For weeks she watched for him in the shop, and finally faced the grim fact he wouldn't return. The only man she'd ever truly cared for: What had she been thinking? Why did she fight him off like that? And what was she to do now? How get him back?

Alana, four years her junior, had proved more clever, proved she knew how to get her man. She was busy preparing for her wedding.

So Vi's dreams of going dancing with Nat, of strolling about town on his arm, being seen in his carriage, were ended. While her family worked on Christmas decorations and her mother baked fruitcake for the relatives, she drooped, sighed, and tried in vain to make sense of life without love. Though Alana sought her advice in choosing bridal gowns, she had none to offer. In the pattern books she saw gowns she would never wear for a wedding of her own. Tears filled her eyes.

When her parents asked what was wrong, she couldn't tell them. They'd say she did the right thing. In response, she'd probably burst out with her forbidden question: How can it be right when it means the end of everything I ever dreamed of? Aren't we women supposed to set our cap for our man? And isn't that what I was doing?

She might as well have entered a convent. Out of fear of what Ma and Pa would say, she'd cloistered herself over a fool notion of purity and virginity she didn't even believe in. She believed she was made for Nat. And she couldn't talk to her family about the incident. Pa would argue that Nat wasn't a nice man, approaching her in the woods that way instead of coming to the house to seek permission and offer a proper wedding proposal.

Yet they weren't labeling Menno "not nice" for doing the same thing. They were defending him. Pa especially. Any man who laid a finger on Pa's daughter was the epitome of evil, but the things Pa's son did—even if they were the exact same things—were normal male responses to a temptress.

Glancing out the window while writing in her diary, Vi wanted to shout to passersby: Don't mess with the Langstons, you people out there. You'll be damned whatever you do.

In the saloon, as Vi later learned, some crony of Nat's spilled the beans to Pa about that woodland ride, making it sound more salacious than it was. His words triggered a battle between Pa and Nat.

From Pa's garbled account, when he finally came home late at night looking disheveled, Vi gathered that when Nat and his friend had come into the saloon together, an altercation developed over who should pay for a round of drinks. Though the two men insisted it was Pa's turn, Pa denied it. To get even, Nat's friend Josiah taunted Pa with the assertion that Nat got into Vi's drawers. In a fury, Pa took a swing at Nat. And for some incomprehensible reason, Nat the Natty, a slim man but muscular and noted for fisticuffs, went down without a fight. Since all bets were on Nat, everyone in the saloon gaped at Douglas of the strong right arm.

Nat went to the hospital. Douglas went to jail for assault and battery and was released on his own recognizance. Rebecca scolded Vi. "How could you? How could you let a man do that to you?"

Vi defended herself. "I didn't, Ma. I don't even know this Josiah person, I can't think why he should tell such a lie. Pa should have asked for my version before he got in a fight."

When it was ascertained that Nat had a serious liver condition, that illness rather than the blow had floored him, charges against Pa were dismissed. He confronted Vi. "All right, let's have the truth now. What really happened?"

"Nothing, Pa. Nat touched me, I stopped him. That's all."

"I won't have you going around with Downer McCurdle." Pa frowned and his moustache twitched. "Downer's a wrong 'un. I hate to tell you, but he's known for how fast he downs both women and drinks."

"Pa, how silly! Nat's perfectly nice. He took me riding around Reeds Lake, and I'm sure his touch was accidental."

"Sure. That's why he boasts of it."

"He didn't boast of it, he only told his buddy." Vi wished Nat had been attracted enough to keep trying. She'd learned a lot from Alana, and would handle things better next time. She'd know to slow him down rather than stop him cold. Keep him guessing.

If, that is, there ever was a next time. With Nat in the hospital, with rumors circulating that his liver ailment was life-threatening, the future became doubtful. Vi longed to visit him, but her friend Clovia, who worked at the nearby Notions counter, claimed that was the worst plan of all. "Never pursue a man in an obvious way," she warned.

"Is there nothing I can do to get him back?" Vi wailed.

"Play it smart," Clovia said. "Be resourceful. Take a volunteer job at the hospital so you encounter him by chance. Then be casual, be indifferent."

The Gibson Girl stance, Vi thought. Of course. Cool, collected.

She stopped at the home of the family doctor, Dr. Lapham, to ask about hospital work. "Could I help the nurses in some way? Evenings and Sundays, that is—I have a day job."

Dr. Lapham brightened. "We always need volunteers. I'm so pleased you're interested."

Though Vi felt guilty about it, she concealed the reason for her sudden decision and asked merely, "I won't catch anything, will I?" She'd always feared that place of fevers and contagion. She'd been known to cross the street before passing the sign: HOSPITAL, ZONE OF QUIET.

"We won't send you to the contagious ward." He told her to report on Sunday after lunch.

She nodded. If she couldn't reveal her love for Nat, at least she could see him one more time, reassure herself he still lived and breathed.

On Sunday, provided with a tray of magazines to carry around to patients, she studied her list and found Nat in 323. Panicky on coming close to his room, she couldn't bring herself to enter it. What was she doing here? Nat would surely know he was being pursued. She feared her motives were obvious. Embarrassingly so.

When she moved on, a nurse reminded her she'd overlooked the previous room. With the woman watching, she had no choice but to go back there. Her stomach churned, her feet dragged. Her heart seemed to beat in her throat. An odd sensation; she'd never believed anyone could really have their heart in their mouth.

She forced herself to walk into the room. In a four man ward, she focused her gaze on the other men, though she was aware only of Nat. Propped on pillows, he looked thin and wan. Wasted, downright bony. His straight hair falling into his eyes hinted at vulnerability. Deeply moved, she felt frantic to have him available to her so she could take care of him. She forced herself to remember: cool and calm.

When he turned his head and spotted her, his lip curled in scorn. "Who have we here? Can it be Daddy's Girl in person? Did Papa Langston send you?"

She couldn't manage a response. He went on in the same tone. "Is he remorseful for putting me in the hospital? Did he send Daughter to apologize?" His tone became harsh. "Tell him to keep his apologies."

She managed a friendly, "Hello, Nat."

He mocked. "Hello, Nat. That's no answer to my question."

She fought tears that threatened to overwhelm her. Thinking *Gibson Girl*, thinking *calm and dignified*, she straightened her back and controlled her features. "I came to offer you magazines. If you don't want them, I'll move along."

He relaxed against the pillows. "The girl with the kewpie-doll smile. I thought sure you were here for my salvation, aided and abetted by your old man."

"I'm distributing magazines," she repeated. "Do you want one or not?"

"Not. And don't go home and tell Pops that poor old Nat is half dead. If word gets out, I'll know who tattled."

She tilted her nose higher. "I don't discuss patients with anyone. It would be unprofessional." They'd lectured her on that rule just an hour before, at orientation.

"Bully for you." Nat's hand shot out and caught hers. A roguish gleam brightened his eyes. She relented and allowed herself to be drawn to the bed.

"Remember, I'm only half dead, Tootsie," he said. "The larger half is very much alive."

She couldn't resist letting her free hand touch his chin. It was square and had a dimple. "You need someone to nurse you back to health," she said.

"I don't deny it. I only deny I want Pop Langston's savior-daughter to do the job. I'm after health, not reformation. Keep that halo for some other guy."

He still held her wrist. She sat on the edge of the bed and clasped his free hand. "Nat, your pride will kill you. You and Pa will drink each other into the graveyard. And for what? What fun is a graveyard?"

"You have a point. Hospital's not much fun either. I may abandon plans to get even with the watchmaker."

"Forget my father. Let it be just us, just you and me."

"Has a nice ring to it." Nat grinned, and his fingers squeezed her arm. "Saved by the savior-girl. Who'd have thought it of old Downer McCurdle?"

When a nurse passed the door, Vi hastily disengaged her wrist, jumped up, and returned to her tray of magazines. The other patients were asleep, or they pretended to be.

"I'll be back," she told Nat as she left.

Hospital rumor had it that Nat had been warned he had only a year or two to live. It seemed his liver was dying and taking him with it. Vi felt confident that, given the chance, she could nurse him back to health. She dreamed of preparing nutritious meals, urging him outdoors for fresh air and exercise, making sure he avoided liquor. She needed to find a way past his pride, to persuade him to let her take charge. Right now he refused to admit his health was bad; in her presence he determinedly maintained his gay-blade act. Yet she could see how effortful each movement was for him. He grimaced in pain. She tried to assure him she loved the real Nat, not the swashbuckler he pretended to be.

"Women always go for swashbucklers," he said.

"Not this woman. I'm different. You can be yourself around me."

"No woman is different, Tootsie. You got a pussy, you act female."

"Nat, *must* you talk so crudely?" She sensed it was a pose. "This isn't you."

He continued to keep his emotional distance. When it came time for his discharge from the hospital, she tried to learn where he lived. She reminded him he would need someone to shop and cook for him.

"I'll get a housekeeper," he said.

From hospital records, she obtained his address, an apartment building close to downtown. She strolled past it. Labelled "Residence Hotel," it struck Vi as large and grand. One of the nurses, who seemed acquainted with Nat, told her he'd been the child of wealthy parents, inheriting money too young to know how to take care of it. "Ran through a small fortune before he was thirty. He lives a wild life."

The statement didn't bother Vi. On the contrary, she loved seeing herself in the role of rescuer of this charming rogue. She believed that, given the opportunity, she could get Nat to settle down and restore his fortunes. She longed to be his goddess, his inspiration.

For that, she needed to be with him. He showed no sign of inviting her to his home.

The last day, he perched on his hospital bed, strength drained by the effort to dress, waiting for the doctor to sign him out. Vi found nothing to say except, "I'll come and help if you need me."

"We'll meet again, Savior-Girl," he promised.

Those words were all she had to cling to.

Though she tried to share her family's Christmas preparations, Vi felt like a ghost at the party. She seemed to lack substance; she could only think: Nat, Nat.

One or two years to live, unless someone could induce him to change his lifestyle.

Since clearly she was not to be allowed to share Nat's holiday, she struggled to put him out of her mind. She helped Millie make decorations for the tree. Soon long strings of popcorn hung over the backs of chairs, while Millie worked on colored-paper chains, gluing strips into circlets. Rob made cardboard dolls and toy soldiers; Millie painted their faces.

As if noting her big sister's restlessness, Millie suggested, "You could paste clothing on these I've finished with." Vi nodded and kept her fingers busy cutting and pasting leftover bits of fabric and braid into uniforms for the soldiers and ruffled or pleated skirts for the dolls.

The following Sunday she worked again at the hospital, just so no one would suspect she'd signed on only for Nat's sake. The hospital corridors seemed desolate. A sense of meaninglessness engulfed her as she pushed the cart with its tray of magazines.

At work in the store, her body went through the motions of selling gloves and strings of cultured pearls to an endless parade of customers while her mind focused on Nat. She remembered with love every small detail about him, even the way his hair stood up in a persistent cowlick at the back and fell across his forehead in front. Day and night she replayed his promise to see her again. But when? When?

She knew he had few relatives nearby, since no one had visited him in the hospital. That meant he'd be alone at Christmas. Surely he needed her. She went out of her way to walk past his building each day on her way home from the store, but he never pushed aside his curtain to wave at her. She didn't know if he saw her.

At breakfast on the morning before Christmas, seeking a spot to place her bowl of oatmeal on a surface covered with sheet music, she snapped at Rob, who was copying out scores for Millie. "Do you have to take up the whole darn table?"

Rob hastily gathered his music papers together. "Sorry, Sis." Rob, who was twelve and belonged in school, instead worked as delivery boy at Baxter's Laundry to contribute money to the household. She felt guilty for being short with him.

Later, when Vi started out the door, she heard Rob ask Millie, "What ails her?"

"She's in love," Millie said. "A man named Nat McCurdle."

Vi rushed back, demanding, "Who told you that, Miss Snoop?"

"I empty the wastebaskets. Yours is stuffed with notes saying, 'Vi McCurdle,' and 'Mrs. Nat McCurdle.'"

"You don't know what they say, you can't read. You're only five."

"I asked Alana."

Vi's face flamed. "So you and Alana have been giggling together about my personal affairs?"

"Don't tell Dad," Rob said. "There'll be hell to pay. Dad hates Nat."

"Oh, mind your own business, all of you." Vi left the house and slammed the front door. Her eyes tearing with shame and humiliation, she walked out into a chill morning fog. Now her whole family, even Alana, knew Nat had abandoned her.

She longed to vanish into the silky whiteness, to lose herself and never come home again. She couldn't bear for them all to witness and talk about her heartbreak.

CHAPTER 5

1901
Vi

At work, Clovia scolded Vi. "Men don't fall for women who pine. It's essential to keep a man guessing. It's not as if—" The tall, bony woman vigorously polished the glass display case as she spoke. "—you lack other opportunities."

Vi scoffed. "The 'other opportunities' are skinny fellows with wiggly Adam's apples who boast about what big-shots they are at work, how their boss can't manage without them."

"That's to show you they're a good catch."

"Who wants a catch? I found love."

"You found a daydream. I hear Nat likes popular girls." Clovia rubbed harder at the glass as she grew more vehement. "I'm telling you, Vi, you have to go out and live. No man falls for a wallflower."

Vi's shoulders drooped. She confessed, "The men have stopped asking."

"See? That happens. You need to get back in circulation. You can start by going with George and me to dancing lessons after work. Meet men who need partners."

Vi shook her head, then suddenly had a vision of herself as a good dancer, popular, in demand, Nat eyeing her wistfully from the sidelines while he rued the day he tossed her aside. Rue the day—such a lovely expression. She said it over to herself. "Nat, you'll rue the day."

"I'll try it," she conceded.

At the dance hall, the instructor assigned her a partner named Jimmy Reeves. He was tall, skinny, red-haired, too large of nose to be handsome, but he knew his stuff and proved eager to show her. In his embrace, she plowed her way through the box-waltz, slide-two-three, slide-two-three, while the instructor droned out the count. Jimmy held a hand against her back and guided her. In time, she caught on and began following more effortlessly. He stepped out faster, whirling her around. To her surprise, she found it fun.

"You're doing fine, New Girl," the teacher said.

Pleased, she told Jimmy she owned a talking machine, and they could try this out in her parlor. "We'd need a dance record."

His narrow face became all smiles. "You and I are great together. We'll practice until we can show all the others how it's done."

It hadn't occurred to Vi she might have a flair for dancing. Now she visualized herself floating around a ballroom with Nat, her long skirts swirling, all eyes upon her.

"We do have one or two waltz records, I think," she said. "I don't know if they're right for dancing, but we can try. How about tomorrow night?"

Jimmy looked as if he couldn't believe his good fortune. "I'll be there. Where do you live?"

"College Avenue, across Washerwoman's Hollow," she told him, adding, with a lift of her chin, "Come for dinner." That would settle their hash, Ma's and Millie's. They'd stop pitying poor Vi.

"Will it be all right with your parents?"

"I have a big family. There are five of us kids at home. Ma won't mind one more mouth to feed." On the contrary, Vi believed Ma would be delighted. Ma had always hoped for her daughter to be popular and have friends in to visit.

"I'll buy a couple of records," Jimmy said. "Is yours a disc or cylinder gramophone?"

"Disc," she said.

Vi went home and announced to her family that a young man named Jimmy Reeves would be coming to practice dance steps, and she'd invited him to dinner. Rebecca offered to bake, in place of their everyday fare, the meatloaf she'd planned for Sunday. Because they kept hens, the family lived on chicken and dumplings.

"Dumplings will be fine." Vi didn't want Jimmy to think he was special.

Millie flew to neaten the house. She seemed eager to encourage this new relationship. "Is he good looking?" she asked. She answered her own question. "Of course he is; my sister wouldn't choose someone homely. She's no dummy."

The following night, Jimmy arrived a few minutes early, bringing flowers and two records. Vi found it amusing the way the whole family put themselves out to be nice to him. He responded politely, praising their new house, raving over the good smell of Ma's cooking, talking about his own home-life. "I have no brothers or sisters. It isn't fun like this."

When Douglas inquired about Jimmy's work, they learned he'd been a bank-teller recently promoted to loan officer. Douglas looked impressed. Vi hadn't even thought to ask.

Vi felt duplicitous when, at dinner, everyone appeared to be charmed by the visitor, even baby Bea who for once didn't play with her food and make a mess. No one seemed to realize Jimmy was a mere dance partner, a means to an end. With their attention focused on him, they appeared to fancy he'd replaced Nat. As if anyone ever could do that!

After dinner, Vi and Jimmy rolled up the rug and went to work in the parlor, Jimmy showing Vi the dance steps he knew, helping her try them out. While they shuffled their way around the room, he told her he'd been invited to a New Years' Eve party the following night and hoped he might take her. Vi agreed to go. Let Nat eat his heart out. No wallflower she, stuck at home to welcome the New Year with parents and younger siblings.

She gave little thought to what she'd wear. Her Sunday best would do, she supposed.

Next morning, when she talked to Clovia, her co-worker went wide-eyed on hearing of the invitation. "Jimmy's going to the Hamiltons," she said. "They're wealthy, they have a ballroom on the third floor of their house. Mansion, I mean. There'll be an orchestra. The event'll be written up in the paper. You'll need a ball gown."

Vi stared at her in horror. A ball gown! She'd never owned such a thing—and there was no time to sew.

"Orchestra? Ball gown?" she blurted. "I never dreamed—! I assumed the party would be at someone's home where they'd roll up the carpet and wind the talking machine." She threw her hands to her head. "I'll cancel; I'll send Jimmy a note."

"You'll do no such thing. This is a great opportunity." Clovia smoothed her already neat brown hair. "We'll shop on our lunch hour. I'll help you pick out something."

"I have no money." Vi always turned over her wages to Ma for household expenses.

When Clovia told her the store would let her buy on time payments and deduct from her salary, Vi panicked. Having succeeded beyond her wildest imaginings, she wasn't prepared for the consequences. She protested that she had no idea how to behave around the Fulton Street crowd, the city's socialites. "They'll know I'm a hick from the country. I'll die of embarrassment."

"Not if you're well dressed. Look your best, keep dancing, smile, don't talk except to say 'Howdy do,' and thank your hostess at the end of the evening. That's all that's necessary."

Though dubious, Vi went at noon with Clovia. They spent their lunch hour in the ready-to-wear shop. Clovia selected for Vi an expensive gown in Gibson Girl style, low cut at the neck, with full skirt and train. Pale lavender, with yellow flowers decorating the shoulder straps, it was the most beautiful dress Vi had ever seen. Her guilt feelings over the expense made her critical. "I'll trip over this train when I dance," she protested.

"You gather it up and clasp it on your wrist, silly."

Vi waffled. Against her will, she admired her gowned image in the mirror. She'd had no idea she could look so much like those socialite girls whose pictures appeared in the Sunday papers. Ma didn't approve of self-admiration, kept no full-length mirrors in the house. All the same, Vi wanted the dress whatever the cost.

Clovia urged her, this once, to throw caution to the winds. When Vi confessed that, were this for Nat, she wouldn't think twice, Clovia warned her nothing would ever be for Nat, "not until you make him mad with desire."

Vi capitulated and bought the dress. She worried all afternoon that Ma would complain of the expense—and the time-payments. Ma never indulged in such things herself.

The store closed early for the holiday. Vi went home at four to face the music. "You'll say it's frightfully expensive," she warned her mother while she opened the package.

"I won't say any such thing. You need a nice dress for Menno's wedding—and to impress your young man."

Those last words sent a new wave of uneasiness through Vi. She reminded her mother Jimmy was only a dance partner. "Don't call him my young man. He's not."

"Of course not." A gleam in her mother's eye suggested to Vi that Rebecca didn't believe her.

She wondered how to clarify her feelings. "It's true."

Rebecca kept smiling. She smiled even when Vi took out and held up the dress. She nodded happily and said nothing about the expense.

Once garbed, Vi realized she ought to have bought slippers. Her everyday shoes didn't look right with this fancy gown. Too late. She would have to try to keep her feet out of sight. She buffed away scuff-marks as best she could.

Rebecca helped her do her hair in a pompadour. Jimmy arrived to find her resplendent in her new dress and elaborate hairdo. He seemed impressed. She looked at the tall, skinny young man with the smoothed-down red hair and thought how ironic it was, such fuss and fanciness for a man she had little feeling for. Had it been Nat standing by the door waiting for her, she'd have died of pure joy.

At the party, she wished she'd paid more attention to those magazine articles that told young women how to behave in high society. She felt overwhelmed by the vast house, glittering chandeliers, the swirl of colorful ball gowns and sparkling jewelry. The other young women were effortlessly gracious, seeming to know the right thing to say at all times. Vi envied them but followed Clovia's advice to say only hello.

Jimmy whirled her onto the dance floor. She felt relieved. Concentrating on movement, she didn't have to wonder what to talk about, nor worry that her dress, with its flowers on the shoulder, might be too fussy in this crowd where classic elegance seemed the rule.

The hours of hard work paid off. Vi and Jimmy danced well together. People complimented them.

There were uneasy moments when, introduced, Vi felt she had to say something more than "How do." She knew herself to be socially inept, at a loss for the kind of clever repartee that seemed to occur spontaneously to the others. Lucky after all she hadn't come with Nat. She needed to acquire social graces before allowing him to be her escort.

"I'm going to the library next week for a book on etiquette," she told Jimmy. "These women have such soft voices, such a graceful way of moving their hands—I need to learn all that."

"You're fine the way you are," Jimmy said. "You're so natural. I love that about you." He took from a tray two glasses of champagne, gave her one, and proposed a toast to the new year. "In five seconds it'll be nineteen ought two."

Promising herself never to tell Ma she'd had spirits, Vi raised her glass. As the clock struck twelve and everyone cheered, she sipped.

When Jimmy took her home, he invited her to go skating with him the following Saturday. She accepted. She was gaining needed experience to become a woman of the world, shedding the shy, diffident persona of the farm girl. She was listening to the talk and memorizing the repartee.

Skating was approved of by Mennonites and had been a popular activity back home. She'd skated often and become good at it. On Saturday, on the private rink Jimmy's friend had made by flooding his tennis court, she showed off her talents and tried to make Jimmy proud of her. Jimmy, who as a banker knew the people of this wealthy neighborhood, kept introducing her. By now she'd read the book and ventured onto some suggested lines of small talk which seemed to work for her.

After skating, they went into the house for hot chocolate. The men played pool in the host's private game room. To avoid lengthy conversations with the other women, Vi, pretending to be fascinated with the game, stood near the pool table to watch. She'd read enough in the etiquette book to learn the word *gauche*, and she feared it described her. She felt conscious that her hands had picked strawberries and tomatoes, washed dishes, scrubbed clothes. The other girls' soft, white hands seemed to have done nothing but embroidery work. Their poise was effortless, natural to them. Their voices were low, their gestures contained, hands quiet—and their language seemed ever so proper. They never said, "Pa," they said, "My fahhther," with an uptilt to their voice that made it sound as if dad were governor of Michigan.

She feared to join them lest she make herself a subject for gossip.

When Jimmy took her home, late in the evening after a snack-type supper, she permitted him a chaste kiss, and hurried indoors to open her book and see if she'd done things right. Not to impress Jimmy, of course. Simply to avoid being gauche. She didn't want Nat to hear rumors that some farmer's daughter had showed up at the ball and skating party acting oh-so-countrified.

The following week, she stopped walking home by way of Nat's house.

Clovia, when she heard of it, approved. "Keep playing your cards right," she said, "and you'll have Nat pining for you."

It did seem to Vi that things might work out this way. She waited hopefully for the great moment.

CHAPTER 6

2002
Ashley

In her diary, in different-colored ink as if she wrote it in later, my great-aunt had inserted the comment: "I couldn't have dreamed what would really happen."

The words piqued my curiosity. I'd have loved to go on reading. But I dutifully put the diary aside. I'd been going through this stuff all morning, and on hearing dishes clacking downstairs I felt I ought to help Laura with lunch. Mom had impressed on me that I wasn't to be a burden to the Langstons.

Cousin Laura remained an enigma to me. When we were together, she talked about the other relatives, not about herself. I didn't feel I'd got to know her at all. Doug had mentioned that for years she'd done the firm's office work, and now she had a computer at home and did the bookkeeping, bill-paying, and payroll. She seldom went to the office any longer.

That's all I know about her. In the attic I found pictures of the original dray, with hand-painted lettering on the side, in which the Langstons hauled lumber and supplies to work-sites. Now the firm has all kinds of heavy-duty equipment, each piece professionally labeled *Langston and Langston*. No more hand-printing.

When I enter the kitchen, I see that the strawberries wait to be washed and de-stemmed. I take over the job. I ask Laura, "Why Langston *and* Langston?"

"The other half is Zeke's family," she explains. "The two older brothers, Zeke and Menno, started the firm together. Zeke's descendants live in Ottawa

Hills now, but they'll be coming to dinner. They're looking forward to meeting you."

Well, damn. More of that phony, so-nice-to-know-you garbage. The very thing I've dreaded all along. I cringe. "Ottawa Hills?"

"It's a classier part of town, out toward Reeds Lake. Junior's brother Howard lives there, too, with his wife Terri."

Uh-huh. There it is. I knew I'd uncover a pillared mansion eventually. All this homey stuff is too good to be true. Laura adds that it's nice out there and she'll try to get Doug to take me for a visit. I force a smile and pretend to be pleased.

"I'm making us toasted cheese sandwiches for lunch," Laura says. "I hope that's okay with you."

"It's fine," I say.

"When you finish the berries, you can slice some tomatoes. For dinner tonight we'll have meatloaf and strawberry shortcake."

She takes the sandwiches out of the toaster oven. I slice the tomatoes and manage to insert a couple of slices together with the melted cheese of each sandwich. She remarks that maybe next week we'll go to the Schnitzelbank Restaurant. "It'll be fun to lunch together, just the two of us. Do you like German cooking?"

I admit I don't know. Never tried it. As I say, at home it's tacos, burritos, tostadas—or soul food. Chinese when we eat out formal. Taco Bell when we eat out casual.

Laura and I take our sandwiches and teapot to the dining room and sit down close to one another at the big table, which is set with two place mats, cups and silverware. Laura explains that Zeke's family used to live right up the street, and she missed them when they moved. "The kids would drop in here all the time; they practically grew up here. In those days Stormland was the heart of the family. It seems lonely now."

"How did the house get its name?" I ask. And remember, before she answers, that my great-grandmother, Millie, told me. The original Douglas had named it Stormland—for her—because when they first moved here the homesick child had angrily labeled it a stormland.

Laura says she doesn't know. It was always called that; it used to have a sign over the back door. I wonder if I should enlighten her, but it's not my place to inform her of the history of her own house. Mom said, "Don't be obnoxious, Ashley." Mom considers it rude to tell people what they ought to already know. She claims I'm too blunt.

"How's the research coming?" Laura asks.

I confess to being surprised by what I read, but I don't tell her why. Actually, I never figured white girls might get dumped the way Vi got dumped by Nat. My observations have been that they generally walk in and commandeer the guy as if they had every right to him. It's us darker-skinned girls who learn to anticipate dumping.

My grandma—the white one—is an opera buff and once dragged me to a performance of *Madame Butterfly.* I learned about the Pinkertons of the world and how they walk away from women of color when a white girl comes along. I decided early on that stuff was not for me. Up yours, Colonel Pinkerton. You're not doing me the way you did Cio-Cio-San. I'm onto you, I won't commit hari-kari over you. Never, no way.

It's black guys only for this chick. Not that they're perfect, far from it, but at least the things they do aren't motivated by skin color.

Laura is looking at me quizzically as if expecting an explanation, but I don't want to tell her all that. I don't know if she cares about opera, and I'm not into putting on airs. I remember those girls Vi complained of, saying, "My fahhther." I'm sure not going to talk of "My evening at the operahh."

"It's just that Aunt Vi seems to have had trouble keeping her man," I say. "From her picture, I assume she was the beauty of the day. I mean, she does look a lot like the Gibson Girl—not my style but, you know, the in thing back then."

Laura still seems puzzled. She confesses she hasn't ever gone through the stuff in the attic. "That is, not to stop and read it. I've moved boxes around trying to make more room up there, but I never plowed through the books and papers."

"Oh, it's dramatic. Besides that shotgun wedding, there were abandonments."

"Abandonments? Not at the altar, I hope?"

"Vi hadn't got the guy even close to the altar." I admit to her I'd thought that, for white women, getting their man was a piece of cake.

Laura laughs. "I doubt it's ever a piece of cake for anyone. It wasn't for me. My family was Holland-Dutch, and I didn't think I had a chance of marrying an old-stock Langston. We lived up the street a ways, and I used to admire Junior as we walked to school and back—but hadn't a clue how to get acquainted with him."

I want to laugh with her. This slim, trim, elegant-looking woman with the blonde hair and boyish haircut thought she couldn't capture her man? Come on!

"What did you do?" I ask.

"Fate intervened," she explains. "A bad windstorm blew the roof off our house, and we called Langston and Langston to replace it. When they sent Junior as part of the crew, he recognized me as a classmate and invited me to the prom. I nearly died of joy. I couldn't believe my good fortune. My father wasn't happy; he opposed my dating someone who didn't attend our church—but eventually we compromised. I stayed with my church, Junior stayed with his, and the children have been back and forth between the two."

See, she only thought she wouldn't get him. In the end, she got him. She's white, isn't she? White girls can have the earth if they ask for it.

Laura went on talking about the town's social life. "Now, of course, no one even thinks about who's recent immigrant stock and who isn't. But it was different thirty years ago when I was in high school. We Hollanders were conscious of the fact we weren't in the social register, and we envied those who were."

I wondered how anyone could tell who was or wasn't. In this part of town people were all white and looked alike. Not like us. At my high school, you glanced at people and saw at once where they belonged; they were either white, brown, black or slant-eyed. We each had our own clique, and there was a hierarchy of cliques, with white at the top, Asian second, brown on the bottom and blacks out of the circle, trying to pretend they didn't care. Oh, yes, there was a Jewish clique, too, right up there near the top.

If you were black, you could do one of two things—keep struggling with no hope of getting accepted, or, if you had too much pride for that, simply choose to drop out altogether and let it be known you wanted no part of the white world, neither its good nor its bad. Or you could become cynical and learn to "play the game" while scorning those you played with.

I could never quite manage that degree of cynicism so, to my mother's dismay, I mostly hung out with the dropouts. Dad seemed to understand my dilemma, but Mother never did. She harped, "Ashley, you're only defeating yourself. No one else cares. It's your life."

"Defeating myself from what?" I'd ask her. "From something I don't want, and probably couldn't have if I did want it?" The truth is, I scorned the idea of trying to prove to a bunch of snobbish teachers that I knew all the stuff they thought they were teaching me. I stayed in college only because Mother insisted, "No schooling, no free room-rent."

To Mom, everything is obvious and easy. You work hard, you get good grades, you graduate, you get a topnotch job with good pay. Well, it worked that way for her; she's white. She doesn't seem to take it in that there's no such guaranteed outcome awaiting you if you're black—or even brown. A lucky few may make it, but the statistics are not in your favor.

"You grew up in such an intellectual family," Laura says. "I felt intimidated about visiting out there. I hear your grandparents both taught college and your mom runs her own firm."

"It's not exactly her own firm," I admit. "But yeah, she's the manager. Keeps her busy. I practically have to make appointments to talk to her."

"They say she has a good job and a beautiful house."

"I guess that's so." I never thought much about it. I just know the walls of our house are bare because Dad won't hang paintings of white people, and artists don't paint black people. Mom and Grandma have hunted in all the art stores but have yet to find any great works of art portraying black people. Grandma solves the problem by filling her home with paintings by weird artists like Miro and Kandinsky, but Mom doesn't like abstract, so we're stuck with travel posters and pictures of flower pots full of geraniums. In California, geraniums don't make an interesting picture. They're everywhere outdoors; you can see them any old time.

"And in San Diego, where property is so expensive!" Laura is still on the theme of our beautiful house.

Sure, Mom helped pay for the place. She figures her dear daughter Ashley ought to have the same ambition for herself. But if she wanted me to duplicate her accomplishments, why didn't she marry a white guy?

While we're eating, some woman in a blue dress comes around the house, passes the dining room window, and taps at the kitchen door. Laura jumps up saying, "Oh, here's my sister, Joyce."

She goes to the back door to let the woman in and offers a gushing welcome and a toasted cheese sandwich. The newcomer says she already ate. Laura's like, "Well, come in and meet Ashley, and have a cup of tea with us."

I manage to stifle a groan. I hate meeting people I don't care about. I long to go upstairs and get on with my reading; I'm dying to know what happened to Vi. Did she learn to love Jimmy? Probably not. Women never do love the approved guy, the guy the family wants for them. My parents never actually picked out a man for me, but I've often had the feeling they liked those skinny dorks with big Adam's apple, Jonah for instance, and hoped I'd fall for one of them. When the guy starts bending over backward to please, it's the kiss of death. I want no part of him any more.

Laura comes into the dining room with this sister who looks a lot like her, except with brown hair. She has the kind of hairdo, back-combed, puffy, with every hair in its right place and glued there with tons of hairspray, that beauty salons create for middle-aged women. Her dress, pale blue, full skirted, seems designed to hide widening hips. She rushes toward me with a simpering smile, her hand out.

"Ashley, my dear, how nice to meet you."

This woman is like a caricature of Laura. She's unreal. She's phony, she's all pretense. I already don't like her, and can't bring myself to be cordial to her. I force myself to stand and tilt up my lip-tips.

Laura says, "My sister, Joyce." Her words seem clipped and abrupt. I suspect she's not too happy with this visit either.

I dutifully put out my hand and say what I think my mother would say. "Won't you sit down and join us?"

"Thank you, I can stay only a little while." A patent lie. She came here from sheer curiosity; I can sense it in the way she looks me over.

She slides into a seat and begins chattering in an unnatural way. We learn that, sure enough, she spent the morning in a beauty salon. It figures. She tells us that Natalie, her stylist, urged her to dye her hair. "Can you imagine? I told her there was no gray in it yet. 'Give me time to get old before you make me over,' I said."

Is she kidding? She looks as if she's been made over ten times already. Everything about her seems fake. Her face is a mask with no expression, a sure sign, I've been told, of a face lift.

She drones on about the salon. I'm amazed she can find so much to say about it. Beauty salons are all alike; you go there, you get your hair worked on, you pay your money, you leave. But to her it seems to have been a great adventure; she has to tell us who came in, who spoke to whom and what they said, ad tedium. Compared to her, Laura's a forthright person, a veritable earth-mother. I wonder how sisters could grow up so different—until I remember Marla and me. But Marla's not phony. Naïve, perhaps, but genuine. Downright, Gran calls her.

I finish my meal in silence, then shove my chair back. I'm like, "If you women will excuse me, I have a lot of reading to do, and I know you two want to chat."

"Oh, Ashley, I hoped we'd have a chance to talk." Joyce positively whimpers.

Sure you did. You're dying to quiz me. I can sense it. I say, "I feel sure we'll meet again. I'll be around for a while."

I go upstairs to that enticing diary. Sitting on my bed, I open the book but don't read. From downstairs the voices drone, then grow louder and angrier. The sisters seem to be working up to a fight.

I hear Joyce say, "You and I have spent a lifetime trying to make a good impression on people in this town. We don't need to ruin—"

Laura interrupts her. I can't hear her response but it sounds angry. Joyce continues her diatribe. Finally, loud and clear, Laura goes, "I'm a Christian, Joyce, I will never turn away a relative as a guest. Never as long as I live."

I'd known all along they were talking about me. Now I had confirmation.

What *were* my mom and dad thinking when they married and dumped their offspring into this predicament? Did they ever for a minute give us three kids a thought?

I feel like calling my mother and telling her I'm on my way home and need to be picked up at the airport. But I know what she'll say. "Ashley, it wasn't Laura's fault. Laura sounded delighted when I asked her if you might visit Stormland. Stick with it, give the woman a chance." I'll argue that I never stay where I'm not wanted, that she shouldn't expect it. Then she'll start on the lecture about how nobody in this world is loved by everybody, and I have to get the chip off my shoulder. Soon we'll be fighting long-distance by telephone.

Oh, hell. Back to the diary. You thought you had problems, Aunt Vi? Men are a headache, not a major problem. You *can* live without them, though it ain't easy. Other women are the *real* problem. Now I have to go along pretending that I didn't hear this conversation and I suspect nothing.

And I still have tomorrow night's family dinner to look forward to. No doubt it'll be a real treat, with a whole fucking—I mean frigging—dining room full of Joyces simpering over dear Cousin Ashley.

CHAPTER 7

1902
Vi

Vi would always think of those months as the Jimmy winter. There were sleigh rides, visits to vaudeville shows, evenings when the young people gathered around the piano for a sing. She saw Jimmy as a friend who gave her access to a wonderful social life. But her dreams were of Nat. Handsome Nat, suave Nat, natty Nat, the man beside whom Jimmy Reeves seemed a mere boy, friendly, open, unsophisticated, and not terribly interesting. Even boring.

She soon outdistanced Jimmy in learning to handle smart talk. Her name appeared in the papers as a guest at parties. Other men asked her for dates but, even at the risk of causing Jimmy to fancy—erroneously—that she was true to him, she turned them down. She hoped Nat read the social news. Let him put her popularity with Jimmy in his pipe and smoke it.

Vi decided, after all, not to wear her new gown to Alana's wedding. On seeing the plain dresses of bridesmaid and matron of honor, she feared the women would think she'd tried to outshine them. It might create hard feelings. She opted for her Sunday dress.

The wedding, held at the O'Brian home, seemed tawdry to one who'd been a guest in the city's mansions. Inside the small clapboard house, the sliding door between dining room and parlor had been opened wide to make space for family and friends. Everyone except Alana and Millie wore street clothes. Menno had bought a suit, the first he ever owned. When he brought it home, Rebecca wept because it was for his wedding rather than for the high school graduation she'd dreamed of for him.

Young Millie looked charming in her lacy flower-girl dress, her long brown hair in masses of curls, a bow at the back of her neck; and the bridal gown was nice if one didn't peer closely at Alana's loose, sloppy stitches. The O'Brian women's outfits seemed slap-dash, a make-do wrenching together of non-matching items. Vi promised herself that she and Nat would do their wedding properly, with music and a ready-made gown. She would begin at once to save up for it. She wouldn't tell Ma that she'd received a raise at work; she'd salt away the extra money.

Ma sobbed audibly while the young couple spoke their vows. Even through his brown whiskers Mr. O'Brian managed to look smug, as if he'd pulled off a coup, getting his last daughter married off. Alana's older sister, the matron of honor, was noticeably pregnant for the second time. Her first child, placed in the care of the next-door neighbor, could be heard through an open window, howling in the distance. Its mother tried to pretend she didn't hear. She kept frowning and then smoothing her brow with a finger.

As if women lived only to marry and reproduce. Not my cup of tea, Vi decided. I want more. I want to travel with Nat, go to parties, share an interesting life.

When the service ended, Vi kissed the bride and groom, helped to cut the cake, observed the opening of unexciting gifts—a toaster that unfolded outward, a canister set, cooking pots, twin flatirons. Only Vi's gift, a cut-glass serving bowl, suggested the possibility of glamour in life, of entertaining in grand style. All those grimly useful household items spoke of work, work, work. The only thing missing was a broom and dustpan.

And Alana was only fifteen. Vi shook her head and promised herself: Not for me.

I'll find a way to make my life more meaningful.

In May, Vi's well-laid plans fell apart. On a buggy-ride home from a dance, Jimmy destroyed her carefully constructed world when, abruptly, he announced, "Vi, I'm crazy about you. I want these times never to end. I want you to be mine for always."

Vi couldn't keep her face from reflecting the horror she felt. She hadn't meant to vamp Jimmy, had in fact persistently held him off, allowing no petting, kissing only as a chaste good-night gesture. She thought he'd understood what she'd repeatedly explained, that she'd merely set out to learn her way around in a socialite world.

Speechless with distress, she listened, above the clatter of the horse's hooves, to his pleading. "I adore you, Vi. You're the greatest. You and I make a perfect team. I sensed the first time I ever danced with you that we were meant for one another."

It was heart-in-mouth time again. What should she say? She'd assumed her rejection of his touch, his kisses, had spoken eloquently of her lack of romantic feelings. Instead, clearly, it had intrigued and enticed him. Ma would kill her for doing this to a nice young man. Yet Jimmy's brotherly attentions aroused no response in her, no thrills to compare to the mad passion she'd felt with Nat, the panting hunger for his touch, his closeness.

What to say? How to explain?

While she sat, open mouthed, seeking words, Jimmy spoke for her. "Sorry. Didn't mean to take you by surprise. Thought you knew I'm gone on you."

"Well, actually I—"

He put a finger over her lips. "Don't say anything now. I couldn't bear a flat *no*. Give it time, let's discuss it later. I see I brought it up before you were ready. It was clumsy of me but—I've never proposed to a girl before." He gave her a manufactured grin which clearly sought to hide his disappointment.

"Yes—well, I have to think." She began to panic. A flat no would send him away and end her social life. But if she kept him dangling, hinting that she might later become interested, Ma would kill her when the truth came out. Ma had no patience with women who toyed with men's affections insincerely; she'd warned her daughter against doing it.

Not wanting to say the wrong thing, Vi kept silent for the rest of the ride. Jimmy tossed her an anxious glance and asked if he'd offended her. She shook her head. "No, you just took me by surprise."

At home, alone in her room, she lay awake and stared at a ceiling lit by a finger of light from the streetlamp. She thrashed, trying to think how to explain, to clarify, to plead that she and Jimmy should go on as they were and leave the future to work itself out. She had a despairing feeling that that couldn't happen. He'd made his feelings known and now she could no longer pretend ignorance of them. Now she'd feel like a Jezebel if she went on with this. She needed to put an end to their relationship at once; it was the honest thing to do.

In the morning, after a sleepless night, she stopped by Clovia's counter to talk to her privately. Her distress must have shown, for Clovia asked what was wrong.

"Jimmy proposed." The words came out in a kind of wail. Vi wrung her hands. "What do I say? It's cold-blooded to tell him I love someone else. It's heartless. But it's true."

Clovia shrugged. "Say you're not ready to settle down. You're young, you want to have fun. That's what I say to George. I still haven't decided if George is the one for the rest of my life."

Vi couldn't see herself allowing Jimmy to go on hoping. Guilt feelings washed over her as she recalled how she used him as her ticket to high society while never once giving thought to his feelings. She'd let him and everyone else, including her family, believe she cared for him. Though she'd been honest, she knew her lack of forthrightness had made the truth sound like false protest from a woman in love.

She returned to her own counter and stood lost in thought while debating what to do.

Soon she suffered a second jolt of surprise. She saw Nat himself striding into the store. She stared. No, she wasn't dreaming, it really was Nat. She'd often fancied she spotted him at some distant counter, but it had always turned out to be someone else. This time, though, his identity was unmistakable and he was coming toward her.

Thrills of excitement shot through her. She straightened and held her breath as he approached. He looked thin but otherwise his old self, Nat the Natty, his color good, his step firm and assured. His smile, however, was formal. Well, she could respond in like manner; she'd had practice. She squared her shoulders.

"Hello, Savior-Girl," he said. "You're just the person to help me. I need to pick out a string of pearls. Something special and expensive, a gift for my best girl."

As if expecting her to be pleased, he produced a wider smile. The breath went out of her body and she gasped. A lump formed in her throat. She feared she'd burst into tears right here under the bright lights of the store, with another customer approaching the counter.

She felt she couldn't endure this. In all her dreams of getting Nat back, she'd never once thought he might have another girlfriend. She now faced her own naivete, her foolishness. She'd assumed it was pride alone that made him reject her offer to care for him in his illness. She'd never considered that someone else might be doing the job.

If Jimmy's all there is for me, she thought, I'll throw myself off the pier into Reeds Lake. Life without Nat isn't worth living.

While she pictured herself leaping off the dock, sinking through green water, she went through the motions of showing Nat the various necklaces for sale. He asked which one she preferred. She was beyond choosing. She watched the other customer eye the merchandise and move on.

"I'll have the one you like best," Nat said.

She chose the most expensive one, with a real gold clasp. She boxed and gift-wrapped it, her trembling fingers doing a messy job with the ribbons, her vision blurring with tears. She untied and started over, but was able to do little better the second time. Finally, she handed over a less than professionally wrapped box. Nat slid some dollar bills across the counter.

"Keep the change, Tootsie. I'll be seeing you."

She stood with the bills in hand and watched Nat turn away, pass the fabric counters, and go out through the revolving door. His image was blurry through her tears. She fought an urge to sit on the floor and weep.

On the sidewalk, Nat suddenly wheeled and headed back. Stupidly, as once again he strode toward her, hair in his eyes, she stood clutching the bills, telling herself he must truly love this new woman, to spend on her what was to herself a full week's wages.

Nat came straight to her counter. Smiling again, he held out the package with one hand while shoving his hair back with the other. "For you, Tootsie."

"Oh, Nat!" Tears gushed out and slid down her cheeks. She accepted but put the package down and fumbled in her sleeve for her handkerchief. When Nat hastily offered his, she took it. She dried her cheeks, dabbed at her eyes. "Nat, why do you—" Her voice trembled, cracked. She took a deep breath and tried again. "—do these things?"

"Hey, I thought you didn't care for me any more." He caught her wrist, lifted her arm, forced her to look at him. "You have a new young man. I've read about the parties you and he attended—"

"You know perfectly well he didn't matter." She struggled to get her quavering voice under control. "I offered to come to you. You wouldn't let me." She wiped away another tear.

"I had to wait until I could give you a man, not a bedridden lump."

"You were never a lump to me."

Her eyes swam, her cheeks grew wet again. He took her hand. She protested. "Don't, Nat. My boss will—"

"Who cares about your boss? From now on, you're working for me. We're getting married."

"Nat, do stop funning about serious matters. You drive me crazy."

"Who's funning? I've decided. Let's get on with it right away, tonight, before Papa Langston prevents us."

Her tears stopped. She began to panic. "You mean—elope?"

Nat seemed surprised by the question. "What else can we do? Papa Langston will never give his blessing. He hates me."

She hadn't anticipated this. She'd always believed she could bring her father around somehow. Given time, she'd ease him into the idea. She'd go to parties with Nat as she had with Jimmy, and gradually get her father used to seeing her with him. She also needed time to explain herself to Jimmy—and to make a wedding gown, send out invitations, arrange for a minister, do things right.

"Hesitating?" Nat frowned. "It's Jimmy Reeves, isn't it?"

"Oh, Nat, no. It's just—so sudden."

"If we've decided, why wait? I've hired the minister for tomorrow morning, and at noon we leave for Niagara Falls—on a sleeper train."

"Nat, I—" She felt frightened yet titillated. Niagara Falls! She'd never been out of Michigan, except once to cross the river at Port Huron into Canada. And she'd be with Nat—forever.

"It's cool there in May. Be sure to pack warm clothes."

"Pa will kill me."

"What for? We'll be properly married, signed and sealed." He released her wrist and slid his hand over hers. "Pack your bags, Tootsie, I'll come for you early tonight while Papa's in the saloon. That way, you won't have to deal with him."

"Why can't you give me time to talk him round?"

Nat shook his head. He said again, "Your pa hates me. Elopement is the only way, believe me. If you can sneak me inside your house, I'll carry your bags out."

"No problem, I sleep downstairs." She was barely aware of making the comment. Her mind was busy planning how she might put this situation to her father. She'd anticipated having to win him over, but not so soon.

"Before midnight. Remember." Nat's brown eyes bored into hers. He put the package again into her hand and turned away.

When he was gone, she stood clutching the bills and the gift. She looked toward Clovia's counter and saw that her friend wasn't there. She must have been away at the rest room and missed this entire event.

Vi debated: Should she tell her? Or say nothing to anyone, and surprise the whole world?

CHAPTER 8

1902
Vi

By the time Clovia returned, Vi had decided to say nothing. Surely Nat was teasing. She had to shed her naivete, stop falling for his jokes.

Next time he turned up, she must be casual, flirty. None of the teary, choked-up stuff. Nat didn't go for tears. She would say, "Didn't you once kid around about elopement? What was that all about?" She'd pretend she hadn't for a moment believed it.

Acquire sophistication, she cautioned herself.

Later, walking home, she had second thoughts. What if Nat meant it? What if he showed up and she wasn't dressed and ready? Hadn't packed so much as a toothbrush?

Perhaps she should prepare, just in case. If he didn't come, she'd unpack in the morning, no one the wiser. Also she'd need to write a letter to Jimmy telling him she couldn't see him any more, didn't feel "that way" about him, and wouldn't want to cause further hurts by going on. Sorry for the misunderstanding. "I'll always think of you as a dear friend; our times together were fun and I enjoyed them. But I find I can't switch from friend to lover."

On reaching home, she decided she must begin to mention Nat to her parents. Get them used to hearing the name, knowing she'd seen him. That way, if someday Nat really should want to marry her, it wouldn't come as a shock.

Nat must care a little for her, she thought. Five dollars for real cultured pearls! An awesome expenditure. She loved his recklessness. She'd loved it since the day he bought the classiest carriage in town.

Anxiety squeezed at her midriff, almost doubling her over. As she climbed the steps up the embankment at home and walked along the side of the house to the kitchen door, she yielded to an impulse to press at her stomach. For all her dread of confrontation, she knew she couldn't keep hiding her interest in Nat. She must be casual. "Today Nat McCurdle asked me to marry him." As if he were just one of her many admirers.

At dinner, while surreptitiously clutching her churning midriff, she waited until everyone was seated at the table and the food had been passed around. She watched her mother cut up the stew meat into tiny pieces for baby Bea. While she prepared to launch her rehearsed speech, she reminded herself: no tearing up, no getting angry or upset. Cool and calm, no matter what they say. Deep breath now; several deep breaths to quiet the butterflies.

In a moment of silence, she squared her shoulders, plunged in, and grabbed the limelight. "Guess what?" She tilted up her chin, smiled slightly, and spoke to the table at large, avoiding the eyes of parents and siblings. "I had two proposals recently. The men are standing in line out there." Small giggle, not too forced. Remember the Gibson Girl. "I expect I'll be getting married soon."

"I didn't know you had more than one beau." Her mother, too, maintained her calm.

Vi shrugged. "I like Jimmy but, you know, he's young. No man of the world."

Millie spoke up, her childish voice piping and clear. "He's no Nat McCurdle, is he?"

At the sound of the hated name, Douglas moved abruptly, scraping his chair back. Vi tossed her sister a look of fury. She'd planned so carefully how to say this. Now Millie had ruined everything.

Her father's fist slammed on the table. "You are *not* going around with Downer McCurdle. I won't have it. The man is a bas—a bum."

Vi jumped to the defense of her beloved. "He's no such thing, Pa. You don't really know him. You and he got off on the wrong foot with one another."

Douglas removed his napkin and turned to confront her. His fingers grasped the table-edge so hard his knuckles went white. "I said you are not to see Downer."

In her anger, she abandoned her resolve about calm persuasion. "Pa, I'm almost twenty, you can't tell me what to do."

"I can while you're living in my house."

Vi abandoned her planned strategy. She pushed her chair back and stood. "Pa, I've grown up. I contribute my income to this household. Between us, Rob and I practically support it. I'll choose my own man."

He flinched at her accusation but stood his ground. "Not to the point of carrying on with a saloon rat, you won't."

"So what do you think *you* are?" she threw at him. "I suppose the cops don't bring you home dead drunk?"

Everyone gasped. He stood. He shoved his chair out of the way, stepped closer to her, and reached out to slap her face. Vi felt a shock. It was the first time she recalled him striking a family member. Her face stung. She cradled her cheek with her hand and backed off. The others at the table stopped eating and, forks in the air, maintained an uneasy silence.

Douglas swallowed hard, relaxed his fists, and visibly brought himself under control. He spoke more calmly. "You are not to see Downer. I won't have it."

She swallowed hard and took a deep breath. "I'm a grown woman; I'll see whomever I please."

"You're still my daughter, and I'm telling you I won't put up with—"

"Your daughter!" Vi couldn't resist the thrust. "What is it to be the daughter of a man who staggers along Bridge Street singing at the top of his lungs?"

"Stop that at once, Vi!" Rebecca too shoved her chair back and stood. "Go to your room!"

Bea began to cry. Millie sat white-faced with fright.

Vi shoved her chair away so hard it tipped over and crashed. She left it on the floor and rushed to her room, tears flowing, promises to herself of control abandoned. She was glad that at least her brothers hadn't heard this exchange. Rob had gone to a band concert, and Menno was now permanently out of the house, living with Alana's family while saving to build a home.

Behind her, she heard her mother pleading, trying to make peace. "Could you have misjudged the man, Pa?"

"He's a bum," Douglas insisted. "He gambles, he goes around with loose women. I won't have my daughter seen with him."

Vi slammed her door. She threw herself onto her bed, sobbing. Her determination strengthened. She decided to pack at once and hope Nat meant what he said about eloping. Clearly, it was the only way. Though she hadn't wanted to believe him, he'd been right about that.

Teary, working off her fury, Vi flung clothing pell-mell from her drawers and wardrobe into the valise, then hid the valise at the back of the closet so that snoopy Millie wouldn't find it. She felt furious with her little sister for precipitating this confrontation, furious with her father for treating her like a child and failing to respect her true and deep love. She decided that if Nat didn't come, she would move out anyway, into a furnished room or boarding house somewhere. Let her father manage without her income. She'd started clerking in a dry goods store at age thirteen, the day after she finished sixth grade, and had always contributed her wages to the household.

Later, somewhat calmed, she managed to write a letter to Jimmy, put a stamp on it, and stuffed it in her coat pocket, to be mailed when she could get to a mailbox. She also scribbled, in shaky script, a note to her parents saying she was sorry things had to be this way. She'd hoped for their caring and support, but she loved Nat and he needed her. He was far from well even yet.

The note was designed to serve whether she eloped or simply moved out. If Nat failed to show up, she would leave at dawn and take her bag to the train station, to be checked in a storage locker while she room-hunted. Either way, she would be gone when her mother came in the morning to call her to breakfast. Her previous week's wages, luckily not yet turned over to Ma, would pay the rent in a boarding house.

Dressed and ready, she lay on her back on the bed, careful not to thrash around and muss her hair. She heard Millie say goodnight and go up to bed. She heard Rob come in and climb the stairs. She heard her parents in the dining room, talking in quiet voices, probably discussing her. The upset had apparently made Douglas cancel his saloon plans. That would complicate matters.

In the dim gleam of the streetlight, she watched the clock. At eleven, the voices still murmured. She worried that Nat might arrive too soon and get caught.

At last, footsteps sounded on the stairs. The house grew silent. The street had long been so, with no clomping of hooves or clatter of carriage wheels. When she heard a low whistle at her window, relief flooded through her. She jumped up, opened the window wider, and leaned out. Nat stood back in the shadows. She could see only his tall, dark form.

She whispered, "I didn't hear you arrive."

"I parked around the corner. Waited ages for the lamps to be snuffed. Are you ready?" He too spoke quietly.

"Here, hold my coat. I'll get my valise." She rescued the valise from the closet, lifted it to the window, and handed it out. Nat took it from her. She grabbed her reticule, which contained all the money she had. After checking to make sure the note was in plain sight on her dresser, she climbed through the window, taking the hand Nat held out to her.

"Dad didn't go to the saloon," she said.

"I noticed. I've been watching the house." Still holding her hand, he slid a ring onto her ring finger. She gasped. Even in the faint light from the street lamp she knew it was a diamond. She whispered, "Oh, Nat!" She held up her finger to admire the sparkle. "Dearest, how beautiful! Thank you."

He took her in his arms for a quick kiss, and she eagerly kissed back.

The night was foggy. Nat said they'd best go the back way so as not to be seen on the street. They trekked along the path through the vegetable garden and across the vacant lot next door, Vi holding her skirt with one hand, carrying her coat and bag in the other. Nat carried the valise.

Through the fog, they made it safely to the buggy, and then had to drive past the house. The clatter echoed in the silent street. Vi twisted the ring uneasily. Through her excitement at being beside Nat, she felt terrified. Even in the hollow where it was thicker, the fog wasn't thick enough to hide them. They cantered up the opposite hill and along silent and deserted Bridge Street toward downtown. She wanted to urge the horses forward faster; she wanted to be safe indoors.

"I made reservations at the Cody Hotel." Nat spoke as if reading her thoughts. "It's close to the Railway Station. The preacher's due at nine in the morning, along with two of my buddies to be witnesses. We'll be married in a reception room of the Cody and then get out of town."

Vi's midriff twitched so hard it seemed about to cut her in half, and once again she bent over to clutch at it. Yet she suffered a sense of unreality. The silent city half hidden in fog, its gas lamps forming circles at each crossroad, seemed an eerie setting for this improbable adventure. Nat wasn't really beside her, his arm around her. He hadn't really given her a ring. This was just a repeat of a recurring dream.

They flew down the hill, all buildings dark except the hospital, where electric lights glowed through the fog. The clatter of the horse's hooves echoed, the only sound until, on Monroe Street, another carriage could be heard some distance behind them. Through Campau Square, they angled back past Wurzburg's, dark and unrecognizable, toward the railroad station and the hotel.

The Cody was lit up as if awaiting them. They entered the lobby, with its gaslight chandeliers, red plush furniture, and potted palms. Even while admiring in the light the glitter of the ring on her finger, Vi awoke from her dream to realize she was in a hotel with Nat, and had only his word that a preacher would come tomorrow. Warning bells sounded in her mind. What if, in the morning, she should awake to find Nat gone, and no preacher?

Though crazy about this man, she didn't wholly trust him. She knew he was a lovable rogue.

"I'll sleep on one of these chairs in the lobby," she said. "We shouldn't share a room until we're married."

He gazed at her in consternation. "Those chairs weren't made for sleeping, just for looks. They're not comfortable. Come on, Vi, I promise not to touch you until we tie the knot."

She shook her head. There was her reputation too to think of. "Easier to manage if I stay here. Easier for both of us," she added, wanting him to know she really did long to be in his arms.

He looked hurt. "Don't you trust me?"

She wanted to fling her arms around him and assure him that of course she trusted him. She restrained herself.

He added, "We'll be married in nine hours, and it's hardly—" His gaze focused on the windows to the street. His voice trailed off; he frowned. He murmured an uneasy, "Uh-oh."

She whirled around. Plunged back into the dream, a bad dream now, she saw her father rush in through the swing door, his moustache twitching. As he strode toward them, she wondered how to wake herself up. This couldn't be happening.

Apparently, her father felt the same way. Arms akimbo, he stood confronting her. His first words were, "I don't believe this, Vi. You wouldn't go to a hotel with this—this—"

She squared her shoulders and faced him. "Nat and I are getting married tomorrow, Pa." She held out her hand to show him the engagement ring.

His face went white. He said, "You're doing no such thing. You're coming home with me." He grasped her arm as if to march her off.

"Here now," Nat reached out to shove away his hand. "This is my betrothed you're talking to. Show a little respect, old man. She'll soon be my wife."

Douglas clenched his free fist and gripped Vi's arm. His moustache wiggled as if he were moving his lips but finding no words. Finally he said, "Over my dead body."

Not knowing how to handle the situation, still feeling like one in a dream, Vi tried to buy time by asking, "How did you find me so fast?"

"Bet Doc Lapham brought him down," Nat said. "I see Doc's buggy outside. Did he pass your house at the right moment, Langston? Did you recruit him as your taxi service?"

Vi recalled hearing the sound of a carriage behind them as they'd turned onto Monroe Street to clatter through the silent downtown. She looked around and discovered that, even at this late hour, the lobby was not empty. There were at least three witnesses to this drama, all men, one hidden behind a newspaper. Off in a corner, one young man scribbled in a notebook. Douglas tightened his grasp until it hurt.

Desperate measures were called for. Vi tilted her chin higher and spoke forcefully. "Take your hands off me, Pa. I have to marry this man." She drew herself up, pulled free, gathered her courage, and announced, "I'm—I'm carrying his baby."

Her father stared. He sagged and dropped his arm. He seemed to turn suddenly old. All the lines in his face showed. Though she knew she'd won, she already regretted the method she'd used. The victory felt hollow. Nat eyed her, open-mouthed.

After a long silence, her father said, "At least come home and let's do this right. Your mother will want to help with the wedding."

Suddenly worried that he might believe her desperate ruse, Vi turned to Nat. She tried to act as if this were a casual conversation. "All right with you, dearest?"

Nat hesitated. "Big weddings are not my thing."

"Not big. Just the family and Clovia, my best friend. Let me have two weeks to make a gown and notify my boss I'm quitting." She tried to give him a wink, but in her nervousness, her eyelid wouldn't cooperate.

He pointed out that he'd bought the train tickets and hired the minister. Suddenly feeling guilty that she'd doubted him, she asked, "Could we telegraph the man? Postpone everything until later?"

He shrugged. "I suppose I could change the tickets. I'll have to cancel the room reservation."

"It would mean so much to me to have a proper wedding," she said.

He sighed, gave her a regretful look, yet swung around toward the desk. "Okay, wait here."

When he'd gone, Vi again confronted her father. "You can go on home with Doc, Pa. I promise I won't do anything without letting you know. If we can't postpone the wedding, I'll send a carriage for you and Ma in the morning."

With a frown and a barely perceptible nod, her father walked away, his steps dragging. While deeply regretting what she'd had to do, Vi yet saw no other way she might have handled the situation. Pa's intransigence left no room for discussion or compromise.

Nat came back to report that he'd canceled the room reservation. Vi watched the young man with the notebook get up and leave the lobby. Suddenly she had a renewed attack of fright.

Nat took her arm and peered at her with a quizzical expression. "So tell me, Vi, which was it? Virgin birth or Jimmy Reeves?"

"Neither." Vi longed to offer Nat an explanation, but she wanted to wait for that familiar form to move out through the swing-door into the night.

"Ooh, a mystery man," Nat said.

Vi shook her head. "I'll explain later." She saw Mr. Notebook stride off toward the *Herald* office. Along with panic came the chilling recollection that he was a reporter from the newspaper, probably taking down every word that had been spoken. She'd seen him watch with interest, glancing up even while his pencil moved. Once or twice, she'd met his gaze.

She recalled that he'd attended and reported on a party she went to with Jimmy. In that case, he knew who she was and could name names.

"I'd just like to know whose kid I'm raising." Nat sounded more perplexed than angry. "It sure as hell isn't mine."

Too upset to deal with explanations right now, Vi wailed, "Dearest, that reporter recognized us! This incident will be in all the papers!"

Nat shrugged. "You don't say?" He seemed unconcerned.

"But Dearest—"

"What can they say about us? We're going to be married, aren't we? So let them put us, all proper, in the society news where we belong."

She continued to feel uneasy. The whole town would believe she was pregnant. She'd meant that lie for her father alone. Now all the socialites who knew she'd been dating Jimmy would think she was having his baby.

How on earth was she to untangle this mess?

CHAPTER 9

2002
Ashley

I couldn't restrain a chuckle over Vi's worries regarding the reporter. I knew it wasn't funny, that for Vi it must have been desolating. Yet it made me feel good to know my twice-great aunt had faced difficulties echoing my own when she tried to fit into a society not made for her kind of person. I hadn't supposed white people encountered such problems.

I'd had no idea what secrets I might uncover when I began reading Vi's diary. Actually, when I first went to the attic and looked at those dusty boxes full of letters, diaries, and fading old photographs, I'd felt so intimidated I'd been tempted to chuck the whole plan. Especially after hearing Laura's sister spout off, I longed to rush home. But I knew I'd only go back to the same old fights with Mom about my future. "Ashley, you manage to snatch defeat from the jaws of success." And the pressing of guilt buttons: "Your forebears, black and white, fought hard to give you the privileges you now scorn."

That wouldn't be good. I'd already heard and argued that, *ad infinitem.* Why should I be held responsible for what my ancestors did? No one seems to have given thought to what my life would be like as a mixed-race kid; no one offers help about that. Not even my dad understands how it feels to get rejected by both the white world and the black.

Vi's diary ended with her almost-elopement and the claim that she was pregnant. I search frantically for more information. Thumbing through brittle, cracking paper, I find a diary that Millie started as a child. The first sentence was written in block printing: MY BIG SISTER IS DUM. SHE SHOOD-*SHOUD* OF MARRIED JIMMY HE WAS NICE.

It's hard for me to imagine my educated great-grandmother writing those misspelled words, but though I see her as forever adult, she had to have been a child at one time. She went on: ME AND ROB PLAYD AT HER WEDDING.

So there *was* a wedding. I can't believe the children would have been allowed to play during it. Then I remember that they were musicians. Of course—of course: they played their instruments, they provided music.

I go through the other papers in the box, hoping for a description of the wedding. And sure enough, I find two more of those unsent letters from Rebecca to her sister. Often, it seems, Rebecca poured her heart out and then couldn't bring herself to mail the outpourings.

Just as I start to read, my mother calls from California. Laura brings me the portable phone, then leaves. When Mother asks how things are going, I squelch the urge to complain to Mom that Laura's sister doesn't want me here. I know in advance what my ever-loving mother will say: "Laura's sister doesn't own that house nor even live in it. Why are you worrying about her?"

Instead I talk about Vi and her love-life.

Mom claims to remember about Natty Nat. "I never met him but Grandma Millie used to mention him. She said he changed her life. Knowing him made her extra cautious who she fell in love with. To avoid Vi's predicament, she always second-guessed herself over her own feelings, always trying to get to know her men better before letting herself become carried away. She said she went too far the other way and lost two of her beaux because of her coolness."

"Even at age six Millie saw through Nat," I say. "She wrote in her diary that she wished Vi had married the other guy, Jimmy Reeves."

"I gather that the 'research' is turning out to be more interesting than you expected?" Mom comments.

"It's different, anyway." What had I expected? A lot of snobby white people I'd have nothing in common with. Yet I feel I understand Vi perfectly. I fell for a guy like Nat—white, of course—in my last year of middle school. He propositioned me and when I said no, he wanted nothing more to do with me. He wasn't up for any sort of committed relationship. My first experience of that sort of thing, and it hit me hard because I really cared for the nerd.

"The surprise, to me, is that Nat even wanted to marry Vi," I say. "What brought him around, do you suppose?"

"I seem to recall that he was dying of cirrhosis of the liver. No doubt he needed her."

I confess to astonishment that Vi worried about being a wallflower. "To look at her, she seemed like a person who'd be naturally popular. By the way, which family members are descendants of Vi and Natty Nat?"

"Oh, I think that would be our Boston cousin. Louisa?—no, Eloise. Della Eloise. I never met her."

"A snobby Bostonian is descended from Natty Nat? Does she know what her forebear was like?"

"I never asked. Get Grandma to tell you about it sometime." Mom adds, "Grandma knows all the juicy stories."

Blown away by this, I protest. "She never told me any of them. She acted like gossipy stuff didn't happen in *her* family."

"Perhaps she just didn't imagine you'd be interested."

When I hang up, I realize my third cousin twice removed has arrived. I hear his voice from downstairs, talking to his mother. Feeling the need of a friend in this house, I long to rush down and say, "Hi."

I sit firmly on that urge and again pick up the letter. Before I can read, I hear footsteps on the stairs, and there he stands in the doorway looking at me. He's sort of cute with his hair in his eyes. It may run in the family to fall for guys with hair in their eyes. I have to watch it.

"How's it going, Ashley?" he asks.

I pretend I hadn't heard him come in. I gaze at his tall form as if surprised to see him. "Oh, hi, Doug. You're here, are you?"

"I have to drive my mother to a meeting this evening," he says, "I thought you might like to ride along and we could go out for a snack while we wait for her."

It sounds like a welcome break. I nod. "Okay. I could do that."

He inquires how my research is coming along. When I tell him I'm still reading about Aunt Vi, he asks, "What about Aunt Vi?" He plunks down beside me. I notice he smells of shaving lotion.

"I'm afraid she married Natty Nat, and that he wasn't really the darling she fancied him to be."

"I've heard that her husband was a gambler." He frowns and fingers the brittle pages. I bend over them and we read together. I can feel his breath on my hand that holds the book. I almost yield to an impulse to slide closer to him, and then decide: Better not. Might send the wrong message. I have to be careful about that. I lean closer to the page.

🍁   🍁   🍁

Rebecca had been thrashing, worrying about Vi, when at one-thirty a door slammed below. She hurried downstairs to find her daughter in the front hall, dressed in street clothes and holding a valise.

"What's going on?" she demanded.

"Nat and I are getting married." Vi's cheeks were flushed, her hairdo awry. "The wedding's in two weeks."

In shock, Rebecca grasped the newel post to steady herself. "Pa'll have something to say about that, Violet. He told you he—"

"Pa has given his consent. Nat and I met him downtown."

Rebecca felt choked up, unable to breathe. "How did you talk him round?"

Vi shook her head. "Tell you tomorrow." She carried the valise to her room and closed the door behind her.

Too nervous and jittery to sleep, Rebecca went to the kitchen to warm some milk, added a bit of cinnamon and sugar, and sat drinking it. Her midriff churned with anxiety about her husband and daughter.

When, more than an hour later, Douglas arrived smelling of liquor, he too, like Vi, refused to talk. He followed his wife to bed and pretended to sleep. Panicked about this wedding which seemed to make no one happy, Rebecca thrashed.

Toward morning she dozed off, to be awakened at daylight by a shout from Rob, whose voice echoed in the hall outside her door. "Ma, did you know Vi tried to elope last night? Pa stopped her. It's written up in the *Herald*." After a knock, he came into her bedroom, proffering the newspaper.

Rebecca sat up and hid her face in her hands. This was too horrible. When Rob thrust the paper against her arm, she pushed it away. She longed to hunch down and draw the covers over her head. Finally she forced herself to get up, put on her robe, and go downstairs. She sought Vi, sought an explanation for the horror-story her family seemed embroiled in.

Events moved along inexorably, and though Rebecca kept hoping something would interfere, nothing did. Time passed, the dreaded day came, and Rebecca awoke to the sound of Vi's singing in the bathtub.

Vi splashed and belted out a song about her wedding day shining in the sky. She seemed in a delirium of happiness, as if nothing could now stand in the way of eternal joy.

How little she knows of life, Rebecca thought. How pitifully, tragically young she is.

The day really was shining in the sky, with bright sun, tree branches leafing out, a robin on the window sill. Everything, including Vi's rich contralto voice, spoke of promise for the future. As if Mother Nature were trying to tell Rebecca she was wrong in doubting her daughter's chance at happiness with the man called Downer.

Vi claimed all young men sowed wild oats. "I'll keep Nat happy after we're married so he'll stay home." When Douglas assured her Nat wouldn't change, she insisted, "Yes, he will. I have so much love to give him. He needs me."

The words were doubly jarring to Rebecca because she remembered saying the same thing about her own wedding. Her parents had been horrified by her insistence on marrying a man not of the Mennonite faith, a man fond of saloons. She'd argued, "I have so much love to give, I can make him happy without the drink." She'd passionately believed her own words, believed she could open a new world of joy to him.

Now, each time Douglas came home drunk, she felt he was throwing her love back in her face.

Nat, she suspected, would do the same. Vi would sit at home, alone with her little one, wondering where she went wrong, how she'd failed her man.

Like me, she thought. Always trying to give more, care more; always discovering that my gift wasn't wanted. Turning bitter, feeling a hard core of anger growing within, gall rising in my throat, interfering when I try to say something kind and caring, making it come out hostile-sounding. Millie always taking her father's side, flashing me protesting looks as if to say: Why are you being mean to my nice dad? Millie patting Douglas' arm to console him for his wife's angry words.

When Bea toddled into the room, Rebecca put on her bathrobe and took the child downstairs to the kitchen. She set her in the high chair and poked into the franklin stove to prod the coals to life and start the coffee perking.

Vi entered, her lily-of-the-valley perfume preceding her, to complain that her hair wouldn't behave. As always after a shampoo, her curly brown locks hung in corkscrews. Rebecca studied them, and a lump formed in her throat as she recalled Vi on Christmas eve, so beautiful in her new ball gown, going off on the arm of the red-haired, freckle-faced man Rebecca had joyfully but naively assumed to be her daughter's new love.

Still in her nightgown, soft brown hair covering her shoulders, Millie followed Vi into the room and studied the problem. "You could do it Grecian," she said. Millie's favorite book, given to her by one of the Sunday School ladies, was about Greece, its gods and goddesses, its buildings with stately columns, its women with draped garments.

Rebecca considered. "Perhaps you're right, Millie, a Grecian hairdo might—"

"You make me sound like a statue," Vi protested.

The thought flashed in Rebecca's mind: from now on you *are* a statue. Your future is frozen.

Millie was excited over her first public performance. She and Rob had played together all year with only the family as audience. Now there would be outsiders—Clovia, Nat and his friend Josiah, and a Mrs. Randolph who'd become a friend of Vi's during her months of dating Jimmy. Mrs. Randolph was organist at the Congregational church and urged that Millie, though she was a year below the required age, be permitted to join the youth choir. Millie, she said, had perfect pitch and knew how to read music. "The other children can't do that yet."

Rebecca wondered if she ought to allow Millie to participate in so many things. She didn't want to push. If the child had musical talent, she felt it should be allowed to grow naturally as Rob's had.

Millie had argued, "It's a *church* choir, Mother."

"But such a big, imposing church. There must be two hundred people in the place on any given Sunday."

Even Douglas joined the argument, saying he saw no harm in Millie's performing. "God gave her a talent, Becky. Presumably she was meant to use it."

"Sure, when she's grown and can handle it. We don't want her to become a show-off kid."

Douglas insisted Millie would never become a show-off.

Shortly after lunch the first guests arrived, including Alana, far along pregnant, and Mrs. Randolph who brought a beautifully-wrapped gift. There was as yet no sign of the groom. Rebecca felt a sudden, sinking fear: Vi could find herself standing alone at the altar. Under the circumstances, with a baby coming, that would not be good, even if the groom was less than desirable as husband material.

When the minister put in an appearance, and still no groom, Rebecca paced and worried. For all her doubts about Nat, she'd never wished upon her daughter the nightmare of a last-minute, public abandonment.

A few minutes before the service, the groom hurried up the steps and across the porch in the company of Josiah Morgan. In her relief, Rebecca greeted the men more warmly than she'd planned. She told Nat, "I'm sorry we had no chance to meet until now."

"There'll be plenty of time for us to get to know one another. I'll soon be calling you Mother Langston." Nat, a handsome man with straight brown hair and a small beard, dressed formally in a suit with pinstriped trousers, took both her hands and gazed deep into her eyes as if she were the only woman in the world who mattered to him.

I understand it, she thought. I see why Vi's attracted. This man knows how to win women over and sweep away their scruples.

Nat stepped through the rows of folding chairs and went to take his place near the improvised altar. Rebecca was left alone with Josiah Morgan, who squeezed her arm and told her not to worry. "Our Downer has changed since his illness," he said. "Doc Lapham put the fear of God into him, told him to give up his high living or he's a dead man. I truly believe he's learned to 'preciate your daughter."

"I hope so," Rebecca said. "I pray so."

She asked how Nat had got the name Downer. Josiah explained that he'd once won a prize for downing liquor faster than anyone else. He added, "Nat knows goddamn well—sorry, I mean, he knows he's lucky. Not many women would have waited for him through a long illness."

"Yes, Vi's a good person." Too good, too loyal.

He went to stand beside Nat. Rebecca helped the last arrival find a seat. Millie and Rob had already taken their places beside the music stands, Millie wearing the lacy dress Rebecca'd made for Alana's wedding. At a signal from the minister, the children began playing. Rob carried the melody on the guitar, Millie accompanying him with chords on the banjo. The room quieted.

After their performance, a borrowed record of "Here Comes the Bride" blared from the Victrola. Zeke stood by to keep winding. Nat, hands folded in front of him, appeared debonair in his pinstriped trousers, a gardenia in his buttonhole. In his high, stiff collar, he looked like an actor playing a role. Rebecca wondered how long his good resolutions would last.

Holding the arm of her scowling but properly dressed father, Vi followed bridesmaid Clovia down the aisle to join Nat at the altar. Rebecca had to admit that they made a handsome-looking couple, Vi slim and shapely, Nat tall and erect.

The couple spoke their vows. The minister pronounced them man and wife. Rebecca wiped tears from her eyes. For better or for worse, it was done. Vi would go off to an unknown future. Millie, at six, would be the oldest daughter of the household. None but Rob was of working age. Loss of Vi's income would mean rigid economies for the family.

The children played a closing number while the young couple hurried to the dining room. Everyone rushed off to kiss the bride and congratulate the groom. Rebecca went to the kitchen, where she made coffee to be served with the cake. Mrs. Randolph followed her to help and to rave over the children's performance.

"Your youngsters are delightful," she gushed. "I'd like to borrow them for our fundraiser for the poor farm. People will love them."

Rebecca winced. Church choir, fundraisers. They were only children. Yet she sensed Douglas would be pleased by all this adulation. She nodded uneasily.

Rebecca served the coffee and waited quietly through the lengthy process of taking a wedding photo, cutting and serving the cake. She watched Vi open presents and thank her sisters-in-law for toaster and cooking pots. There was a set of Waterford crystal from Clovia, and two beautiful cut-glass bowls from Mrs. Randolph. Except for her own gift of a talking machine, and Milllie's, an opera record of Caruso, all others were functional. She couldn't imagine a home without music. In her own childhood people owned music boxes with different records, and the calliope at the park in the center of town could be heard everywhere. Here the calliope was attached to the carousel out at Reeds Lake, and couldn't be heard in town at all.

Soon it was time for the bride and groom to leave. Vi had changed into her traveling clothes, and Menno had carried out valises already packed. Zeke drove the rented surrey with tin cans tied on behind.

Rebecca gave Vi a kiss. "Take care of yourself. Drink plenty of milk for baby's sake."

Vi frowned "Ma, there *is* no baby. I said that to win Pa over."

Shocked, speechless, Rebecca gasped. She flopped into a chair and fanned herself with a handy envelope. She could hardly believe her daughter capable of such duplicity. It seemed to her that she'd never really known this woman who stood before her.

"Pa would never have consented to the wedding if he'd suspected," she sputtered.

"Of course not. That's why I lied. I *had* to marry Nat. He needs me and I love him."

Exactly what I said about Douglas. Rebecca felt her spirits sinking. She asked, "How will I explain this to Pa?"

"Say I had a miscarriage."

Lie piled upon lie. Rebecca went faint contemplating breaking the news. When he learned the truth, Douglas would be furious—and disillusioned. Just thinking about it, she ached for him, for his coming disappointment.

Vi justified herself. "Pa and Nat were like two boys in a schoolyard; they didn't know how to stop fighting. They kept tearing me apart." She wiped her eyes with her handkerchief. "I love them both. Why can't they put aside their anger and make the effort to get along for my sake?"

It was no time to scold. This was Vi's day, maybe her only day. Rebecca forced herself to reach for her daughter's hand and squeeze it. "Go along. Be happy."

Vi nodded and turned away. The surrey waited before the house, and the guests held their rice at the ready. Rebecca watched her daughter bend her head in anticipation of the deluge soon to be tossed her way.

❧   ❧   ❧

"Wow, I can see why you like this job," Doug says. "This stuff is fascinating."

I gaze at him curiously. "You mean you never read any of it before?"

"Not a word."

"I always thought of attics as the rainy-day place where kids retreat to seek out mysteries of the past."

"I never figured my family had any mysteries," Doug confesses. "There were no pirates or smugglers among the Langstons."

"Are you sure? Sounds like Nat's past would bear some investigating along those lines. I wonder how the marriage turned out."

"Good question. Let's go on reading. Are there any more of those letters?" Doug reaches up and with his fingers flips his hair out of his eyes. His shoulders touch mine. I remind myself not to let him play Natty Nat, nor to let myself play Vi. Once around for all that was enough.

CHAPTER 10

1902
Rebecca

On an Indian-summer day in late October, the woods beside the hollow had turned gaudy with the reds of maples and yellows of oak. Busy at her sewing, Rebecca saw Vi come around the side of the house and pass the dining room window. Still smart and fashionable, the younger woman wore a new fall dress of rusty red, along with her large hat and ostrich plume. Rebecca was pleased to note that Vi had not let herself go after her marriage. A better man than Nat might have been proud to have her for a wife.

There were moments when Rebecca wished she dared dress as Vi did. Of course, it was out of the question. She'd worn gray Mennonite clothing for so many years she now felt conspicuous and uncomfortable in anything bright-colored. She knew she'd even feel uneasy wearing the dress she was making. She'd chosen dark blue with tiny lavender flowers for Rob's and Millie's sake, so as not to embarrass them at their big performance.

Giving a light tap, Vi entered by the kitchen door. She stepped into the dining room, unpinned and removed her hat, and surveyed the work in progress. "Ma, don't tell me you're actually making yourself a dress? That looks too big for Millie."

"I'm recruited to go to the WCTU shindig tomorrow night. Pa says he won't go alone to a women's affair."

Vi squinted in thought. "WCTU—Women's Christian Temperance Union. Their annual convention or something." She stared at Rebecca. "Pa's going to *that*?"

Knowing Vi resented such reminders, Rebecca squelched an urge to tell her daughter not to frown and cause wrinkles in her brow. She explained. "Because of the kids, you know. They're performing." Rebecca shrugged at Vi's obvious astonishment. "Mrs. Randolph's done so much for the youngsters, booking them for performances, giving them a start in music—we have to show our gratitude."

Thoughtfully, Vi fingered the dark blue shantung with the tiny flowers. "Mrs. Randolph didn't aim to do the kids a favor, Ma. She needed music to spice up their meetings and provide accompaniment to the singing. You and Dad don't owe her."

"She could have chosen someone else. She didn't have to pick Rob and Millie for the jobs."

"Ha! Who else would work for fifty cents an evening?"

Rebecca shrugged. "Kids have to expect to work cheap until they get a start. How many six- and thirteen-year-olds do you know who are paid to perform?"

"Fifty cents apiece? Call that pay?"

"For children, that's good. Lots of grown men only earn a dollar a day. Besides, it buys their sheet music."

Rebecca knew Douglas was right. She had to show up. The occasion offered an opportunity for Rob to become known in his field, and the lad had his heart set on one day starting his own musical ensemble. Yet she did so hate to mingle with those well-to-do church folk. She felt out of place. Worse, she felt like a specimen. She always wondered how much those women knew of her problems, whether they'd seen Douglas staggering about on Bridge Street.

"I never did figure out how you managed to visit so freely among those wealthy folk, Vi," she remarked. "Those women have been to finishing schools. They're educated; they've traveled in Europe. Don't you worry that they may've noticed Pa around the saloon?"

"I see no reason that should reflect on the rest of the family," Vi said. "Men do those things—drink, gamble, seek prostitutes. We women have to be their conscience. Isn't that what WCTU is all about?"

Rebecca didn't know how to explain her concerns. She wanted to be part of the alcohol solution as Mrs. Randolph was, as those other ladies were. It embarrassed her to be part of the problem. When she went to WCTU meetings, she longed to hide her head in shame.

She put the dress aside. "Now you're here, you can pin up this hem for me. Let's have coffee first. I'll make fresh."

Vi carefully laid her hat on an end table. "It's quiet around here. Where is everyone?"

"Bea's napping, Millie's at school, Dad and Rob are at work."

Rebecca went to the kitchen to fill the blue coffee pot, stir the embers in the stove, and add paper and wood. Vi sat at the kitchen table, straightening the red-and-white checked oilcloth cover, pushing aside the bowl of cucumbers soaking in vinegar.

"How's Downer?" Rebecca asked

Vi frowned. "Why can't you call him Nat? I hate the name Downer." With a sigh, she added, "Doc still claims he has only a couple years to live, but I know I can add several more to that. I'm taking good care of him, feeding him well. We go for rides in the country almost every day, and I urge him to stop the horse so he can get out and walk. Yesterday we strolled around John Ball Park. It's putting color in his cheeks."

"That's good." Now that Vi was married, Rebecca hoped for Downer to live on and become a decent husband. So far his illness had prevented his return to the saloons.

"Ma, I have news." Vi hitched her chair closer to the table, and helped herself to a cucumber-slice. "I'm *really* preg—in the family way, at last."

"Pregnant?" In her shock, Rebecca came right out with the word.

Vi only smiled. "Isn't it great? It's been five months. I was beginning to worry."

Though she tried to hide the fact, Rebecca panicked. Even if Vi could expand Downer's life-expectancy to three or four years, she'd still be a young widow with a small child. A terrifying thought in view of the fact Downer seemed to have run through most of his large inheritance. Rebecca had no idea, and even Vi didn't seem to know, how much money he still had, whether there would be enough to support a family after his death. And Vi couldn't go back to her job if she had a child to look after. What would become of her? Would she end up in Washerwoman's Hollow, taking in washes for a living?

Rebecca longed to inquire into Downer's finances, but feared that Vi, if she knew, wouldn't tell her. She forced a smile and said what she sensed her daughter wished to hear. "How exciting. I hope all goes well."

"Alana and I will be raising our kids together," Vi said. "She's in the family way again, too."

Rebecca turned from the stove to stare at her daughter in surprise. "But Sean's only three months old!"

"Five months tomorrow, Ma. He was born right after my wedding."

Rebecca felt cold all over. Children raising childen. It wasn't what she'd wanted for her offspring. Menno was now seventeen, Alana a year younger. One child would have been more than enough for them to cope with.

"They're both so young!" she protested.

"Alana says it's easier when you're young and have lots of energy."

"I don't know as that's true. It's tough to settle down when you haven't yet lived your life." Rebecca brought cream from the ice box, cups and saucers from the cupboard. To Vi's comment that she herself started young, she responded that she often wished she hadn't.

"Child-raising will be hard on you," she added. "You've already got Downer—Nat—to care for. Now you'll have two charges." Her hands were shaking; she clattered the cups as she set them in the saucers.

"It's not hard to care for people you love, Ma. Nat's pleased that something of himself will go on in this world."

"I just hope it works out." Rebecca tried not to sound dubious. She still believed Nat married mainly to gain free nursing care.

The coffee perked noisily; the kitchen grew fragrant with its aroma. A late robin hopped onto the porch and peered in through the screen door. Rebecca felt she ought to welcome the future, the coming of her grandchildren, but she couldn't stifle her worries. Alana with two babies and a teen-aged husband. Vi with a child and a dying man. Rob working full time at age thirteen to support the household. Millie and Rob performing for the very organization designed to fight the conditions existing in the Langston family—children working and earning money, father drinking it up. And she so helpless to change the situation.

She sighed again. "Life seems to rush like that roly-coaster at Reeds Lake, flying wildly, taking us all with it, but going nowhere. Ending where it started."

"Even if life's a roller-coaster, I want to have Nat's baby," Vi said. "I too want something of him to go on forever."

The hall was lit by electric lights which seemed glaring to Rebecca, and its rows of folding chairs were already almost filled. Rebecca chose an inconspicuous seat at the back. When Douglas slid in beside her, she whispered that they could have brought Bea instead of getting Annie to mind her. There were other people here with toddlers.

"You can't pay attention to the skit when you're fussing over Bea," Douglas argued. "The youngsters worked hard on this."

Though proud of her children, Rebecca wondered if she'd be eternally compelled to attend these functions in which she felt both overdressed and underdressed: overdressed for her own comfort yet underdressed for the occasion. She always wondered, did she choose the right material, the right pattern?

"How late will this 'do' run?" She was already looking forward to going home.

"Not too late, with all these little ones."

"I'm afraid my clothes are too plain."

"Nothing wrong with plain," Douglas said. "Shows you're free of vanity."

"I should have let Vi buy me pearls while she worked at Wurzburg's and could get them wholesale."

"Relax, Becky, you look fine."

Rebecca didn't believe him. Her hat was small, her shoes old and worn. She watched well-dressed women coming in, chatting with one another, and felt dowdy by comparison.

When Mrs. Randolph went to the podium to make the welcoming speech, Rebecca wondered how the woman found the courage to stand up before all these people. However would a person learn to do a thing like that? Hadn't this woman always been told, as Rebecca had, not to make herself conspicuous? Rebecca couldn't imagine herself getting up in front of folks under any circumstances, not even, were she to smell smoke, to yell, "Fire!" Most likely, she'd nudge some man, politely point out the smoke, and let him do what had to be done.

Yet here was Mrs. Randolph, introducing people, seeming poised and gracious. A second woman stood and thundered against the saloons, while a third pleaded for child labor laws, urging people to work for their passage. Rebecca could only think about Rob and how desperately the family needed his income. Child labor laws would desolate them.

At last it was time for the children's skit. Millie would have to stand up in front of all these people, not only to play her instrument, but to sing and even speak lines. Rebecca wondered if the child could do it. What would happen if she lost her courage?

Carrying her banjo, Millie stepped out with aplomb, as did Mrs. Randolph's daughter, Eloise. A cardboard saloon-front had been hauled onstage, and hand in hand, the two girls approached it, pretending hesitance. They paused, pointed, dared each other.

Following instructions, Rebecca had made for Millie a costume from one of Vi's old dresses, cut down but still touching the floor. It made the child look quaint. Eloise was even more of a waif, all rags and smudges.

Pretending fright, Eloise touched Millie's arm and spoke her lines loud and clear. "I don't think I can do this, after all. We'd better go home. We shouldn't hang around a saloon."

In a voice lower and stronger than her natural one, Millie urged, "Come on, this was your idea; you talked me into borrowing this banjo." Before all those people, she spoke up with no hint of timidity. So unlike my shy child, Rebecca thought.

Eloise went on. "I believed we should sing for our dads and lure them out of this place. But Ma would kill me for coming here."

The children argued back and forth. Eloise said, "Our dads won't even notice, and other people will think we're silly." Millie countered, "We're here now, so let's try your plan."

She raised her banjo and strummed. Rob and his newly-recruited friend Harvey, seated below the stage, provided accompaniment, while Millie struck chords and began singing. "Oh Father, dear Father, come home with me now." Eloise shrugged and joined in.

The "bartender," a woman dressed as a man, hurried out with a broom and mimed shooing them off. They moved away a little distance and started the song over. The bartender pursued them, raised the broom and threatened. "Go away or I'll call the police." They retreated further but sang on. She/he grew belligerent and, tossing the broom aside, grabbed Eloise by the shoulders to shake her. At this, the two "fathers," actually teen-aged boys made up with lines drawn on their faces to look older, came out, pulled the bartender off, and shoved him back inside his saloon.

Returning, they joined the girls in a second verse. "Oh, yes, dear children, we'll come with you now." Then, while Millie strummed, the four sang a rousing drinking song with words changed to vow a farewell to taverns and liquor. The fathers commented to one another that they must cease and desist from putting their children through this awful experience. They took the children's hands and escorted them off-stage, saying, "Let us go home and tell our dear wives we've sworn off booze."

Lovely, Rebecca thought, raising a finger to wipe a tear from her eye. Too bad it never happens like that in real life. If only it would!

The audience appeared moved. Around her, she saw people dab at their eyes with handkerchiefs. The younger children had been incredibly convincing. The audience applauded wildly when the pair came out to take their bows. Bouquets of flowers were presented to each of them. Rebecca saw Douglas dry his eyes—her Douglas who never abandoned the saloons no matter how often his children came to get him.

Rob and Harvey stepped up on stage to share, along with the four young actors, the applause and shouts of approval. When the meeting broke up, people crowded around the performers and congratulated them. Mrs. Randolph remarked to Rebecca and Douglas that they were "onto something here," that the skit was so good it should be performed for groups all over the area. "We plan to do this again for a fund-raiser at the County Poor Farm. After that, we'll take the show to Kalamazoo—maybe even Muskegon."

A woman grasped Rebecca's hand, saying, "What gifted children you have. How do you get them to practice so much?"

Rebecca shook her head in bafflement. "I never tell them to practice. They just do it." She herself felt astonished at their talents, and had no idea why two of her brood should have distinguished themselves like this.

"Aren't you lucky!" the woman said.

Rebecca nodded but privately thought she could have been luckier. She could have had a husband who really stayed away from the saloons, and a son who was getting an education instead of supporting a wife and infant. She wondered if any of these women had seen Douglas being escorted into the paddy wagon by the police.

And as for child labor laws, how in the world would the family survive if Rob were no longer allowed to work? These days Rob was their sole wage-earner. Douglas was still slow at his new trade, still learning. When the Polish and Hollander immigrants brought in their fine old European clocks for repair, the American parts didn't fit, and Douglas had to make new parts, a day's-long job for which his clients couldn't possibly pay him adequately. In lieu of money, they gave him other clocks or their European recordings. The Langstons were now the proud possessors of a large collection of marching-band records with names in Polish which no one in the family could read, and which couldn't be traded for groceries.

Millie came up to her mother, clutching her flowers and glowing with the thrill of success. She'd perspired under the bright lights, and the dampness made her hair curl in tendrils around her face. Her brown eyes, flecked with green, turned solemnly to the women who hurried over to praise her.

Millie was a beautiful child. Rebecca permitted herself a brief moment to recognize that fact. She hoped her little girl would not awaken to the irony of the situation, that she'd literally played herself, the abandoned waif of a drunken father.

If Millie hadn't had a talented brother to teach her music, she'd have no future beyond that of a working child.

Rebecca smiled as, hair awry, carrying his instrument in its case, Rob came toward her. She reached out to pat his shoulder and remind herself that all the family's hopes rested on these two gifted children and their performing abilities.

She and Douglas, when they married, had had such big plans. She would never have believed it could come to this, that the children would have to be the money-earners in the family and she'd go places worried that someone might recognize her husband as the town drunk.

She forced another smile as Millie, with her brown curls bouncing around her head, stood nearby in her waif outfit. She fumbled in her paper sack for Millie's street clothes and took the child to the rest room to change.

❧   ❧   ❧

I know just what Millie must have looked like. Gran has a portrait of her as a child, with her masses of curls. I tell Doug about it. He comments, "She must have been beautiful—and so talented besides. Mom calls her the Shirley Temple of her day."

"I wish I'd known about all this," I tell him. "I'd have got her to tell me how she felt about all those performances." Funny, she told me so much about her childhood, about the egg babies she played with instead of dolls, about Lake Michigan shipwrecks and the stories she heard from her mother of terrible wildfires, of Saginaw burning, Chicago burning—but she never told me about those performances of hers. I wonder why. Did something terrible happen to make the memories become unpleasant? I wish I'd questioned her back then when I had the chance.

CHAPTER 11

2002
Ashley

When Doug and I go for our drive after dropping Laura off, I ask him to take me to the black section which he claims exists. So far I haven't seen a black face. My impression is of a lily-white town. Yet while driving around, sure enough, we see a few blacks coming out of stores. It's hard to tell black sections from white because in Grand Rapids people don't use their sidewalks. No one is strolling, running, jogging or doing any of the other things we do on sidewalks in California, from making out to walking the dog. I couldn't be sure I really saw a black "section" though I saw black shoppers.

Afterward he drives me to Reeds Lake, where, as he warned, I find the amusement park gone without a trace. No hint that it had ever been here. No remains even of the pavilion with its theater where Millie once performed, no pier, no rental canoes. Nothing here but grass, trees, water and a picnic table. Too bad, it sounded like great fun, with its "roly coaster" as my twice-great grandmother called it, its carousel, its calliope, its excursion steamer. Sparkling and scenic, the lake would have been a great place for such a park. Grandmother Del says it was the Disney World of her childhood, the high point of her summer days.

On Saturday, helping Laura with preparations for the dinner party, I allow myself to reinstate a long-ago dream and pretend to be the white girl of the household. Knowing Mom would consider it self-defeating, I hide my uneasiness over the forthcoming event. Yet butterflies batter at my midriff. When my friend Keisha calls on my cell phone and gives me a chance to think of familiar things, I excuse myself to Laura, take the phone upstairs, and close my door.

Keisha and I have been friends all our lives; she's one of the people Mom fusses about. At fourteen she got pregnant on purpose so she could drop out of school. She lives with her mom and her son Jordi, now five, who's named for Jordi LaForge of *Star Trek*. She lost track of Jordi's father before the kid was born, and never demanded child support. Mom calls her a loser; Mom and I fight over whether I should be best friends with that kind of people. I tell her Keisha's not a kind of people, she's just Keisha and I like her.

The way Mom carries on about Keisha, you'd think nothing out of wedlock ever happened in her own family. Ha! What about Alana and Menno and the shotgun wedding? What about Vi and the trick of the pretend-baby? I have news for my family: Keisha didn't invent teen-age pregnancy.

Keisha catches me up on our mutual friends, then asks how things are going here. I tell her about my third cousin twice removed. "He's cute, especially when his hair falls into his eyes, but of course that's nothing to me. He's white."

"Watch out for him," Keisha says. "Fucking white guys can cause *mucho* pain."

"You're telling me!"

"I've been dating a Mexican guy lately," Keisha confesses, "and though his skin's as dark as mine, he still acts like he thinks he's better than me."

"That's the Mexican culture," I say. "Pure macho. With them it's not color, it's the fact you're a woman. Who needs that stuff?"

"I do, I'm afraid. Mom keeps saying she's fed up with raising and supporting two generations. She's like, 'I want you to marry and get out of the house.' So far, Mario's the only dude who asked me."

"Are you in love with him, Keesh?"

"I'm in love with the idea of having my own apartment. And Mario's in love with the idea of marrying an American citizen. He's an illegal." She giggles. "I can't get over the surprise of finding myself in demand because I'm a citizen. I never thought of myself as one. Guess I'll have to go register to vote."

"It all sounds pretty cold-blooded for a marriage," I protest.

"It's not that bad, Ash. We like each other a lot, and Mario and Jordi get along great. Mexicans are wonderful with kids. I wish they were as good with women. Hey, Ash, I'm learning Spanish, would you believe it? Today I told the Mexican custodian at our apartment complex to take out the trash." She rattles off the words. "*Venga a la calle con la basura.* I learned *basura* from your gran's Mexican gardener and *calle* from Tijuana street signs."

"Hey, that's great, Keesh. Maybe it'll work out after all. You'd have to turn Catholic, I suppose."

"Oh, well. Mario never goes to church anyway, so what does it matter? So I say I'm a Catholic—what the hell. Fact is, I haven't yet told him I'm not, though all I know about Catholics is, they eat hot cross buns at Lent, and get ashes smeared on their foreheads. And they spoke Latin in church but no more. I once went with a black dude named O'Neal who was Irish Catholic on his dad's side—and no, he was not Jordi's father, in case you're wondering." She's never admitted even to me who Jordi's father was. "He got ashes smeared on his forehead every year, and he taught me that Latin Hail Mary prayer: *Ora pro nobis nunc et in hora mortis nos*—uh—*nos*—"

"That's okay, Keesh, I'll take your word for it." Though I feel dismayed that she's abandoning black guys after we promised each other we never would, I pretend enthusiasm. "Let me know when the wedding is to be. I'll come home for it." I wish it were tonight. It would be an excuse for me to escape the Ottawa Hills crowd and head for California.

I can't seem to find words to tell Keisha of my apprehensions regarding the upcoming dinner party. Keisha never had white relatives, never observed the painful politeness that doesn't tell the truth. In Keisha's experience, the people who don't like blacks come right out and say so, along with dumping trash on your lawn and garbage in your mailbox. Well, I've had that done to me, too, by kids in my high school, but I think this subtle pretense is worse. You can't fight an invisible enemy.

Keisha drones on about Jordi, about how he's fussing over having to go to school in the fall. I tune out. Since I don't know a damn thing about raising kids, I can't help her. I loved Jordi when he was a cuddly baby, and even when he was a cute toddler, but now that he's about to become a schoolboy, I don't know how to talk to him any more. I suppose that's something you learn when you have kids of your own.

Keisha says, "You're so lucky, Ash, to have your dad at home. I wish my dad were still around. He could give me away at my wedding." She makes me feel guilty, remembering those years when I wouldn't let Dad come to pick me up lest the white girls see him. How could I have done that? I squirm with shame to remember.

When we hang up, I stop to check out my hair in the mirror, and before I can leave the room, the phone rings again. It's Dad, wanting to know how things are going. I tell him stuff I wasn't able to tell Mom or Keisha. "There's this big dinner party tonight for the whole extended family, and I'm having jitters about it. I feel it's crucial that people here should like me—and you know me, Dad. As soon as I try to make people like me, I get—well, what Mom calls caustic. Like, I go rigid and uptight, can't be charming to save my life."

"It's not essential, Lee." Dad chops off the first half of my name the way Keisha chops off the last half. "You're not required to be nice. Don't think of it that way; it's pressure that causes you to freeze up. Just think about acting natural, being the person you are, and let them like it or lump it."

"And if they don't like it, I'll have to come home. And Mom will carry on about how I always defeat myself at everything I try to do."

"You didn't defeat yourself in college," Dad says. "Your grades came today and they're good. In fact you got A in both psychology and English Comp."

"You're kidding!" Psychology was easy, but—surprise, I could have sworn my English instructor didn't like me. She did say I could be a writer or reporter, maybe even a television anchor, if I tried harder. But I didn't try harder, and I assumed she'd be turned off about that. English teachers tend to grade on what they believe the students *can* do rather than what they actually do. Then when you complain about your grades, they say, "You didn't realize your potential. You could have done so much better."

I *could* have done better in that class, and now I wish I had. I never dreamed she'd give me an A. I could easily have made it A plus. I mean, I even read *Beowulf*, I just didn't want her to know. Sometimes I like to annoy my profs.

"I guess I've never gotten over my high school phobias," I tell Dad. "Like, I still feel the girls are looking over my shoulder and will consider me dorky for getting good grades. Smart isn't cool in high school, you know." Not with anybody except a few brains that no one wants to emulate. Certainly not with blacks.

"Time to jettison all that," Dad says.

"Oh, I don't know. I still wouldn't want to tell Keisha or Bertie about those two A grades." Bertie's my other life-long buddy. She's gay but she knows to leave us alone.

"Your friends want you to be a loser?"

"Well, I wouldn't put it like that, but—like, they don't want me to get too far ahead of them. We couldn't hang out together." I spend a lot of time reassuring them that I'm still me, still the same old Ashley, even though I'm now a college girl.

Dad doesn't say what Mom would say, "You need new friends." He says, "By the way, Keisha called here. She wanted your number. Seems she's thinking of getting married."

"I know. Some Mexican dude named Mario. I'm concerned about her, Dad, I don't believe she's in love with him. She just wants to get out of the house because her mother's on her case."

"Well, you do kind of lose your options when you have a kid." Dad sighs. "But I won't say, 'Poor Keisha.' She chose her way to go." He wishes me good luck with the dinner party, tells me to let him know how it goes, and promises to call again in a day or two. We hang up.

Now I have to go back to figuring out what to wear to this event. Something nice and proper, skirt not too short, something Mom would approve of. No spiky hair, no belly-button ring, no leather tank-top or metal choker, no platform shoes—yet I don't want to be a total loser either. I mean, I want to be *noticed.* Especially by my third cousin twice removed. I mean, just because I'm not into dating white guys, that doesn't mean I don't want them to come on to me. Life would be boring if you dressed to turn guys off.

So how do you dress to be approved of by Ottawa Hills and still noticed by the opposite sex? Is it possible to do that?

I go back downstairs to finish helping Laura. She tells me everything's under control and I can shower and get ready. So—upstairs again, with a few free minutes to read Millie's childhood diary. I skim through it but find no more juice about the family. It's mostly about their "gigs," my word, not hers. Don't suppose they had the word then. Seems they performed their skit for WCTU meetings all over the southern part of the state, and were driven to them in—guess what?—*automobiles*, which she found thrilling. She became popular in school as everyone sought to get to know the "Banjo-girl." This caused chagrin when other girls came to the house, since in those days, as she explained in her capital-letter printing, WE HAVE NO INDOOR BATHROOM. Having to send visitors to the outhouse was a great embarrassment for her. She celebrated when Rob managed to pay for indoor plumbing.

I have to admit, plumbing was not a major concern when I was in school. Our worries had to do with cliques and being in or out of one. Black girls had to placate other black girls because we had nowhere else to go. The white cliques didn't want us. Well, maybe briefly, so they could have a token black—but that never lasted more than a couple months, and then we were out again, falling far and hard because our black friends weren't in a hurry to welcome us back. We'd become oreos.

We finally learned not to respond when white girls played friendly. Like, we'd been through it all before. Me and Keisha and Bertie—excuse me, dear English instructor, I mean Keisha and Bertie and I—formed our own clique and stayed in it. We didn't deign to notice the so-called Fab Five, the social leaders of the school, the girls destined to marry the bankers and the CEOs in town. Everyone else tried to commandeer their attention, but not us.

Millie described in great detail the performance at the county poor farm, which was run by a Mrs. Kingsley whom she seemed to admire. Or maybe it was Mrs. Kingsley's son she admired. His name was Warren and she wrote that she thought he was sweet on her. After the performance, he came to sit with her on the County House porch while they ate their meal. She claimed the County House had great food, including an abundance of ham and something called apple grunt, whatever that was. Warren explained to her that this was because they couldn't sell the produce. It wouldn't be right to compete with local farmers. They could only give food away in charity baskets to the poor.

Millie's first diary, covering the gigs and the embarrassments over that bathroom, ended after about six months, and I could find no more childhood diaries. Apparently she stopped keeping diaries until after she graduated eighth grade. The next diary began when she was fourteen. Though I longed to read it, I decided to put it aside for tomorrow. It was time, as Laura had said, to shower and make the weighty decision about the right clothes to wear.

I decided on my persimmon dress. It fit my form—for the guys, and came almost to my knees—for the Ottawa Hills folks. And it made my skin look a nice bronze color, not too dark or too light. I liked that because it didn't place me in a category. I hate being told I have to fit myself into a category. I can't do it without denying one parent or the other.

In this room my great-grandmother had dressed for her performances and worried, as I was doing now, about her appearance, especially for that trip to the poor farm, where she'd longed to wear her new dress yet hadn't wanted to make the poverty girls look bad. She'd wondered, would they want their performers to seem grand, or to be like them? She'd consulted her mother, who'd assured her she never made clothes "too grand" for her daughter.

The visit to the poor farm seems to have been a big occasion. I wondered if the farm was still there. Since Millie was no longer around to ask, I'd have to ask Laura. It would be something to talk about at the dinner party. It seemed an innocuous question; I couldn't have known it would cause trouble. But then, I have a genius for creating trouble. Mother always questions, "Ashley, why can't you *anticipate* these things?"

I used to kind of enjoy causing chaos but I guess I'm outgrowing my taste for it. I find I have no urge to do it now.

I'd learned from Laura that the Ottawa Hills cousins have two boys, one of whom works for the family construction firm while the other is studying to be a dentist. So when I hear a shouting in the side yard, I go to the window mid-way down the stairs—a small, diamond pane—and look out. Two guys are with Doug in the side yard, the three of them pitching horse shoes. I realize our dinner guests have arrived and it's time for me to put in an appearance. I go back to work on my hair, and finally decide I look demure enough to make my entrance.

The boys' parents are in the living room with Laura and Junior. The father is one of those hale-and-hearty guys with what Grandma calls a "corporation," a large, protruding stomach. Their mother reminds me of Laura's sister, Joyce, beauty-salon perfect, with brown hair teased into curls, held rigidly in place with so much hair-spray it shines like it's coated with shellac. I feel wary, and after shaking hands with Junior's brother, whom Laura introduces as Cousin Howard, I turn to his wife, Teresa or Terri, and offer just my finger-tips. I've noticed that older women who don't like each other do a kind of fingertip-drip that doubles for a handshake, and I imitate it. Terri fingertip-drips right back.

"Ashley, how nice to meet you," she says, and I think, *Yeah, you bet.* Then in my head I hear Mom say, "Watch that chip, Ashley."

"We were so pleased to learn you were coming," she adds. "We looked forward to meeting you."

"Me too," I lie. I never heard of her before.

"I hear you're in college."

"Just finished my second year." No point in telling her I dropped out.

"Our son Jason's starting his fourth year," she says. "He plans to go on to dental school at the University of Michigan." Terri's skin is so white it's clammy, and she has a turned-up nose. No doubt she was "cute" as a teenager, the girl-next-door type everyone loved. Now she probably wonders where she lost that charm. I've heard that type fades fast. She adds, "Ray has one more year in high school."

Laura says, "I just have a little more to do on dinner. Why don't you go out and meet the boys, Ashley?"

"Yeah, I guess I will." I notice Cousin Howard eyeing me with interest—maybe too much interest—so I turn quickly and hurry to the fragrant, steamy kitchen. Through savory cooking odors, I head for the back door.

When I step outside, the horseshoes stop flying and *three* cousins eye me with too much interest. So far this is not a good evening. I've read about white guys and "high yellow" girls. Great-Gran used to sing about "The Yellow Rose of Texas." I don't wish to be the Yellow Rose of California.

"Hey, Ashley, come on over and meet the gang," Doug says. When he introduces me, he puts an arm around my waist and acts possessive. The others continue to look intrigued. I start to wonder if I might have to fight off all three.

"I just wanted to meet you all," I say. "Don't let me interrupt your horseshoe game. I'll go ask Laura if I can help set the table or something. See you guys later."

"We should have planned a barbecue so you wouldn't have to bother with all that table setting," Doug says.

I slip out of his grasp, wave a farewell, and despite their disappointed expressions, go back inside. The table is already set with real silver in place of our everyday stuff, and elegant dinner plates. I fold the napkins fancily into the stemware. Then I work at helping Laura. Salad veggies were never so clean as those I scrub for her. In my vigor I take much of the red off the radishes.

When we've assembled at dinner, with the grace spoken, candles lit, food passed, Terri asks about my research. I tell her I was just reading about my great-grandmother's visit to the poor farm. She looks alarmed. I think, Oh-oh. Have I done it again?

"Poor farm?" she says to the table at large. "What has *our* family ever had to do with a poor farm?"

"I think that was merely the place where Millie got her start as a performer." Junior, extra-mashing his mashed potatoes, sounds offhand.

"I don't remember hearing about any Langstons involved with the poor farm," Terri insists.

"It was just a performance, dear," Howard says. "Aunt Millie didn't stay there."

She frowns. "I'm beginning to wonder what kind of stuff is in that collection. Has anyone checked it out to see if it's fit material to be given to our young people? Those old-time actresses were so awful."

I stifle a giggle. Is she serious? Protecting my innocence from my bad old great-grandmother?

Laura looks uncomfortable and says that *she* certainly hasn't had time to go through everything.

"Well, somebody ought to," Terri insists.

I bite my tongue. I long to say: you have to be kidding. I bet I know more about life than you do. I wish I could talk black to you for two minutes; that would wake you up.

I don't speak. Let them fight it out. Sooner or later Terry'll have to learn about the elopements and the shotgun weddings.

I catch Doug's eye and realize that he too is on the verge of laughter. I control the corners of my mouth and force them to stop twitching. I cut a piece of steak and lift it to my mouth with my left hand, English style. I am to the Manor born, after all. Gran has spent a lot of time trying to transform me into a "lady." I pretended not to listen to her, but if I had to, I could pull off a good performance as Lady Ashley Pennington. I bet I could even manage an English accent.

There is silence around the table as everyone looks embarrassed for not having thought to protect poor little me from the bad stuff in the diaries. Doug chokes, coughs, and reaches for his glass of water. I decide to take a break from eating so as not to do likewise. Terri glares around the table and remarks that it's high time the adults in the family take it upon themselves to check out the contents of the attic.

"I don't think it does any good to indulge in ancestor worship," Laura ventures. "It sets an impossibly high standard for the young people without doing a thing for the ancestors. I doubt anyone wishes to be worshiped."

"I'm not talking about worship, I'm talking about *respect*," Terry snaps. "I'm talking about preserving the highest values in the family."

Feeling uncomfortable, I count the minutes until the guests go home and I can get back to Millie's second diary, the one she wrote at age fourteen. I have a horrible premonition that Terri may try to snatch it away before I can dip into it. I sense she sees me as a threat, the one member of the family who'd tell the whole world that our two illustrious musicians got their start with gigs at the county poor farm. And that they were driven to earn money because their dad was a lush and big brother, aged sixteen, was supporting a family of his own.

Terri doesn't know the half of it. She hasn't yet heard the real juice. I decide not to tell her. She might talk Laura and Junior into sealing those diaries in some inaccessible place, or even destroying them.

"We want our young people to see their forebears as fine, upstanding people," she says. "It's important—it's essential—to provide good role-models."

The three boys are struggling as hard as I to stifle laughter. None of us dares to look at each other for fear we'll choke up with it.

Laura pointedly changes the subject to ask the high school kid about his plans for fall studies. He chokes back laughter to answer. The argument starts up again later when the two women go to the kitchen to clear up the dishes. I hear Terri say, "We were lucky, you and I, Laura. We married into a fine old family with veterans in every war the United States ever fought. Our boys are eligible for Sons of the American Revolution. We should never let scandal compromise the family's position."

I can't hear what Laura answers to that, but she must demur. I hear Terri say, loud and clear, "Well, if you won't do something about it, I will!"

Her tone makes me uneasy. I vow to get back upstairs as soon as I can excuse myself and escape, to make sure those precious letters and diaries are safely locked in my suitcase. They belong to me. My great-grandmother, no blood kin of Terri's, is none of her business.

In fact, I feel downright proprietary about them. It's as if Fate—or great-grandmother—had sent me here to protect them from Terri.

I have no fear of battle. All those fights I got into with white girls at school, those sessions in the principal's office waiting for my parents to arrive and take me home for a three-day suspension—maybe they made sense after all. Maybe they were preparation for this moment, this conflict.

Mom will kill me if I get in a fight with Terri.

But what the hell. The prize is worth it. Those diaries are precious. Let the battle be joined, Mrs. Howard Langston. Pick your weapon of choice. I'm ready.

CHAPTER 12

1911
Millie

Four days after her eighth grade graduation, Millie participated with Rob and their newly-formed orchestra in its first paid performance. The occasion hardly gave cause of celebration; the venue was the chapel of Holmes Mortuary.

After adjusting the big black bow on her pigtail, Millie lifted her banjo from its case. She heard someone in one of the pews comment that Nat McCurdle's luck had finally run out. Millie didn't agree that luck had been involved. She believed her sister had kept Nat alive by sheer willpower. Eight years—six more than the doctors had promised him. Eight devoted years during which Vi hovered over him and nursed him while weeping over miscarriages. She'd finally produced young Edgar, aged five, and she now faced widowhood with a small child.

The six-piece orchestra sat off to the side. From her position midway of the strummers, Millie could look over at the closed coffin—Vi had insisted it be closed to hide the corpse's gauntness and the ugly liver spots generated during Nat's final illness—piled with flowers. Millie pinched her nose to stop a sneeze over the cloyingly oppressive scent. Wanting to be inconspicuous in her borrowed dress of the hated black, which she believed made her skin look sallow, she inched her chair back.

She glanced over the assembled mourners. Vi, at front left, seemed more swathed in black clothing and veils now to bury Nat than in white years ago to marry him. As if, thought Millie, this funeral were a kind of dark wedding, marrying her forever to the dead. Millie shuddered as she watched her sister bend over and weep. Flanked by their mother in plain black, and nine-year-old Bea in borrowed gray, Vi covered her eyes and shook her head, refusing to let herself be cheered even when Bea patted her arm and Rebecca whispered what must have been comforting words.

Millie gazed at the huddled black figure and wondered what would happen next. Vi's very dedication to Nat, her long struggle to keep him alive, had worked against her, the illness having used up most of Nat's financial resources. Had Nat died when the doctors expected him to, Vi would have been a well-off widow free to resume her social life. But thanks to her care and devotion, Nat lived on and on, his illness costing much money, his good humor deteriorating as death inched toward him. He'd grumbled all the while that "the damn woman" kept smashing the liquor bottles friends smuggled to him.

Now the family could only hope that the deceased, who never discussed money, had secreted a bank-account somewhere. The lawyer was to come at dinner time and inform them about the will. Would Vi be a well-to-do widow? Or an impoverished woman with a five-year-old boy? Millie eyed her sister and wondered. Vi'd insisted she cared nothing about money, only wanted Nat himself. Dad had scolded, "You'd better start caring about money, you have a boy to raise."

Millie's gaze scanned the mourners. Most were related to the Langstons. Annie had brought her mother and her older sister, Flora. Alana was with her father. Dad and Millie's older brothers, Menno and Zeke, stood at the back with the other pallbearers, former saloon buddies of Nat's who now acted properly sober and solemn for the occasion. Millie recognized one man from the long-ago wedding. Josh? Josiah?

The organ, playing quietly as people filed in, now silenced. The musicians raised their instruments and focused on Rob, awaiting his signal to begin. There was tenor mandola, mando-cello, first and second mandolins, and Millie's banjo. Ruth Pearson, the pianist, set her fingers on the ivories.

It had been Nat's own idea to have a dance orchestra at this funeral; he'd even put aside money to pay them. He'd claimed he wanted no sad songs, no "Abide with me." "Let my funeral be joyful," he'd said. "For most of my life I lived the way I wanted to live, and I'm leaving part of me behind in Edgar." Millie remembered how he'd reached out to rumple the boy's hair as he spoke, the only time she ever saw him touch Edgar. On the whole he'd seemed intimidated by the child and hadn't known how to be a dad.

The funeral posed problems for the orchestra which, despite Nat's orders, could not play dance music at a solemn occasion. Luckily Rob had discovered a few dignified classical pieces, Haydn and Mozart, transcribed for mandolin orchestra. Thus the musicians proved able to avoid the kind of farce the irreligious Nat had envisioned. "We do have to think of the living as well as respect the dead," Rob had argued.

Rob raised his mandolin to signal the musicians to lift their instruments. The pianist played her introduction, then was joined by the others. Mourners hushed. Millie thought Haydn sounded less than great on their kind of instruments, but Nat's orders had to be carried out. The musicians strummed bravely. Millie's gaze met that of Harvey Hubbard, the second young man in the group, and she saw an amused glint in his eye. So he shared her views about Haydn-cum-mandolin! She squelched an impulse to giggle. She and Harvey had performed together for years at WCTU meetings, and along with the poorhouse boy, Warren Kingsley, who attended the affairs with his mother and his prim-and-proper sister, often shared irreverent thoughts.

When the music ended, the minister offered a eulogy in which he piously described Nat's so-called reformation. "Though this man started out as profligate and gambler, he later saw the light and, thanks to the efforts of a good woman, turned his life around. His wife, Violet, proved able to show him the senselessness of his path, and for the last eight years, under her guidance, he lived a life no one could fault him for."

Good reason why, Millie thought. He'd lacked the strength to do otherwise.

Millie herself had seen no sign of reformation. A year or so ago, when she'd developed breasts, Nat had begun leering and pawing. If he'd been stronger, not staggering so much, she'd have had to remove herself from his presence. Yet she knew she was supposed to think kind thoughts about the dead. Her mother would urge her to forget the bad things.

"He ended his life a good man," the minister concluded. "We must forgive the scapegrace years, and pray that God will accept this repentant sinner into heaven."

Heads bowed for prayer. Millie would have loved to question whether God rewards people for enforced goodness, but she knew her mother would consider the thought blasphemous at this solemn moment.

The orchestra played another number. When, at the end of it, the pallbearers came forward, Rob eased himself out of his seat to join them. Floral wreaths were removed from the casket. To the sound of Vi's sobs, Nat in his coffin was carried to the hearse.

Though Millie tried to feel sad about losing her only brother-in-law, she could generate no tears. During her childhood Nat had ignored her. In her teen years, he'd been obnoxious. She couldn't remember that she'd ever had a sensible conversation with him. Obviously, he'd had no idea how to relate to a young woman as a person. To him, young women were prey.

The orchestra members replaced their instruments in the cases and followed the mourners down the aisle, Millie and Harvey in the lead. Against Vi's express orders, the organist played "Abide with Me" as a recessional—but only after Vi had left the chapel.

Millie and Rob were to go on to the cemetery. The other musicians, who'd never met the deceased, departed. Harvey had promised to drop off Millie's banjo and Rob's mandolin at Stormland where a neighbor minded young Edgar.

So, for the second time since their arrival in Grand Rapids, the Langstons drove to the cemetery. In the carriage, Vi kept saying, "I can't live without Nat. Nat was my life; he was all I cared about."

"That's gol-darn hard on Edgar," Dad scolded. "Don't let the boy hear you talk like that. Believe me, I know what it's like to have a grieving widowed mother turn against her sons. No child should be put through such an experience."

"I didn't mean it like that," Vi sobbed. "Of course I want Edgar. Didn't I suffer three miscarriages before—"

"See you remember that. Pull yourself together and think of the future."

"A future without Nat is no future."

"There you go again."

"Pa's right," Rebecca said. "You have a son who needs you; you have to live for him now."

Vi wept harder. When they reached the cemetery, she stumbled, blinded by tears, on the walk to the open grave, which had been dug beside Zeke's deceased newborn in the family plot. Both parents grabbed her arms to help her along.

When Nat, without a single tear from his young sister-in-law, had been consigned to ashes and dust, the family went home and Rebecca set out food. The crowd snacked, hugged and consoled Vi, and finally departed. Alana offered to let Bea and Edgar stay overnight with her, to give the chief mourners time to themselves. Pa warned her she was taking on a lot. "Those two kids fight worse than siblings."

"Not at my house, they won't. I'll keep 'em busy. Edgar and Roan will play together; they're like twins. And Bea's old enough to be a help with baby Rory. Aren't you, dear?" Portly now from childbirthing, Alana turned to Bea and held out a hand which was promptly grasped. Nine-year-old Bea loved overnight visits to her grown up sister-in-law's multi-child household. Sean was only a year or two younger than she.

With the family alone in the parlor, Vi abandoned her brave pose. She sobbed and insisted she couldn't go on. Pa argued that she could and would. "You've shamefully neglected Edgar, always sending him outdoors to play. A hundred times in the last year I heard you order him out of the house."

"Had to, Pa. Nat needed quiet."

"And now Edgar needs attention. He's coping with the death of his father. He's trying to understand something new and awful to him."

Vi flung herself out of the chair and stood. "Oh, leave me alone!" She rushed upstairs, and the family heard the creak of springs as she fell onto the bed. Her sobs were audible below.

"You're too hard on her, Pa," Rebecca said. "You don't understand the girl; you never have. She's the type who needs someone to cherish and care for, needs to be needed. Her whole life was wrapped up in Nat."

"I have no quarrel with her needing to be needed. She *is* needed—by Edgar. Let her wrap herself up in him now."

"Give her time."

"When a boy who's just lost his father seeks the consolation of his mother's arms, he shouldn't suffer a rebuff and be foisted off on an aunt while his ma indulges herself in weeps and wails." Dad's fingers worked nervously at his moustache, curling the ends.

Millie hadn't noticed Edgar seeking consolation; in fact, before Alana took him away, he'd been tearing around the house with seemingly boundless energy, ignoring his grandmother's protests.

"We'll all help to look after Edgar and give Vi a chance to mourn," Rebecca said.

"Mourn!" Douglas sounded bitter. "Believe me, Becky, I know how easy it is for grieving widows to turn to another man as a replacement instead of standing on their own feet and caring for their children."

"Oh, Pa, don't judge everyone by your mother. Vi wouldn't do a thing like that. You'll see, it'll be years before she'll bring herself to look at another man."

"For Edgar's sake, I should hope so, even though Downer doesn't deserve that kind of loyalty. I don't want Edgar to go through what I went through."

"Pa, you're unfair to your mother. You need to forgive. In the days after the Civil War, women had little choice. They *had* to be supported by a man even if it meant sending their sons away, like you, on the orphan train."

Dad scoffed. "Millie and I can introduce you to a woman who took her two children to the poorhouse so she wouldn't have to place them in an orphanage or send them away. It may not have been pleasant for her—I'm sure it wasn't—but she had a roof over her head and she raised her own kids. Her name's Lorraine Whaley; she's now on staff at the County House."

"I suppose that's an option," Rebecca conceded.

"Unless you're the type to set store by preserving your position in society." Douglas' voice dripped scorn.

The cat, Donatello, had wrapped himself around Millie's neck so that she wore him like a living fur piece. When he purred, his chin vibrated against her collar bone. She sat with the other family members at the dining table where the lawyer had spread out the papers from his briefcase. Minus veils but still red-eyed and weepy, Vi sat opposite, their mother beside her. Dad sat near the lawyer to read his papers.

Millie had expected to be sent to her room during this conference, but no one said anything about her leaving. Apparently, either her status as the best-educated person in the family, or her age, which was fourteen, permitted her to be included.

The lawyer, a formally dressed gentleman, burly, jowled and moustached, hemmed, coughed, and came out with his news. "I'm sorry to report that Mr. McCurdle's long illness used up most of his resources. Mrs. McCurdle, there won't be enough money, I'm afraid, for you to maintain your home. I have the exact figures here, of course, but—my advice would be to sell the house, invest the income, and arrange matters so you can manage on the interest. If, for instance, you and your boy might live with your parents—"

To Millie's alarm, Rebecca spoke the words her middle daughter had hoped never to hear. "Millie can share Bea's room, and let Vi and Edgar have the big front room."

Millie protested. "I can't room with Bea. She's a child—and messy."

The lawyer eyed her with disapproval, yet he spoke in an impersonal, taking-no-sides tone. "It would enable Mrs. McCurdle to make a most generous contribution to the household, Miss Langston." Millie had never before been called Miss Langston, and on hearing, she drew herself up and squared her shoulders. The lawyer went on, "If she had no expenses beyond room, board and clothing, her income from the sale of her home should keep her going for years."

"With the extra money, you could go to high school, Millie," Dad pointed out.

Since Millie felt she absolutely must go to high school, could in fact not imagine her life without an education, she knew she could no longer protest the arrangement. Right now, getting to high school was her top priority.

"We must train Bea to be neat," her mother said. "She's old enough to clean up after herself."

Millie stroked the furry black and white paw lying between her breasts. "Only on condition I get to go to—"

"We all want you to go on in school," Dad said. "We need an educated person in the family."

"So that's settled." The lawyer gathered up his papers. "I'll see about putting the McCurdle house on the market. Will you want to store your furniture, Mrs. McCurdle, or sell it?"

"I'll never sell Nat's things." Vi broke down in a sob. Her mother hastened to embrace her. Millie ran her fingers over the soft fur between Donatello's ears. When she pictured Edgar in the house, she couldn't restrain a grimace. He was the worst tease in the city of Grand Rapids. Added to that, she would have to room with a nine-year-old who was herself a nuisance and a pest. It would be hard to take. She'd have to stay out of the house and study in the library. Her one consolation was that she would be attending Central High with her old friend Eloise, and Doc Lapham's daughter, Hazel.

She decided she'd buy herself a Chinese screen to divide her part of the bedroom from Bea's. Also, she'd need a desk. She assessed her savings from WCTU performances and tried to guess how much a desk and screen might cost. She'd scour the second hand stores, of course—but still, it would be an expense.

"At least young Edgar will be well cared for, with five adults in the house to look after him." Her mother spoke while getting up to leave the table.

Dad was seeing the lawyer out. When he returned, Millie patted his arm, remembering his bitter comments about his mother. "I bet my back-East grandmother misses you now, Dad, and wishes she'd kept you at home with her instead of putting you on the orphan train."

"I think she could find me if she wanted me." Dad wiggled his moustache. "She knows where she sent me."

Mother paused in the kitchen doorway to comment that the woman was probably dead by now. Dad shook his head. "Not she. Only the good die young."

Millie wished she could afford a trip to Maine. She'd have loved to locate her paternal grandmother and demand to know how the woman came to terms with sending her young son away alone. What was she thinking? How could anyone do this awful thing?

CHAPTER 13

1911
Millie

It was a summer of dying and funerals. On looking back, Millie would wish she could have skipped her late-July fifteenth birthday.

Though she'd bought two second-hand screens and a desk, she had trouble communicating that Bea's belongings and person were restricted to the far half of the room. Bea kept stepping around the screens, interrupting Millie as she worked at copying music for the orchestra. Millie's insistent reminder, "I need to concentrate here," never stopped Bea from telling tales of the doings of her friends. A natural-born storyteller, Bea hated to write and refused to keep a diary, but she loved to talk.

Five-year-old Edgar, surprisingly, had so far not proved to be a problem. On storing her furniture, Vi had brought Edgar's bed and toys and moved with him into the front bedroom, but Edgar didn't choose to hang around this household full of women. He took off with his cousin Roan, Alana's second-oldest son. The boys spent their days exploring the woodlands on the hill above Washerwoman's Hollow, collecting treasures of rocks, fallen bird eggs and "critters." Edgar often stayed overnight with Roan.

To lure Edgar home, Dad and Rob pitched a tent under the elm tree, and the boys filled a jar with fireflies to light the place. Yet the fun lasted only until total darkness set in. Then, wrapped in blankets, the weary adventurers trooped indoors to camp on the dining room floor. The next night they returned to Alana's.

In mid-August, Menno came to the house early one morning with his suit-case and announced that the two boys took sick in the night. He hesitated before admitting that the doctor, when called, had diagnosed the dread scarlet fever. He'd placed the boys under strict quarantine.

On hearing, Vi let out a scream. Scarlet fever, as everyone knew, was life-threatening to children. "Dear God, I can't lose Edgar, too! Please God, not Edgar!"

"You'll want to go over and help with the nursing," her brother Menno said. "I'll borrow your room. I have to stay out of quarantine so I can go to work."

Millie asked about Alana's two older children, Sean and Maggie. "Are they all right?"

"They've been exposed." Menno sighed. "We must pray they don't get sick."

Rebecca clutched her hands together. "Scarlet fever's a ghastly—"

"If I have to bury Edgar, I'll kill myself." Vi started for the door.

Rebecca followed and shushed her. "Don't talk that way. You'll tempt fate." She reminded her daughter she'd need to pack clothing and sleepwear. "Take food for yourself and Alana. There's leftover pork roast in the ice box. And don't worry. Doc Lapham will take good care of the boys."

"Oh, I can't think what I need." Vi held her head. "I just want to get to Edgar, fast."

Rebecca helped her pack. Millie walked with her, carrying the suitcase while Vi carried the roast and other groceries Rebecca had assembled. Despite the big red quarantine sign on the door, Vi was admitted to the house. Millie shivered as she watched her sister step inside, and thought of the words of Dante that she'd studied in English class: "Abandon hope, all ye who enter here." She felt sure something dreadful would happen in that grimly marked house.

She set the suitcase close to the door so it could be pulled inside, then talked to Alana through an open window. Alana handed out a glass jar. "Take these darn frogs back to the crick, Millie. I'll forget to feed 'em and they'll die."

Millie followed the woodland path down to the creek at the far side of the Hollow, where she turned the creatures loose and watched them hop toward the water. The feeling of foreboding lingered. She tried to shake it off.

Everyone worried about Edgar, the child who'd suffered stress over the illness and loss of his father. No one thought to worry about Roan, the healthy child whose life had been stable. Even as the boys' fevers rose, the family felt confident Roan would come out of this all right.

A week later, around midnight, there was a pounding on the front door. Millie in her nightgown followed Menno downstairs and watched him open the door, watched Dr. Lapham, gray and exhausted, step into the foyer. The doctor shook his head and placed a hand on Menno's shoulder. "Edgar's all right. I wish I could say the same for Roan. He—well, fact is—brace yourself, man—your son didn't make it. We lost him about an hour ago. I'm so sorry. I did all I could."

Millie's mother, coming downstairs in her bathrobe, froze on the bottom step and stood in stunned silence. Menno moaned. "Roan? Not my boy, not Roan!" He flopped into the overstuffed chair and hid his face in his hands. Rebecca stared at the doctor. Millie knew her mother and her older brother were thinking, as she was, that Roan was Alana's healthiest child, with never so much as a cough or sniffle. When the other children were sick, Roan helped his mother nurse them.

As if belatedly grasping the doctor's news, Rebecca stepped down and wrung her hands. "The camping out! It killed him!"

"No, the boys caught a germ somewhere. There are other cases in town. Roan's fever kept soaring in spite of all our efforts. We even tried an ice bath." The doctor hesitated, took a deep breath, and offered more bad news. "I can't let you have a regular funeral. It will have to be graveside, family only, closed coffin. Danger of infection, you know." He opened the door behind him. "I'll stop by the tavern and inform Mr. Langston."

Millie's face flamed with embarrassment over his assumption that her dad was at the tavern. The others seemed too much in shock to notice.

When the doctor left, Rebecca clasped her hands together and keened. "We'll never see Roan again. This has to be a bad dream."

Millie didn't believe it. Surely Doc Lapham had confused Roan with some other boy. Everyone claimed Roan was the sturdiest child in the family. Just over a week ago he'd lunched with Edgar at Stormland, and they'd played in the Hollow all afternoon.

The next afternoon, sans music, sans pallbearlers, the family gathered again at their plot in the cemetery. Roan's grave had been dug on the other side of that of Baby Langston, Zeke's and Annie's unnamed firstborn, opposite Nat's. The new closed coffin had been placed beside the ominous hole in the ground. Millie shuddered, convinced that Roan was about to be buried alive. He couldn't possibly have died so suddenly.

Though Vi and the youngsters were still in quarantine, Alana, who'd had scarlet fever as a child, was allowed to attend the funeral. She walked from the carriage to the grave like one in a trance.

"Roan is my only towhead." She peered at the half-sized coffin as if she, like Millie, couldn't believe her perpetual-motion boy could be contained in it. "The other children are black Irish like me."

"Roan and Edgar were so cute together." Between dabs at her eyes, Rebecca twisted her handkerchief. "More like brothers than cousins. I used to stand in the window admiring them as they played outdoors."

The women clung to one another. Zeke's wife, Annie, let her arms encircle them both. Millie saw her father grip Menno's shoulder. Everyone pretended to listen while the minister talked of the joys to be found in heaven and offered consolation none could accept.

After six weeks, the quarantine ended. With Edgar no longer contagious, the family visited. The five-year-old, thin and pallid on his bed, kept asking where Roan was. No one ventured an answer. Vi complained she had no idea how to explain two deaths to a child. He'd say God was getting greedy, taking two members of the Langston family. He'd already demanded to know what God wanted of his dad.

Millie heard her sister attempt a consolation. "We can't know why God needs people, dear, we just have to accept that He does."

"I need him more," Edgar insisted. "We're to go to school together. Tell God to send him back."

"We don't tell God what to do. You'll make new friends to go to school with."

"I just want Roan. I don't like God very much."

"Edgar! Don't say that; it's blasphemy!"

Edgar persisted. "Does God know Roan's my only playmate? Sean never wants to play with me. Maggie's a girl, and Rory's only two. You can't play with a toddler." For once in his life, the five-year-old looked ready to cry. He fought the impulse and curled his lower lip instead.

When school started, Edgar was still asking questions. "When will God be finished with Roan? Why doesn't He send him back? I don't want to start school until he comes."

"This is much worse than with his father," Vi commented to the family. "He never asked all these questions about Nat."

"He knew Nat wasn't well," Rebecca said.

Dad took Edgar on his lap and explained. "Sometimes people just go out of our lives and we have to accept that. It's hard, but we must get used to the fact they aren't there any more."

Millie felt tears flood her eyes. She sensed her father was talking about his own losses as well as Edgar's. She knew Douglas had never entirely gotten over losing his father and being severed from his family, being sent off on that orphan train at age seven—just a little older than Edgar, never to see his mother or brother again.

Having no choice, finding himself escorted to school by his mother and firmly placed amid classmates, Edgar went to kindergarten. The teacher complained he woolgathered. Vi excused this on the grounds of his recent illness. "A high fever takes away gumption."

Millie felt sure Edgar still awaited the return of Roan.

Millie and Rob had a busy summer even when not mourning deaths or planning funerals. The orchestra was booked for every weekend evening, along with frequent midweek parties and several weddings. Since it was not easy to buy sheet music for a mandolin orchestra, Millie had to learn to transcribe and copy.

Though at first she found it exhilarating, performing in those elegant homes, she soon began to feel socially isolated. Polite but never warm, the wealthy young people hovered around Rob but showed little interest in knowing his sister. And these were the people Millie would have her high school classes with. They'd be cliquish and she'd have trouble making friends.

Of course, there'd be her old friend Eloise. And Thelma Cunningham, who'd participated in WCTU skits. And Hazel Lapham, the doctor's daughter. If all else failed, the four of them could form their own clique.

A few days before school started, Millie received an invitation to a party at the County House, the poor farm at Eastmanville where she'd often performed. It was to be a farewell for the Kinglseys, who after serving as Keepers for many years were now moving to town.

"It's so their son Warren can attend high school in Grand Rapids," Eloise explained, when Millie stopped by her house to show off the invitation. "He lived with his aunt and uncle last year, but now those folks are not well and can't have him."

Warren, only a few months older than Millie, was a year ahead in school. There'd been no kindergarten for him in the country. Now it seemed his father was returning to his former job as a salesman, selling the newly developed asphalt roofing for the Reynolds Shingle Company. Eloise too planned to attend the party. "You'll ride out with us, I hope," she told Millie, who assured her friend she looked forward to it.

The occasion, when it arrived, proved gala. Though familiar with the County House from many performances, Millie had never before seen it festive with decorations. Colored steamers hung from the ceiling in the parlor and dining area, while flowers graced the big table. The kitchen counters were loaded with thick ham and turkey sandwiches made with bread so new-baked the aroma still filled the air. There were large bowls of potato salad, tossed salad, sliced tomatoes, and the first of the sweetcorn, shucked, stacked and ready for boiling. Huge pans of what Millie called apple betty, and the County House folks called apple grunt, waited on the stove.

The County House always had an abundance of food, probably, Millie thought, because of the many people available to help grow and harvest it. Upwards of thirty men, and a few women, lived here at any given time.

Mrs. Kingsley came from her private cottage to hug her good friend Mrs. Randolph, who'd driven the group out here. She even hugged Millie and Eloise. "So good of you all to come. I hope we'll see more of each other in future, when I'm in town." At Mrs. Randolph's comment that the decision to move seemed to have been sudden, Mrs. Kinglsey explained what Millie had already heard, that her brother-in-law had a heart attack and couldn't cope with a teenaged boy in the house. "We had to make arrangements quickly, before school starts."

"I can't think how this place will get on without you," Eloise's mother said. "It's been—what? Fifteen years?"

"Seventeen. I worry, too." Mrs. Kingsley lowered her voice to a near whisper. "The new keeper has harsh ideas. You drink, you're out of here. I've learned that some of these men are addicted and can't help themselves. The new man says, if they want a warm bed, they'll knock off the booze. Unfortunately, it's not so easy. When the craving hits, they don't care if it's freezing outdoors. Throw them out, they'll go right on drinking in the frost and die of pneumonia."

It was true, as Millie knew. She'd seen her father blue with cold and unaware of his own suffering.

"The supervisors will have something to say about that," Mrs. Randolph asserted. "Relax, Liz, you've done your share here."

"But the men are like family now. Warren was born here. Even Maddy's forgotten her other home. And there's Blanche's grave in the nearby cemetery, my baby—all alone out there." Mrs. Kinglsey choked up and couldn't continue.

"You'll come back to visit. It's only twenty miles from town." Mrs. Randolph squeezed her friend's arm.

Chairs had been set out in rows for the entertainment, and the women went to find seats. This time the County House residents did the entertaining, offering songs from the lumber camps. The men in particular seemed to enjoy hamming it up, contriving exaggerated gestures. The Kingsley boy, Warren, recited a humorous poem he'd written and received a round of applause for it.

When the brief program ended, everyone gathered around the piano for a sing. Then the food was brought out. Millie stood juggling her plate with her ham sandwich, ear of corn, sliced tomatoes and two salads, together with a glass of lemonade. Left with no free hand for eating, she stood looking around uncertainly. When Warren came up to her and whispered a suggestion that they go out to sit on the back porch steps, she nodded. She followed him through the kitchen and outside, where the sun was still warm. He held both plates while she tucked her skirt under her and eased herself down onto the top step. Their glasses of lemonade were perched precariously on the porch railing. Warren handed down plates and glasses and sprawled his long form down beside her.

"A doctor was once attacked by neighbors on this porch," he said. "He used diphtheria antitoxin on kids when it was new and untried. Scared their parents so bad they threatened to cut off his fingers in revenge. There was big excitement; the vigilantes camped out here and Ma fought them off with a borrowed gun. Can you picture my mother doing that?"

Millie smiled. "Your mother's the kind of woman who could handle such a situation."

"I guess you're right. Ma's no slouch. Ironically, the antitoxin worked. The inoculated children lived, and my sister, Blanche, who hadn't been inoculated, died." Warren shook his head and thrust his long legs down the steps. "Mother never got over that. She still talks about it." Tall and gangly, he wore his brown hair combed straight back off his forehead. "I hear you're headed for Central High, Millie."

"That's right. I look forward to it. You'll be a sophomore?"

"Yup. I'll stay with a friend for a few days until the folks get moved into our new house."

"So how do you get along at school? I've heard there are cliques."

"Shucks, I clique right back. I don't let them get my goat." He buttered and attacked a long ear of corn, holding it with both hands as he bit into it. Chewing, he added, "Mostly, they're cliquish by church membership." He wiped butter from his lips with the back of his hand, then, as if remembering he'd put napkins in his pocket, he brought them out. He offered one to Millie.

She took it and wiped her lips. "Church membership?"

"Sure. The Episcopalians think they're the school leaders because they're almost Church of England and serve high tea. Presbyterians claim the honor because they're the wealthiest in town. Congregationalists claim it as the Pilgrim church."

"Serving afternoon tea, too?" Millie smiled and sipped her lemonade.

"Heck, Congregationalists haven't touched tea since the Boston Tea Party. They hate everything Tory. So do Unitarians, who scorn everybody except A students. Which I'm not, by the way. I attend the Unitarian Church but I don't get straight A's. Far from it, I'm a practicing lowbrow." He grinned. "I don't go to Chicago for opera, I don't take in the openings at the Art Institute—not even their summer shows in Saugatuck."

"Is that what Unitarians do?"

"So they claim. But who knows? Talk's cheap…Anyhow, you must join the Sock and Buskin at Central. That's the drama club. We have our own clique. You and Eloise, with your experience as performers, will be welcome."

Millie gazed at him curiously. "I didn't know you were interested in drama."

"I wasn't until I got a job as usher last year at the vaudeville theater. Then I even took tap-dance lessons. Great fun. I guess I'm a natural-born clown."

Millie felt she wouldn't have consented to play a clown if she were starving, but Warren seemed to like the idea. Actually, she'd thought of him as a tease. He'd often pulled her pigtails. She was surprised to be having this serious conversation with him. She told him, "I could see you had a flair, the way you recited poetry just now."

He put his plate aside and sipped his lemonade. "Finish your meal, Millie, and let's go get some of that apple grunt. I smelled it baking, and my mouth has been watering."

"You'll miss this place."

"Yes, especially the food, and my pals, Roaming Roger and Rattlechain Charlie. I'll tell you about them sometime." He offered a leftover piece of ham from his plate to an approaching tabby cat, who promptly attacked it. "Tell you what, Millie, I'll get apple grunt for both of us while you finish your sandwich. Do you like cinnamon cream on it?"

"Yes, it sounds good." Millie reached out tentatively to pet the cat, who first shied, then permitted her touch.

Warren scrambled up. "Be right back. Don't go away."

CHAPTER 14

2002
Ashley

So even then they had to worry about cliques at school! I guess, the more things change, the more they stay the same.

On Sunday morning the family decides that in my honor we'll all go to church together. Seems they want to show me the church Millie attended as a child. I always hesitate about going into all-white places, and also I'm uneasy about leaving those letters and diaries unattended. I well recall Terri's threat to do something. Yet I can hardly refuse the honor. I lock the suitcase and hide it under my bed, pulling the bedspread low to conceal it, and off we go. Laura seems unworried; she claims Terri, who grew up in poverty, is just insecure. "Like my sister, she 'married up' and wants to preserve her position in society."

As we leave, I notice that the dining room window has been raised a crack. Though I debate with myself whether to suggest we close it, I decide it's not my business.

Fact is, I mostly go to church for youth groups and the chance to meet guys, and the church I attend is modern. Still, I have to admit that those big old-time churches are awesome. The moment you step inside, you feel you're truly in a House of God. With their colored windows, they seem so *enclosed*. The very atmosphere, the odor, is of the spiritual, a combination of candle smoke, old pews and mildew. You've stepped out of the secular into the sacred. And here the stained-glass is indescribable. These windows are enough to make a Christian out of anyone. Christ holding out his hand to the children; Christ talking to his disciples, Christ praying alone on Gethsemane, all back-lit with a kind of holy light streaming through—who could refuse to believe? Then there's the beautiful rose-window at the rear, and the altar with its hand-carved figure of Christ and its flowers. And there's the organ playing soft music as you enter. It all adds to the sense of holiness. No wonder my great-grandmother claimed to be a Christian even after she stopped going to church. She used to tell us kids about this place. I knew it would be something special.

Modern churches often have big windows opening to earth and sky, and that's nice, too, but these old places create an atmosphere that the new ones can't duplicate.

Everyone is polite. I'm the lone black person but no one eyes me as if I don't belong here. The service is familiar, with hymns and responsive readings. There's a choir, and on watching them in their red robes and white cottas, I think of Millie, of how she must have looked as a child standing at the front of the choir stall to sing a solo. Did she wear a robe like this?

Everyone seems friendly. After the service, people come up to shake hands with us, and at the door the minister tells us he hopes we'll return. Junior admits he hasn't shown up lately and promises to do better.

As we leave, Doug points out, across the street, another building of beautiful architecture with broad steps and enormous arched windows. "The old Ryerson library, where Millie worked," he says. "They've just restored it."

I'm like, "I think classical architecture is nicer than our modern glass-and-steel stuff." Doug promises to bring me for a visit to the library when it's open. I claim to look forward to the visit—and really I do—but in truth my mind isn't on this conversation. I still worry about those letters and diaries at home. The library can wait. Right now I'm in a hurry to check under my bed. I keep thinking about the dining room window; I keep wishing I'd mentioned the fact it was ajar.

When we reach home, I notice immediately that the window is open wider than when we left. I point it out. "Look, it's about four inches up. It was less than an inch this morning."

Junior pauses, studying it, scratching his head, looking puzzled. "Are you sure? We've never had a break-in."

Laura stops to look and asks how it got open in the first place. "I never touch that window," she says. "It has no screen."

"Maybe the boys opened it last night," Doug suggests.

I insist. "I noticed as I passed it this morning—it was open only a crack." I feel Terri had something to do with this but I don't want to accuse her until I know.

"Doug and I had better go inside and check to be sure no one's in there," Junior says. "You women wait out here."

They go back along the walk and enter by the front door. We hear footsteps and the inserting of the key. We stand listening to bird chirpings, and presently Doug comes to the window, flings it up, and leans out.

"No one's here and nothing's been disturbed," he says. "No sign of a break-in. Dad's checking upstairs but I guess all's okay. I'll let you in the back door."

We hear Junior calling that no one's up there. Doug opens the door. On entering the kitchen, I smell the roast and the spicy casserole Laura left cooking in the oven. All seems normal. I remind myself I should help with dinner. But first I need to check on that suitcase hidden under my bed. I take the stairs two at a time. In the upper hall, Junior, ready to start down, moves aside to let me pass.

"I even went to the attic," he says. "As far as I can see, nothing's been touched."

I don't believe him. Windows don't open themselves. I'm certain I saw it almost shut.

I hurry to my room. The suitcase is right where I left it, locked, the unread diaries within. With a sigh of relief I re-pack and hide it. Then I go to the attic to check out the material I'd already read. Millie's childhood diary is still there but there's no sign of those unsent letters of Rebecca's. I check everywhere; I feel sure I brought them back here after reading them. They're not here now. Panicked, I search the boxes frantically. Nothing. Did I put them inside the diary? I open it to see—and discover some missing pages, torn out hastily so that tatters remain. Terri! Just as I thought! She *said* she'd do something about those papers—and she did.

"I knew it, I knew it!" Aware of an acute sense of loss, I say the words aloud under my breath. I blame myself; I saw through the woman right away and ought to have protected this material. I wonder: What do I do now? I can't go to Laura and accuse her sister-in-law.

Thumbing through, I ascertain that the missing pages all have to do with gigs at the poor farm, and with Douglas and his drinking, Millie and Rob collecting Douglas at the saloon, Douglas being brought home in the paddy wagon. These were the only things Terri knew to look for. In her haste, she must have lacked time to read extensively enough to learn about the other bad stuff, shotgun wedding and Vi's duplicity.

I take the book to my room and sit on the bed, pondering. I decide I have to say something. Not even Mom would want me to keep quiet about this. Still, I have to avoid sounding accusatory. Things go better when you handle them without anger, Dad always says. Unfortunately, I *feel* angry. I feel furious. Terri had no right to mess with that material. She's only an in-law, she's no blood kin to Rebecca or my great-gran, Millie.

I take the diary downstairs. Junior and Doug are in the living room hiding behind sections of the Sunday paper. Laura is in the kitchen. Since those open newspapers look intimidating, I decide to tackle Laura first. Amid warmth and enticing cooking odors, I find her in her apron, poking a thermometer into a roast on top of the stove. Without looking up, she remarks that the roast is not quite done. "In this family, we don't like it bloody." She glances at me, sees my expression, and does a double-take. "What's wrong, Ashley?"

"I'm afraid there *was* a break-in, after all." I try to keep my voice calm, to avoid sounding accusatory. I want to handle this diplomatically. "Some letters are missing from the attic—and several pages have been torn out of Millie's diary." I hold up the book.

She pales and gasps. "Torn out? Are you sure?"

I open up to show her. "There were no torn pages yesterday."

"Terri!" Her hand goes to her chest. "I can't believe it of her! I always think of her as all bark and no bite." She takes the book from my hand, glances through it, and heads for the living room. I follow while she breaks the news to the men. "Junior, guess what? Your sister-in-law came here and tore pages out of an old diary."

Both newspapers are put aside, both faces emerge. The men gaze at her—then at me—in astonishment. Junior says, "She did *what?*"

Laura flips to the missing pages. "She broke in and tore up a diary. Also some—what did you say, Ashley?—letters?"

"Yes, letters Rebecca wrote to her sister and apparently never mailed."

"Those letters are gone?" Doug gazes at me in horror. "The ones you and I read?"

I fling out my hands. "Every one of them."

"We'll just see about this!" Frowning, Junior flings his paper aside, rises, and marches to the phone in the dining room. Laura protests. "Don't call in anger, dear. You know Terri's sensitive about our family history. She was devastated when she was denied admission to the DAR."

"She'll be more sensitive when I get through with her," Junior says. "We can't put up with this kind of destruction." We hear his voice, loud and angry. "Terri, some letters and papers have gone missing from our attic. Do you know anything about them?"

After a brief silence, he says, still in fury, "My dear sister-in-law, it wasn't your decision to make. That material belongs to me; I was heir to this house and its contents. Nothing gets destroyed until I say so. I want everything brought back here at once." He clicks the instrument and yells, "Hello? Hello?"

Terri must have slammed down the phone. Junior hangs up, sighing. "Well, she's mad but hopefully she'll bring the stuff back."

"She didn't deny taking it?" Laura asks.

"No, she actually sounded proud. She said someone had to do something, and we didn't seem inclined to."

"I told you she's sensitive about—"

"Sensitive—or criminal?"

"I can't believe she'd break into the house," Doug says. "She must have cracked the window last night when no one was looking, so she could let herself in this morning."

"I wish I'd mentioned it earlier," I wail. "Since I had no idea you never opened that window, it didn't occur to me that something was wrong." Not quite true. It *did* occur to me, but I hesitated to accuse their relative. I worried all through church services.

"Terri feels strongly about the family and likes to keep the bad things secret," Laura says, "but I never thought she'd go that far. How can it hurt for Ashley to read that material? It's not as if she's writing it up for the newspaper or something."

No, I hadn't meant to—but now I'm having second thoughts. I'm suspecting maybe it *should* all be written up, at once before more of it is lost. I don't, however, mention this. The idea might appeal to that English instructor who gave me an A in comp, but I fear it won't appeal to this family.

Shaking her head, Laura returns to the kitchen. Junior quizzes me. "What were those letters about?"

I shrug. "Nothing that awful."

"They were about great-great-grandfather's boozing," Doug says. "It seems the man hung out in the saloons with his buddies and was often brought home in the paddy wagon. I feel sorry for the guy, sent away from his family, put on the orphan train and shipped out to Michigan to work for Mennonite farmers. A little kid of seven! Everything must have seemed strange and frightening in his new surroundings, and just think, poor guy, he never saw his family again. No wonder he took to drink when he grew up, and founded a dysfunctional family."

I knew it was me Terri didn't trust. She wouldn't have minded Doug reading the material but she saw me as an outsider who wouldn't scruple to tell the world our forebear was the town drunk. I had news for her. That fact was already known to me. My great-grandmother, Millie, to the end of her life remained bitter about her father's drinking, and more than once she'd come right out with her anger. "What little Dad earned went for booze, and we three younger children had to support the household," she once told me. "Rob went to work at age twelve, Bea at fifteen. Besides that, Rob and I contributed the money we earned performing." I remember her saying that the family often had nothing to eat except bean soup, and that when she wasn't busy with the orchestra or her studies, she did housework for a neighbor just to keep food on the family table.

We wait for Terri, and in less than half an hour we see her car pull up at the curb. Lips pursed angrily, she marches up the embankment and the porch steps. She carries only a small white box which can't possibly hold all those papers. She flings open the front door, strides straight to Junior, and thrusts the box toward him.

"Here are your precious papers," she says. "They're ashes now, shoveled from my fireplace. I burned them. You want them back so take them. They're all yours."

Frowning, Junior stands to confront her. "Terri, you had no right to do that. Those papers belonged to me; I authorized the young people to read them."

"Then you're a fool," Terri says. "And I don't suffer fools gladly." She puts down the box and adds, "Someone has to protect the family honor. Looks like I'm elected." She turns and marches out through the open door, which she slams. Laura comes in from the kitchen and we all watch Terri climb into her car, slam that door, too, and drive off.

"I suppose she'll never speak to us again." Laura sighs.

Junior's shoulders slump. "I'm not sure I ever want to speak to *her* again. I don't like her methods."

"I wonder what Uncle Howard thinks of all this," Doug says.

"I'm not sure my dear brother thinks at all," Junior says. "A thinking man wouldn't have married that busybody."

"She's not a busybody, she's an insecure woman," Laura argues.

Later, while we're eating a subdued dinner, no one showing much sign of appetite, the phone rings and Junior answers. We hear him say, "No, I damn well won't! Forget it, I'm not about to do that." A silence, then, "I'm sorry you feel that way, Howie." He comes back to report, "Howard says he doesn't care about the stupid papers but he has to offer his wife his backing and support, and he wants me to apologize. I'm damned if I will! She's the one who broke in and stole priceless heirlooms—and burned them. What do I have to apologize for?"

"Of course, you shouldn't apologize, Dad." Doug folds his arms across his chest. "I still can't believe this happened. Terri breaking in, destroying letters—it's unthinkable."

"Terri's Polish," Laura reminds us. "The Polish immigrants suffered put-downs in the days when we were all growing up. In school I wouldn't associate with Terisa Milkowski even when she changed her name to Terri Milk. I feel guilty about that now. She tried so bravely to join the DAR and learned that merely marrying into an old-line family doesn't count. I'm sorry for her. We need to recognize that we all contribute to what each of us becomes."

I wouldn't know about that; there was no Polish clique in my high school that I knew of. But I don't feel so forgiving. Worse, I can't help squirming a bit. I know I wasn't at fault in all this, yet I keep remembering what Mom always says when I get into those fights at school. "It's never your fault, Ashley, but somehow you create chaos wherever you go."

Sometimes it does seem that way. I was doing what she told me to do—researching my roots—and now there's a family fight.

What do you want me to do, Mom? Just overlook all this? Well, I can't—and won't. I speak up. "I'm going to write down every word I remember from those letters and papers so we'll have a record of what was in them."

"Yes, I think you should." Junior says, "The truth never hurt anyone, at least in the long run."

Doug adds, "After dinner I'll go up and read with you, Ashley. Then two of us will know everything that's written in those diaries—in case the thought-police come again."

I feel grateful to the family for supporting me. If they'd taken Terri's side, I'd have been in deep doo-doo over all this. I feel sure my mom would not be happy with me.

"We may have to live in a fortress but we'll keep those papers safe." Doug squeezes my hand.

He's not drop-dead handsome, but he's cute with his hair in his eyes, and he's on my side. So what the hell. I squeeze back. If Keisha can have a Mexican, I guess I can have a Scotsman for a while. And I can still read Bea's and Millie's diaries that I so carefully preserved under my bed.

CHAPTER 15

1916
Bea

At last, at last, fourteen-year-old Bea had a room to herself again! No more sharing with a snooty big sister who isolated herself behind Chinese screens.

The longed-for event occurred because Vi, after four endless years of widowhood at Stormland, had finally consented to marry a partner in the construction firm, Don Dexter, and was moving to a home of her own, returning the front room to Millie.

The Chinese screens had been folded up and propped against the wall. Bea felt tempted to thumb her nose at them. All this time they'd kept her out of half of her own room. Millie kept busy, busy, busy, always having to study or transcribe music for the orchestra. You wouldn't get Bea into that orchestra, not on your life. When Rob urged music lessons on her, Bea nixed the idea. She liked listening to music but her mind refused to translate sound into little black notes on paper. Her brain turned off when she saw clef marks.

Bea put on her new sheer lavender dress and hurried downstairs to the dining room, where the three sisters worked on their wedding outfits, Vi's bridal gown, Bea's and Millie's bridesmaid dresses. The work was finished except for a last-minute fitting for Bea. Millie was so slender she could wear rags and look good; in fact she'd often done so in those WCTU skits, where people had raved over her because she was so cute in the waif costumes. Chunky Bea faced problems in the way her dresses hung over her newly-rounded breasts and hips. She stood still while Millie re-pinned the hem more evenly, and vowed to go on a diet.

"Okay, got it." Millie stood off to assess her work, and looked to Vi for approval. Vi nodded.

Bea hurried back upstairs and changed into a work-dress. Vi's furniture was to come out of storage this very day; in fact, the men had already arrived with the dray. It was time for the sisters to stroll up the street to the new house and unpack.

Downstairs again, Bea found Vi shoving her sewing basket into a drawer, remarking that she couldn't wait to see her stored things again. "They'll all be new to me; I've forgotten what I had."

Their mother came from the kitchen in her gray hoover dress, drying her hands on her apron. "You girls run along. I'll clean up here." She reached for the broom, kept handy during sewing sessions, and attacked the scraps of cloth and snippets of thread on the floor. Millie and Vi hung their new dresses on hooks on the backs of the doors.

It was a warm Saturday morning. The sisters walked up the street smelling damp-earth odors left by a rainstorm the night before, bypassing the puddles on the sidewalk. On arrival at the house, they found the dray partly unloaded, its flatbed half empty. Zeke and Don were inching a large wardrobe toward the porch steps. Behind them the horses stamped impatiently.

"Where do you want this thing, Vi?" Don asked.

"Upstairs. Front bedroom."

"I was afraid you'd say that."

"Too big for the stairs?" Vi studied the wardrobe. Bea knew Vi's former house had been much bigger, and that Vi, though she wouldn't express her concerns in front of Don who'd built this house for her, feared her furniture would be too massive for this small place.

"We might take it through the front window," Don said. "We'd have to remove the pane."

Of course, Vi wouldn't need all her furniture from the big house, but Bea knew her sister wanted her belongings.

"Wouldn't take long to unglaze the window, with the glaze still soft." Zeke, a short man, shoved his hat to the back of his head and looked up. While he studied the window, Bea studied him. She tended to think of him as her uncle rather than her brother. Nineteen years older than she, he'd left their town of Fargo, Michigan, before she was born. During her lifetime, he hadn't ever lived in the family home. Her mother spoke of his childhood in the same way she spoke of her own, as something long gone.

"We'd need a crane. Let's try the stairway first." Don leaned his weight against the wardrobe. "Come on, up we go."

They wrestled the massive piece onto the front porch. Bea opened the screen door for them.

The three women entered the tiny house which still smelled of fresh plaster and paint. They found the small parlor cluttered with boxes. Vi gazed around, saying, "I don't know where to start."

The boxes were labeled. Millie suggested they first unpack pots and pans. "We need to fill the kitchen shelves so you can cook."

Vi hovered over the box labeled *treasures*. "Wedding presents from my first marriage," she explained. "My crystal and stuff."

"Leave that for now," Millie said. "It'll upset you to see it again."

Too late. Vi had already ripped the box open. She dug among yellowing newspapers and brought out a china teapot. "Look at this. From Aunt Ruth and Uncle Ephraim. Isn't it beautiful?"

Bea could see what was coming. Recalling her first wedding, Vi would grow teary. To divert attention, Bea picked a box at random and opened it. "Look, your Christmas ornaments!" She snatched a holly wreath from on top and held it up.

Wrong box. Vi grabbed the wreath and hugged it. "My final Christmas with Nat! Our last happy time together! Three months later, he went to the hospital and then—and then—." Tears sprang to her eyes. She sat down on a wooden crate. "Guess you're right; I shouldn't unpack."

Millie urged again that they concentrate on the kitchen things. "It's pots and pans you'll be needing, and broom and mop, not crystal and holly wreaths. This stuff can be stored in the attic."

Pale, splotchy-faced, Vi shook her head. "I never dreamed it would be so hard." Tears ran down her cheeks. "The wreath—teapot—it all comes back." She delved into the treasure box and retrieved a butter dish in the shape of a setting hen. She held it up. "From Nat's great-aunt, a family heirloom."

"Time to forget all that. You have Don to think of now." Millie spoke quietly; the men were not far away. Their bumping and scraping shook the house as they wrestled the wardrobe up the stairs.

Vi too spoke in a near-whisper. "No one can replace Nat. I feel that the happy times of my life are over."

"Vi, pull yourself together." Millie scolded in half-voice. "Of course, no one can replace Nat. You can't have first love twice. But you can make a home for a man who needs you in a different way."

"Sometimes I want to ask the same question young Edgar used to ask," Vi admitted. "Why was Nat taken from me? What did God want of him?"

"Oh, Vi, be real! You knew he was dying. When you married, you knew what you were getting into."

There was scraping overhead, a bump, more scraping, then silence. The wardrobe, presumably, had arrived at its delegated position. The men clattered downstairs in their heavy work-shoes.

"We did it!" Don mopped his forehead with a large handkerchief.

Zeke fanned himself with his hat. "That was the biggest piece. The rest should be easy."

To hide her tears, Vi bent double and touched forehead to knees. The two men stood eyeing her in bafflement.

"What happened?" Don asked. "What's wrong?" He was paunchy, with a bald spot at the top of his head. Though not handsome, certainly not natty, he was good-natured and likeable. A man who often kidded around with Bea and Edgar, he treated Vi with respect.

"She got something in her eye," Millie said. "She'll be okay in a minute."

"Can I help?" Don approached, his hand out.

Vi shook her head, one hand on her mouth as if to stifle sobs. Don seemed uncertain but moved to the door behind Zeke. "We'll bring in the overstuffed chair so you can relax in comfort, dear."

Millie spoke up. "That's thoughtful of you."

When the men were gone, Vi sobbed. Her shoulders heaved. "I feel I'm being unfaithful to Nat."

"Vi, snap out of it," Millie scolded. "You've been doing great, keeping busy. Now's not the time to—"

Bea put in a reminder that Vi had been successfully running the office of the construction firm and doing the payroll. "I thought that was swell. I want to learn that sort of work myself. That's useful in the world."

"But it's not enough for a lifetime," Millie said. "Now, at last, Vi, you have a good man interested in you."

"In just a week I'll be married to him, and have to—have to—" Through her sobs, Vi muttered something of which only the word "bed" was audible.

"Of course, you have to live up to your marital commitments." Millie was now almost nineteen, and Bea supposed she knew exactly what marital commitments entailed. Bea herself was unclear about them, and certainly her Mennonite mother would never tell her. But Millie had been performing for the feminist organization, American National, with those sophisticated women who knew about things like how to meet marital commitments while avoiding conception.

"And betray Nat." Vi's voice shook.

"Holy catfish!" Bea suddenly grew angry. "Look who you're mourning for! From all I've heard, Nat only married you because he was sick and needed a nursemaid." She clutched her head. "You're a fool, Vi McCurdle!"

"That's not true! Nat loved me. You don't know, you were a child." Vi dried her eyes. "Oh, I realize I have to forget him. It's just—so hard."

"Sure it is. You were a socialite around town, with a big house and fine carriage." Millie patted her shoulder. "Those days are gone."

Bea looked out the window and saw the men returning with an overstuffed chair. "Come on, now, the pots and pans," she urged.

A week later, less than an hour before the wedding, Bea sprang a surprise announcement of her own. As she and Millie dressed, she said, "Guess what? I've decided not to go to high school." Actually, the decision had been made right while she talked to Vi of her role as office girl, but she hadn't until now worked up the courage to say so.

Millie turned to stare at her. They were in the front bedroom, helping each other fasten up their new dresses. Since some of the guests had already arrived, they could hear voices from downstairs.

"You *can't* not go," Millie said. "Dad has his heart set on an education for us both."

"He'll have to get his heart unset. I've signed up for business school. I start the summer term in mid-June."

"What on earth led you to that decision?" Millie fastened a last button, turned Bea around, and stood off to inspect her.

"I'm tired of not having money."

"You can go to business school after you graduate high school. Sit down so I can do your hair."

Bea remained facing her sister. "Truth is, Millie, I don't want to be like any of you. I'm no Vi, to mope for a dippy dead man. And no Alana, with a passel of kids to raise. I've grown tired of kids, watching my sisters-in-law wipe snotty noses and change shitty diapers."

"Bea!" Millie looked shocked.

Bea stuck to her guns. "Shitty is the word for them. What kind of life is that?"

"And me?" Millie asked. "What are you tired of about me?"

"Frankly, since you ask, I don't see what those French and Latin lessons are going to get you. So you read Virgil, so what? How is that going to earn you money?"

"It may well earn me a college scholarship. My English teacher is working on getting me one."

"So after another four years, you'll be able to read Virgil without a Latin-English dictionary. Then you get to spend the rest of your days teaching it to kids who don't want to know it. That's a life?" Bea shook her head emphatically. "Not for me. I want to earn money, wear nice clothes, meet well-off, sophisticated men, do exciting things. Maybe even take a trip to Europe on a big ocean liner." And have a *real* romance, not one with an impecunious musician or a boy from the poorhouse who's sweet on me, as Millie had with her Harvey and Warren.

Bea glanced out the window and saw Menno and Alana climbing the front steps followed by their troop, Menno carrying baby Richard wrapped in a blue blanket. Across the street, Annie and Zeke strolled toward Stormland, their two little ones clinging to Annie's skirts.

She stepped closer to the window and gestured. "Just look at them! That's not for me, that baby stuff. Getting your kids grown so they can start growing more kids—for what? What's it all about? Where's the sense in it? All Alana's done, her whole life, is care for kids. First her little brothers, then Sean, Maggie, Roan, Rory—and now Richard. And she's in the family way—again!"

"Mother must think there's sense in raising kids," Millie dryly remarked, "or you and I wouldn't be here."

"Well, I have a life ahead of me, and I plan to do something with it. I don't intend to fall for some guy and start raising his kids. Neither will I suffer through four years of Latin and English. I want to have fun, see the world."

"Dad will be devastated. He comes from a well-educated family; he lives for the day when we—"

"Dad has you for the scholar in the family. He'll get used to having me for the money earner."

"Come on, it's almost time." Millie pulled out the desk-chair. "Sit down and let me do your hair."

Bea sat, and Millie took her hair down and brushed it. Vi called from the hall to ask if they were ready. "You have eight minutes." Millie whisked the hair back up and began jabbing in hairpins.

They soon heard the opening notes of the Lohengrin Wedding March from the downstairs Victrola. They hurried out to the hall to take their places ahead of the bride, who, since this was her second wedding, had dressed in yellow instead of white. Bea noticed that, if Vi didn't look exactly radiant, at least there was no sign of weeping.

Bea and Millie went to the top of the stairs. Bea turned to see Dad come out in his only suit and give Vi his arm. The procession moved downstairs and into the front room. The bridesmaid and maid of honor stood back to let the bride join the groom before the makeshift altar. The vows were spoken.

Bea felt relieved that the wedding had come off as planned. She'd worried that Vi might back out. That would have meant continuing to have that nuisance, Edgar, in the house, not to mention again surrendering half her bedroom to Millie.

She hurried to be first to kiss the bride. Vi turned to her with a smile. "My baby sisters are all grown up! Next you'll be Millie's bridesmaid, Bea."

Bea couldn't imagine that happening. Millie lived for the orchestra; neither she nor Rob had eyes for the opposite sex. Bea'd long ago concluded that her next-oldest siblings would never marry. They were already married—to the Royal Mandolin Orchestra.

CHAPTER 16

2002
Ashley

Bea's my kind of person! I ask Doug if she's still alive. He shakes his head and tells me she died years ago. I'm disappointed; I'd have loved to meet her. Tempted to ask if she realized her dream, I decide the answer would be too much like sneaking a peek at the ending before you read the book. Spoils the impact when you reach the last page.

Great-Aunt Bea, you are one white person I'd have loved to know. I feel just the way you did, I don't want to be stuck raising kids. I also hope for glamour and excitement in my life, no going to school forever to learn irrelevant stuff.

Bea expresses my thoughts so well, I can't help wondering if I'm a reincarnation of her. Is it possible for white people to be reincarnated half black? I must ask my brother. Mike knows esoteric stuff like that.

"Do you believe in reincarnation?" I ask Doug, who's squeezed up beside me, reading over my shoulder.

"That's a big question." Doug frowns, shakes his head. "My mother would say it's not possible. It would give the soul a second chance at salvation. She'd figure you'd best act like a Christian the first time around, and not look to a second life to get you off the hook."

"I guess my dad would agree. What do you think?"

"I don't know; that second chance seems unlikely, though a lot of people believe in it. Karma, it's called."

"It's just so weird the way things recur in families. Bea reminds me of myself. She does what I'd have done, says what I'd have said. When I read her diary, I feel as if I'm her."

Doug agrees she's a dynamo.

I can't wait to find out what happened when she announced to her parents her news about quitting high school. I flip ahead. Blank. I let out a small scream. "We'll never know! She stopped writing!"

"That's a bummer." He turns pages and finds more scribbling further along. "This is two years later," he says. "It's dated 1918."

"Bea's too much like me altogether," I say. "That's exactly what I do, lose interest in my diary for years at a time and skip stuff."

He thought we might get lucky and Millie would have mentioned the quarrel. He reaches for Millie's diary, flips through it, and nods. "Ah, good old Millie describes it in detail."

We bend over, heads together, reading. Predictably, there was a fight.

"Dad thundered," Millie wrote. "He kept yelling, 'I won't have it, I won't have it!'"

"I've already registered at business school," Bea informed her father.

"Then cancel. You're too young to sign up on your own. A fourteen-year-old, by golly!"

"What d'you mean, too young? I'm two years older than Rob when he went to work at the laundry and began supporting the family. I'm a year older than Zeke when he came on his own to Grand Rapids."

"They're boys."

"What are you saying?" Bea raised her voice to an angry protest. "You always claimed girls shouldn't be treated differently! You made Rob hire women for the orchestra. You made me learn to swim and to bellyflop on the Flexible Flyer sled, all because—"

"Yes, in matters like that—"

"Alana was only a year older than I when she gave birth to Sean." To calm down, she took a deep breath. She put hands on hips. "Dad, face it, I'm no scholar. I don't care a fig for the *Odyssey* or *Iliad*. I wouldn't read Virgil if you paid me. Anyway, typewriting and bookkeeping are what employers shell out shekels for. No one hires people to read *classics*."

"Tell 'em, Bea!" I can't help shouting a bit myself. "Right on!"

Doug laughs. "I guess you're not big on classics?"

"I'm as small as you can get on them. Like Bea, I feel sure I could live my whole life happily if I never read the *Odyssey* or *Iliad*. I struggled through *Beowulf* but that's it."

Doug admits he eased his way through both books fairly painlessly. "Still, I can see why you mightn't like them." He bends over the diary again to read ahead. "Aha. The fight goes on. Bea says she wants to earn money, live the good life, vacation at the Grand Hotel on Mackinac Island. Listen to this: 'I'll never live in a tiny house like Vi's, or an unfinished dump like Alana's. Neither will I rear snot-nosed kids.'"

Doug raises his head, looking amused. "I'll have to ask my mom if any of those horrible things happened to her. I don't think so. No kids, I'm pretty sure."

I take the diary in my own hands and go on reading. This is getting to be fun. I fancy I might become a researcher after all.

Bea complained to Millie, "Our family's always waiting for some great and wonderful future. Waiting for Dad to become more skilled in his craft so he can earn more money, waiting for Rob to get the orchestra onto a paying basis. Well, I'm tired of waiting. I'm going for a job that will pay now. I'll have something the rest of you won't have—nice clothes, interesting friends, travel, a life."

Millie expressed hope that the excitement of her own graduation might change Bea's mind. Seemed Millie had loved her high school years. Voted Class Entertainer, she'd played for all school organizations. She'd won the *Sock and Buskin* award for participation in the most school plays, the Virgil award as best Latin scholar. She'd received a book of Shakespeare's plays presented by the English department for best poetry writer. At the graduation ceremony, the principal announced that she'd won a tuition scholarship at the University of Michigan. She'd have been valedictorian except that the principal apologetically informed her he had to give the job to the Episcopal bishop's daughter, the school's social leader.

"You see what I'm up against!" I wail to Doug. "That's my great-grandmother who won all those awards. Besides that, my grandparents were college instructors, my mom's top manager in her firm, my dad was a Naval officer, my aunt is publisher of a magazine for black business people. And—oh, yes, big brother Mike is in his last year of college, studying neuroscience, which is said to be one of the hardest fields. I'm supposed to compete with all that? Come on! Sometimes I wish I was someone else's kid."

"I know the feeling," Doug admits. "I have four generations of successful builders behind me. Dad's so passionate about fresh-cut lumber he gets excited when he goes to a lumber yard. To him it's the raw material of creative work. I've spent my life watching him and wondering what's wrong with me that I don't share the excitement."

We chuckle at the thought of someone being passionate about lumber. We go on reading. It seems that though Millie was walking on air after all her success, her mother felt uneasy. She claimed Ann Arbor was a long way off. Four hours by train. She didn't want Millie to go so far from home.

"And Millie was my age," I comment. "I'm four hours by *plane* from my mother."

"Times have sure changed." Doug reaches over to turn a page in the diary, points. "I suspect we're to read about a boyfriend. A mysterious Mr. Loomis appears just ahead."

"Ooh. Sounds juicy." I bend over the book again. Millie's a good writer, she puts in the dialogues. She makes me picture the scene.

❦   ❦   ❦

Holding her swishing skirts as they walked home from the graduation ceremony, Rebecca remarked, "We should do something to celebrate all those honors. I have a roast ready for the oven. I could invite Vi and them, Zeke and them, Menno and them."

"Not tonight," Millie said. "The orchestra's playing a dinner-hour concert at the Cody Hotel, and afterward I'm stepping out with Mr. Loomis." She tried to sound casual as she mentioned the name.

"Mr. Loomis. Hm. You see a lot of him lately." Rebecca studied her daughter. Millie knew her mother remembered problems with Vi and worried about her girls' beaux.

"I only met him two weeks ago," she said.

"He's keen, though. He's been to the house three times."

"He walked me home, that's all."

"What about the poor-farm boy, Warren Kingsley?"

"Warren's taking summer classes at Valparaiso," Millie said. "He wants to finish college fast, in case we get into the war and he has to go."

"Oh, dear. Horrible thought. I hope and pray that doesn't happen."

"But it could. Ever since the sinking of the *Lusitania*, there's been talk of war."

"We can't manage without Rob," Rebecca said. "He's our sole support these days. If he has to go, I don't know what we'll do."

"Rob's a Mennonite," Millie said. "Everyone knows Mennonites are conscientious objectors. Even the government knows that."

"All the same, we must pray for peace."

I ask what the *Lusitania* was. Doug explains that it was a great ocean liner. "A German U-boat sank it off of Ireland, and thousands drowned, including some very wealthy Americans. The disaster caused a lot of people to feel we should get into World War I.

Doug describes the shipwreck, how all those bodies washed ashore at Cobh in Ireland and were buried in the graveyard there. I can see he's fascinated. On our drive home from Grand Haven he'd told me about the wreck of the ore boat *Edmund Fitzgerald,* which broke apart in a storm on Lake Superior. He now admits he wants to learn to scuba-dive so he can explore Great Lakes shipwrecks.

"Sinkings of those huge ships must have been terrible," he says. "Just think, bedding and suitcases floating amidst the corpses."

I shudder; I saw the movie *Titanic,* and I can picture it vividly. We go on reading. After the shipwreck description, I'm glad for something pleasant like Millie's visit to the now-defunct Ramona Amusement Park. It seems so real I can't believe the place isn't still there.

Since mid-June brought almost the longest day of the year, full daylight reigned when Millie and Charlie Loomis arrived at Reeds Lake. Blue water glittered in the westering sun. Ramona Park, newly opened for the season and freshly painted, sported colorful pennants flying from the peaks of buildings. The big pavilion that housed the theater and picnic tables loomed over all, a mother hen surrounded by her chicks. Calliope music and the smell of popcorn filled the air. People strolled, eating cotton candy. The excursion boat *Ramona,* also with banners flying, nosed its way toward the dock and announced its arrival with a toot of its horn. Ragtime music from a player piano on its deck mingled with the breathy sound of the calliope at the carousel.

Millie and Charlie sauntered along the midway. On the shelves behind the duck shoot, kewpie dolls in bright red skirts and gold blouses proffered their closed-mouth smiles. Charlie tried to win one, failed, vowed to try again later.

"How about a roller coaster ride, Miss Graduate?"

Millie confessed, "Miss Graduate is scared to death of those things." The screams of people flying down the drop-off were sufficient to convince her that the ride was not for her.

"The Tunnel of Love, then? That's only half as high."

"Give me time to work up my courage." Millie was dissembling now. She'd ridden the Tunnel of Love with Warren, and the water-shoot at the end had ceased to frighten her. It was the other part she worried about—the boat ride through the dark tunnel, alone with Charlie.

They strolled on along the midway toward the pavilion at the far end. Hawkers approached them selling everything from hot-dogs to jewelry. At the Wheel of Fortune, Charlie tried and failed to win a box of candy.

"Oh, well, the night is young," he said. "Better luck next time. Why don't we see the play at the theater? When we come out, it'll be dark and we can sail around the lake and dance on the boat deck."

"What's the play?" Millie asked.

"It's an operetta. *The Dollar Princess*. Good songs, I hear."

"I believe I know them." She sang. "'There is Egypt in your dreamy eyes/A bit of Nile's paradise. And gleaming lights are in your hair/While fragrant incense seems to fill the air.'"

He nodded and finished with. "'And the orient is in your smile/As dreamy as the River Nile.'" Their voices joined as they sang together, "'And you stole my heart/With your charming art/And the Egypt in your dreamy eyes.'"

People glanced at them. They laughed and, hand in hand, climbed the steps of the large pavilion with its steeply-pitched red roof and its wrap-around porch, the latter enclosed with latticework, newly painted and gleaming white. Pictures of cast members, posed with glamorous smiles, filled the spaces beside the ticket window. While Charlie stood in line to buy the tickets, Millie waited by the theater door and eyed him surreptitiously. He looked handsome today. In his high collar and formal gray suit with buttoned vest and gold watch chain, he seemed a different person from his usual sporty, collegiate type. He struck her as more mature than her other two beaux, Warren-the-tease and Harvey who boyishly mooned over her.

Charlie was in town for the summer from the university, where he studied architecture. He'd come up to her at a party and asked her to put her instrument aside and dance with him. She knew Rob frowned on that sort of thing, believing musicians should remain aloof, but she was flattered, and after all, since Charlie was the nephew of the people giving the party, she could hardly refuse.

They'd danced. Millie enjoyed playing guest. Charlie told her he'd been offered a summer job as draftsman for a furniture designer and would be in town for three months, staying with his aunt and uncle. He planned to return to Ann Arbor in the fall.

Several times afterwards he'd met her at school functions and walked her home. This was the first time he'd asked her to step out with him.

He now guided her ahead of him into the theater, stopping only to buy popcorn. Inside, they slid into seats while the theater darkened.

It was Millie's first musical, and she felt inspired to become one of those beautiful people onstage. She began dreaming of life as a musical comedy star. Also, she suspected the music would sound better from the Royal Mandolin Orchestra. At intermission, she commented on this fact to Charlie, who argued that the Royal Mandoliners needed to be more aggressive about advertising. "No reason your group shouldn't perform at this theater. It's all in getting known."

Millie daydreamed: perhaps, if the orchestra performed here, one day the young woman playing the lead might be sick, and a desperate management would ask who knew the lines and the songs. Millie would raise her hand and say, "I can do it." Recruited, she would be discovered and would become a musical comedy star. They'd be impressed on learning that, from her years of doing skits with WCTU, she was already an experienced actress.

Leaving the theater when the play ended, they found that the daylight had faded to a faint glow in the western sky. The lights of the midway shone brightly, outlining each building and ride. They strolled to the dock and boarded the steamer *Ramona*, festive now with colored lights strung above the rails.

On a broad rear deck, the player piano hammered out ragtime music. Three couples danced. Offering his arm to Millie by way of invitation, Charlie swung her onto the floor.

With a hoot of its horn, the boat chugged outward onto the silver-gray water, circling the lake until the passengers could look back and see the lights of the midway like a string of jewels along the shore. Between dances, Millie stepped to the rail with Charlie following. She felt his breath on her neck. It all seemed romantic.

"Isn't it beautiful?" she said. "I was never here at night before. I've hiked around the lake in the daytime, but I had no idea it would be such a fairyland after dark."

She felt Charlie's hands touch her shoulders. "If you like, we'll do this a lot during the summer," he said. "This will be our special place. We'll drive over to the big lake, too, and ride that excursion boat. And how about going with me to the John McCormack concert next week?"

"I'd love to." Millie turned to him and confessed, "This has been one of the best days of my life. Thank you for bringing me here."

"The day isn't over yet," he said. "We still have the Tunnel of Love."

This time Millie did not demur. When they left the *Ramona*, and crossed the midway to climb into the small boat that would take them through the tunnel, Charlie sat close to Millie and put his arm around her. On entering the darkness, she felt his arm tighten across her shoulders, his head lower. She turned her face to him and he kissed her. She permitted it, knowing they would come out to light and splash down into the pool of water, and she would scream and cling to him, pretending to be terrified. It was what one did in the Tunnel of Love, if one were with a properly romantic person. She'd never screamed when riding here with Warren, nor clung to him. Warren was a pal, not a lover.

When she saw ahead the light at the drop-off, she flung her arms around Charlie's neck, closed her eyes, held her breath, and prepared for the plunge. Charlie's arms enfolded her.

She went home at midnight carrying a large kewpie doll, her fingers clutching a box of candy. Charlie had finally got lucky at both the duck-shoot and the Wheel of Fortune. He'd also promised to buy her the record of *Egypt in your Dreamy Eyes*.

"And I believe he did just that," Doug says. "In fact, I believe the recording is still in the pile of old 78s in the attic. I used to play them when I was a kid. The attic was always good for a rainy day."

"You mean you can still play those things?"

"Sure. They don't sound so great by modern standards."

Still, I thought it would be fun to hear them. "We'll have to go through that stuff some time," I say.

He suggests we go out for a snack at McDonald's and I agree. He says that though Ramona Park is gone, we could drive to Cedar Point next weekend; it's also a place with carousel and roller coasters. We discuss again the possibility of reincarnation, of whether I could be Bea. I'm still marveling that she's such a twin of mine. Though I never had the *Odyssey* inflicted on me, I always hated those Odes on Grecian Urns and poems about the Great God Pan that we read in English class. I felt just as Bea did, what's the point? The Great God Pan piping in the reeds by the river? Come on!

"I guess they figure, if you're to be educated, you need to know about that stuff," Doug says. "I didn't find it as exciting as Millie seems to have done."

After we eat, he asks if I'd like to come to his house for a while to watch television. At the invitation, I freeze up. "No, thanks." He looks disappointed, but he drives me back to Stormland.

I like Doug a lot, and we've had some good talks about our forebears, but I'm not eager to be alone with him at his house, or any house. I've had no end of trouble with white guys. I dated one my last year in high school and had to smash a coke bottle and point the jagged glass edges at him to fight him off. He was just another of those sex-without-commitment dudes who seem to think black women are free and easy.

No more of that stuff for me. I'll talk to Doug, I'll drive to the beach with him, possibly even to Cedar Point, but I won't be alone in his house. I'm not the Millie-romantic type. I'm Bea, the realist.

CHAPTER 17

Autumn, 1915
Millie

On coming to Ann Arbor a week early for freshman orientation, Millie had grown homesick almost at once. There was so much to give up if she attended college, not least her position in her beloved orchestra. Already she worried what might be happening to it.

She consoled herself that things would look better when Charlie arrived. He was due this very day. She'd see him in a couple of hours.

Hastening across the diagonal walkway called the Diag, she startled a robin into flight and sent a squirrel scurrying up a tree. Thinking back, she could hardly recall the excitement of winning her scholarship. At the time she'd fancied it a blessing, having her tuition paid, but she'd soon learned that tuition was only a small part of college expenses. Charges for room and board seemed to her astronomical. Besides, there were student fees, gym clothes, costly textbooks. At best, her savings might see her through her first year. After that, she would have to begin working her way, and as she'd recently learned, that would be difficult. Two women who'd tried it had ended up waiting tables at campus restaurants and warned her to anticipate a struggle. One of the women reported being expelled for falling asleep in class, after days and nights of working for eight hours and studying for ten. "The human body isn't made for that kind of punishment," the woman asserted.

Why go through all that, Millie asked herself, when she'd already helped to build up a successful orchestra and longed to perform with it?

She'd begun to think that perhaps, for this one great year, she should have it all. She'd even allow herself to be rushed for a sorority. Time enough later to decide about the future.

This morning, she'd awakened recalling how Rob and her mother made long faces when they saw her off on the train. She kept hearing in her mind Bea's scornful, "What will college get you? The chance to teach Virgil to kids who don't want to know it?" She missed rehearsals and kept wondering how Rob and the group were managing without her.

I should go home, she told herself.

She was surprised that the idea should occur to her. All summer she'd talked of little else besides her upcoming college life. At those rare moments when she'd suffered doubts, Charlie's enthusiasm had carried her along. Charlie had claimed he couldn't wait to take her walking in the Arboretum and canoeing on the Huron River.

This was Charlie's senior year, but it was to be followed by graduate work in architecture. She'd boasted about him to her sorority-sisters-to-be. She sensed they were impressed that a freshman should be stepping out with a senior; they'd asked how she met him.

When she explained, "You get to meet lots of people when you play in an orchestra and perform at parties," she knew she'd aroused their envy.

On the steps of the Administration Building, she was joined by a blonde future sorority sister named Helen, also on her way to sign up for classes. Helen paused to wait for her, smiling, commenting, "I'm glad you're here; we can go in together."

Millie confessed to having second thoughts about registering. "I'm undecided; I don't know if college is for me, after all. It means abandoning the orchestra my brother and I worked so hard to make a success of. I mean, I started when I was fourteen. Five years of hard work. Now, with no time to practice, I could lose my musical skill."

Helen gazed at her and frowned. "Surely your brother will hold a place for you. And musical skill can be regained."

Millie pursued the question. "Who knows what will happen in four years' time? Rob may not be able to keep the orchestra going by himself. I took charge of advertising and wrote the letters arranging schedules." She stopped herself just short of explaining that Rob, with a mere fourth-grade education, couldn't do that sort of thing, that her help was essential. A sorority girl like Helen, raised in wealth, wouldn't understand that poverty children had to quit school and work to support their families.

Suddenly, Millie felt she didn't belong here. She wondered why she'd come. She explained, "We're entertainers, we have to know popular music, not classical." Millie had become painfully aware of the gap. This wasn't her world. Of course, Dad would claim she'd merely moved back into a world which should have been hers all along, that if his father hadn't died in the Civil War, he himself would have been sent to college and would have become a professional man, able to educate his children well.

She remembered Charlie. If she left, she wouldn't see him. They'd looked forward to sharing college life; they'd talked of it all summer.

"Don't give up before you start." Frowning, uneasy, Helen stood on the top step gazing at her. "There are so few of us women at the university as it is. We need to stay and support one another."

Millie noticed that a lock of Helen's hair had worked loose from the bun in just the way Vi's hair always did. The sight brought a longing for home. Helen seemed to read her thoughts; she grasped her arm. "Everyone gets homesick. It passes. Let's go register." She opened the door and held it.

Millie still hesitated. "You go ahead, Helen. I want to think about this for a while." If she signed up, then left, she would be a drop-out, her award wasted. If she opted out now, before registering, perhaps someone else could use her scholarship.

Helen gave her a protesting look. Millie understood her new friend's bafflement. Scholarship, sorority, beau on campus—no one should drop all that. "Just give me a few minutes," she urged.

Helen opened her mouth to argue, shrugged, went on inside. Millie decided to walk down the hill to the train station to meet Charlie, who was due on the 11:20. She felt sure all would be well when she saw him. Those great plans they'd made during the summer would all come back to her. "It's great canoeing on the Huron River," Charlie had said. "And in winter there's ice skating. We'll have fun together."

At the station, she learned the train had been delayed. She wandered back and forth along the platform, among students in collegiate clothing awaiting their friends. She perched on an empty luggage-carrier, swung her legs, and resisted a temptation to bite her nails. She wished time would pass more quickly. She needed Charlie here to reassure her.

The train arrived an hour late. Charlie stepped off carrying only a small overnight case. When Millie waved, he waved back and came toward her. He looked boyish in his collegiate checked tweed jacket. She took a few running steps, hesitated, walked more sedately. It struck her Charlie didn't seem as eager as she'd expected.

He smiled a bit wanly when he said, "Hello, Freshie, how's it going?" He appeared uncertain whether or not to embrace her. She felt him holding off. He took her hand.

"I thought it would be fun to come and meet you." She spoke demurely. "I had nothing urgent to do at the moment."

"I'm glad you came. I have news."

Hearing a somber warning note in his voice, she gasped. "Is something wrong?"

"Don't panic, it's not a disaster." He gave her his arm and walked beside her. "It's just that—well, an opening turned up at the Yale School of Architecture. I've decided to grab it. I'll finish sooner; I can skip the general courses required here." He seemed abashed. "You know how I'd love to be with you in Ann Arbor, how much I counted on it. But I thought—well, speed is important, especially now with the war and all."

She felt her blue mood plunge lower. Tears threatened. She tried not to show her disappointment. "Of course you must do what's best for your education. I can understand that." She seemed to have known he'd say something like this. From the moment she'd awakened, she'd been suffering the blues and sensed disaster ahead.

Charlie set his bag down and took both her hands. "I came to get a few things I stored at the dorm. I'll be heading east tomorrow morning. I'm sorry, Millie—for both of us. But because of the war—we could get into it any day and I'd have to go—I need to finish college quickly."

"Of course. I understand." She swallowed the lump in her throat.

He grimaced. "I feel I've let you down. We had great plans."

"Fact is," she admitted, "I've convinced myself I don't belong here."

He frowned. "Oh, Millie, don't ever think that."

"You see, I've discovered expenses I never anticipated." The words tumbled out of her. "I've saved my orchestra earnings thinking they'd see me through. Now I realize my bank-account won't stretch far here. I'll soon have to begin working my way, and I'm told that's almost impossible. I've talked to two women who flunked out."

"You need to apply for a second scholarship. Don't just give up." He picked up his bag. "Let's have lunch and talk about it. And this afternoon we'll go canoeing. We planned that all summer. Can't miss our big adventure." With his free hand he squeezed her arm.

They walked up to State Street, entered a small restaurant, found a table in a secluded corner, and ordered creamed chip-beef on toast with tossed salad. Charlie urged Millie to reconsider. "In the sorority, you'll make friends and conquer this homesickness. You'll forget me and—that is, I hope you won't forget me, I hope we'll write to each other and get together again soon. I mean, you'll forget I'm not here. You'll be busy with classes and social life."

Millie felt she'd been handed a consolation prize. She fought her depression and tried to sound forceful. "This is not homesickness, Charlie, it's a realization of who I am. I'm a musician, an entertainer, and there are no university courses here to help me."

With a frown, Charlie reminded her, "Your orchestra is small potatoes compared to what might open up for you in college."

Millie didn't admit to him that the only thing stopping her from leaving this morning had been the assumption that she'd share her college experience with him. She shrugged. "Music has always been my life. My brother taught me to play the banjo when I was five. I've dreamed of being in vaudeville and operetta. All during *The Dollar Princess*, I kept wishing to be up on stage, performing with the other actors. You don't learn that stuff in college."

He gave her a rueful smile. "I don't doubt you'd be great at it, Millie, but it's not a lifetime career. Musical comedy performers get too old almost before they get old enough."

"Not orchestral musicians, though. I'm lucky, having a brother willing to hire women. He's one of a kind. Our dad always taught us that women should have the same rights as—"

"But think if Rob should give up the orchestra. What would you do then?"

"He won't quit. Music is his life."

"—or fail—"

"But that's precisely the point. He needs my help so he doesn't fail. Oh, I know what you're saying. I'm putting all my eggs in one basket. But things succeed when people care about them and fling heart and soul into them. My heart and soul have always been with the orchestra."

"Just give it thought." Charlie frowned again and attacked the salad placed before him. He speared a cucumber-slice, lifted it, studied it. "Competition's fierce."

Millie toyed with her own food and reflected. Fierce competition meant Rob needed her. He couldn't hire people with her kind of loyalty, people who'd work without pay if necessary.

Rob had been loyal to her for a lifetime. He'd watched over her as a child, taught her all he knew about music, given her a place in his orchestra. She owed him.

There was another reason she wanted to go home, one she didn't care to discuss with Charlie. Her father's drinking. Many nights she'd sat up with Douglas and kept him away from the saloons. They'd listened by the hour to the recordings people gave him in lieu of payment for watch repair, everything from Polish marches and polkas to Caruso and Madame Schumann-Heinke singing Verdi. Millie'd cranked the Victrola while her dad poured the coffee.

Also, this past summer, she'd got involved in the Woman Suffrage movement and longed to continue her work in that arena.

"I do know how you feel," Charlie said. "The university offers so many courses that seem pointless. I've often asked myself why an architect needs to know the Roman and Greek literary classics. The buildings, the columns, the pediments, the aqueducts, yes—but why Homer and Virgil? With a war on, we need to learn to draw up plans and build."

"I guess that's what I'm feeling." She recalled Bea's comment: *What use will it be to you to know Virgil?*

He put his hand over hers on the table. "I support you in whatever you decide, Millie. Just remember, an opportunity for university study comes only once." He eyed her thoughtfully. "What brought on all these doubts? I hope it wasn't my change of plans."

Millie thought about it. "I guess it started yesterday when I tried to play my banjo and found my fingers stiff. With no practice, I'd lost flexibility. Made me realize how much I'm giving up."

"Well, it's your life. You know best what's important to you." Charlie added consolingly, "In any case, I'll meet you at Christmas—unless war comes."

"I'll look forward to it." Christmas was far off, and she felt sure she'd be on the 7:10 tomorrow. She forced a smile. "You go east, I go west."

He squeezed her hand. "After all, we have our whole life ahead to do things together, don't we?"

She felt tempted to say, "Not if war comes," but she squelched the dark thought and said nothing.

CHAPTER 18

2002
Ashley

Though it's time to dress for my lunch with Laura at Schnitzelbank, I sneak a peek ahead in the diary to see what Millie decided. I find that her idiot brother Rob wrote her a letter complaining at length of his problems with the orchestra. It seems he'd hired an agent who wanted him to stop playing for those piddling parties and go for big bucks. Rob felt there weren't enough big-bucks offers to keep the group in gigs, but since he lacked the education to do his own advertising, he couldn't fire the agent unless Millie came home to handle the work.

What got into him to write all that? Why couldn't he have shut up and let her enjoy college?

I guess you know what Millie did. She went home. Good old reliable Millie couldn't let her brother down. I feel furious with her for giving up her scholarship, so furious I can't focus my mind on what I want to wear today. I go through the limited wardrobe I brought with me, look at everything, shake my head, can't decide. I want to slap Millie; I want to yell at her: *Do something for yourself for once in your life, for God's sake. Stop thinking about what's happening to Rob and your father. Let them worry about their own lives.* I feel frustrated at my inability to communicate across the years. I need a time machine.

I pull out a slinky dress that falls off one shoulder and drops to a point at the opposite knee. I almost lay it out, then decide no, that's a guy kind of dress, not for wearing to a women's party. For lunch with Laura, better find one with covered shoulders and an even hem. But I have few of those, and I've worn them all at least once, some twice. Finally, in desperation, I come up with a tie-dyed blouse I made last year at camp, and a skirt Mom would say is too short. Still fuming at Millie, I put them on and re-do my makeup.

Laura drives us downtown to the Schnitzelbank, a German restaurant which looks like something out of Washington Irving, decorated with paintings and figures of the Little Men who played ninepins and got the better of Rip van Winkle. I order the only thing I recognize on the menu—knockwurst and sauerkraut. Laura orders something with an unpronounceable name like Wienerschnitzel. While we await our food, I talk about Millie. I can't get my mind off her.

"My mother wouldn't want to hear me complain about my great-grand-mother," I admit. "But I went ballistic when I read that she gave up a scholar-ship at the University of Michigan. It seemed so self-defeating."

Hearing my own words, I cringe at their hypocrisy. Hadn't I myself chosen to drop out of college? Why should I feel angry at Millie for doing so? I can't analyze it, except that it seems to me Millie was the right sort of person to get an education.

And I'm not? Well, I have to think about that.

Laura, who also dressed for the occasion in her tan church-going suit and pimento scarf, smiles at my vehemence and reminds me that a woman's role was viewed differently in those days. The woman was expected to be the angel in the house, the savior and do-gooder. "I remember reading where even the writer, Virginia Woolf, complained of it. It would have been difficult for Millie to buck that. Millie probably felt responsible for her family, felt she must hold things together because no one else would."

"But, I mean, a scholarship! To the university! I wouldn't give it up."

"Of course you wouldn't. You're a twenty-first century woman."

"Would you have walked away from it?" I ask her.

"Probably, if my family needed me. I'm a twentieth-century woman; I still feel caught in the ties that bind." She smiles. "I don't honestly know, Ashley. I had a conventional upbringing, I wasn't exposed to much Women's Lib. I'm for it, of course—but I wish the Libbers weren't so shrill."

"Maybe they have to be, to get heard," I venture.

"That's possible. Anyway, I believe Millie was involved in a lot of things here in Grand Rapids, not least the earlier women's movement. Also, I seem to recall hearing that she was active in WCTU. She didn't return home to do nothing."

I admit I'd read about that. "What *was* the WCTU? I mean, I know what the letters stand for, but—"

"I read somewhere that it was the forerunner of the women's movement. It was organized to fight the saloons, and at first the women had a problem just holding meetings and giving speeches. They were refused podiums. In those days it was thought that no decent woman would get up to talk in public." She shook her head thoughtfully and explained that Frances Willard, the head of the organization, had to do battle with everyone, men, public opinion, even other women, just to be allowed to speak. She fought, won, and got herself heard—but others facing the same problem decided women would never be taken seriously until they had a vote. "Only political clout can make for equality. So—they became Suffragettes."

I read in history class that WCTU was the laughing-stock of the nation. When I remark on this to Laura, she assures me that came later. Under Francis Willard, it was a legitimate organization doing a good job fighting alcoholism. Later, unfortunately, a woman named Carrie Nation took over and made herself a comical figure, waving her hatchet and attacking taverns. She became the butt of cartoons with her ridiculous slogan: lips that touch liquor will never touch mine.

Our meal is served and we sample our food. Laura has what appears to be a breaded pork chop, but she claims it's breaded veal. She also has curly homemade noodles that she lets me sample. They're good! I decide I'll be more courageous next time. I never know what to order in foreign restaurants—except Chinese. I know exactly what egg foo yong is, and gotlet chicken.

Anyway, I like knockwurst and sauerkraut, so it's okay. Laura reminds me that though she skipped college, Millie didn't waste her life. The orchestra was successful, and for a time she was their solo singer. She also became a librarian. "The family has every reason to be proud of your great-grandma," Laura says. "She was ahead of her time."

I'm still steaming about the college business. Maybe it's because it hit home; it's what I'd been about to do: drop out. But Millie was multi-talented. I didn't inherit her gifts.

Though I can't bring myself to admit to Laura about the dropping out, I do admit to confusion about my major. She says she thinks psychology would be ideal for me. I consider it. The word *psychology* tripped off my tongue when I could find nothing else to say, but I'd never really thought of it as a career.

"What would I do with a psychology major?" I ask.

"You could do counseling."

Me? A counselor? That's laughable. I can't even get my own life together, let alone others' lives. Not wishing to tell Laura this, I shrug and protest that I wouldn't know what to say.

"Sure you would, you have good ideas. You'd tell Millie to stay in college and fight her tendency to focus too much on her family. You'd tell my sister-in-law she has no right to what isn't hers. You gave all of us courage to fight Terri. Without your input, we'd probably have let her get away with what she did."

"Really?" I'm astonished. It never occurred to me someone might applaud my outspoken qualities. At home I'm told my mouth will get me in trouble.

"I think you're a very bright girl; you see through subterfuge. You'd make a great counselor."

Well, I need to give it some thought. No one ever before suggested such an idea.

While I ponder, Laura goes on to tell me I also gave her courage to send away for a potter's wheel and a kiln. She says she's wanted to be a potter ever since she visited Santa Fe back in the nineties and admired the hand-crafted ceramics. She'd even taken lessons and attended workshops at a ceramics center up north somewhere. Seems she never had the guts to buy equipment for herself. "I guess I'm like Millie; I have a hard time spending money on myself. It feels wrong to me. I always put family needs first."

"Of course it isn't wrong." I'm amazed she'd worry about such a thing. After all, a potter's wheel is hardly a luxury item. It's not as if she's spending money on expensive clothes or luxury spas.

When we get home, there's an exciting message, a dream of a message, for me on Laura's answering machine. It's from Kevin Rogers, an athlete at my college and a dude I've met at rallies and meetings but never dated. His fault, not mine. I'd have dated him in a hot minute if he'd asked. Naturally, I call him back immediately. For me, it's a turn-on just to hear from him.

I access only his answering machine, so I leave a message saying I'll be home for the rest of the day and giving him my cell-phone number.

I obsess about why Kevin would call me long distance like that. It's not as if he were a close friend. I wanted him to be, I dreamed he might be, but I thought it was all one-sided. At the parties and team rallies we both attended, he never seemed to notice me. I admired him because he was big on helping black orphans get adopted, convincing black families to take on an extra child. Once he was even on television talking about it.

Finally, after I've paced for a half hour, it occurs to me he must have got Laura's number from Dad. I call Dad to see if he knows what Kevin wanted. Dad says he understood Kevin was heading for Detroit and hoped for me to meet him there for a day of sightseeing.

Exciting, but it causes complications. I remember that Doug suggested our going to Cedar Point, which is somewhere near Toledo, which is somewhere past Detroit. But I don't suppose I ought to ask Doug to pick up Kevin and take him along. I mean, at home I wouldn't think twice, but here I'm a guest.

"If you did go to Detroit, you could maybe locate the Pennington house," Dad says on the phone. "It's one of those old Victorians, elegant in its day. Might be fun to see if it's still there."

At the words "Pennington House" I envision a white family of slave-owners. "You mean our old Southern mansion is in *Detroit*?" I ask. "How can that be?"

"It's not an old Southern mansion, it's an old Michigan mansion."

"Come on, Dad, Detroiters didn't own slaves."

"Who said anything about slaves? Our Pennington forebears were runaways who fled to Canada. They made a bit of money, moved back to Detroit after the Civil War, and bought a Victorian or Queen Anne or something."

I'm astonished. He'd talked so often about his grandmother who'd been a slave, I just assumed that the Penningtons were in the same category and had belonged to a family in a southern mansion.

"I never heard that before," I say.

"You didn't? How come? Michael and Marla knew it."

That's the problem of being the youngest. Your siblings learn things when you're too young to understand, and later no one thinks to update you on all that stuff. I confess I hadn't a clue. "Are you telling me that the Pennington mansion never belonged to a white family?"

"Oh, maybe it belonged to white folks at one time, but they weren't Penningtons. Lee, you need to research your black roots, too."

I think about it. "I could meet Kevin in Detroit and go searching for our family mansion," I say. "But I don't know what I'd do about Doug. I can hardly tell him I don't want him to come along. He's the one who offered to take me to Cedar Point."

"I'd recommend separate trips," Dad says.

"I guess I could take the train to Detroit and say I'm off to research the Penningtons."

Dad claims he has a cousin in Detroit I can stay with. "I'll give him a call."

I feel relieved at this suggestion. I've been getting antsy just thinking about that jaunt in the company of two guys, one black, one white. It sounds to me like a tense situation where I'd be caught in the middle, trying to make the guys like each other.

"Could you get in touch with the cousin right away and let me know, Dad? I need to have suggestions ready when Kevin calls."

"I'll try." Dad chuckles. "Just remember the old saying, *Oh, what a tangled web we weave/When first we practice to deceive.*"

"I'll keep it in mind, Dad."

I pace around my room wondering if it would be okay to walk away from the Langstons, who've been so nice to me, and go to Detroit to meet a guy. When Dad calls back to tell me I'd be welcome to visit at his cousin's house, I ask his opinion. He suggests the Langstons might be glad to have a break from a steady visitor. I'm not so sure Doug will be glad. I suspect he might be coming on to me, but I don't tell Dad that. Dad says he notified his cousin to expect me this weekend, so I leave it at that. I jot down the cousin's name, address and phone number. When I hang up, I go at once, without waiting for Kevin's call, to tell Laura about my trip to locate Pennington House. No mention of Kevin.

To my relief, Laura says, "This is a good weekend for you to go to Detroit. My relatives in Traverse City are holding a family reunion and have been urging Junior and me to come. I've put them off because I didn't want to leave you here alone."

"Then everything will work out perfectly." I feel relieved to know I can get away without leaving hurt feelings behind me. "Doug will go with you, I expect?"

"I don't know about Doug," she says. "I haven't asked him."

I hope and pray Doug is dying to go. I wouldn't want to appear to walk out on him for another guy. I mean, Doug and I were never an item, but even so, it wouldn't seem right.

When Kevin calls, I'm ready to say yes. "I can meet you in Detroit this weekend. It'll be great to see you again. I'm glad you thought of me." I try to sound cool and not let him know I'm dying of pure joy at his invitation, had scrambled to arrange to be available for it, or that I can hardly wait for the weekend. Promising to meet me at the station, he hangs up.

I find it almost impossible to settle down and read the diaries. I just want to go out and shop for new clothes. I mean, I'd shopped for new clothes before I came to Michigan, but those were prim and proper outfits with high neck-lines and knee-length skirts. They wouldn't do for Kevin. Of course, there's the slinky paisley for dress-up—and I do have a couple pairs of shorts, slung low to show my belly-button ring, with halter-blouses. I decide I'll have to settle for those.

I'm sitting with the diary on my lap, trying my best to get my mind off Kevin long enough to again pay attention to Millie, when the doorbell rings. Laura calls to say the potter's wheel she ordered has arrived. I go downstairs to see it, while Laura debates where to put the thing. "I guess the back porch will do for now," she tells the delivery man. She adds, to me, "I'll need to build a studio."

"My guess is, you'll need a shop," the delivery man says. "You make pots, you'll want to sell them."

"You may be right." Laura giggles. I realize she's acting girlishly excited, as if this were Christmas and the delivery man Santa Claus. When he returns with two large plastic bags of gray clay, she tells him to place those, too, on the porch.

When he leaves, after setting the kiln in the corner away from the house-wall, she looks around for a heavy-duty extension cord, runs it out from a kitchen outlet, and starts the machine spinning. She goes in search of a plastic apron and returns wrapped in it.

"This will be fun, Ashley," she says. "I'll let you try it out if you wish."

"You go ahead, I'll watch." I'm not sure I want to mess around with that gooey-looking clay. I've outgrown my nursery school days. True, I work with ceramics at camp, but those are ready-made pieces that only need painting. I've never begun from scratch, with wet clay and a wheel.

Laura says she can't wait to get started. She attaches the hose to the machine, slaps a wad of clay onto the wheel, and sits down on the bench. She lets the clay form itself into pot-shape under her fingers, and shows me which fingers she has to insert—the middle two—in order to hollow out the pot. The thing flies around and seems to hollow itself.

"This is such fun!" she says. "My very own potter's wheel!" She happily guides the clay into a leaning, irregular pot.

Recalling her husband with his passion for lumber, I want to say, "It takes all kinds." But I don't. I go back to thinking about Kevin and my weekend.

"No good, too tippy," Laura announces of her creation, and whooshes the clay back into a lump. "I need to try again—unless you want to have a turn, Ashley."

"No thanks, I enjoy watching." I look up to see Doug approach. He wears a white shirt and blue slacks. Truth time—or rather, lie time. Ugh, I don't want to do this.

"What have we here?" he asks, walking up to us. "Ooh, a potter's wheel. Mom will keep busy now. No more fancy dinners. We'll be eating peanut butter and jelly sandwiches from now on." He grins, says, "Hi, Ashley. Some fun, huh?" and gives me a quick hug. I feel guilty when Laura tells him I'll be going to Detroit for the weekend. His face grows longer.

"And I suppose we're stuck to go to the family reunion?" he grumbles.

Laura upbraids him. "*Stuck* is not the right word for your relatives, dear."

"No, Mom. But let's face it, we're stuck." He adds, to me, "I'll miss you, Ashley. I wish I could go with you instead."

"Yeah, me too." I speak the words, but under my breath. I know my response is not what it should have been. Awash in guilt, I force a smile and try not to notice that cute cowlick. Damn, why did I hang out with this guy so much? I should have known I'd end up regretting it. Why didn't I stick to my resolve to be remote and impersonal?

Of course, I never dreamed that Kevin, football-hero Kevin, Denzel look-alike Kevin, Kevin the chair person of the Black Condor Club at our community college, would get in touch with me. Kevin, you dreamboat, I'm yours.

I'll need to do a washing and pack, but that won't take all evening. I'll read a few more sections of the diary. I'm up to war-time now—World War I. The War to End War. What a crock.

CHAPTER 19

1918
Millie

I've made it, I've made it, Millie sang to herself while she descended the stairs at the Hotel Macatawa. *So much for the nay-sayers. I proved I'm good enough to be soloist with the orchestra. I'll make it to the stage, too, I'll be in vaudeville. I've been in vaudeville at the Ramona Theater. I'll do it again. It worked out after all to leave college. It was the right thing to do.*

At the bottom of the stairs, she stood with her hand on the newel post and glanced across a lobby deserted except for a cleaning lady at work. She exulted when she saw, prominent on a stand near the desk, the giant poster with her picture at the top. *Millicent Langston, featured singer with the Royal Mandolin Orchestra, appearing nightly in the hotel ballroom except Sunday and Monday.*

Even yet, after three weeks. Millie tended to keep checking on the poster to make sure it was there, it was real.

Granted, the war had something to do with her success. Until recently, Rob had rarely let her sing solo. Probably, if his regular singer, Bud Hansen, hadn't gone off to join the Army, he'd still refuse. Like their father, Rob believed in opportunities for women yet had strong feelings about what was "suitable." Banjo, yes. But singing struck him as an activity best reserved for dancehall girls, not for his properly brought up sister, who he thought should limit her singing to WCTU performances, or the County House, or at the very least Grand Rapids locales like the Ramona where she was known. Despite her years of experience in skits, he'd remained reluctant to permit her to sing until circumstances forced him into it.

Arguing the point, she'd told him not to be so protective. "How about opera singers? Call Madame Schumann-Heink a dancehall girl?"

"Opera's different," he'd asserted. "That's sort of—you know—uppity."

When Bud quit, she'd happily taken over and proved her mettle. The audience at the hotel loved her—and they were mostly well-to-do Chicagoans who could afford the best. She knew how to put a wistful note into her voice and to mimic Alana's dad's Irish accent. With songs like "My Wild Irish Rose," and "Rose of Tralee." she, who was half Scottish, half Swiss, could bring the audience to the verge of tears with nostalgia for a land she'd never seen. She felt ready for duets with John McCormack, the great Irish tenor.

In the grand entrance hall with its chandelier, the cleaning woman, who swept at the ubiquitous sand forever blowing or being tracked from the beach, raised a white-capped head and waved. "That there's a good pitcher of you, Miss Langston."

Millie smiled her thanks and again studied the poster. Her eyes focused on Harvey in the group photo below, and she shuddered as an unpleasant memory invaded her mind. Harvey had proposed to her the previous evening, causing her embarrassment. Knowing he was soon to be called up, she hadn't wanted to hurt his feelings with a blunt refusal—but Charlie remained her man of choice. Before he'd joined the marine corps, she and Charlie had shared a second and even more wonderful summer. Of course, she didn't want to admit the fact to this departing friend. She struggled to be kind, to be diplomatic. She waffled. "Let's wait, Harvey. The future is so uncertain right now. I'll write to you; we'll keep in touch." His disappointment was palpable. It hurt to see it.

She also worried about the fate of the orchestra. Wylie Blake, a married man with children, probably would not be called up, but there was bachelor Josh Graham—and there was Rob himself, a conscientious objector who might well be recruited as ambulance driver or for other non-combatant duty. What would happen then? Could she and Wylie keep going by themselves?

"Did it take you long to learn them instruments?" The chambermaid leaned on her broom and studied Millie with interest.

Millie admitted she didn't remember a time when she couldn't play. She added, "My brother started teaching me when I was a tiny tot. I could read music before I learned to read words."

"My, ain't that something?" The portly woman drew a handkerchief from her pocket to wipe perspiration from her brow. It was already a warm day. She added, "Some brother you got there. My brother never taught me nothing, he only pulled my pigtails and swiped my desserts."

"There aren't many like Rob," Millie agreed.

"Pretty name, Millicent. Is it really your'n or one of them whatchacallits, stage names?"

"It's on my birth certificate."

Clearly longing to chat, the chambermaid put aside her broom. She stood, feet apart, gazing at Millie. "We've got a actress staying here, Laddie Munn; you ever hear of her?" When Millie admitted she'd met Laddie briefly the previous night, the woman went on, "Checked in, or I should say swooped in, all swank. They say she was born Gladys Munnafee but changed her name for the stage. Laddie sounds like a boy but I hear she chose that on purpose. She's one of them, you know, suffragettes."

Millie suppressed an urge to correct the put-down term, suffragette. Instead she pointed out that Gladys was scarcely a memorable name. "I guess she figures people will notice a girl with a name like Laddie." Millie moved closer to the poster. Her own face gazed back at her, thoughtful, unsmiling, good-looking but with features she considered too regular to be captivating. Beauty, Millie felt, required some slight variation from the norm. Young Bea, with her brown hair and snapping brown eyes, showed promise of becoming a beautiful woman, and Vi was often compared to the Gibson Girl, but Millie believed that she herself, the middle sister, had to settle for mere prettiness.

Two little girls thumped down the stairs and shyly approached to ask for an autograph. One held out an open book, the other proffered last night's menu. Millie smiled, signed both, and handed them back. Then, with a wave of farewell to girls and chambermaid, she went into the dining hall and walked through to the table at the rear reserved for the more distinguished employees, orchestra members, desk clerks, and the concierge. Waitresses, bell-hops and chambermaids ate in the kitchen.

The sun had hidden itself in a fog-bank on the Eastern horizon, and tinted the clouds over the lake salmon-pink. Through the dining-hall windows, the broad expanse of Black Lake, or Lake Macatawa—the name changed depending on whom one spoke to—was gray-blue in the early morning light, dotted with white rowboats full of fishermen.

On entering the small enclosure, Millie saw Rob sitting alone near the window. Relieved that she would not have to face Harvey so early, after last night's contretemps, she hurried to the table. While she seated herself, Rob commented, "You're up early."

"Couldn't sleep. Worried about Harvey. He proposed to me last night."

"Did he?" Rob eyed her with curiosity but not the dismay she'd anticipated. He failed to offer a thundering protest; he didn't complain that her marriage would devastate the orchestra, didn't remind her he couldn't afford to lose her. She waited in vain to hear the words.

Rob hadn't shot up tall during his teen years; he remained a short man like Zeke, a bare inch taller than Millie herself. Yet he was slimmer, less burly, more handsome than his older brother. He simply gazed at Millie as if awaiting more information. When she remained silent, he asked. "And you said?"

She placed her napkin in her lap, half-folded. Clearly her brother must trust her, to show so little anxiety and concern. She hastened to confirm that trust. "You know what I said. I have no intention of leaving the orchestra to get married. I love what I'm doing. I just wish Harvey hadn't muddied the waters by becoming *personal*. We were good friends all these years."

"It won't be long until he leaves."

"Which is precisely why I couldn't remain cool and indifferent. I had to sound caring while making it clear I'm not considering marriage right now."

Cook brought her a steaming cup of coffee. Millie thanked the portly woman and ordered a light breakfast of toast and fruit. When the woman hurried off, Millie snacked on a strawberry from her brother's plate.

Rob pushed the creamer in her direction. On turning to reach for the sugar bowl, she saw the chambermaid hurrying toward her, waving a telegram. She felt a stab of panic. Telegrams for her always meant bad news. Good news came addressed to Rob and involved engagements and contracts.

Approaching, the chambermaid confirmed her fear. "Black border means death, Miss Langston. You have someone in the military, maybe?"

A chill went through Millie. It would be too horrible if—But no, not Charlie, her true love. It couldn't happen. And not her old friend Warren. Too awful, she couldn't bear it. She'd known Warren since age five when they first eyed each other with interest across the large dining area at the County House. Liz Kingsley's only son.

The chambermaid placed the yellow envelope before her. With trembling fingers she tore it open and read.

BABY RICHARD DEAD STOP ALANA DISTRAUGHT STOP
NEED YOU COME HOME LOVE DAD

She stared in disbelief. What could have happened? "Richard was fine when we left." Puzzled, she handed the telegram to Rob. To the chambermaid she explained, "Seems our baby nephew died. My brother's child."

The woman shook her head, clicked her tongue, said, "Dear me, how sad." Before she left, she touched Millie's shoulder consolingly. Rob studied the telegram with a frown of bafflement and asked, "Flu? This terrible epidemic?"

"Alana's careful not to take the children into crowded places."

"Diphtheria? Scarlet fever?"

"No epidemics of those that I know of."

"I suppose you have to go," Rob grumbled. "Our first two-month contract, and it's been one thing after another. Hanson drafted, Hubbard about to go, you summoned home."

Millie dismissed Harvey from her mind. She needed to think what to do. This death defied belief. "I can't believe it's true. You don't suppose Edgar would pull a prank like this? Send a telegram just to scare us?"

Edgar, Vi's twelve-year-old son, had recently moved back to Stormland because he didn't get along with his stepfather, Don Dexter. He was now being pampered by his grandparents, who doted on him despite his mischievous ways.

Rob admitted he wouldn't put it past him. "But I don't see him spending his allowance on a telegram when he's not here to witness the result. He likes to watch the reaction to his tricks. Maybe Richard was hit by a car. There are so many rigs on College Avenue these days."

She sighed. "I suppose I'll have to go. Lucky you, you never get asked."

"I have a contract here. I don't see how you can help, either. I agree you should go on Tuesday, for the funeral, but—"

"I'm sure Mother is frantic and feels she needs me."

"The folks depend on you too much. I've always said so." Rob was frowning. "This is our big break. All these Chicagoans at this hotel, someone with big-time connections may turn up to offer us a great job. We don't need interruptions."

She put her fingers over his to squeeze his hand. "I won't stay long, Rob. I'll console everybody, then catch the first interurban train back here. Poor little Richard, he's your nephew, too. We have to show some concern. And poor Alana, another child-death. Bad enough about Roan, the scarlet fever—" She struggled to find comforting words; she shared Rob's concerns. Rob had recently quit his job to devote full time to the orchestra. She well knew his future depended on its success, and that he'd had endless worries as the men were called to military duty.

"They won't want to let you go," he said. "And I don't see you insisting, Millie. Not around a bunch of weeping women."

"It won't be easy," Millie admitted. "Mother and Alana both go to pieces over the death of children. We all do."

The cook brought a plate of toast, jelly and fruit. Millie wrapped it in a napkin to take with her. "I do have to go find out what happened to Richard," she said. "But I promise I'll make it short. I'll return right after the funeral."

"Give Alana and Menno my sympathy. I didn't mean to sound callous."

"I know." She touched his shoulder as she stood up. "And I realize you're worried about the big dance here tonight. But you'll manage without a soloist this once."

"I hope so." He waved her away.

In her gray travel suit and the Chinese red blouse so dramatic against her dark hair, Millie leaned toward the mirror and touched her powder puff to her face. A knock on the door set her to hastily replacing the puff and snapping the compact shut. She stepped to the door and opened it.

Rob stood in the hall, accompanied by a young woman Millie recognized as Laddie Munn. Laddie—short for Gladys—wore her hair in a loose bun that made it look bobbed, while her fringed skirt showed off, below the knees, legs that Millie thought looked a bit like pillars. Laddie and Rob were both smiling—one could almost say grinning—toothily. Millie found those grins unsettling, chessy-cattish.

Clearly a dynamic person who knew how to make herself noticed, Laddie had come up to the orchestra members the previous evening and introduced herself, explaining that she'd been on the vaudeville circuit and just finished a show in Chicago. "I'll soon be on my way to Mackinac Island for performances at the Grand Hotel," she said. (Boastfully? Millie wondered.) "This is a rest period."

Millie struggled to return the smile. She'd taken an instinctive dislike to Laddie, from her shortened name, which should have been Gladys Munnafee, to her seemingly faked charm.

"Miss Munn has kindly offered to help us out." Rob, so long-faced a few moments ago, had suddenly grown cheerful. "Don't worry about a thing, Sis."

"Yes, I can take your place—and glad to do it," Laddie said. "Resting bores me."

"Take all the time you need, Millie," Rob added. "I know how Mother depends on you."

Millie experienced a sharp pang of jealousy. Miss Munn seemed too willing, Rob too happy. Millie didn't want anyone substituting for her; she liked being the sole singer with the group. And she wasn't ready to compete with an experienced performer from vaudeville. She felt strongly tempted to change her plans and refuse to leave.

As if he sensed her hesitance, Rob reminded, "Bus is waiting at the door for you."

She told herself she was being foolish. With dispatch, she picked up her satchel and reticule. She hastily descended the stairs, her brother and his new friend close behind her.

She felt a chill as she climbed onto the bus but assured herself she worried too much. She made herself wave to the pair outside her window. When the bus started, she forced her mind toward thoughts of home, of what might have happened and what she'd be expected to do about it. There seemed to be, in fact, little she *could* do except offer consolations—and hurry back here before Rob and Laddie grew too chummy.

She tried to relax and look out the window, but she saw only her own face reflected back at her from the glass, a frown-line creasing the forehead.

CHAPTER 20

1918
Millie

Riding home on the interurban, Millie steamed with anger. Surely Rob could have managed for one evening without a singer rather than bring in a seasoned professional who'd make his sister seem amateur by comparison. Management couldn't cancel his contract over a death in the family. At worst they'd dock him Millie's share of the orchestra salary.

Well, she'd settle Laddie's hash. She'd rush back later in the day; she'd catch the last interurban train and arrive in time for tonight's performance. She'd offer whatever help she could at home, then be on her way. With Richard already dead, there was nothing she could do for the family except hold hands all around to console and mourn.

She pictured herself walking into the Macatawa Hotel just in time for the evening's opening number, smiling sweetly at her brother, telling Laddie, "We're so grateful for your offer of help, Miss Munn, but you won't be needed after all. I'm here, I'll carry on."

Yes, that was it; that was what she'd do. Hold everyone's hand, pat their backs, offer regrets, then leave. The family really didn't need her, they had Annie and Vi—and even Bea, seventeen now, was old enough to lend a hand.

Through the window of the Grand Rapids station, she saw Zeke outside, sitting on the dray with its two gray horses, waiting for her. She hurried out to him.

"Why are you using the dray?" she asked. "I thought you fellows bought a truck."

Abashed, Zeke admitted, "None of us knows how to drive. Don was supposed to take lessons, but the learner-car jolted when he started it. Gave him a bad scare."

"So what about you? Why don't you learn?"

"I'm no good with machinery. Mennonite prejudice, no doubt." He leaned over to offer her a hand up. When she was seated beside him, he said, "Thank God, you were able to get away, Sis. You don't know what we've gone through. Alana's out of her mind, and mother's close to it."

"What on earth happened?"

"I thought Dad wired you."

"Only that Richard was dead. Not how or why."

He frowned. "I don't want to be the one to talk about it. It's not my place."

"Come on, Zeke, I came home because of this; I need to know what happened. Richard ran into the street and got hit by a car? He played with matches and set himself on fire?" Those were the most terrible things Millie could think of.

"It's not for me to reveal it, Sis. Dad or Menno should do that."

Millie protested that she didn't think this was fair. When Zeke remained silent, she demanded, "So what am I supposed to talk about? The weather? With a child dead? What did I come here for?"

"We need help because Alana's in the hospital. She'll be released today, but she won't be up to taking over. Right now, Dougie and Rory are at our house. Vi's minding Sean and Maggie. Bea can't take time off; she started her new job only a few weeks ago."

On finishing business school the previous spring, Bea had taken a beginner job at low wages. Now her boss had made her his personal secretary at a much higher salary. Her prospects had been so good that she'd agreed to take on the support of the household, leaving Rob free to quit his laundry job at long last and concentrate on the orchestra. At present, she was the family's sole breadwinner.

"Am I allowed to know what happened to Alana?" Millie couldn't quite keep a note of sarcasm from her voice. She'd begun to think the house must have burned down or something. Just three weeks before, Alana had brought a perfectly healthy toddler to the train station to see the orchestra members off. Millie recalled his red-cheeked smile, his chubby hand waving to her and Rob from the station platform.

"I don't want to talk about it, Millie. I might sound like I'm accusing Alana, and I wouldn't want to do that. What with her being in the family way and all—"

"Zeke, no! Another child coming? She can't handle the ones she has!" Millie felt ready to come around to Bea's point of view about Alana's childbearing proclivities.

Zeke seemed to agree. "Bad, isn't it?" His shoulders drooped. With obvious effort, he lifted them to switch the reins and get the sluggish horses moving faster. "Ma didn't sleep all night. Sent Dad out at the crack of dawn to telegraph to you."

"Zeke, I can't fix anything. I'm not a magician. And Rob needs me, too. I had a great act going; I'd hoped to have Alana show me how to make an Irish costume. I do wish, just once, I could rely on my family to help—" She stifled the complaint. Selfish thought! At a time like this, with Richard so mysteriously dead, she shouldn't be worrying about costumes, performances, or even Laddie.

"You know how Ma gets when babies die. Wants her brood nearby. It's like she has to check on all of us, like she's holding her breath until you come. Lamenting that she can't have Rob here." Zeke flicked a glance at her. "Glad to hear that things are going well in Macatawa. It was a worry for all of us when Rob quit his job at the laundry. Bea's young to be the sole support of the family."

"Knowing Bea, I doubt we need be concerned. Bea has always known exactly what she could and couldn't do." Millie sighed, thinking again of Laddie Munn, the experienced performer who could so easily upstage local talent. Laddie would replace Millie while she struggled to do the impossible, console the inconsolable mother and grandmother of little Richard.

"Rob has help." She forced out the words. "He met a woman named Laddie who's in vaudeville. She'll take my place while I'm gone."

"Rob met a woman?" Zeke turned to her with sudden interest. "I'd become convinced it would never happen."

Millie froze. "He recruited a substitute, not a fiancée." She snapped out the words.

Zeke remained phlegmatic. "Now he's got her, he'd better keep her. He's been too single-minded about that infernal orchestra. A man can't be a bachelor forever. He's what? Twenty-eight?"

"He's seven years older than I, and I'll be twenty-two in three weeks, so he's twenty-nine. But he never seemed interested in meeting women. He hasn't lacked opportunities, you know. Girls hang around orchestra leaders."

"Those are worshippers. He doesn't need idolatry, he needs a helpmeet."

"Oh? He's told you so?" Anger had crept into Millie's voice; she found this conversation upsetting. She looked around at passing houses, at the shanties of Washerwoman's Hollow, and tried to focus on what might have happened to Richard.

Failing to notice, Zeke shrugged. "We're brothers; we talk. He often said he wanted to marry if he could meet the right woman."

Millie had given little thought to the possibility of Rob marrying. On the rare occasions when she did so, she'd envisioned for herself a congenial sister-in-law, perhaps even one of her own friends, Eloise or Thelma. She certainly hadn't foreseen being upstaged by Laddie Munn.

"What nonsense," she said. "There are plenty of 'right women' available. I've introduced Rob to all my friends. He's not interested, whatever he may say."

Yet she remembered Rob's broad smile as he stood in the hall with Laddie. At that time, the smile had been unsettling. Now, in retrospect, it seemed downright worrying.

A somber wreath graced the front door at Stormland. Looking at it, Millie shuddered. Though baby Richard had not been a resident, the grandparents clearly wanted to notify the community of the tragedy. No wreath had gone up here for Roan. Millie sensed that this was different, not an act of God but the family's responsibility, calling for public penance. Someone was at fault.

Millie braced herself to enter and face her mother's gloom. The wreath awoke in her mind echoes of days of quarantine, at Stormland when Menno suffered from smallpox, at Alana's when Roan died of scarlet fever. She walked around the house to the rear entrance and on the back porch found Alana's daughter, Maggie, playing jacks with a neighbor child.

"Aunt Millie," Maggie said, looking up, "did you hear the news? Richard fell into the boiling washtub and got cooked, and Ma's in the hospital with burned hands from fishing him out."

Cooked! Millie stood on the narrow walkway feeling as if her heart had plunged down into her abdomen. She could almost feel it beating down there. She breathed, "Oh, my God! Oh, you have to be kidding!"

"No, I'm not, am I, Uncle Zeke? The clothes were boiling on the stove and Richard tried to swish them around with a stick—and he fell in."

Millie felt her legs shaking. She had to sit down on the top porch step. "But—but how could that happen? A toddler can't *fall* onto the stove."

"He dragged the step-stool over and climbed up."

Zeke, who'd come up behind Millie, said, "I don't think you and I should be the ones telling Millie all this, Mag. That's for Menno—for your dad—to do."

Maggie demanded to know why. Millie said, "I think it's high time someone told me. How could this happen? Wasn't Alana watching him?"

"She was vomiting and she rushed off to the bathroom." Zeke finally admitted the whole truth. "She was gone for no more than a minute when she heard Richard's howl. She rushed back to pull him out, but he died in her arms. Then she choked on her own vomit. We almost lost them both. Luckily her earlier screams brought the neighbors running to pound her on the back."

Millie said again, "My God!" She'd imagined everything from street accidents to house fires, but nothing so awful as this. Her hand went to her forehead. She could think of no comforting words to say; her mind couldn't wrap itself around such a horror story. She asked a mundane question of the eleven-year-old, "Why are you here? I thought Vi was minding you."

"Aunt Vi went to buy the coffin. Me and Sean are staying with Gram today. Know what, Aunt Millie? I picked up nine jacks before I dropped one."

"You're getting good." Millie wished she could think about jacks instead of about death. She herself had once been a champion and rarely dropped any jacks. This was due to the fact that, as a little girl, she was allowed to play only quiet games. No hopscotch or jump-rope for her; her mother worried about the leaky heart-valve which was supposed to have killed her long ago.

Shakily, she squeezed Maggie's hand and waved briefly at the child's blonde-haired companion from next door. She just wanted to sit still and recover from the shock, but realizing she was delaying the inevitable, she stood and forced herself to enter the house. Her mother, seated at the oilcloth-covered kitchen table beside the ever-present bowl of cucumber-slices in vinegar, held her head in her hands. She reached for a handkerchief, wiped her eyes, and got up to embrace her daughter. Millie gave her a consoling hug.

"Thank heaven, you're here," Rebecca said. "I couldn't wait to have you at home. This death is almost too much for me to deal with."

"It's unthinkable, Mother. It's almost beyond belief." Millie gently reminded, "But I can't fix it."

"If only Alana had asked me to watch Richard while she boiled the clothes! She knows she's subject to morning sickness."

"I'm sure, if she'd imagined what would happen, she wouldn't have done the wash." Too obvious to need saying, but Millie felt a response was called for. "Who'd have thought Richard would try to stir the clothes?"

"A single moment and a life is ended—horribly." Rebecca shook her head. "Alana can't take it in. She keeps insisting it was just a bad dream."

"It doesn't seem to have upset Maggie. She's playing jacks out there."

"To her it's a holiday, a chance to stay with Grandma and Aunt Vi. What does a child know about death?" She got up and pulled out a chair. "Sit down for coffee, Millie. It's good to have you here. Things go better when you're around."

Still in shock, Millie didn't admit she'd been reluctant to leave Macatwa. She eased herself into a chair and asked, "How long will Alana be in the hospital?"

"She'll be out today. I don't know what we're to do with her; she's all to pieces. Any chance Rob will get home for the funeral?"

Millie thought about it. "With me gone, he has full responsibility. Has to keep track of music, set up for performances. Also, he's trying to recruit musicians. We're losing two orchestra members to the Army. Bud's gone, Harvey's been called up."

As if she hadn't heard her daughter, Rebecca remarked, "Another child to be put in the graveyard!" Her hand shook as she poured coffee from the blue pot.

Trying to set a tone of normalcy, Millie commented, "We need a Langston Family tombstone. Maybe Rob and I will earn enough at Macatawa to pay for it. By the way, I hear Alana's in the family way again." She drew the creamer closer, looked for the sugar bowl, realized that sugar, being rationed, was probably used up for the month, and decided to drink the coffee black. She made a face at the bitterness of it. Her mother, she knew, used corn syrup for a sweetener but she felt the stuff altered the flavor of the coffee.

"Lost the baby early this morning." Rebecca wiped her eyes. "Just as well, she had enough to do. Dougie not even a year old yet."

"She's tough, she'll survive."

"She blames herself for this one."

Millie frowned. "What about Menno? Doesn't he share the blame? Why can't he leave her alone for a while? Five kids are enough."

"Young men have strong drives. Mother Nature made them that way. Besides, I'm sure she didn't expect to get in the family way while nursing. No woman does."

The subject was too depressing to discuss. Still pretending to normalcy, Millie remarked, "I looked forward to being picked up in the new truck. Zeke claims no one can drive it."

"Don Dexter is supposed to be learning." Rebecca wiped her eyes and nose with a handkerchief, but proved not ready to stop talking about her middle son's affairs. "Alana and Menno married too young. What did two sixteen-year-olds know of child care?"

"Mother, they did fine with Sean and Maggie. Rory, too. As for Roan, the scarlet fever, no one could help that."

Head in hands again, Rebecca stared into her coffee cup and spoke as if she hadn't heard her daughter. "I don't know how we let that child-marriage happen. Things just seemed to fall apart when we first moved here. Menno met Alana, Vi met Nat. Pa started drinking. Nothing seemed to go right. Rob had to quit school and go to work. Seems like we've been Job's children ever since."

Millie thought back to the small town of Fargo, Michigan, where they'd lived before. Though barely five, she'd understood that, with train service discontinued, the town was doomed. The mill was forced to close because shipping routes ended. People lost their jobs and moved away. There were no customers for her father's apothecary shop. She recalled seeing her parents stand behind the counter in the empty store, awaiting customers who failed to materialize. Young as she was, she'd felt sorry for her father, who could no longer support his family.

"Dad had lost his profession," she reminded her mother. "It must have been shattering for him to come here and find he lacked qualifications to work in a big-city pharmacy. At age forty he had to start all over, learning watch-repair. It'd drive any man to drink." She grew heated. "You should blame the railroad for destroying the town. And blame Dad's mother and stepfather for shipping him out to Michigan in the first place. He shouldn't have been here; he belonged back in Maine. It's monstrous, throwing away your own children." She wiped a tear from her eye.

"You're telling *me* all this?" Rebecca straightened up. "I was there, I knew him. A lost, lonely little boy who tried to freeze himself to death in a snowbank. I rescued him, I dug him out. All I wanted in the world was to provide him with a happy home. It was my goal in life."

"I know." Millie reached across the table to squeeze her mother's arm. "You did try hard."

"I'll never understand how his parents could do that to a seven-year-old. I felt guilty when Zeke left home at thirteen. But that doesn't let your father out of responsibility for drinking up the family income. Last year, when they voted in prohibition in Michigan, he managed to stop his drinking in a hurry, didn't he?"

"Because two of his friends died from drinking bathtub gin."

"Proves he could quit if he wanted to." Rebecca sounded bitter.

Again Millie jumped to her father's defense. "Why blame Dad? Blame the Civil War. Blame the slave-traders."

"Now you're being silly."

"Why? Talk about monstrous. Enslaving our fellow man is surely the most monstrous thing anyone can do. I'd have gone off to fight, too, if I'd been Grandpa."

Rebecca swallowed the last of her coffee and got up to pour another cup. "Actually, I do blame the slave-traders." She sat with her steaming cup and gazed at Millie. "They caused problems for the whole country, especially the black people. And called themselves Christians!"

"People think first of money, then of justifying their activities." Millie's mind drifted from the subject. She began pondering how to bring up the fact she wanted to leave on the five p.m. interurban, to return to Macatawa and her evening performance.

As if sensing the thought, Rebecca said, "I'm proud of all my children but I do worry about you and Rob, there with those high-living Chicago folk." She got up again, took a frosted white cake from the bin and brought it to the table. "May as well eat this. Berdina de Groot up the street made it for us last night when she heard the news. Her son in the Navy brought her sugar."

"Looks good to me," Millie said. "I ate a stand-up breakfast while waiting for the 9:20 interurban." She leaned back in her chair to peer at the grandfather clock in the dining room. "Past noon, Mother. Have the kids eaten?"

"I forgot to check the time," her mother admitted. "Maybe you should bring some canned stuff from the cellar, tomatoes, peaches. I'll make tomato soup and fruit salad."

On opening the screen door, Millie heard shouts from the children outside. Maggie called, "Grandma, Aunt Millie, guess what? Ma's home!"

Millie stepped onto the porch, followed by Rebecca. Alana and Menno were making their way along the walk, passing the trumpet vine beside the porch. Menno held Alana's elbow while his wife thrust bandaged paws before her. Millie noticed that her sister-in-law appeared to have aged in the weeks since she'd last seen her. Not yet thirty, Alana already had lines in her face, along with a squat, matronly figure and hair gray at the temples. Millie wondered: had all this happened overnight or had she merely failed to notice until now?

Maggie rushed to her mother, who spread her arms for an awkward embrace that avoided use of her hands. "Where are the boys?" She looked around.

"Sean's playing in the woods with Edgar. Rory and—"

"I want to see the little kids." Alana peered, looking confused. She eyed her own skirt as if expecting Richard to be clinging to it.

"They're with Aunt Annie," Maggie said.

"I told you, Lan," Menno put in. "Don't you remember?"

"I want to see them." Alana caught sight of Millie as she approached. "Millie, I'm so glad you're here! I must tell you, I had this terrible dream. I thought Richard fell into a boiling washtub. It was so horrible I can't get it out of my mind. I keep seeing him in that bubbling water, and hearing the awful howl and gurgle."

Not knowing what to say, Millie gently hugged her sister-in-law. Maggie spoke up. "But Ma, Richard *did*—"

"Hush, Mag." Menno gave the girl a warning wink. "Let your ma rest now."

Waving her bandaged hands, Alana cried out. "No, it didn't happen! I don't believe it!" She looked around. "Where is Richard? I want to see Richard!"

"We're getting lunch on now," Millie said. "After lunch, you should rest."

"I'm not hungry. I want to see all my children."

Menno tried to nudge her toward the porch. He told Millie, "Doc gave me something to make her sleep. If we can get her to swallow it, she'll be all right. Come on, Lan."

"Put her in Rob's room downstairs." Rebecca held the screen door open. "I'll brew mint tea."

Alana protested. "I don't want to lie down."

Menno urged her along. "You need rest, you're badly burned."

She gazed at her bandaged hands in bafflement. "How did I do that?"

"Hot water. Come on, Doc's orders."

They pushed and prodded until they got her into the downstairs bedroom and persuaded her to lie down. They brought her mint tea and cookies. She drank the tea, refused the cookies, but under protest finally swallowed the medication.

When at last she dozed off, Millie followed her mother to the kitchen. She had an uneasy feeling she wouldn't be able to leave today after all. With Alana helpless, the family would need her. She tried not to think of Laddie Munn.

CHAPTER 21

1918
Millie

A letter from Charlie Loomis had been placed on Millie's dresser to await her arrival. On entering her room she found it, tore it open, and read.

Charlie offered no news of himself. He talked about Macatawa. "Chicagoans will hear you, and who knows, you may wind up with a contract in the big city. I wish you well, Millie. They do say radio will be the coming thing after the war. People will own sets in their own homes and music will be broadcast all over. You'll sing and the world will hear you."

That was nice, but seemed impersonal. There followed a description of the scenery in the town where he was stationed, and a statement that he was helping to design and construct barracks. He signed the letter, "With love." Always before it had been just, "Love, Charlie." *With love* sounded like an expression one would use to a maiden aunt. In fact the whole letter sounded to her like something one would write to an aunt. She bit her lip and worried. She'd been careless about her correspondence. Busy making her clothing for her summer engagement, then preoccupied with her experiences at Macatawa, she hadn't written as faithfully as she once did, to either of her men in the military. She vowed to write Charlie a long letter and apologize for her dereliction, to let him know her ardor hadn't cooled.

She also puzzled over the strange absence of mail from Warren, who'd been her most faithful correspondent. What could have happened? Might he have been sent overseas and into battle? On changing her clothes and returning to the kitchen to help with lunch, she asked her mother if mail had come from Warren. Rebecca shook her head. "Not since you left."

"Lordy, I hope he hasn't shipped out to France. I can't bear to think of him in the trenches."

"You might attend the Unitarian church tomorrow and ask his father. Warren once told me his father never misses the Sunday service. Pa'd go with you, I believe."

Uneasily, Millie broached the question of her departure. "I hadn't planned to stay until tomorrow. Saturday's our big night in Macatawa. I'm to sing for the dance this evening."

"We can't spare you," her mother insisted. "Alana will need help; she can't use her hands." She added complacently, "Don't worry, Rob will get along."

Millie couldn't bring herself to mention the threat of Laddie. Her mother would think her foolish to be jealous. She felt awash in frustration, impatient to leave yet all too painfully aware she was needed here. She whacked at the ham her mother asked her to slice, came up with thick pieces, tried to concentrate and slice more neatly.

Her brother, Menno, came into the kitchen carrying a bucket of coal which he dumped into the franklin stove. He told her she was too dedicated to that orchestra and should focus on other aspects of her life. "Remember, that's Rob's group, and he may someday want to do something different with it."

Despite her struggle to remain calm, a note of impatience crept into Millie's voice as she responded. Everything seemed to conspire to annoy her today. She fretted over why Rob wanted Laddie as his singer, why Alana had been so careless of her toddler, why Warren hadn't written, why Charlie sounded dismissive. Now her brother wanted to pile on another unpleasant thought. She snapped, "Different? How different?"

"I can't guess, I'm not a musician. But if he—"

"Rob would never make plans that failed to include Millie," Rebecca asserted.

"I should think not." Millie forced a note of finality into her voice. She couldn't picture Rob not needing her in the orchestra. Laddie had a contract at Mackinac and would soon leave. At worst, Millie would lose a few performances to her. It was foolish to perceive the woman as her nemesis.

"Rob can surely get along without you for a few days, until Alana's hands heal enough for her to cope on her own. We really need you here, Millie." Rebecca, too, managed to sound assertive, something rare around her talented middle daughter. She brusquely spread out slices of bread, buttered them, and added the ham chunks.

Millie sighed, frowned, bit her lip, whacked at the ham, and held her peace.

On Sunday morning, Alana awoke confused, not knowing where she was. While Millie accompanied her to the bathroom, she asked what had happened to her hands.

"You burned them." Millie didn't elaborate.

"And the children? Where are they?"

"They're being looked after. Sit down and let me comb your hair."

While Alana submitted to having her hair dressed, she asked, "What happened to Saturday?"

"You slept through it. Doc gave you sleeping pills." Millie fastened Alana's hair into a neat bun, helped her back to bed, and propped the pillows so she could sit. "I'll bring your breakfast."

As Millie turned away, Alana tried to grab her skirt but only flipped it. "Wait, I want to tell you about my horrible dream. I was boiling sheets, and I fancied Richard climbed on the stepladder and grabbed the stick and—Oh, dear, I can't talk about it!" She collapsed back against the pillows. "It was ghastly."

Millie didn't enlighten her that it was no dream. Time enough for that. The funeral wasn't until next day.

When Alana fell asleep, Millie, her mind still on Warren, approached her father about attending church. He nodded. "Went once or twice, myself, years ago. Never got around to going back." Since he didn't ask the reason for her sudden interest, she didn't confess it. She pointed out that her mother labeled the place a mere lecture hall.

"Well, Unitarians generally don't spend big bucks on buildings. They're more into good works. Abolitionists, one and all. That's why my father volunteered for the war. You won't hear much about God. Guess they figure, if you do good works, God and heaven will wait for you."

Later, walking downtown with her father, Millie remarked to him, "You never talk about your childhood, or about growing up Unitarian."

"Didn't really grow up Unitarian," he said. "Our church had no Sunday school. Dad usually went alone, and over Sunday dinner would tell Mother about the sermon and discuss it with her. At Christmas and Easter when we children were allowed to go, it was a special occasion, with candlelight and singing."

"So you don't know much about it?"

"I do remember that once Mr. Emerson came to visit. There was great excitement, with housecleaning for days in advance. I didn't witness the visit; I was sent out to play."

"Too bad. What a conversation piece that would make: The Day I Met Emerson!"

"Dad told me Emerson's philosophy was too difficult for a child. When I finally read him, I thought he was too difficult for a grownup."

Millie nodded; she'd placed Emerson on her list of people to study at leisure, allowing time for comprehension.

Passing through the area of fine old homes, Millie didn't feel intimidated. She and Rob had played for parties in many of these houses and found the interiors dark and dreary.

Approaching downtown, Millie on impulse pointed to a shoe-polishing stand. "Dad, let's get your shoes polished. My treat."

He raised an eyebrow. "Unitarians don't care about spit and polish."

"I want you to look nifty."

She felt sure her father had never before had his shoes polished. He dutifully climbed to the seat and put one foot and then the other onto the footrest and allowed the attendant to polish and buff.

"Now let me straighten your tie," she said when he climbed down.

He complained, "You're worse than your mother." Yet he stood still for her ministrations.

Finished, she stood back, approved, then posed for him. "How do I look?" While he inspected her, she fluffed her skirt and tilted her hat at a rakish angle.

"You look great, Millie. I was lucky, the women in my family are all beautiful."

"Oh, Dad." She laughed and swatted his arm.

They walked on. At the church, Millie recognized Warren's father, John Kingsley, standing on the front steps in a tan summery suit. Creases crisp, he appeared a very upright citizen compared to her own father, who always seemed dressed for a hike in the woods. Emerson and Thoreau, she thought, must in their day have offered similar contrasts, strolling together near Walden pond. She wished she could have been a bee buzzing around them, hearing their talk.

Millie wondered if John Kingsley would recognize her. He was speaking to another gentleman, reminiscing about the blizzard of '98. She heard him say, "Running the County Farm, I was, back then—with the wife's help, of course.

Snowbound. No way out for two long weeks. We had to manage as best we could on our stores of home-canned food. Tunneled through the snow to the barn to care for the animals."

The words took her back. Millie well remembered the days when he'd run the County Farm, when she'd performed her skits there for fundraisers and dined with Warren on the porch.

When John Kingsley became aware of Millie at his side, he swung around, grew silent, blinked. A tall man, clean-shaven, he was slim but sported a slight paunch. Like his son's, his face tapered to a narrow but firm chin. He eyed Millie. "Know you from somewhere. Hey, aren't you Miss Langston?" His eyebrows lifted. "The very person I hoped to see! I need to talk to you about Warren."

His tone was not cheerful. The niggling anxiety in Millie's midriff tightened into a knot. She caught her breath. "What happened to Warren?"

"He's in the hospital. Hit by electricity, several thousand volts, I hear. You knew the Navy put him to work as an electrician? With little training, of course. Typical of our armed forces."

Millie instinctively reached out to touch the older man's arm. "Is he—I mean, will he be okay?"

"We hope so. Arm burned to the bone. His mother went out to be with him. She's due back on the two o'clock train today. The doctors say he was in great pain for a while but is better now."

Millie persisted with her questions. "His arm will heal? He won't lose the use of it?"

"Lord, I pray not. A Navy parent can do so little. I feel helpless. No doubt he's hoping folks will go to Glenburnie for a visit. It's near Baltimore. Wish I could go myself, but summer's my busy season. I'm in roofing. Maybe you—"

Millie recalled hearing that Mr. Kingsley was now a traveling salesman—a highly successful one, judging by his beautiful home and the fact that in high school Warren was the only student who always had access to a car.

"Warren's stuck in the hospital, bored with lengthy therapy, hoping for visitors. I'm sure he'd love to see you, Millicent. Think you could go out there?" He gazed at her speculatively.

"Perhaps later." She spoke sincerely; she'd always regarded Warren as a dear friend. In their high school Sock and Buskin Club they'd done plays together. "Right now our orchestra has a two-month contract at Macatawa. I'm home for a nephew's funeral."

"Oh, sorry to hear. Child deaths are so sad. Lost a little one myself some years ago."

"Diphtheria, wasn't it? Warren told me."

"Yes, a major epidemic. Many deaths, adults as well as children. Cemetery filled up fast. Gruesome times, those. The doctors knew so little. Antitoxin was unfamiliar to folks."

Millie turned to include her father in the group. She introduced him. "My father, Douglas Langston." When Douglas stepped forward and reached out a hand, she rejoiced that she'd insisted on the shoe-polishing. Paunch-free, with his small brown goatee and his softly curling brown hair, her father looked natty enough to compete with Natty Nat. At this moment she felt proud of him, and forgave him for all he'd put the family through in his drinking days.

The men shook hands and chatted. John Kingsley said, "Langston. Scotch-Irish?"

"Pure Scots, I understand."

"That so? Scotch-Irish myself. Folks came from Belfast long ago, back at the time of the Revolutionary War. I believe Millicent mentioned you're a watch-maker?"

"That's right. Used to be a pharmacist, but when the railroad closed down, my drug store business got wiped out along with the rest of the small town of Fargo, Michigan."

"Oh, foul luck. Common problem, though. Depression of '93, I expect? Railroads went out along with a lot of other things. I remember those times. Had a wife and child, a second baby on the way. My brother Roswell and I traveled all over the county, job-hunting. Worked a day here, a day there, sometimes at nothing more than fruit-picking for a few pennies. That was before I landed the Keeper position at the County House. Millicent here knows about that, she used to come and perform for us."

"Yes, I went with her once or twice."

"Oh, then we've met before? Sorry, I didn't remember. There used to be such crowds at those events."

The sound of organ music hinted that services were starting. Mr. Kingsley suggested they go in. He briefly introduced his companion, and added, "Didn't know you were a Unitarian, Millicent."

Douglas spoke up. "My folks were Unitarians back in Maine, but I'm not a church-going man myself. Millie sings in the Congregational choir."

Following Mr. Kingsley and his friend into the building, Millie saw what her mother had meant. The place was indeed a lecture hall. No altar, no cross.

Forewarned, she wasn't bothered by the lack. She'd already done what she came to do, learned about Warren. She didn't know whether to be relieved that he wasn't in battle overseas, or worried that his arm-injury might cause serious complications. But one thing she did know—she'd write him a long letter this very afternoon. Him and Charlie.

The church service, mainly a scholarly speech on the politics of Rome and Judea in which Jesus of Nazareth had gotten caught up, proved to be all Rebecca had predicted—informative but scarcely spiritual. Millie didn't come out of it feeling inspired to go home and act more Christian. On being introduced to the minister, she assured him she'd enjoyed the talk—and politely neglected to point out that it was no sermon but a lecture.

On the way home, she spoke of Warren and her worries about his recovery, the possible loss of use of his arm. Her father sympathized but reminded her of the more immediate problem with their own patient. "Alana must be told the truth. We can't pussyfoot around any longer."

"Yes, I need to get back to Macatawa. I can't stay here and shield her. She'll have to come to terms with reality." Millie tried to sound emphatic and forceful.

When they reached home, a family conference was convened. Rebecca urged that they give Alana one more day. Millie and Douglas argued that you can't protect people from life. "To be alive is to face pain as well as joy," Douglas said. "Let Alana come to terms with that."

No one seemed able to convince anyone else. When Alana awoke, the family was still split, Douglas and Millie against Rebecca and Menno.

Millie went to attend to the injured woman, who again asked to see her children. Millie told her Sean and Maggie would be allowed to visit her. Obedient to her mother's wishes, she claimed the younger ones were happy at Annie's and shouldn't be bothered just yet.

Rebecca brought the meal on a tray, but Alana made a face over it.

"If you'd eat, you'd recover faster," Rebecca said. "I've fixed a lovely dinner, pork roast, garden peas, hot biscuits and honey. It's impossible to buy roast pork in wartime; it's saved for the troops. We only got it because Menno is renovating the local butcher shop, building a walk-in freezer."

Alana still gazed at the tray with indifference. When Millie fed her, Alana dutifully took a few bites and then pushed the tray away with the back of her bandaged hand. Worn out and feeling stuck here, unable to escape, Millie sighed with relief when Alana again drifted off to sleep.

In mid-afternoon she received a telegram.

LADDIE DOING GREAT STOP NO NEED FOR YOU TO HASTEN
BACK ROB

Millie fought an overwhelming urge to walk out on everyone and go at once
to Macatawa. Laddie seemed to be insinuating herself into her own place in the
orchestra.

❦   ❦   ❦

I push the diary aside in frustration. I demand of Doug beside me, "Why
didn't the crazy woman just go back to her job and use her paycheck to hire a
nursemaid for Alana? That's what a sensible person would do. Her career was
far more important—"

Doug shakes his head. "Not in that day and age. She'd have seemed cold and
impersonal." He stands up and stretches. "How about some hot chocolate,
Ashley?"

"That sounds wonderful." I too stand to stretch. "Lucky I didn't live back
then. I couldn't have put up with the demands and expectations. If I'd been
Millie, I'd have run away."

"I agree it's hardly fair she should have had to give up so much for a sister-
in-law. Hold on, I'll microwave our chocolate." On his way out, Doug pauses in
the doorway to ask, "Shouldn't we stop reading? It's getting late, and we're all
traveling tomorrow. You need to catch the early train."

I shake my head. "I have to know what happened. While you get the drinks,
I'll sneak a peek so I can tell you the next installment." I wave him away.

CHAPTER 22

1918
Millie

On Monday morning, Millie stepped into Alana's room and drew up the shade. Alana awoke, raised her head, and gave her sister-in-law a hard stare.

"Tell me the truth, now." Her voice, too, was hard. "It happened, didn't it? It was no dream."

Moving toward the bed, Millie froze, her hand already out to smooth rumpled sheets. She hadn't wanted to be the one to tell. That was Menno's job.

Too late. Alana knew. Her grim expression proved that.

"It was no dream," Millie admitted.

"Richard's dead. Scalded in boiling water."

"Yes. Funeral's today."

Alana stared out the window at a view of nothing but gray clapboard, the siding of the house next door. "I'll see that horror picture in my mind for the rest of my life. It's burned into my brain. The only way I can forget is to die."

Though Millie herself vividly recalled Maggie's imagery of the cooked baby, she consoled. "Give it time, Lan. All things fade."

Alana shook her head. "I can't live with it. Every time I close my eyes I see my baby in that tub, turning red, water steaming and bubbling around him. How could I have fancied it was a dream?"

"Alana, you have four other children who need you. Not to mention a husband. You must pull yourself together."

"My sister Fiona says God is angry with us for abandoning the Catholic church."

"Superstition. God doesn't judge people by the church they go to. You've been a good mother. Sean, Mag and Rory are delightful youngsters, and Dougie is a loveable infant."

"I failed Richard. I turned my back. And I'd already failed Roan by allowing—"

"No one can be in two places at once." Reaching above the burned area, Millie squeezed Alana's arm. "Today you get those bandages changed. You'll have hands instead of paws. Come on, let me help you to the bathroom and then I'll do your hair."

"You've been good to me, Millie. I appreciate it. I hope I can soon go home and stop being a nuisance here."

"If you're tired of lying in bed, why not sit in the living room and listen to the Victrola?"

But when Alana tried it, she found Rob's dance music jarring, and as for Millie's opera arias, Caruso and Scotti vowing eternal friendship which was not to last, Caruso in *Lucia* agonizing on seeing his beloved marry someone else—even though she didn't understand the Italian, she labeled the scene heart-wrenching. Grand opera, she declared, was not for her. Preferring silence, she sat by the dining room window to watch the children at play outside. Millie, she said, could keep her Caruso recordings and welcome to them.

When Dr. Lapham arrived, he insisted his patient needed a vacation. Except for birthings at the hospital, she hadn't had a day off from housework and child-care since Sean was born fifteen years before.

"Physical and mental exhaustion," the doctor diagnosed. "Menno should take you on a second honeymoon."

"It would be a first, Doc. We never had one. Too bad Menno can't get away."

"You could go with Millie to Macatawa," Rebecca suggested.

Millie sought frantically for an excuse to escape that plan. To her relief, Alana herself protested. "I can't go off without Menno and the children. What would I do there while Millie and Rob are performing?"

Bea joined in promoting the idea. "Sun yourself on the beach. Have a ride on the excursion boat."

"I'd need nice clothes for a fancy resort."

While Millie chewed her lip and searched her mind for even more excuses, Dr. Lapham ran his hands through graying hair. "You must take care of yourself. A distraught mother can't be a good mother."

Millie stopped fighting her conscience and decided to bite the bullet and offer the invitation. She took a deep breath. "Rob and I will pool our money and buy you a new outfit, Lan. Macatawa is beautiful this time of year."

Alana shook her head. "Music, dancing, everyone else having fun; that would drive me crazy."

"At least you must take a walk, go shopping, sit in the park," Doc Lapham said.

Since no one else mentioned it, Millie asked, while accompanying Doc Lapham to the door, "Should Alana go to the funeral?"

He twisted his moustache-tips and thought about it. "She'll have to come to terms with what happened. There's no way to protect her." Pausing on the porch to turn back, he again urged Millie to keep after her sister-in-law about taking a trip. "She needs a break, needs to see different scenery, get her mind off house and children for a while."

"I'll do what I can." Millie knew she sounded dubious but she hesitated to take on Alana's problems. She felt she had enough of her own. Worrying about Laddie as her replacement was keeping her awake at night.

With the doctor gone, Millie and Alana, along with Bea who'd requested a day off for the funeral, walked to Annie's house for a reunion with the two younger children. Alana hugged baby Dougie so hard he squawked a protest; then she hugged five-year-old Rory who submitted more dutifully.

She insisted on going to her own house. The three women strolled to her street a block away. Sean, Maggie, Rory, and Edgar trooped along, stopping to admire fallen birds' nests. Edgar pondered how, lacking fingers, the birds managed to weave the nests.

Until they entered the kitchen, Alana had acted normal enough. Now she looked toward the stove, screamed, and threw bandaged hands to her face. "My baby! Oh, no! Please God, no!"

Bea embraced her while Millie put a hand on her arm. Alana sobbed on Bea's shoulder.

The big kitchen had for years been the only finished room in the house; the others were tarpaper and lath, which Menno seemed to find neither the time nor the money to complete. Last year the house had finally acquired a plastered living-dining room, but the plaster, still unpainted, remained mud-gray. The kitchen had always been the center of the household, the eating area, the place where Alana worked at paring fruit, cutting up vegetables, washing and ironing clothes, the room where the children played.

"Think of happy times," Millie said. "The fruity smell of canning berries. The steaming coffee pot. Children building a fort in the corner on cold winter mornings while you prepared breakfast. Jack Frost painting the windows. The family gathered around the table eating roast pork and string beans." She'd often walked in on such scenes when she came here on some errand from her mother.

"The time that ripe watermelon exploded when you cut into it and the children ran around grabbing and guzzling chunks," Bea put in.

Nobody smiled. The children stood by the door, subdued. Alana pressed her head with her bandaged wrists as if to squeeze her thoughts out and be rid of them. Maggie patted her mother's shoulder. "We still have Dougie, Mama. He'll be your baby."

Alana hugged the girl. Millie blinked back tears. Bea ventured to mention the funeral. "It'll be right after lunch, Lan. Are you up to going?"

"How can you ask?" Alana wiped her eyes on her bandages. "Of course, I have to go. I'll find my black dress, and you girls can help me put it on."

At the funeral, the closed coffin was piled with flowers. The three older children came with Menno and Alana. Baby Dougie had been left with Annie's sister, Flora. A subdued Edgar came with Vi.

Alana sat through the service like a zombie, dry-eyed, clearly taking in none of it. Only Menno wept. Rebecca and Douglas hovered near and tried to console him. Millie supposed the others, like herself, couldn't believe that another perpetual-motion child could be forever immobilized in that tiny white casket. Vi's son, Edgar, wide-eyed, clung to his mother's skirt.

People gathered at Stormland afterward, bringing baskets of fruit. Everyone, even distant neighbors and employees of Menno's construction firm, came up to misty-eyed Menno and hypnotic Alana to offer condolences. Millie's friends from the Women Suffrage organization stopped by, as did Vi's friend Clovia with her new, elderly husband.

Alana remained passive, indifferent, occasionally forcing a faint smile and managing a thank-you. Doubting the couple would even remember who came, who spoke to them, Millie tried to get people to sign a visitor-book so Alana and Menno could thank them properly later.

While planning her imminent departure, Millie hurried around setting out bread and cold-cuts, making pots of coffee, telling the children to be quiet, reminding them this wasn't a party, and no, they could *not* blow up balloons. She put baby Dougie on Alana's lap so his mother wouldn't have to use her hands to lift him. She gathered cups and plates and took them to the kitchen, where Maggie washed up.

It seemed the whole town dropped in, even Dr. Lapham with his wife and daughter. Dr. Lapham again urged Millie to take Alana on a trip, at least to Macatawa. Millie suppressed a grimace, fought her conscience, and asserted, "She doesn't want to go."

"You'll need to insist. It's important she get away from the scene of the tragedy."

Millie squirmed with guilt over her own reluctance to take on this problem.

When everyone departed, Millie let out a sigh of relief. The children had acted wild despite her best efforts to quiet them, and she was glad finally to be able to allow them to bring their games and crayons into the parlor as they'd teased to do. The parlor floor was soon awash in toys. Children played; things seemed normal. She could leave tonight on the five o'clock train.

Collapsed in a chair, wiping her brow with the back of her hand, Rebecca remarked that there'd be no need to cook dinner, since plenty of fruit and cold-cuts remained.

"We should at least make soup." Alana got out of her chair, shuffled through the clutter, and started for the kitchen. "Richard and Rory always like soup for their evening—." She caught her breath in the middle of the word *meal*. She stumbled and almost fell, catching herself by grasping a chair, and screeched in pain. Her face crumpled. "I won't ever again feed Richard his evening soup!"

Tears poured down her face. Her outburst set Dougie howling. Millie picked the child up from the floor where his mother had put him and soothed him with pats on the back. Annie hugged Alana and reminded her, "Richard's in good hands."

"I'll never see him again," Alana wailed.

"When my baby died, I knew he'd have care like I could never give him," Annie told her.

This proved insufficient consolation to Alana, who broke away from her sister-in-law and clutched her head with bandaged hands.

Glancing out the window, Millie saw a stately car pull up before the house. The children noticed it, too, and wild with curiosity to know who could be arriving after the last guest had departed, rushed to the door. Shoving at one another, they stood on tiptoe and peered out through the diamond pane. The car was unusual and unique. Tall and square, with large windows all around, it looked more like a traveling parlor than a transportation vehicle. Two ladies sat within, wearing dark dresses and large flowered hats, facing each other as formally as if seated in their own living rooms. Millie almost expected to see them sip tea.

"An electric car," Bea said. "It must be the WCTU folks."

One woman stepped out, her long skirt swirling to the pavement. She spoke to the other briefly, then turned and climbed the steps, her bearing erect.

"It's Mrs. Kingsley!" Recognizing the new arrival, Millie panicked. Why would Mrs. Kingsley come here except to bring bad news of Warren?

She shooed the youngsters aside and hurried out to the porch to meet her visitor. Her hands seemed to work of their own accord at smoothing her hair and dress. She felt incapable of duplicating the impeccable manners of her guest, who'd climbed the steps and was now crossing the lawn to the porch.

She tried to keep the anxiety out of her voice. "Mrs. Kingsley, you're home from your trip! How nice of you to stop by. I hope Warren is all right."

"Hello, Millie, good to see you." Mrs. Kingsley came onto the porch, paused to catch a breath, then held out her hand. Slim, well dressed if somewhat old fashioned in her over-long skirt, she presented a commanding figure.

"Warren's still in the hospital," she admitted. "We were lucky, the electricity hit only his arm. Would have killed him if it had gone through his body." She released Millie's hand and reached up to adjust a large hat trimmed with fake flowers, a pre-war model she still wore.

Apparently, then, his condition hadn't worsened. Millie commented, "It was a dreadful accident. Mr. Kingsley told me about it in church yesterday."

"I hear your family had a worse one. I want to offer my condolences."

Millie felt relieved. This visit wasn't about Warren after all. "Thank you. Do come in and meet everyone." Millie couldn't imagine what Mrs. Kingsley of the neat and tidy house would make of the tumbling masses of Langston children, not to mention the clutter of toys and games in the parlor. Yet she could hardly avoid inviting her guest inside. "Won't your friend come, too?" She gestured toward the electric car.

"We can't stay long," Mrs. Kingsley said. "That's Mrs. Durham. She's in charge of the statewide training session American National is hosting." American National was the suffrage organization Mrs. Kinglsey and Millie both belonged to, one for which Millie often led sings.

Her guest accompanied Millie into the house. Millie was glad to see that Bea and Annie had hastily cleared children and toys out of the parlor. Only Alana remained, and she stood as Mrs. Kingsley entered. Bea came from the kitchen. Millie managed the introductions. "My sister and sister-in-law." Alana smoothed her hair with awkward, bandaged hands.

"I was so sorry to hear about your loss." Mrs. Kingsley stood in the middle of the room looking regal, as always, with her hat tilted at a rakish angle. She addressed Alana. "I know how hard it is to lose a child. Years ago, I lost a baby."

Alana's eyes teared. She swallowed hard, nodded, couldn't seem to speak. Millie helped her to a chair and offered one to their guest, who shook her head.

"I have to hurry; my friend is waiting. I wanted to tell you, Millie: Warren is homesick and longing to see old friends. He sent along two train tickets, first class with sleeper. He hopes you and your sister Bea can use them to go out for a visit. John can't get away right now, and my daughter Maddy's in California with her soldier husband. So if you—"

"I've just started a new job." After shaking her head, Bea suddenly brightened. "Alana could go with Millie."

"Oh, but I can't go, I have to—" Millie spoke simultaneously with Alana, who protested leaving her babies.

Millie gathered her courage, fought her impatience, and forced aside thoughts of Macatawa. "Bea's right, Lan, it's just the thing for you. Just what the doctor ordered." It wouldn't matter much, after all, if she missed the weeknight performances. Selfish to think of the orchestra when two people she cared for had been injured and needed her. Let Laddie have a few more days.

"It'd be a rushed trip," she added. "I have to be in Macatawa by Saturday."

"Oh, yes, I believe John mentioned you were performing there." Chewing her lip, Mrs. Kingsley thought about it. "If you leave tomorrow, Tuesday, you'll have Wednesday, Thursday and Friday with Warren—returning Friday night."

Alana repeated her protest. "I couldn't possibly. My children—and Menno. Who'd cook for him?"

"Menno can stay here with us," Bea said. "The children are already being cared for."

"Well, then, it's settled." Mrs. Kingsley shoved an envelope into Millie's hands. "Tickets and reservations. I'm so pleased you can use them. I feared Warren might be making a mistake in planning something like that without asking you. Travel tickets are so hard to get in wartime. The Red Cross had to arrange this for him."

"Oh, my, I—" Millie suddenly realized she ought not to accept anything so expensive. First class train tickets! But she could think of no way to refuse politely at this point.

"You're to stay at a guest house on base," Mrs. Kingsley told her. "You leave at two-thirty p.m. tomorrow. Enjoy yourself and give Warren my love."

She waved and departed, leaving Millie speechless. Bea saw the visitor to the door and closed it after her.

As the car drove away, Millie wondered aloud, "Why me?" She stared at the tickets in her hand. "It's not like I were—I mean, Warren and I were never anything but friends."

❧   ❧   ❧

I hear Doug say, "Ashley, that's enough reading for tonight. It's getting late." I look up, blinking. Doug had been reading with me while we sipped the hot chocolate. When he'd returned with the steaming cups, I'd caught him up on what happened in the past.

So Millie is off on a train trip and so am I—and both for the same reason, a guy we're interested in. I wasn't snowed by Millie's pretense of concern about Alana; I knew it was really Warren she worried about. Of course, she wanted to go to his Navy base to check on him. I would, too.

Doug reminds me again that I leave on the early train. As if I'd forget! Kevin, my true love, wait for me, I'm coming. Not that I want to tell Doug. Doug looked disappointed enough just hearing of my departure.

I wonder, though, if I can ever get the disturbing image of the boiled baby out of my mind. I ask how in the world a toddler could fall into a pot. Surely just his head would go in.

Doug explains that those old fashioned clothes boilers used to be huge, the width of the entire stove, taking up at least two burners. "We still have one in the basement. I can show you."

What awful things happened in those days! I'm so glad I live now.

So on to the Pennington Mansion and my black roots. I'll take Millie's diary with me and read on the train.

I walk downstairs with Doug to the front door. As he leaves, he wishes me a good trip and tells me he'll miss me. I respond with a perfunctory, "Me, too." I'd like to sound more enthusiastic, but it would seem disloyal to Kevin.

CHAPTER 23

2002
Ashley

Just before train-time next morning, I receive a phone call from my ex-boy-friend, Jonah Roberts. My *boring* ex-boyfriend. Pissed, I demand to know how he tracked me down. We parted after a big fight about my leaving college. When he told me I shouldn't become a drop-out, I told *him* my life was none of his business. I intended to make my own decisions without his help, and so farewell.

The problem with Jonah is that he's wide-eyed naïve. Though he's my age, I always feel like the big sister. He's a child, open, always ready to take people at their word. If someone tells him he should stay in school, he stays. Doesn't think for himself at all. Believes that all older people are telling him things for his own good. He actually goes about asking for advice—even from my Kings-ley grandmother. He claims she went to college, after all. I tell him, yeah, about sixty years ago.

Not only that, the guy actually doesn't mind being a token. He has white friends and he *knows* he's their token black. Incredibly, he thinks that's okay. They're learning about black folks, he says. They have to start somewhere.

No doubt Gran was the one who spilled the beans about where I am. She loves Jonah; she raves over him. Well, she's right, he's nice. Too nice to be fun.

I tried several times to break up with him but he didn't get it, didn't believe I meant it. In time he began getting on my nerves. At this moment he's dis-tinctly annoying. He tells me he just finished his first summer course, which lasted only three weeks, and instead of enrolling for another, he wants to come to Michigan and visit me.

I give way to an urge to let my anger show. "Don't even think of it. I'm a visitor here myself; I can't have guests. Besides, I'm leaving for a few days."

"I could meet you wherever you plan to be," he says.

"Jonah, we broke up, remember? We're not going together any more."

"Over that stupid tiff? Come on, Ashley, you don't discard people out of your life over a silly little argument. I can't even recall what we fought about."

"I didn't consider the argument either little or silly. I don't put up with people telling me what to do with my own life."

"Ashley, I didn't mean to come on like a boss-man. Surely you know I don't—"

My temper rises as train-time nears. I haven't time to hear his apologies. I cut him short. "We'll talk about it some other time. Right now I have to run." I put the phone down firmly so he'll hear a loud click in his ear. I want to communicate that it's over, that we're not an item any more.

After a last check of my makeup, I sling my purse, heavier with the added weight of Millie's diary, over my shoulder and call to Laura that I'm ready to leave.

On the train, with Millie's diary in hand, I steam while I think about Jonah. What do you do with a guy who won't take a hint? I've tried every possible way to communicate that I'm not attracted any more. Nothing seems to get through to him. We had sex a few times so now he owns me. Like that makes us married or something.

With Kevin waiting for me at the other end of this train track, I definitely don't want re-involvement with Jonah. I try to forget the guy and think about my new honey, my handsome football player. How many times in high school and college, as he raced for the goal-line, the football tucked under his arm, expertly dodging the other team's defenses, I watched from the bleachers! Stood and yelled myself hoarse. "Go, Kevin, go!" Wished I were the one he'd come looking for after the game. And how often, at Black Condor Club meetings, I tried to think of something witty or clever to say, to get noticed by the chair—and never could. And now, like a miracle, he awaits me. I must have caught his eye after all.

Thank you, God. My prayers are answered.

It's a gray, cloudy day, nothing much to look at out the train window, a few farmhouses, an orchard, endless fields of corn. If I were a little older I could have rented a car—but you need a credit card for that, and I'm a student sans credit rating, sans employment. Seems like I've spent my life waiting to grow up.

When I calm myself enough to concentrate, I open the diary and get busy reading about Millie and Alana on their train trip. It was all new and exciting to Alana; she'd never traveled by train before. She raved over the 'cute' little bars of soap provided in their sleeping compartment. I wonder if trains still offer those. Mostly, I think, recalling Amtrak trips to L.A., they now provide liquid soap. I'll check when I go to the restroom.

It seems some woman on their train asked what was wrong with Alana's hands, and Alana began talking about what happened to Richard. The woman claimed to remember seeing the story in the newspaper. Alana started to weep, and Millie couldn't get her to stop. She wept for hours. It must have been hectic. In the end, Alana fell asleep and slept the rest of the way.

They arrived in Baltimore next morning, and Warren, in his white summer Naval uniform, his arm in a sling but looking tall and handsome, awaited them at the station. They all took a bus to Glenburnie, to the Naval base where Millie and Alana stayed in the guest house. Later that day, and each day, they went sightseeing or strolled along the shore of Chesapeake Bay. Alana kept telling Millie to grab Warren while he was available. She called him "peachy," a good catch. Millie grew annoyed. She still liked Charlie and hoped to mend fences with him, and anyway she wasn't ready to settle down. She wanted to have her singing career first. Though she doesn't admit it, I think she would really have liked to be in vaudeville. I get the feeling she envied Laddie Munn.

Millie described Baltimore at length, saying that all the houses had beautiful doorways with pillars and fanlights. I skip a few pages of description; I'm curious what went on between her and Warren. But wouldn't you know—that's precisely what she doesn't tell. She claims Warren teased her but she didn't mind because he was never mean, always good natured and funny. She says she and Alana laughed a lot.

When we pass through Lansing, someone remarks that we're halfway to Detroit. At the stop, I acquire a seatmate, a white girl who tells me she's a student en route home from Michigan State, where she stayed on for part of the summer, working. She has a week's vacation so she's going back to Saginaw. She looks at me questioningly. "Where you off to?"

"Detroit," I tell her.

"Live there?"

"No, I'm visiting from California."

Right away she starts asking questions about California. Have I been to Hollywood? These midwesterners seem to think we see movie stars walking down the street out there. I'm forced to disillusion her. "Sure, I went to Universal Studios, but they don't take you on the sets where they're shooting movies. Once or twice I watched a movie shot in San Diego, not with anyone famous." Since she clearly awaits more information, I confess, "I hate to tell you, but Hollywood is looking seedy these days, and even Beverly Hills is not what it was. You have to go to Orange County for the classy places."

She wants to know where in California I live, and what I do. Since clearly this chick wants to talk, I slide the diary back into my purse. I wouldn't be able to keep my mind on it anyway. I'm now just a couple of hours away from Kevin, and anticipation is making me restless. I tell her about community college, and how I'd decided to drop out because I didn't know what I wanted to major in. She tells me she plans to go into nursing "We're guaranteed a job in that field," she says. "There's such a shortage these days."

I agree that's true, and remark that it's very practical of her to make her choice based on job needs rather than her own interests. I doubt I could manage it. I want to feel passionate about what I do. She says she likes to take care of people, likes to feel she's making a difference in their lives.

Talking does make the time pass more quickly. Finally, we begin to see buildings in place of fields. We're coming into Detroit. My seatmate, who told me her name though I promptly forgot it, says, "My parents are meeting me here. We'll drive to Saginaw." I know about Saginaw from reading Rebecca's description of the Great Fire there, and from the Simon and Garfunkel song, one of my mom's favorites. Mom has a CD of Simon and Garfunkel that she plays in the car.

Kevin, you lovely man, you honey-pie, what will we talk about? Shall I tell you how I yelled and screamed from the bleachers while you ran down the field? The loudest voice you heard was mine. Or shall I play it cool and pretend *you're* the lucky one, calling at just the right moment to find me free and available?

Everyone, including my seatmate, is stirring around, getting suitcases down from overhead. I've checked mine so I sit still. It's not easy to do, with excitement churning within. My seatmate asks if someone will be at the station for me.

"My boyfriend is meeting me." I try not to sound boastful, but I can feel my chin tilting upward as I speak. I waited a long time to call Kevin my boyfriend.

When I hop off the train, I see no sign of my true love, and I suffer a horrible, sinking conviction that he's been fooling me all along. It must be tempting for big time football stars to do that sort of thing, maybe not in cruelty but just because they're so much in demand. I mean, every girl in my community college wants to know Kevin.

But no—I spot him, coming out of the station with a rolled newspaper under his arm. He's tall and muscular, wearing a gray sweatshirt with a sports figure on the front. His head is shaved; his skin is swarthy, darker than mine. He strides toward me with a welcoming smile that shows off strong white teeth. When he looms over me, I experience an impulse to be in his arms. I smile back and hope the day will soon come when I'll know him well enough to rush up and embrace him.

He doesn't worry about not knowing me. He reaches his free arm around me for a hug. "Sugar-baby, you look even more delectable here than you did at home."

"That's because at home you're surrounded by admirers," I tell him.

"Oh, I don't know about that."

"I remember legions of them," I say.

He bites his lip and comments, "Only when I make a lot of points for the team. They like winners." I assure him I'm for him whether he wins or not.

Kevin keeps his arm around my waist while we walk through the station. He says his car is out front. "I could only find a ten-minute parking spot."

"So why are you in Michigan?" I ask.

"Visiting an aunt and uncle. What about you?"

"You'll laugh when I tell you," I say. "My parents sent me here to 'research my roots.' It seems there's a Pennington House somewhere in Detroit and I'm to look for it."

"Come on, you're kidding." He raises an eyebrow. "Black Penningtons, in Detroit?"

"Hard to believe, isn't it? I always pictured them as white slave-owners in a pillared mansion. Turns out they were black brothers who lived in Detroit for generations."

"Well, you never know." He shakes his head.

We stop to get my suitcase, and Kevin carries it. In front of the station, he points out his car, a gold-colored sports model Toyota, a welcome change from that uncool Renault of Doug's I'd been riding around in. I'd admired this car in our school parking lot when someone pointed it out to me, so I know Kevin drove out here from California.

After he deposits the suitcase in the trunk, we both climb in. He asks me, "Where to? You getting a hotel room?"

"No, I'm staying with my dad's cousin, Carr Pennington."

"Hey, that's not good." He grimaces. "You with cousins, me with aunt and uncle. We'll be supervised."

I laugh. "All we want is a room somewhere." Instantly, my face flames with embarrassment as I realize how that sounds. I hastily add, "That's a quote from a song."

"All the same, you got it right, Sugar-baby."

I start to protest being called Sugar-baby, but tell myself to let it go. I wouldn't allow anyone in the world but Kevin to call me that. On anyone else's lips it would seem put-down, but Kevin says it so nicely. Coming from him, it sounds friendly and kind of sweet.

Kevin consults a map, then drives toward the address I'd given him, complaining the while how relative-visiting involves too much polite conversation. "Folks don't like it when you use their house for a hotel. You gotta pretend you really came to see them, even though you both know you came for a good time. It takes patience. I really like old Badass, don't get me wrong, but sometimes it'd be fun to go places without him and his ever-present wife."

"Luckily, my dad's cousin and his wife both work. They promised to leave the key under the mat for me."

"Good. We'll drop off your suitcase and then go have lunch. You didn't eat on the train, did you?"

I assure him I didn't. Anyway, the club car sold only snacks.

Away from San Diego, every place seems grimy to me. Detroit looks particularly slummy. All the houses need a good wash with a high-pressure hose. I remark on this to Kevin, who grins and says, "You're not in Kansas any more, Dorothy."

I try to analyze the difference. I'm sure San Diego has slums, but they're hidden behind red bougainvillea so they don't seem so grim. In Grand Rapids there are trees. Here, the houses stand exposed to the world, dreary, dirty-faced and depressing.

After miles of these, we enter an area of newer tract homes, all alike. We drive through winding streets of two-story brick houses that look fresher and cleaner than those we'd been passing. Dad's cousin, Carr, and his wife Renata, live in one of these. When we locate it, Kevin parks in the driveway. I hop out, climb the steps, search under the mat, and find the key. It doesn't readily open the door. I try a few strategies like pulling up, yanking out, pushing in. Kevin locks his car and climbs the steps to help me. When finally we get the door open, Kevin brings my suitcase and follows me inside. A ginger cat comes running to meet us, and while I stoop to pet it, Kevin sets my suitcase by the stairs.

This seems a pleasant house, fairly new, neat, comfortably furnished. We walk through the rooms, and in the kitchen find a note: *Make yourself at home, Ashley. There are turkey sandwiches and cokes in the fridge. Your room is upstairs, second door on the right. Love, Renata.*

"Make yourself at home, Ashley," Kevin quotes, reading over my shoulder. "That sounds to me like good advice. Turkey sandwiches, too. It's going on two o'clock. Let's locate the bedroom."

I start to protest that I don't need his help in locating the bedroom—then warn myself: don't be another Millie, don't turn guys off. We climb the stairs and enter the second room down the hall. It's a girlie room, bright, with curtains, matching flowered dust-ruffle around the bed, and a floor-length tablecloth on the small round table by the window. I surmise that it was Renata's daughter's room. "I seem to have heard she went to New York to work."

"It's perfect." Suitcase deposited in the closet, Kevin stands behind me near the bed, so close I can feel his breath on my shoulder. He reaches his arms around me and whispers. "The ideal place to spend an afternoon."

His breath caresses my cheek. Feeling horny, I press back against him and put my hand over his. Then suddenly I remember all those women I'd seen him with in the halls at school. He seems to change women as often as he changes shirts. I don't want to be one of a long parade; I want to be the permanent one, the one who hangs in there.

Don't be easy, Ashley, I caution myself. Remember the rule Clovia gave Vi—always keep a man guessing. Smart girl, Clovia.

Kevin leans even closer; his chin touches mine. He talks black to me. "I'm a fling you on that bed and fall on toppa you, girl. I'm a light your fire so bright this house will be ablaze and the fire truck will have to come."

I remove his hand from my midriff and start for the door. I say, "Of course—but not now, Kev. Right now I want a good lunch, no dry turkey sandwich. I want to go out to eat somewhere glamorous."

His face falls. "This opportunity might not come again. Tomorrow's Saturday; your relatives will be at home."

"I'm here for five days," I remind him. "Weekends come and go."

He confesses, "Sugar-baby, I don't know the restaurants nearby."

"We'll look in the yellow pages." I leave the room and head for the stairs. He follows with a groan of protest. We go downstairs and out the door. I grab the yellow pages from their place by the phone, wave to the ginger cat, then close the door and replace the key under the mat.

Clearly, my handsome darling is not used to having girls say no to him. He stalks ahead of me. I can't restrain a smile.

CHAPTER 24

2002
Ashley

It's no problem visiting with Dad's cousins, Carr and Renata; I don't feel uncomfortable here as I did with the Langstons. Since these two Penningtons spend their vacations in California, I've known them all my life. As a kid I looked forward to their visits because it meant we got to go to Disneyland, Sea World, the Wild Animal Park, all the tourist places Dad wouldn't otherwise spring for. This is not mind-your-manners time for any of us, even Kevin who's familiar with the places we talk about. We spend the evening chatting and reminiscing. Carr tells us about Pennington House, how it's now abandoned and he's often been tempted to buy and restore it himself. I ask if there are a lot of black Penningtons in Detroit. He says there were at one time, because the white Pennington, who had no heirs—his wife and children died in a yellow fever epidemic—used his money to buy abused slaves so he could bring them north and free them. He was a good man, Carr says. Our forebears were lucky to encounter him.

Around midnight Kevin gets ready to leave but promises to return next day. Renata lists all the places in and around Detroit that we might visit. She claims their own weekend is packed and they can't take us around town. She apologizes, says she hadn't known I was coming. I assure her it's no problem. Kevin and I want to be alone, but of course I don't mention that.

"You'll have no trouble getting around on your own," she tells us. "I'll give you a map."

Kevin shows his relief more than I think he ought to. We agree that he'll pick me up before lunch. He suggests we do the Detroit stuff quickly so we can go to Cedar Point on Sunday. I'm all for that; I hear the rides at Cedar Point are even faster than those at Six Flags.

Next day, when Kevin comes, he's with his aunt and uncle who propose to take us sightseeing. We don't get to be alone after all. When I tell them about Pennington House, they offer to help me find it. I show them the map and, sitting together in the front seat, they both nod. The uncle, a man with a skullcap whom Kevin introduces by the nickname of Badass, though he's called Bud by his wife, says he knows exactly where the place is. He and his wife have looked at houses in the area—old houses which can be bought for one dollar but would cost hundreds of thousands to renovate. "Your family home is probably one of those."

Kevin echoes, "One *dollar?* Did you say one *dollar?*"

"Yes, but don't rush to purchase," his uncle cautions him.

"Why not? I'd give them a dollar just to say I own the pile of rubble."

"To get it for that price, you have to homestead—that means you agree to live there for a few years and fix it up. *And* you'd have to start renovating immediately. Most of these houses are not fit for human habitation; they've been vandalized, stripped of everything including windows and floors."

"Even so, I gotta see this," Kevin insists.

So we drive over—and on a post-holocaust sort of street of ruined houses, the place looks like what was once an impressive Victorian—or rather, Queen Anne—with a three-story tower room and big porch. Granted, it's decrepit—horribly so. The unpainted pillars on the front porch are leaning, and though the windows aren't actually gone, they're cracked and broken, with glass missing in a front one. Obviously, this was a bad neighborhood before it became a largely deserted one. Most of the other houses in the area are in even worse shape, abandoned, with a lot of added outside stairways indicating that they'd been used as rooming houses. A few are in the process of renovation, newly painted and with windows replaced, roof repaired.

I have to admit that Pennington House must have been awesome in its day. It has wide grounds and evidence of long-gone flower gardens beautifully laid out, with stone walkways still in place. I'm impressed to think that my forebears owned it. Badass remarks that servants were easier to come by in those bygone times. I confess I hadn't thought of my ancestors as people with servants.

"They must have had servants in order to keep up this big place," he says. I theorize that more likely they had nine or ten kids to help with the work.

The house is locked but easy to enter through that gap in the large front window. We step inside. A damp mustiness assails us, combined with the unpleasant odor of dead and decaying rodents. The floor is warped and stained beyond repair, and the plaster has fallen in great chunks. Yet Kevin seems hot to buy and restore the place. He looks around in awe, his expression almost as starry-eyed as Jonah's would have been.

"I've always seen myself living in a house like this—fixed up, of course," he says. "I'll give them a buck for it any day; you know what I'm saying?"

"You're out of your mind, Kev," Badass tells him. "It'd cost more to renovate this big place than to go to the moon."

"But it's basically well built." Kevin, hands in pockets, jumps up and down. "The floor don't squeak, the house don't shake."

"Forget it, Nephew. Your bank account couldn't replace the two front windows, let alone repair twenty rooms. In this place, everything's outsized and would have to be made to order. No going to Home Depot to buy ready-made."

The fixtures are missing, of course, but I can visualize beautiful crystal chandeliers in these large rooms. We could buy them in Tijuana pretty cheap. Kevin's aunt, whose name I've forgotten, wanders into the bright, multi-windowed tower room and comments that in Victorian times these areas were filled with ferns. "I've been on home tours of places with tower rooms like this."

"Hey, we could add this to the home-tour lists," Kevin says. "People pay good money to take those tours. We might earn enough for the restoration."

"Earth to Kevin," Badass says. "Time to come out of the clouds. People don't pay for home tours until the places are *already* restored."

Kevin insists that with both of us working, he and I together could restore this pile. I'd have a job and earn money; he'd do the carpenter work himself. It's an exciting thought, Kevin/Rhett Butler and I together working on the estate of heiress Ashley Scarlett O'Hara Pennington. As I stand admiring the beautiful sweeping staircase, worthy of Scarlett's Tara, I'm tempted to agree with him.

"Have you ever done carpenter work?" Badass asks him.

"No, but they show you how at Home Depot. They have seminars."

"Sure, they do—and they make it look like a breeze. But when you go off and try it, you find it ain't so easy. Things don't fall into place for you like they do for them guys on the Old House shows on TV. Believe me, I know."

"A guy can learn," Kevin insists.

Badass lists off all the things needing to be done before the place becomes habitable. As he goes on and on, my enthusiasm flags. Not Kevin's, though. Even when we're back in the car, he's still figuring. "We'd just need to get one or two rooms livable, so we could stay there—then we work along at the rest as we can."

"There are no light fixtures," his uncle reminds him, "not to mention bath-room fixtures."

Kevin is unstoppable. "I've helped dad replace those at our house."

"Kev, you don't even know if the plumbing and electricity work well enough for you to hook up the appliances. If they're bad, you could have a flood or a fire."

"So big deal. So we'll check. This place would be worth big bucks once it's fixed up. Paint, wall-paper—it'd be palatial."

Kevin is still talking about the possibility when his aunt and uncle take us to dinner. I'm amazed and flattered that he's so interested in my former family home. Yet I can't fully share his eagerness. Not that it wouldn't be fun to fix the place up, mind you, and especially working with Kevin. I love the idea. It's just that I find it hard to believe we could really see it through. We can't live there with it smelling so bad and lacking water, lights and facilities. Besides, it's a long way from home, and neither of us has a job at the moment. I incline to agree with Badass, it's unrealistic. Not wanting to rain on Kevin's parade, I pretend to side with him but can't manage to sound as enthusiastic as he.

We locate a restaurant that offers video games. After we eat, the rest of us forget the house and get absorbed in the games. In time Kevin appears to do likewise. Later, we all play pool and Kevin wins. I make sure of that.

The next morning, at Cousin Carr's house, I dress and tiptoe downstairs in the gray of morning twilight for breakfast. Kevin had promised to come for me at the crack of dawn to head for Cedar Point. To my surprise, on glancing out the front window, I see the gold Toyota already parked before the house. I go out to ask Kevin why he came so early.

"I want to get going." He rolls down his window to talk to me. "If we're to have a full day there, we need to hit the road. It's a seventy-five mile drive."

"I haven't eaten breakfast yet," I protest.

"Neither have I. We'll stop along the way. And Sugar-baby, bring your suit-case."

I stare at him. "Why on earth do I need my suitcase?"

"You never know. We might want to stay overnight or something."

I again start to protest. He urges me, "Just grab your stuff and come, okay? You don't even need to stop to put a face on. There's a mirror behind the visor in the car."

I can't see the reason for so much haste, but if Kevin thinks we should do it, I'm willing to go along. I head upstairs, hastily repack my suitcase, and scribble a note for Carr and Renata saying we might stay over. No doubt Kevin's right, we'll want more than one day at Cedar Point.

I snap my suitcase shut, grab my makeup case, sling my purse over my shoulder, and carry everything downstairs and out the door. The ginger cat runs in as I run out. I sling the cases in the back seat, then leap into the front. With the motor already running, Kevin pulls away from the curb even as I close the door on my side.

"Okay, now tell me the *real* reason we're in such a rush," I say.

"Sugar-baby, I'm not kidding, the lineup for Cedar Point can be miles long. It's a traffic nightmare."

"But you knew that last night."

He sighs and confesses, "My aunt and uncle were talking of going with us. I had to get out of the house this morning before they decided. You know what I'm saying?"

So that's it! Handsome Kevin, Dream-boat Kevin, Superstar Kevin, wants to be alone with me! How can I object to that?

I can't, of course, any more than I could have objected the day before when he proposed helping me restore the family mansion.

Somewhere south of Detroit, we stop for breakfast at a McDonald's. I'm just poring syrup on my pancakes when Kevin offers a startling proposal. He says that, in view of the predictable traffic at Cedar Point on this warm, sunny day, we ought to go somewhere else instead. "We're sure to spend hours inching in slow-and-go stuff."

Naturally, I ask him where he wants to go instead.

"How about Las Vegas?" he ventures.

I pause with plastic syrup-container in mid-air and stare at him. "*Vegas?* Did you say *Vegas?*"

"That's what I said. Great place, Vegas. I think we could make money there. I have a cousin who told me how to beat the slot machines."

"Kevin," I remind him, "we're in Michigan, not California. Vegas isn't four hours from here, it's more like three days away."

Without so much as a blink, he snaps right back at me. "Two, if we take turns driving and go right through. You do have a driver's license, don't you? Of course, we'll have to wait for that room somewhere, but in the end—wow!"

I realize this plan was in his mind all along. That's why he urged me to bring my suitcase. I shake my head. "It would be crazy. Driving day and night just to test some friend's theory? There must be Indian gaming in Michigan if you're so hot to find slot machines."

He gives me a rueful smile. "Sugar-baby, you don't cheat *Indians*—uh, Native Americans. They need their money."

"And the Las Vegas people don't?"

"Nah, they're rich, they won't miss a few hundred."

"Good. If they won't miss it, we'll stay away from there and not give it to them."

The rueful smile turns into an amused grin which shows all his white teeth. He does have the world's snowiest pearlies, I have to admit that. To pretend this is a casual conversation, I go on eating while he pleads.

"Come on, Ash, it'll be fun driving across the country. You don't see nothing from up there in the sky. You crossed the continent and I bet you saw only clouds."

Not true. I flew out on a clear day and saw the Rocky Mountains, even the Grand Canyon—though I must admit they looked like bumps on the landscape and a big ditch from thirty thousand feet up. I saw the Missouri and the Mississippi and Lake Michigan, not to mention the green and beautiful Grand River Valley. When I start to tell him all that, he only shakes his head and repeats his urging. "Sugar-baby, I'm talking super adventure, just the two of us driving across the country. And think of the fun we can have when we get there, the classy hotel. New York, New York, or Paris or Venice. Cedar Point is a kid's park compared to Vegas."

"I guess I'm a kid," I tell him. "I trust rides more than casinos." Actually, it's Kevin's idea of jimmying slot machines that I don't trust. If that could be done, someone would have found out before now. We'll wind up in the pokey, as Gran would say.

"Think of the shows we can see."

"Are there shows in the summer?"

"There are always shows in Vegas. Come on, let's do it!"

The idea of driving across the country with Kevin does have a certain appeal, but I don't see how you can just decide and go, on the spur of the moment. I mean, that sort of trip has to be planned for—clothes assembled, car checked over, bank account reviewed. I say, "Kev, I don't have cash. I have only my return ticket and a few bucks of spending money. I didn't plan on our driving across the country; I thought I'd be staying with relatives."

"I have enough," he says. "Well, not for a lot of motel rooms and stuff, but we won't need those. We'll take turns driving and go straight through."

Though I'm beginning to share his excitement about the idea, I still raise objections. I point out that it's hot in the desert in summer. He says, "We'll buy cases of cokes."

I remind him that soft drink cans explode in great heat. He shrugs and says, "Okay, make that gallon jugs of water."

"I only have a few clothes. I left most of my stuff at Stormland."

"Shit, you don't need clothes in the desert." He grins more broadly. "You can go bareass naked if you want to; I won't complain. The best part is, we'll be rid of our *chaperones*," he adds.

"All right, let's go." What the hell. I never in my life set off on a wild adventure. Everyone should do that sort of thing at least once. It'll be a chance for us to get to know one another better and perhaps cement our relationship, to guarantee I won't be just one of his harem.

Kevin nods, looks relieved, opens and consults an atlas. "South of Toledo we hit a fast toll road. All we gotta do is make a right instead of left and head off across Indiana. We'll soon come to an Interstate that will take us southwest to avoid the Chicago traffic. I figure we can be in St. Louis by nightfall, Texas by morning, driving across the desert *manana*. How does that strike you?"

I have to admit it does sound like fun. His enthusiasm puts me in the mood to go. Besides, it'll be a cool trip to talk about when I get home. Wait till I tell Keisha! She often claims college girls don't have fun, just classes and books and term papers and boredom. Ha, is she wrong!

By now we're both so excited we wolf down our food, make a hurried visit to the facilities, then depart and climb in the car. Remarking that we'll need entertainment en route, Kevin puts on a CD of Puff Daddy. We pull out of the parking lot.

We entered McDonald's as a stop-over on a seventy-five mile trip. We leave it as a stop-over on a two-thousand-mile trip.

Kevin is turning out to be one dynamo guy to know! This time I got myself a *man*, not a Jonah.

The drive through Indiana proves tedious even for enthusiasts like us. Since we bypass the cities, we see nothing but corn and wheat fields, plowed land and pasturage. And farmhouses with barns. I can't seem to get a conversation going. I ask about Kevin's work with the orphan-placement outfit. He says it's something his cousin first got involved in, and he tries to help out. Next I talk about his victories on the playing field, but he's modest over them and complains that his teammates didn't cooperate enough. "Shit, I could have made two more points both times if them guys had shaken their asses a little faster." When I ask about his family, he says he moved out after high school. "My folks are oreos and yassirs."

"Yassirs?"

"Like, they say 'Yassir' to every white face. They preach at me to live straight and do right. Problem is, we don't agree about what's right."

"I get the same stuff. My parents are on my case all the time. I dropped out of college, and to hear them go on about it, you'd think it was the end of my life."

"Stick to your guns, girl. I'd drop out if it weren't for football."

We listen to stacks of CDs. Still struggling for conversation, I talk about Vegas, how often I've been there, what I did. I begin to fret over the fact I haven't notified my family about this trip and remark that I should phone home when we stop again. "My parents will kill me for going off and not letting them know."

Kevin says not to worry. "You're of age, you're no runaway."

Well, I *did* leave a note for my cousin, so no one will be looking for me. I follow Kevin's advice, I relax and stop worrying. When it's time for the ball game, we tune in and soon become absorbed. The New York Yankees and Boston.

Claiming I don't drive fast enough to suit him—"The trick is to keep ahead of the cops"—Kevin does most of the driving. I study the mileage charts and periodically inform him how far we still have to go. It takes us ten hours to reach St. Louis, which, after crossing the Mississippi, we approach at five in the afternoon. The ball game ends; the news comes on; the giant arch rears up in the distance. I consult Kevin's atlas and suggest that from here we take the northern route through Kansas City, which on the map seems to be the most direct road to Vegas.

"Nah, southern route's better," he says. "Highway Forty all the way."

"Highway Forty swings south of Vegas." With a finger, I follow it on the map.

"Not far south, and it misses the high mountains in Colorado. Takes us through Albuquerque which isn't quite so high." He glances at me. "No, believe me, that's the old Route 66, easiest way across the Rockies. We don't want to climb to the Mile High City."

I study the map again. "Well then, we join Forty at Oklahoma City, and after that comes Amarillo." I consult the mileage charts. "It's sixteen-fourteen to Las Vegas from here. Five-fifty-five to Amarillo. Don't you think we should stay over?" The westering sun is in my eyes, I've begun to feel sleepy, and the motels we pass literally hold out their arms to me.

"Nothing to it," Kevin says. "We'll make Amarillo by morning, easy."

"Kevin, I don't think we should go straight through without rest. We'll get road-hypnosis; we'll have an accident."

"Nah. I'm not tired. We'll stop for dinner and run around the block couple of times to get our exercise. Then you can crawl in the back seat and have a snooze while I drive on. After you wake up, I'll grab a nap."

"What's the rush?" I ask again.

"It's just—we don't want to run out of money. I don't have a lot, and you say you have none."

We race through St. Louis on a bypass route, seeing the town's skyline and arch only from a distance. On the far side, we stop for food and gas, and following Kevin's suggestion, run around the block. It feels good to move a bit. When we return to the car, I climb into the back seat and find a blanket and pillow there. Surprised, I ask Kevin if he planned this trip all along.

He's like, "That stuff's left over from my drive out here. I only came a week ago."

"You sure must like to tear back and forth across the country."

"Nothing to it," he insists. "Truck drivers do it all the time."

I find I can't fall asleep; I keep shifting my position. Finally I abandon the attempt and sit up. "I can't sleep in the car," I complain.

"You gotta learn to do that, Sugar-baby," Kevin says. I suddenly feel turned off. I'm beginning to wonder if he even knows my name. Or did he just bring me along to help with the driving and maybe be available when he feels horny? I remember that I have a valid return ticket in my purse and could have flown out west.

Too late now to change my mind. Michigan is six hundred miles behind us. I argue with myself; we're both tired and out of sorts. I need to make allowances.

It's getting dark when Kevin turns the wheel over to me. He crawls into the back seat and, as far as I can tell, falls asleep immediately. I fight weariness. In Missouri there seems to be nothing alongside the road except woodlands. No houses, no fields. I begin to think I'd prefer Indiana, where at least I'd see a light in a farmhouse now and then. The only lights here are from passing cars. I blink often to stay alert.

When finally, at midnight, I can't keep my eyes open any longer, I locate a McDonald's and go in by myself to order two large cups of black coffee. I carry these out to the car. Kevin wakes at my return and offers to take over the driving. "Better let me have the coffee, Sugar-baby. You sure as hell won't fall asleep if you drink them big gulps."

He takes the coffee, and I settle into the back seat and drift off to sleep. Next thing I know, the car is slowing to a stop. I open my eyes to the gray light of pre-dawn. Kevin's like, "Yikes, the engine lost power. Something's wrong." He lets out a curse.

I agree. Something surely is. I knew we should have checked out the car before we started on this long trip, but I don't want to inflict on Kevin an, "I told you so." Instead, I remark, "Dad always calls Triple A at times like this."

"Hell, I don't have Triple A. Lucky we're approaching Amarillo. I know a guy here can help me find a good mechanic who won't eat me alive." He pulls over, consults a small address book from his glove compartment, then brings out his cell phone. I hear him talking. "Connor, that you? It's Kevin. Sorry I got you up so early, but I'm in trouble, man. My car broke down. Where am I? I'm right here in Amarillo, man. I wouldn't be calling you otherwise. My car died on the Interstate, Highway Forty, just coming into town from the East. Can you meet me out here? Connor, you're a pal. I'll be looking for you, man." He turns to me in the back seat. "My friend Connor is coming out here. Thank God I got through to him. He knows cars; he'll help."

We'd stopped near a roadside motel and restaurant, one of those mom and pop places, open, brightly lit and inviting. Though I'm still rubbing sleep from my eyes, we decide to walk over to it and go in. We lock the car and cross a grassy verge to the frontage road.

"It'll be a while," Kevin says. "I got Connor out of bed and he has to dress before he comes. We may as well have breakfast."

It turns out to be a surprisingly large and good breakfast, pancakes, eggs, bacon, biscuits and honey. You never know about these roadside places. Some are great, most are awful. This time, just when I'm getting fed up with McDonald's, we luck out.

Before we finish, Kevin's friend Connor, who's tall and lanky and wears an Afro, shows up and agrees to give us a push. Seems he knows a mechanic on down the road who opens at seven, just fifteen minutes from now. Kevin wolfs down the last of his food; I abandon the remainder of mine; and we go out to the car. We drift over to the frontage road, which luckily has little traffic, and in time, with a final bumpy push from Connor's truck, roll toward the mechanic's shop just as he's pulling up the big garage-door. When Kevin explains about the car losing power, he offers to look under the hood. He points me to a waiting room where already I see coffee dripping into the pot from the coffee-maker.

Entering the room to the tempting smell of my favorite morning beverage, I remember Millie's diary in my purse and bring it out. I'm glad I have something to amuse myself with. It could take hours to locate and fix the car problem. I choose the most comfortable chair and settle down to read while I wait.

I have a hunch about what happened to Millie on her return from her visit to Warren in Glenburnie, and it's not good.

CHAPTER 25

1918
Millie

On the final leg of their homeward journey, Millie and Alana transferred at South Bend to the Pere Marquette Railroad. Without their compartment and its luxury, they dozed in coach seats, and ate fruit pilfered from the dining car of their cross-country train.

"I'll leave you at Kalamazoo," Millie told Alana. "I may as well go straight to Macatawa." She was in a hurry to cope with the Laddie situation, whatever it might prove to be, and get it over with. "Will you be all right?"

Alana chuckled. "I'm grown up now. I can get from Kalamazoo to Grand Rapids on my own."

"It's nice to see you smiling again. The trip did you good. Sure you won't revert to gloom when you're alone?"

Alana sighed. "Life must go on, I know that. I've played hooky too long; it's time I relieved Vi and Annie of the care of my children. You've all been wonderful, and I appreciate it. Can't think how I'd have survived this ordeal without you. But after this trip, I'll be ready to roll up my sleeves. Doc Lapham was right again."

"Menno worried. We all did."

"I know. I refused to believe the horrible thing had happened. I tried to turn the clock back, make it not so."

In Kalamazoo, with no time at the stopover for lengthy farewells, Millie gave Alana a quick hug and wished her luck. Alana said, "Take care, and marry that handsome sailor-boy."

Millie waved and climbed off. At a stand near the station, she got a cup of coffee while she waited for the shoreline train. The day was cloudy, Macatawa seemed remote, and her fingers felt stiff. Had she known she'd be away for a week, she'd have taken her banjo. Now it would be a chore to limber up for the evening's performance.

On reaching Macatawa, she decided to go directly to the dining hall, to fortify herself with a meal before she faced Rob and Laddie. When she headed for her usual seat, the waitress produced a puzzled frown. "Miss Langston? You're back?"

Millie paused, surprised. "Surely you expected me."

The young woman looked distressed. "Oh, Miss Langston, I guess you haven't heard the news." She frowned and touched Millie's arm in concern. "Your brother said he wrote to you."

"I was out of town and didn't get my mail." Millie's uneasiness grew. "What happened? Rob's all right, isn't he?"

"Yes, but—I hate to tell you—the orchestra disbanded."

Millie stared at her. "*Disbanded*? Impossible! Rob wouldn't do that." Nothing so awful could happen.

"He hadn't much choice, I understand. Mr. Hubbard and Mr. Graham were both called up and had to leave. Mr. Wylie rushed home to his wife and children who are down with flu. Miss Munn and Mr. Langston carried on alone. And oh—Laddie's so great! Everyone loves her! Have you seen her act?" Apparently failing to notice Millie's frown, she raved on. "You're in for a treat tonight! She promised to do her suffragette skit. It's a riot."

"Tonight? She's on tonight?" But surely Rob knew of Millie's return and her plans to reclaim her stage role! She'd sent him a postcard about it.

The waitress clasped her hands and winked knowingly. "I feel sure those two are in love. They're so sweet together, holding hands, laughing. You'll soon be having a wedding in the family, mark my words."

The floor fell from under Millie. Her heart constricted. This couldn't be happening! She felt herself plunging and grasped the back of a chair. She fought for breath. Rob in love? Orchestra disbanded? All in one week?

No, not possible. It couldn't happen, not so quickly. She forced herself to calm down and draw air into her lungs. Rob never showed great interest in women. His only thought was of promoting the orchestra. How much money to allot for advertising, how to keep up with the latest trends in music while still retaining popular oldies in the repertoire, that sort of thing.

"We're serving macaroni and cheese for lunch," the waitress said. "And Bavarian cream. I remember that's your favorite. Sit down and I'll—"

"I'm not hungry." Millie tried to step away from the table. Her legs shook. "I need to talk to my brother."

The waitress touched her arm to stop her as she inched away. "He's not here right now, Miss Langston. He and Miss Munn ate an early lunch and went canoeing. You may as well sit down and eat. Canoe rentals are for three hours." As if belatedly noticing Millie's look of dismay, she consoled, "I doubt they expected you so early."

"Obviously, they didn't." No doubt Rob had assumed she'd take Alana home, and wouldn't arrive back here until late afternoon. She slid into the chair. "All right, bring me the macaroni and cheese." She forced herself to act normal, to conceal her distress from the late diners, several of whom had noticed her indecisiveness and were eyeing her curiously.

Incredibly, the sun had come out. The lake sparkled like a great blue gem. At the marina beyond the dock, people were wasting no time in launching boats. The whole world was enjoying life while she sat here devastated.

The waitress brought the macaroni, along with a salad and hot biscuits. Millie toyed with the food but couldn't eat. She kept telling herself this couldn't happen. Rob wouldn't betray her like that. They'd always done things together.

It struck her that she was acting just like Alana, refusing to believe in something that had really occurred.

In her wildest worries of the future, Millie had never imagined the orchestra disbanding. Rob had planned to replace with women the men who'd be called up for military duty. He'd even begun advertising for women musicians. What had happened to that plan?

If Rob walked around holding hands with Laddie, as the waitress claimed, he must indeed be in love. Yet she couldn't imagine him making a sudden decision about marriage. Not Rob.

Two elderly ladies, on their way out of the dining hall, stopped by Millie's table to welcome her back. She forced a smile.

"We've so longed for you to come." The tiny one raised a shaky hand to tuck stray gray locks into her bun. "You need to speak to your brother, dear. We worry about him. He's letting Miss Munn make a fool of him. She has designs on him, and he's too nice to see it."

"These theater people," the taller one said. "Absolutely shameless. The woman throws herself at him. Open about it, smiling up at him like a hussy."

Despite the welter of feelings storming within her, Millie jumped to her brother's defense. "Rob's old enough to have a girlfriend if he chooses."

The women raved on as if they hadn't heard her. "That costume she wears—you can see her *limbs*, covered by a mere fringe."

"Don't forget to tell about the cigarettes, Jessie," Tiny added. "I don't hold with women smoking."

Under other circumstances, Millie might well have repressed a smile over the two old biddies with their high moral tone. Right now, with her midriff churning with anxiety, she felt bereft of humor and only longed to be rid of the pair. She made her voice curt and dismissive. "Sorry it bothers you. I really can't tell my brother what to do."

"No, but if you're clever, you can drag him away from that—that *Jezebel*."

When they were gone, Millie faced a bleak time ahead with nothing to do. After pushing her lunch aside largely uneaten, she sat trying to calm herself, pretending to watch the boaters, wishing Rob would hurry back to deny the rumors.

One thing she could do: she could see the manager about the orchestra contract. She hurried to his office. The manager looked up from his paper work and indicated a chair for her.

"Yes, the orchestra disbanded," he said in response to her inquiry. "We had no choice but to agree. What can you do when the military summons? It's wartime. Contract or no contract, we had to let the men go."

"So what happens now?"

He shrugged. "We're looking for another orchestra, but I doubt we'll find one soon. Older musicians aren't familiar with the modern ragtime stuff our guests demand. We may have to settle for the Victrola."

"Rob and I can play duets," she said. "Banjo, guitar and voice."

"I understand Mr. Langston plans to go with Miss Munn to Mackinac next week."

Millie gasped. "Mackinac? Oh, that can't be! Are you sure?" How could all this have been arranged so quickly? It was as if, during her few days of travel, months had passed here. Years, even. She'd returned, like Rip van Winkle, to a different world.

"Miss Munn needed an accompanist and was pleased to get your brother." He smiled at her. "Sorry about this. Kind of leaves you out in the cold. Not much I can offer to a woman alone."

A woman alone. The words were devastating. They eliminated her career; they wiped her out.

Trying to reclaim the last vestiges of her pride, she said, "I'm needed at home anyway."

As she left the office, she felt light-headed. She staggered and leaned against the wall for support. Orchestra and future gone. Nothing for her but a return to her library job. Not what she'd had in mind as a lifetime employment.

She climbed the stairs to her room and took out her banjo, hoping at least to keep her fingers limber. But when she strummed, the effort hardly seemed worth making.

Her fingers went wrong, she knew, because her mind refused to concentrate. She couldn't strike the right chords. She could think only of Rob, wanting him to hurry, to reassure her. To tell her things weren't as people claimed, that gossip and rumor had created a chimera.

She gave up on the banjo and went out to walk on the beach, where she paced up and down until at last she saw a canoe returning with two people who looked from a distance like Rob and Laddie. Then she went up to her room, again picked up the banjo, and tried to pretend she'd been practicing all along.

Rob didn't come upstairs at once. It was nearly four o'clock when he finally showed up at her door. Nervous and uneasy, he moved his fingers across his chest as if over the strings of his guitar. He reached up to shove back his hair, and finally clamped his hands onto the edge of the door. He forced a smile which seemed a grimace.

"Glad to see you back, Sis. I hadn't expected you. I thought the family would still need you."

To cut through these preliminaries, she blurted, "I hear you disbanded the orchestra."

He looked sheepish. "Had to. I'm so sorry. I *did* write you. Harold and John are gone, and Wylie's wife and kids are sick."

"So you decided to go to Mackinac with Laddie Munn?"

He released the door and sat down on the chair beside the bed. He reached out to take the banjo from her. Laying it aside, he grasped her hands. She felt his fingers tremble. "Millie, I know this will come as I shock, but I need to tell you. Laddie and I are getting married."

She suppressed a gasp. The despair she'd been fighting flooded through her. Icy fingers clenched her midriff until the pain seemed unbearable. Bile rose in her throat. She thought she might retch.

"On Sunday morning," he added. "We'll have a quick wedding and then take the train to Mackinac."

Sunday? *This* Sunday? Not possible! She gasped out a protest. "Rob, Mother can't plan a wedding that fast."

"Mother won't need to. We decided to have the ceremony at a church near here."

"You're not even going home?" Millie seemed to be drowning in ice water, yet at the same time her brow felt inflamed and her roiling stomach couldn't decide which direction to send its contents.

"We don't want fuss. Meeting each others' families—that's for after the wedding. Right now we need to stay focused for our performances here and at Mackinac."

Through waves of panic as her world came to an end, Millie kept her voice calm. "Mother will be devastated."

"I don't think so. I've already written to her. I've promised her we'll have a *real* wedding in the fall, flowers and all."

"I see I missed a lot, not going home for news." Millie swallowed hard and fought to keep her tone light, to betray no hint of her despair. Rob had a right to marry. As Zeke had said, he was more than old enough. She should have anticipated this.

"I feel rotten about leaving you high and dry," he said. "I'll finance a trip for you to visit Charlie if—"

"You don't owe me anything, Rob." She withdrew her hand from his. "You've paid me a salary all these years."

"Except for the devoted effort I couldn't begin to pay you for. Maybe, after the war, we'll get going again."

"Sure, maybe." She forced a smile. She knew she would never play second fiddle to Laddie. "Anyhow, congratulations."

"You'll stay and attend the wedding, of course?"

"I don't know about that." Her impulse was to rush home, to seek consolation from mother and sisters. She had to remind herself they could do nothing. Her career had ended. A woman alone could not make her way in the music world, not unless, like Laddie, she had training for vaudeville.

"Laddie's counting on you to be bridesmaid," Rob said.

Millie worked up her courage and asked, "Isn't this awfully sudden? You've only known Laddie a week."

"But what a week!" Rob flung his arms out; his eyes shown. "It's been miraculous. We have so much in common—music, goals in life. It's like we grew up together—well, actually, we lived close to one another but didn't know it. Laddie's father's dead; her mother paid for her singing and dancing lessons by selling candy."

"Mrs. Munnafee's Homemade Fudge!" Millie had been given boxes of it by all three of her beaux. "She's not a Chicagoan, then?"

"Grew up in Grand Rapids, just a few blocks from our house. Went to Michigan Street school. If I'd stayed in school I'd have known her."

So this was catch-up time for Rob, making something right that had gone wrong a long time ago, when he had to quit school in fourth grade. Though Millie tried to feel happy for him, the despair, the sense of betrayal, persisted. "You never hinted you were looking for a wife." And she'd thought they were so close! She remembered with embarrassment how she'd told Rob about her beaux. Clearly, he hadn't in response shared confidences with her.

"It just happened," he said. "I didn't plan it. Couldn't have dreamed of such a thing—or that she'd feel the same way about me. It still seems too good to be true."

"So you performed together and found that—"

"—that we're great together. Laddie suggested we travel the vaudeville circuit as a team. We started at once making plans. I could hardly believe she wanted me in her life, but I took the chance and asked her to marry me. At first she urged that we wait until fall when she'd finished at Mackinac, but when the orchestra fell apart, it seemed Fate was telling us to hurry. Today we canoed over to Holland and made the arrangements."

Millie felt herself spinning downward into a void. She couldn't remain here all week watching Laddie in performances that were rightly hers. That would be unbearable. Empty days stretched ahead with nothing for her to do.

She managed to blurt, "If you'd get married at home, I could go on ahead and make the arrangements."

Rob shook his head. "Too confusing for Laddie, meeting so many people at once. Annie and Zeke with their three, Menno and Alana with their five—four, I mean. Lordy, it's hard to remember about Richard's death. Vi, Don and Edgar. Mom and Dad. Bea."

"Well, I don't see the point in my hanging around watching you and Laddie spoon." Millie stood up. "I'm going home. I'll try to come back for the wedding if you wish."

Rob obviously sensed the barb in her words. His face went white. "If that's what you want, Sis. You're welcome to stay."

Millie longed to get away. There was no one her age in this hotel, which catered for business and professional men and their wives.

"You sure you don't want to visit Charlie Loomis? I'll pay for the trip. Call it your severance pay."

"What would I do there? Charlie doesn't have leave."

"I don't want you to feel I dumped you."

But you did dump me, dear brother, she thought. And I gave up so much for you. My scholarship, my college education.

Unbelievable that Rob would do such a thing—after all those years, their joint skits at the County House, WCTU performances, all held long before the orchestra was formed. Their combined efforts to locate a drunken father and bring him home before the police did. They'd done everything together. It was always Millie and Rob. She'd left college so as not to break them up.

Rob wanted her to greet Laddie. She dutifully followed him downstairs to Laddie's second-floor room, where she showed off her teeth in what felt to her like a witchy grimace. The room-door was opened by the young woman in the fringed skirt. Millie started to offer congratulations, then remembered one doesn't congratulate the bride. She forced out words. "Rob told me the news. I'm so glad he met someone he cares about. I hope you two will be very happy."

"Thank you, I believe we'll make a great team."

It seemed to Millie the final insult. She and Rob had been a team all their lives.

Laddie seemed ecstatic; her eyes glowed. She talked of looking forward to the wedding, and to acquiring a family with sisters and brothers. Millie kept showing her teeth. When at last the chore was done, and she could leave, she added, "I'm going home, but I'll try to return for the ceremony."

"I'm so sorry about the orchestra," Laddie said. "This wartime stuff is so sad, all the men going off to the army."

"Yes, isn't it?" Millie turned her painted smile on Rob. "See you Saturday."

"We'll miss you," he said.

She bit her lip. *I just bet you will,* she thought.

Duty done, she fled upstairs to pack. She fought tears. Rob called up the stairs after her. "I haven't forgotten your birthday's coming, Millie. We'll celebrate when you come back."

She'd forgotten. Some birthday, she reflected. May I never have another like it.

At home, she learned that her mother had received the letter from Rob but had not believed he'd go through with the wedding. "It's so unlike Rob," she said. "He never does anything in a rush. He'll postpone this, you'll see."

"I doubt it," Millie told her. "He has stars in his eyes."

She climbed the stairs to her room, where she found a letter from Charlie awaiting her. She tore it open and read.

Dear Millie:

I don't know how to tell you this so I'll just say it. I've decided to get married. I'll be shipping out soon, and there's a girl here I've come to care for. I do feel I'll want someone waiting for me. They say it means a lot when you're in the trenches.

I may not return to Michigan as my girl wants to live near her family. Luckily, there's lots here for an architect to do. Beautiful old homes to restore. I'll keep busy. I know you will too, with your orchestra.

All best,

Charlie

p.s. It was fun, Millie. I'll remember.

CHAPTER 26

❀

2002
Ashley

Across the years, I feel for Millie and wish I might somehow reach back to her. Everything hit her at once. I know the rejection must have been terrible for her; she never talked about the orchestra or her years as a performer. Couldn't bear to recall, I guess.

Of course I'd known something was destined to go wrong with both Charlie and her musical career. For the first thirteen years of my life, I lived near my great-grandmother, and her last name was not Loomis. And, though she strummed on her guitar, I never heard she'd recently retired from an orchestra.

Flipping ahead, I discover that Millie had not commented on Charlie's letter, merely inserted it into her diary. Nor did she have much to say about the wedding, stating only that she and Bea had attended. Luckily, Bea had written two long letters to Alana which someone had retrieved and stuck into the diary.

I take out the first letter and am unfolding it when Kevin returns. I refold it and hastily insert it back into the book.

"It's the alternator," Kevin says. "It went bad and the battery died." He looks at the diary and, sounding annoyed, demands, "You still reading about them stupid white folks? You should knock that off, girl. You got loyalties to think of."

I ignore this comment and ask, "The alternator? On a new car? I thought those only went bad on old cars."

"My car's only two years old but I bought it from a friend who'd been in an accident. I guess maybe he damaged the alternator. Anyhow, it has to be replaced and the battery recharged. The mechanic says to count on at least three hours. I figure we should ride back with Connor to that restaurant/motel place and rent a room. Crash while we hang around. That okay with you?"

"Sure, it's cool." I've been waiting for the moment when we'd have a room. Oh, lovely dream, oh long-time fantasy dating back to high school! I tuck the diary into my purse and stand up. "Let's go."

Kevin and I squeeze next to Connor in the front seat of the truck and drive the five blocks to the motel. When Connor leaves us off, saying he has to go to work, Kevin tells him not to worry, we'll walk back later to the garage. We enter the office, where Kevin dickers with an elderly woman at the desk and urges her to give us a bargain since it will be for only three hours. "We been driving all night," he says. "The wife and I just want to get a little shut-eye while our car's being fixed. We won't use no towels or nothing. Know what I'm saying?" While he talks, I smile and try to look wifely.

They agree on a cut-rate price and we go to the room. Kevin immediately forgets his promise not to use towels; he claims he needs to take a shower. It's getting to be a hot day.

"Oh, hell, I'll pay her a buck extra for the laundry," he says when I protest. He peels off his shirt, drops his pants, and stands naked for a moment looking muscular and sexy. Then, leaving his clothes in a pile on the floor, he jumps in the shower and promptly steams up the room. I bring out my makeup case and start to work. The mirror fogs over.

Soon Kevin climbs out, and still bare-ass naked, grabs me. He pulls off my t-shirt and drops my jeans. This isn't the great scene I'd anticipated, not the realization of my dreams. But after all, we have to accommodate to the circumstances. His damp flesh feels good against me. I grab back, and shedding panties, press against him. We move toward the bed. When I stretch out on it, he jumps on top of me.

His hand starts feeling me, and it's good. But too soon, a great hard lump comes whacking at me. Much as I'd hoped for our first sexual encounter to be memorable, clearly that's not fated to happen. On the contrary, he barrels in like rock. I feel impaled. He hardly thrusts at all. It's over before I've relaxed enough to savor it. I suffer a let-down. Not only is this not what I'd dreamed of, it won't even be something to brag to Keisha about.

Kevin says, "Hell, we're both too tired. Don't worry, Sugar-baby, I *will* light your fire, like I said—but not after twenty-four hours of driving followed by a car breakdown. You gotta give me a little down time. When we get to Vegas, we'll find a good hotel and have a sleep. Then—wow! Just you wait!"

Remembering my lovely fantasies of Kevin in bed, I hope that's true.

Having promised, he rolls over and has his sleep right then. Feeling used, while at the same time guilty for not sympathizing with his weariness, I go to the bathroom to shower, grabbing his damp towel so as to limit the breakage of our promise to the desk-clerk. Then I return to the bed—where I find that, having slept for six or seven hours in the car, I'm not sleepy.

After thrashing for a while and trying to relax, I get up and put on my clothes. I sit by the window, stare out, think about Kevin. He's not shaping up to be the glamorous guy I'd envisioned. Are real people ever like our dreams, I wonder? Probably not. Reality, even when good, is different from what one imagines. I caution myself to let things develop naturally, not try to force them into my dream-scenario.

For a while, I just sit watching a fly go up the screen, then drop down and start over. I think about sex, how disappointing it was with Jonah—and now with Kevin. Does it ever live up to its promise? Is there really a wonderful person with whom the experience is great and memorable? Yes, there has to be. There wouldn't be so many songs and stories about it otherwise. It must be true what Kevin says—we're both too tired right now. I glance at him on the bed, and he still looks desirable, stretched out there under the white sheet against black skin. I find myself again fantasizing about great moments with him.

In time, I open Millie's diary and again bring out and unfold Bea's letters. At first I can't concentrate, can think only of Kevin, what didn't go right with him, what I might do to make things right. I wonder if the slower response is my fault. I can't discuss this with my mom or dad; they don't like to believe I'm sexually active. Keisha and Bertie think that's wildly funny. At nineteen? Keisha would say. Come on, get real!

No answer comes to mind, so at last I concentrate on my forebear and her sister.

❧   ❧   ❧

Bea and Millie walked to the train station carrying luggage filled with filmy yellow dresses and suitable footwear. Millie was to be maid of honor, Bea bridesmaid. They'd had to buy everything as there wasn't time to sew. It was Bea's first store-bought outfit, and she was proud of it. Clothes Millie defined as hand-made, Bea defined as home-made, a term synonymous with imitation, with having things less good than those of other people.

At the station, with no one to see them off, they checked their own luggage. Though Don Dexter claimed he'd learned how to drive the truck, the women had declined the opportunity to be his first passengers.

"Finally," Bea remarked, when they'd boarded and located seats on the train, "finally I'm the one leaving instead of the one left. I've waited years for this."

"Rob and I were never off to have fun, just to work." Millie stood back to let Bea take the seat by the window.

Seated, Millie adjusted her hat. Bea waited impatiently for the train to start. She pondered how she might get Millie to talk about boyfriends. She sensed there'd been a disaster with Charlie Loomis. On reading his letter, Millie, already droopy because of Rob and the orchestra, clammed up and refused to talk about anything. Had Charlie been sent overseas? Bea wished her sister were less reticent about her love life.

Bea herself had yet to have a love affair. The men had left for war just as she reached the age to step out. She'd planned to be popular, have hordes of beaux, but refuse them all. She didn't wish to end up like Alana, stuck to bear child after child, nor like Vi, caring for an ailing husband, watching him die by inches.

Millie was so secretive she wouldn't even talk about her visit to Warren. Everything Bea knew, she'd learned from Alana—or from sneak-peeks at Millie's correspondence.

Only that morning, Millie had received a letter from Warren, read it briefly, and while Bea watched from the hall, shoved it into her drawer without comment. Bea'd pretended to leave for work, called out her farewell, slammed the back door, but remained in the house. While Millie bathed, Bea tiptoed upstairs to her sister's deserted bedroom to search the desk drawer.

The train started with a jolt. Watching the city slide past the window, Bea recalled the letter with its scribbled left-hand writing. Disappointing. No flowery language, no romance. Nothing to hint at a man in love.

All the same, she'd committed it to memory, and now reviewed it in her mind.

❧

Hello there, Millie, how's the world treating you? What's new in old Grand Rapids? If anything is ever new there. I think of G.R. as the place where time stands still.

I hear something has changed in Macatawa though. I hear the resort is bereft of Millicent Langston. Poor them! But never mind, you can always keep busy helping Ma save the world for the ladies. Great cause, Millie! I see you on a platform, fire in your eyes, lambasting old duffers who won't give votes to women. Make them eat their refusals, Millie! Give them what-for!

I'm practicing to be a lefty. Don't worry if you can't read this. True, you're missing gems of profundity, but there's more where those came from. We Kingsleys have no trouble "opening our word-hoard" as old Beowulf put it. Remember Beowulf in English class? Didn't he swim to the bottom of a lake to fight Grendel? And no diving gear!

Don't take any wooden nickels, Millie.

Yours till the South Pole thaws.

Warren

Bea had read the letter three times but found no hidden passion. She wondered what Millie thought. Of course, she couldn't ask. Millie would be furious to know her sister had peeked.

Millie talked about how, while riding the interurban as a child, she'd had her first real conversation with Alana. "She was taking me to Ionia for my WCTU performance at the fair. I was six. She told what it was like having a baby growing inside her. Scared me to death. I couldn't figure any way the baby could get out; I thought they'd both die, growing together like that in one body."

"You must have been relieved when Sean got born."

"I was. I'd watched Alana's stomach get bigger, and didn't dare ask Mother about it. I thought it was something that ought not to be happening, and Mother would be upset if I told. I vowed that no baby would ever grow inside me. I still feel repelled by the idea."

"You mean you're never going to marry and have children?" Bea turned from the window to gaze at her sister in shock. "But Millie, you'd be like Annie's sister Flora, a dried up old maid with frown lines."

"Bea, you sound like Alana. Marriage and babies!"

"Not at all. You were the one," Bea reminded, "who said women are no longer forced to choose between having babies and being an old maid."

"True, there are ways to prevent babies from getting started. The suffragists know how. But even so, I'm not sure I want to be with a man. They say it changes you forever."

"Well, of course it does. You're no longer a virgin."

Thoughtfully, Millie added, "Don't get me wrong. I'm not against babies; I just don't want to be a man's plaything or housekeeper. I want to be his companion and friend."

"Oh, Millie! Companion, friend!" Bea shook her head. "A man should fall in love with you, madly, passionately—and tell you so. Give me moonlight and roses all the way." She started to hum, "Moonlight and roses/Bring beautiful memories of you."

Bea paused in her singing. For a moment she feared she'd given herself away, all too obviously criticizing Warren, with his breezy, bantering approach. But Millie failed to pick up on it. In fact she changed the subject. She remarked, "It's like another death in the family, losing the orchestra. No more rehearsals. No more weddings and parties."

"Rob sure made a quick decision. I guess Laddie bowled him over."

"She twisted him around her finger." Millie spoke dryly.

"Well, they say that when you meet your life mate, you know it. I think it's exciting. What's Laddie like?"

"I can't say, I didn't talk to her much."

"She must be special. Rob's used to having women pursue him. He never cared before."

Millie admitted that Laddie seemed worldly and sophisticated by Grand Rapids standards. "She knows how to make a play for a man. I remember what Clovia told Vi: Men don't fall for women who pine over them. Maybe Rob's other admirers were too swoony."

No one could ever accuse Millie of being swoony, Bea reflected. Far from it.

The two women arrived at the hotel around dinner time. They found the lobby a swirl of activity, guests arriving, well-dressed people in groups waiting for the dinner gong. Rob was seated on a love-seat with his arm around a young woman Bea thought less than beautiful, eyes too far apart, cheeks broad, tapering down to a chin too pointy. Seeing his sisters, Rob waved and took his companion's arm to help her up. She was almost his height.

The couple hurried over. Bea suffered vague disappointment. Laddie didn't look all that special.

Bea soon changed her mind on that score. As the couple crossed the room, she saw that Laddie had the stage flair, the larger-than-life quality of an actress. She walked with superb self-confidence; and she looked at people, smiled at them, touched their shoulders in passing. In return, people noticed her; heads turned in her direction; admiring smiles lit all faces. Laddie's dark hair framed a gamin face alight with eagerness for this encounter with her new relatives.

"Bea, this is Laddie." Rob laid his hand on the woman's arm. To her, he said, "My youngest sister. And Millie, whom you've met."

Laddie grasped Bea's hand, then Millie's. "Hello, Bea, nice to meet you. Millie, great to see you again. I'm so glad you both came. I'm going to love having sisters." She sounded warm and sincere.

"We feel the same way." Bea politely included Millie, though she doubted Millie felt any such thing.

"Brothers, sisters, nieces, nephews—I never had any of those before, and I look forward to meeting everyone. One or two at a time, so I can savor each. Twenty at once seemed overwhelming. I hope the family understood."

"I'm sure they did." Bea spoke the lie stoutly, without embarrassment.

"Shall we go in to dinner?" Rob asked. "Or do you girls want to go upstairs and freshen up? I believe the bellhop has taken your bags up already."

"We can use the ladies' room downstairs." Millie grasped Bea's arm.

"We'll go in and get a table. We're all eating in the big dining room tonight; it's a celebration party." With a wave, Rob guided Laddie toward the line of people. They entered through the double doors into the big room, bright with western sun, its multiple chandeliers not yet lit for the evening.

Millie led the way to the rest room, deserted except for themselves. Inside, Bea remarked, "Laddie looks great. I'm going to get a skirt like that to show off my legs."

"Mother will have something to say about that."

"Hey, Sis, Mother needs to get used to the Twentieth Century. Things are different now. *You* want men as companions, Rob wants to marry a vaudeville girl, I want shorter skirts."

"Bea, you look great just the way you are. Your clothes are fine. And everyone loves your hairstyle, those thick braids wrapped around your head. Powder your nose and let's get out of here."

Millie disappeared into one of the booths. Bea ducked into the one next to it and heard her sister tearing off lengths of paper to cover the seat. Good old

Millie, always meticulous, even in a spotlessly clean place like this. Bea lifted her skirts, lowered her knickers, and plumped down onto a paper-free oak ring.

Later, when they entered the glittering dining room, Bea paused to admire the panoramic view of Lake Macatawa, then hurried to join Rob and Laddie, who were already giving their orders to a waitress. Millie followed more sedately.

"We're having prime rib," Rob said.

"I'll have the same." Bea didn't want Laddie to suspect she'd never before ordered a meal in a restaurant.

Millie chose the lake trout. When the waitress left, Laddie talked about the wedding. It seemed her mother was to arrive early next morning, bringing with her Laddie's grandmother's wedding gown, which, passed down, would now be hers. "I'm keeping my fingers crossed that it will fit." For flowers, the hotel was donating those currently decorating the ballroom.

After dinner, while Rob and Laddie prepared for their performance, Millie and Bea strolled on the beach. Seagulls screamed overhead, and sandpipers with long beaks explored holes in the sand left by receding waves. Bea breathed in the fresh air and confessed she envied Millie those three weeks she'd spent here.

"The Kingsleys have a cottage on the beach," Millie remarked.

Bea told her that if she played her cards right, she might get them both invited. She added to herself: Not unless you show more interest in Warren. You don't land a fish by turning your back on it.

She dared not speak for fear of revealing her knowledge of the letter.

Returning to the hotel, the women went to the ballroom, where guests were now dancing to Victrola music. A man with a large moustache approached Bea and asked her to dance. Though she doubted her mother would approve, she accepted. The man was thin, agile, a good dancer. She followed effortlessly.

When he said, "Call me Slim," she told him, "I'm Bea."

"Are you from Chicago?" He guided her to the center of the dancers.

"Grand Rapids."

"Oh—I don't recall ever meeting a Grand Rapids girl before." Was there a note of disappointment in his voice?

To recapture his interest, Bea said, "I'm the musician's sister. I'm here for his wedding."

"How exciting." Yet he didn't sound excited. Bea had the feeling he considered Grand Rapids folk unsophisticated, even boring.

Well, they *are* boring, Bea thought rebelliously. They pay their taxes, go to church on Sunday, and play by restrictive rules. They spend their lives conforming. You're safe leaving your doors unlocked anywhere in town. No wonder Vi was attracted to the one man who didn't conform. Downer McCurdle was a rare bird in Grand Rapids society.

She eyed the women swirling around her in their high-style summer frocks of lavender, powder blue, pale green. She felt envious.

"I plan to move to Chicago as soon as I save up the money," she told Slim. "I hear it's a great city."

"I wouldn't live anywhere else," he asserted.

When the dance ended, Slim walked Bea back to her sister, and while she waited for Laddie's performance to begin, she tried to think how she might sparkle as Laddie seemed to, attracting attention without doing anything coarse or unladylike.

The hall darkened; the spotlight focused on the orchestra platform to reveal Rob strumming his guitar. Abruptly, it swung to the stage-door and Laddie entered. Bea hardly recognized her. In a man's tuxedo and top hat, she sported a cane in one hand, a long cigarette holder with smoking cigarette in the other. To Rob's accompaniment, she sang a humorous love song about spooning by the light of the moon. The audience laughed and applauded.

Now Laddie swung into a comedy routine, strolling across the stage, smoking, talking about how she'd chained herself inside some all-male hall women weren't allowed to enter. As the audience chuckled, Rob strummed. Waving the long cigarette holder, Laddie sang.

> I'm a suffragette,
> I'll get votes for women yet.
> You see if I don't!
>
> We women are finer than men,
> We'll fix your morals when
> You gentlemen won't!

She winked broadly. Again everyone laughed and clapped. Bea felt relieved to see that Millie, so dedicated to the suffrage cause, didn't frown over this satire.

More comedy routines followed. Later, Laddie put aside her cigarette and did a tap dance. When she ran off the stage, it was to wild applause—though not from Millie, who contrived to slap her two hands together lightly.

Rob played a solo. Laddie returned wearing the dress Millie had described to Bea, silver-blue with a fringe covering her knees. Bea loved the dress and vowed to get one like it.

Laddie sang another love song, this time serious, romantic, and then was joined by Rob in singing war-songs, 'Tipperary' and 'Long Road Awinding.' The audience sang along.

When the pair left the stage, there were shouts and whistles. They returned and, after they'd taken bows, Laddie announced that they were to be married in the morning. The audience stood to applaud.

Bea felt awe-struck at having such a talented and popular new sister-in-law. At the same time, she worried about Millie, who she sensed must be suffering at being so thoroughly upstaged. The chagrin must be unbearable. Only two weeks ago, a similar crowd must have applauded Miss Millicent Langston.

"You could do as well if you went to a performing arts school like she did," Bea whispered.

Millie stood. "Let's leave. We have to get up early." She slid past several people to the aisle. Bea followed rebelliously, wishing she could be rid of Gloomy Millie and have this exciting resort and its guests to herself. She wouldn't mind if she stayed up all night. She vowed to come back by herself soon.

At dawn, Bea dressed quickly and helped Millie with her hairdo. They made it to the dining room by half past six. They joined Laddie who was already there. Bea congratulated her on her performance of the previous night. "You were great!"

"I was inspired." Laddie smiled. "Just fancy coming back to Michigan to find the man of my dreams." She added, "I've already ordered for us; we need to hurry. Bacon, eggs and toast all around. That okay?"

"Just so they bring coffee. Where's Rob?" Bea unfolded her napkin.

"He was to meet my mother at the station. I made a point of not seeing him off. Bad luck to see the groom before the wedding, you know."

"Speaking of luck, do you have something old, something new, something borrowed, something blue?" Bea asked.

"Old dress, new shoes, blue handkerchief. Nothing borrowed, though."

"I'll loan you my garters. We'll trade."

"Marvelous! I love having sisters!"

After a hurried breakfast, they boarded a hotel carriage which took them into town. There, they entered a church decorated with the flowers sent from last night's ball. They were introduced to Laddie's mother, a portly woman with rosy cheeks and prematurely graying hair, whose smile, on meeting them, seemed a bit forced. Bea suspected that, like her own mother, Mrs. Munnafee felt perplexed about this wedding so suddenly thrust upon her.

The woman confirmed Bea's guess by remarking, dubiously, "The young couple must have decided to marry just days after they met."

"Rob says he knew, the first day, that Laddie was the one he wanted to marry." Bea hoped her words would reassure Laddie's mother, let her know the marriage was fated to be.

Laddie's uncle joined them and was introduced. There followed a brief conversation about the lovely weather and beautiful flowers. The two sisters were shown to the ladies' lounge, where they—or at least Bea, since Millie was moving at half-speed this morning—helped Laddie dress in the bridal gown she'd inherited. Since she was of a less stocky build than her mother and grandmother had been, it proved to be loose on her. She used a wide white ribbon to draw it in at the waist.

"I'll have it altered by a seamstress before our public ceremony next fall," she said.

Hotel guests who'd come to watch the wedding now sat listening to the organ prelude. At the signal, Millie and Bea strolled down the aisle in their yellow dresses. On the arm of her uncle, the bride followed, wearing her pearly-satin gown. Rob and the minister waited at the altar, Rob looking formal, his hands clasped behind him. He moved to join the bridal party facing the minister.

As the vows were uttered, Laddie spoke up loud and clear. "I, Gladys Munnafee, take thee, Robert Langston—" Rob mumbled his lines. His typical shyness, Bea thought.

The minister pronounced them man and wife. The organ played the Mendelssohn wedding march. The bride and groom kissed and ran down the aisle, with Millie, Bea and the Munnafees following. There were hugs and congratulations. Laddie's mother wiped tears from her eyes.

After seeing the young couple off on the interurban, heading for Grand Rapids and the Pere Marquette train to Mackinac, they returned to the hotel. Bea saw that Millie too was fighting tears—but not, she suspected, of joy. Bea sensed her sister felt abandoned.

Millie confirmed Bea's suspicions. In a shaky voice, she said, "I got Rob his start. I arranged those WCTU performances for him."

"He gave you music lessons," Bea reminded. "You helped each other."

Checkout wasn't until two. There was time for a swim and a leisurely lunch. Millie didn't want to stay on, but Bea insisted. She meant to enjoy every minute Rob had paid for. It was, after all, her first overnight away from home. She had no intention of arriving back in mid-afternoon. She remarked that after checking out, they could leave their suitcases in the lobby, stroll on the beach until dinner time, and have one last meal in this beautiful dining room. They'd still catch the seven-twenty interurban.

She intended to see the world, all of it, even the sinful city of Chicago which her father railed against. Next paycheck, she would start saving. Dad couldn't stop her from spending her own money. She thought about Millie's statement: Being with a man changes you forever. The thought was scary, but all the same she wanted to have adventures; she wanted to use up the time she was allotted on this earth and not have to look back and feel she'd wasted it.

CHAPTER 27

2002
Ashley

Poor Millie. I wish I could have her here so I could give her a hug. Her brother's wedding must have been a nightmare for her. I ponder about her statement: having sex changes a woman forever. Does it really? I don't think Keisha changed until she had Jordi. I don't think I changed after those pallid experiences with Jonah or this one venture with Kevin. I think it's pregnancy that changes a woman forever. Whether you decide to have the baby or not, whether you choose to adopt it out or not, you never forget the child and no one ever seems to feel right about their decision. They second guess themselves on and on: Did I do the right thing? Was I foolish? Should I have made a different decision? After six years, Keisha still debates whether Jordi would be better off in a wealthy adoptive family.

The telephone rings; I answer. The mechanic from the garage tells me the car will be ready in a half hour. When Kevin stirs, I relay the information. He bats sleep from his eyes, peers at his watch, and remarks that we should go to lunch at once so as to be finished when we pick up the car.

Having said that, he snuggles down and falls asleep again. I sit there wondering if I ought to shake him awake, and decide I shouldn't. I feel sleepy myself. This is a trip, not a marathon. I crawl in beside him for a little shut-eye.

The next thing I know, Kevin is shaking *me* awake, telling me it's two p.m. "Why didn't you wake me? We gotta hit the road, girl, we ain't ever going to reach Vegas at this rate."

There's a banging on the door. The chambermaid wants to clean the place. I sit up, rub my eyes and confess that I'm hungry. Kevin says we'll do a take-out lunch. In his jeans and t-shirt, he phones the restaurant and puts in an order for hamburgers to go. I gather up my makeup from the bathroom, grab the diary, slip into my shoes and stumble after him. In the hall, the chambermaid tosses us a glare.

We turn in the key at the office and get our bag lunch from the restaurant. Kevin admits that it was good to have a snooze. "You were right. I feel great; I can drive all the way to Los Angeles." He swivels to look at me. "You're an okay chick. I had my doubts—you with that white mother—but you're a sister." I feel good that I'm finally accepted, white relatives and all. He reaches out and hugs me, and whispers that he'll light my fire; that's a promise. I tell him I'll hold him to it.

When we step outside, the weather is sweltering. There seems no way we can walk five blocks in this hot sun. Kevin suggests we hitch a ride. I demur. I never hitchhiked and I feel uneasy about it. While we argue, a man from the restaurant comes out and offers us a ride in his air-conditioned car. Kevin accepts for both of us. In two minutes we're at the garage, where a broiling hot gold Toyota awaits us. I open the doors to air the car while Kevin pays the bill.

From then on it's heat and tedium, heat all day, tedium at night. Toward morning, driving, I get so sleepy I have to pull over to the side of the road. I hear Kevin complaining, "We'll never get there at this rate!" Too near asleep to bother fighting back, I slump down and doze off. I'm vaguely aware that he shoves me to the other seat and takes over the driving, and that he turns the music up until it blasts at us. None of it keeps me awake.

On the third day, the car's air-conditioning conks out. We swelter toward Las Vegas, so hot we have to keep wetting our lips from our bottled water. I never felt heat like this; I worry that we'll collapse, or the car will. When I mention the fact to Kevin, he cheerfully remarks that it's good practice for hell when we get there. I'm convinced we're there already.

About five o'clock that afternoon, we finally pull into Vegas. Kevin apologetically admits we have to go to a cheap hotel the first night, until he figures out his money-making scheme. "Just give me a couple of hours to work this thing out, and then we'll move to our luxury quarters at New York, New York."

I try to pin him down about how this magic is to work, but he doesn't want to tell me. He seems to think he's latched onto some great secret and needs to guard it with his life.

So we go to the Clairmont, sign in, find our room which is a dreary gray with gunky carpets. Still, the bed looks inviting. When we crash, we hear the sounds of Las Vegas outside our window but they fail to lure us. After our driving marathon, we only want to catch up on our sleep.

Kevin wakes me about three in the morning and announces that this is a good time to try out his scheme. Few people will be in the casino at this hour, few employees around. I worry that we'll get caught, but he assures me he'll be careful. "It's just fast-forwarding a machine to payoff. I'm not going to damage or destroy anything."

He wants to go right down. I insist on showering first, to join him downstairs in a few minutes. He promises to wait for me at the nearest snack or coffee shop. "I think I remember seeing one to the right of the elevator."

I open my suitcase, take out a clean outfit, and go into the bathroom. A half hour later, feeling refreshed, I join Kevin at the coffee shop. It turns out he ordered for both of us, sweet rolls and coffee. My coffee is tepid by now but I gulp it down. Kevin signals the waitress to pour more for both of us. I look out toward the casino, where it seems to me there are just as many people playing the slot machines at three-thirty in the morning as there'd been at six in the evening when we checked in—they even look like the same people—and just as many bar-girls running around bringing drinks.

When we've eaten, Kevin searches for a deserted corner of the casino, well hidden from the coffee shop and bar. He brings from his pocket a credit card, pliers, a small screwdriver, and a handful of quarters. He explains that he needs me to sit at the machine, play, and act natural.

"Kevin, they won't let me play, I'm not twenty-one." I hope that's true. I don't want to be involved in his tricks.

He disappoints me by saying, "Eighteen is old enough. You're older than that, aren't you?" He sits at the machine, puts in a coin, pushes the button, and tries to act nonchalant. He doesn't win anything, of course. He then begins poking around with the credit card and the tools. I worry that we'll wind up in jail. Whatever will Mom and Dad say if I call from Las Vegas to ask for bail money?

Twenty feet away, an older woman with salt-and-pepper hair sits at another machine pushing the button. I keep an eye on her in case she's been planted by the management as a spy. She never glances in our direction nor seems to know we're there. Neither does the bearded man behind us, nor the younger woman to our left. It's eerie, the total absorption of these gamblers. They seem hypnotized, or perhaps they're zombies or wax figures put there to make the place look busy. As I watch them, I begin to wonder if they ever lose their concentration. The woman wins a few coins, doesn't even count them, simply sweeps them into her lap and goes on feeding them into the machine and pressing a button.

A tall man walks toward us. I hiss, "Someone's coming!" Quicker than a fast gun in an old fashioned western, Kevin whips the tools into his pocket and comes around to sit and play. Before he can bring out his coins, the man, his focus apparently on finding his favorite machine rather than on us, has wandered off without making eye contact. I tell Kevin I think his cousin was putting him on. I don't believe this trick is doable. Kevin shakes his head and resumes work. I people-watch. These gamblers are incredible; each one totally alone and related only to the machine. They don't even wait to see what the machine does before readying their next coin.

Kevin curses under his breath. I sense the trick is not going as he hoped. Shoving everything into his pockets in disgust, he says, "Let's try another machine. This freak's no good."

We wander around again. I notice Kevin checking overhead and realize he's searching for hidden cameras. He finally zeroes in on a machine in the far corner and tries again. This time it's only minutes before the tall guy strides our way. As before, he stalks on past, not really looking at us—yet it dawns on me he must be a security guard. He's too omni-present to be a player, and I haven't seen him sit down anywhere. I begin to panic.

"Kevin, that guy's watching us," I whisper. "You'd better knock it off."

"Ah, hell, let's go somewhere else," he says. "These old machines are built like goddamn bank vaults."

We go outside, where it's hot even at this hour, and walk down the well lighted Strip. We enter a newer-looking casino and Kevin tries again. To distance myself from him, I claim to be still hungry and locate the snack bar. Not being a big coffee drinker—I love that first cup but don't want to go on and on, as Millie would have done—I order hot chocolate. Not looking at Kevin, pretending I don't know him, I sit on a stool. He soon comes over and tells me that these machines are even worse.

"I guess we gotta walk all the way down to New York, New York," he says. "That's where my cousin made out. Well, not there but in some new casino like that."

"Kevin, can't we forget this business? It's not cool to get busted."

"No reason that should happen, girl. My cousin pulled this off and made the machine vomit up eight hundred dollars. You gotta fast-forward to when the thing's ready to pay off. These old machines don't have computer parts so they can't be fast-forwarded."

"How do you know your cousin's machine wasn't ready to spew out money anyhow?"

"I know because he told me."

To me, that offers no proof.

We hike up the strip what seems like ten miles to the newer casinos. By now it's starting to be daylight and more people are showing up on the streets. When we enter a casino, I immediately spot burly guys standing around looking like security guards. I again try to convince Kevin to forget all this. "There's nothing wrong with the Clairmont except a grungy rug. We can stay there."

"That ain't the kind of luxury I planned to provide for you," Kevin insists. "We want to *live*, not exist."

"Jail is not the best place to do our living."

Kevin gives me a dark look. "Come on, girl, don't get to be a drag."

"I'm trying to save your ass from the jailhouse, Kev."

"The hell you are. You're trying to be a trip-wrecker. Succeeding, too." He grabs my arm and yanks me into another casino, where he goes through the same routine. Stumbling after him, I decide that this time I'll really play the slot-machines so that at least I'll look like a player rather than like Kevin's partner in crime. I sit at a machine, feed in some coins, push the button a few times—and lo and behold, the machine pays off. It dumps about ten dollars into my lap, all in coins. Kevin stares and tells me, "Girl, you found our lucky machine! Now to fast-forward. Move over and give me a crack at it."

I sweep my coins into my purse and wander off to locate the snack bar, hoping it's far away from Kevin. I'll get fat if this goes on much longer.

Kevin soon shows up and tells me he quit fooling around because a guard was eyeing him. "We'll keep track of that machine for later. I marked it." We go out to the street and Kevin looks for another casino to hit on. I urge we go back to the hotel. It's broad daylight now, and traffic is heavy. There are too many people around.

"It's you I'm trying to get money for," Kevin reminds me. "I promised you a fancy stay in Las Vegas, and I'm trying to deliver."

"No need. I can enjoy the Clairmont. It has a pool."

Kevin frowns in annoyance. "Why don't you go on back by yourself?"

"Good idea. I think I'll do that." And just to show him, I step to the bus-stop as a city bus approaches and hop aboard, leaving him standing open-mouthed at the curb.

In the hotel room, I bring out the diary but find I can't read it. My mind won't focus. I worry about my situation. By now, I'm convinced Kevin hasn't a prayer of succeeding at his crazy trick, and I fear he'll go to jail, leaving me alone with not enough money to get home. I realize I was insane to ride off with him when I lacked funds.

I pace. I stare out the window. I debate what I'll do if Kevin goes to jail. The few dollars I won't take me far. I keep wondering how I got myself into this predicament.

After a while Kevin returns. He's scowling so I know he failed. He grumbles, "Security guards everywhere. This is the damnedest city. I called my cousin and he says it was in Laughlin or somewhere that he done that trick. I guess maybe we should travel on." Kevin spots the diary on the dresser and freaks out. "There you are with that cursed white-chick book! I told you to dump it." He grabs it. "If I could find a good hot bonfire, I'd burn the damn thing."

I panic. "Kevin, give it to me!"

He holds it over my head. "You don't want this book, Ash. White folks are the enemy. Haven't you learned that yet?" I realize that when he's angry, he knows my name.

I wonder if he forgot I have a white mother. "Not these white folks," I say. "They're my relatives."

"If I was so unlucky as to have white relatives, I'd have to kill myself," Kevin says. "I never did figure how you could put up with them. Haven't you heard what they done to us? They made slaves of us, beat us, broke us in like so many wild horses. When they couldn't get away with enslaving us no more, they stuck us in ghettos. They segregated us, they lynched us, they even sterilized some brothers and sisters. I could tell you horror stories. They dragged a guy behind a car—"

I think of my great-great grandparents, Douglas and Rebecca, both struggling just to keep going. Of Vi, caring for a dying husband, and Millie who lost the place in the orchestra she'd worked for all her life. I tell Kevin my forebears were in no position to enslave anyone, lynch anyone, or any of the rest of it.

"Sugar-baby, you are one naïve kid," he says. "You believe all the lies they write in their books."

"Not true. I took black history; I know that stuff you're telling me. I was shocked, too, but—"

"So why you reading their garbage. Let's toss this shit in the swimming pool!"

He starts toward the door, the diary still in his hand. I jump in front of the door to stop him. "Kevin, give me that diary! It's mine!"

Still plunging forward, he crashes into me. My head bangs against the door. Too mad to feel the pain, I fight to get the diary back. He grabs my arm with his free hand to hold me off. Even though it brings searing pain, I twist to break loose and try to slide past him and reach the doorknob.

He catches me around the waist. I bend down to bite his arm and sink my teeth in. He curses, lets go, and drops the diary. I stoop to grab it.

"I was wrong about you!" He holds and cradles his arm. "I thought you were a sister, but you—"

I'm already out the door and on my way to the elevator, the diary in my hand. Though my arm aches, the back of my head aches, I ignore the pain and run. I punch the elevator button—and I'm in luck. The elevator is there; the door opens. I jump in and ride downstairs. When I find myself in the casino, I rush to a security guard.

"A had a fight with a guy," I pant. "He's in room 406."

He returns with me to the room. By now Kevin has cleared out. Even his bag is gone. My bag and purse are still there. The security guard tells me to check the purse, and when I do, I find that Kevin has taken the coins I won, along with my few leftover dollars.

"My money's gone," I say.

"You can report it to the police," the guy says, "but it's hard to trace cash."

I root around in my purse and find two quarters. That's apparently the sum total of my present finances. Not even enough for a cup of coffee. Just enough, if I reverse the charges, for a phone-call home. There seems nothing for it but to contact my parents and confess everything. It's the last thing I'd wanted to do. I can't imagine what they'll say.

I stuff the diary and my makeup into my suitcase and, not wanting to risk another encounter with Kevin, accompany the guard downstairs. I try my cell phone, and even though I haven't recently charged it up, by a miracle it's working. I call my parents. Of course they're not home. I get their answering machine. What to say? I'm stuck in Vegas; come and get me? Hardly. I try their cell phone and find they haven't turned it on. But then, why would they? They must figure their daughter is far away in Michigan.

I try my grandmother's number. She doesn't answer either. I have another answering machine to cope with. Making it casual, I say, "Hi, it's Ashley. Sorry I missed you." You'll never know how sorry!

One last chance—Grandmother's cell phone. I try that. She never turns the thing on. But this time, wonder of wonders, she has done so. She answers! I'm so relieved my words tumble all over themselves.

"Gran, it's Ashley. I'm here in—uh, I've been trying to call my parents—uh, can't reach them. Do you have any idea where they are?"

"They're in Santa Barbara, visiting Michael," she says. "What's up, Ashley? You sound breathless."

Do I dare tell her? Or will she read me the riot act for coming on this trip?

I take courage in hand and make myself say the words. "The truth is, Gran, I'm penniless in Las Vegas."

Predictably, in her astonishment, she yells. "*Vegas*? Did you say *Vegas*?"

"That's right."

"I thought you were in Michigan."

"I was, but I met this guy I know, and he offered to drive me here, so I thought—well, of course I had a ticket to come home, but I thought it might be fun to—. Anyhow, we got as far as Vegas and I lost track of him."

"Ashley, you have a genius for getting into the most incredible predicaments."

You don't know the half of it, Gran. I've only told you part of the story.

Kevin, my dream-boy, how could you do this to me? My head hurts, my arm hurts. Yet when you talked of restoring my old homestead, you seemed so sweet about it. I thought seriously of getting involved with you.

"You're in luck," Gran says. "I'm in Victorville, halfway to you. I can drive over and get you."

My relief mingles with concern. She'll notice my sore wrist and know what happened. But I certainly can't tell her not to come. To make conversation, I ask, "What are you doing in Victorville?"

"I came here for a conference," she says.

Gran's a Unitarian Christian, always going to conferences and promoting the cause, even though a lot of people, including my dad, think that's an oxymoron and there can't *be* Unitarian Christians. I mean, Unitarians believe in one God and Christians believe in three, right? Don't ask me how Gran figures that out. It may have something to do with *her* gran being a Mennonite, and her wanting to preserve family history.

I hate to reveal my sordid tale, but, well, even Gran can't berate me too much. I fought to save her mother's diary, after all. I tell her, "I'm at the Clairmont. I'll wait for you by the front door so you won't have to park."

"It'll take me a couple of hours, even from here," Gran says.

I decide I'll spend those hours hovering near the guard, wherever he might be. Just in case Kevin shows up again.

When the guard asks if I contacted someone to help, I tell him my grand-mother is coming for me. "She's in Victorville; it'll take a couple of hours." He studies my wrist—it's starting to turn all colors of the rainbow—and asks if I need the paramedics to check me out. I shake my head. They'll only offer pain pills, and I'm no pill-popper.

He brings out a folding chair, places it against the wall for me, and promises to keep an eye on me in case my assailant returns.

My assailant. What a strange word for Kevin. The last thing I ever envisioned was Kevin as an assailant. Was he one, or did I attack him when he grabbed the diary? I suspect maybe I was the assailant.

I sit, relax, and telephone Keisha. She thinks I'm kidding when I tell her I'm in Vegas. Laughing at her reaction, I say, "Girl, have I got a story to tell you!"

While talking to Keisha, I eye the zombies at their machines and watch for Kevin, still hoping for an apology. He doesn't come. Later I go to get the free cup of coffee the hotel had given us a voucher for. Sipping it, I bring out the diary. In case of trouble, the guard is close by. Shaking a bit, I try to relax and concentrate.

I pretty much know what happened to Millie, but it's fun to read her own words and get her take on it all. And Warren's words—in his letter which she included.

CHAPTER 28

1918
Millie

July 20, 1918
Great Lakes NTC

Hello, there, Millie. Old Lefty here. Guess what? I'm transferred! The Navy got fed up with my goldbricking and gave my bunk to a fighting man. Since Lake Michigan has no surf to ride, I don't find much to entertain myself with. I sure need a pal. Hope you can take a boat across the Great Briny—oops, I mean the Great Unbriny.

I could meet you at the Navy Pier in Chi to do the Field Museum. Also White City—I hear it's much bigger than our Ramona Park.

As I recall, you have a birthday coming up. We'll celebrate that great event, the arrival on earth of Millicent Langston. I fear the suffrage movement may fall apart without you, but we can trust Ma and her cohorts to carry on. So come!

Yours till Hell freezes over,

Warren

Once Millie had deciphered the left-handed scrawl, the message was clear. Warren wanted her to visit. She'd have loved to go, but of course it was out of the question. Her parents wouldn't hear of it. They'd be shocked to know she considered such a thing.

She'd read the letter aloud to her ever-curious sister, and now regretted the impulse. Bea insisted, "You have to go."

"I'll do nothing of the kind," Millie snapped. "With no chaperone? What would Mother say? Not to mention that Dad would have a fit!"

"Millie, grow up, for pity's sake. You're twenty-two, you don't need a chaperone. Did you see Laddie worry about a chaperone? Of course not. She runs her own life."

"Laddie didn't go to Macatawa to visit Rob—she just happened to meet him."

"So you'll vacation in Chicago and happen to meet Warren."

Millie stared at her sister in shock. "You'll get in big trouble, Bea, the way your mind works."

"Fiddlesticks. Your suffragist friends would be ashamed of you, being so timid. Another thing, Millie, you're digging your own grave the way you treat men. This business of keeping them at arm's length—you'll regret it. One of these days Warren will find himself another girlfriend, like Charlie did."

Shock turned to cringing embarrassment, then anger. Millie demanded, "What do you know about Charlie?"

Bea's face flamed. Millie realized her sister had snooped and read her mail.

Bea defended herself. "You asked me to help move your stuff into Rob's room. I peeked a little. It was for your own good. I knew something was wrong. Your face was so long your chin almost touched your chest."

"So Miss Nosey decided to fix my love life!" Millie clenched her fists in fury. "I won't have this, Bea! It's intolerable!"

"And soon you won't have boyfriends either!" Bea shot back. "You can shutter the house and sit in your room wearing your wedding dress, like Miss Havisham in *Great Expectations*. You can take on the support of the family and develop frown-lines, like Annie's sister."

"Oh, shut up! It's none of your business what I do about my beaux. I won't have you reading my mail." Yet even as she spoke, she recalled that she herself had done the same thing to Vi, reading those scribblings, *Vi McCurdle, Mrs. Nat McCurdle.*

She slammed the door of Bea's room and rushed to her new bedroom, formerly Rob's. The argument had given her the shakes. It was true that from having three beaux, she was reduced to one, and the one revealed no great passion. At Glenburnie, she'd approved of that, since she'd anticipated a return to her orchestral duties and wanted no marriage proposal to deal with. Now, the question had become important. Was Warren seriously interested in her or was she only a pal?

She'd been determined to avoid her older siblings' lifestyle, so focused on children and the money to support them that it allowed no room for adult activities, for travel, for meeting interesting people and seeing the world. She'd repeatedly watched them all, Zeke and Annie, Menno and Alana, even Vi, suppress their own interests to place their children's welfare first. Until a year ago, both Annie and Alana had coped with outdoor toilets and well-water from pumps. Food bills, clothing bills, doctor bills had overwhelmed their resources so that they couldn't upgrade their homes. Millie had said, "Not for me, not for me!"

At the same time, she dreaded the thought that she might indeed wait out her life amid the ruins of her wedding, hoping for the return of a lover who never came. Nor did she care to emulate Annie's sister, the woman the family referred to as Aunt Flora, devoting her life to her parents and sister, paying their bills, helping to care for their children. That was not at all what Millie had in mind when she'd made her youthful vow to avoid her siblings' mistakes. She'd meant to marry later and well, like Vi's friend Clovia, who at age twenty-nine married a college professor while retaining her job as a buyer at Wurzburg's.

Should I go? Millie wondered. To the evil city Mother and Dad disapprove of? With no chaperone?

The idea seemed frightening. Yet not going was equally scary. Obviously, the men in the service needed to know they had someone waiting for them. They were anticipating trench warfare and the horrors of war. She couldn't bear to think of Warren, recovered, facing such dangers.

If not me, it will be some other woman for Warren—as with Charlie, she reminded herself.

Her decision-making abilities frozen, Millie immersed herself in preparations for the suffrage training session. For two days she stuffed envelopes with flyers full of slogans: "Michigan in '18, the nation in '20. Urge your menfolk to vote for women's vote." She helped make placards saying, "Michigan loves its women; let them vote!"

With Rob's wedding over, she faced two more endless weeks of her leave-of-absence from the library, and restlessly sought ways to fill in the time. Things seemed promising on the suffrage front. Clovia had exulted, "I believe the country is ready for us women at last! I hear no more scoffing about petticoat government."

Millie cast her gaze over the hall she'd helped decorate with red, white and blue streamers. A group of women including Clovia and Eloise had gathered at the piano for a sing, with Mrs. Kingsley playing the accompaniment. Millie listened to their voices rising in a popular prohibition song: Oh, 'twas not my father who did the bad deed/'Twas drinking that ruined his brain./Oh, let him go home to dear mother, I pray/I'm sure he'll not do it again.

After two verses the group broke up, laughing, and urged Millie to join them. Clovia suggested she bring her banjo next day. "We'll have a great sing, you at the banjo, Liz at the piano."

Eloise suggested putting them on the program. "Let our audience join the fun."

Clara Durham, the chairwoman, turned to Millie. "How about it, dear? Would you consider it?"

Millie hesitated. "My fingers are stiff. It's been over two weeks since I played the banjo." After the orchestra breakup, she hadn't wanted to touch the instrument.

"We'll give you time to rehearse."

"My stars, I'm not a professional pianist," Liz Kingsley protested. "I've only played for small groups."

"We want fun, not a concert." Tall, slim Eloise tossed a shapely head with circlets of blonde braids above each ear.

"You and I will have to get together on this, Millicent," Mrs. Kingsley said.

Millie blushed when Warren's mother's brown eyes met her gaze. She felt sure the older woman could read her mind about her projected visit to Chicago, unchaperoned. Whatever would the Kingsleys think?

Eloise urged they do another song. "Join us, Millie."

When Millie stepped into the circle, Clovia and Eloise flung their arms around her waist. Mrs. Kingsley turned pages of the song book, found what she wanted, and began to play a "home front" song: "Somewhere in France is Daddy."

The women sang with gusto. One woman with a son overseas dabbed at her eyes with her handkerchief. At the end of the song, Mrs. Kingsley urged that they return to their work, but when someone pleaded for one more song, she turned pages and played. The group sang along with her. "Keep your head down, Fritzi boy." In her mind, as she sang, Millie heard Warren's humorous version of this song, which he'd sung for her in Glenburnie.

Keep your shades down, Mary Ann,
Keep your shades down, Mary Ann.
Late last night by the pale moon light
I saw you, I saw you.

You were combing your golden hair,
And you hung it upon a chair.
If you want to keep your secrets from your future man
Keep your shades down, Mary Ann.

That was Warren, always irreverent, always ready with a kidding version of any song. She could almost hear his voice. Tears came to her eyes at the memory. She dared not mention his humorous version here, among these tearful mothers with sons overseas. Only Warren could joke after a near-death experience.

The group disbanded. Eloise poured three cups of coffee and handed one to Clovia, one to Millie. Millie creamed hers, and remembered that no one had sugar available. She drank the beverage unsweetened and tried not to make a face. Clovia, who never sugared hers, smiled sympathetically at this predicament.

While they finished their drinks, Millie gathered her courage and confessed that Warren had urged her to visit him. She wanted to explore the question whether these two old friends would find the idea shocking. She told them, "My sister Bea is all in favor of my going, but I don't feel it would be right."

"Twentieth Century women ought to be free to travel and meet any man they wish," Clovia asserted.

Millie lamely protested. "It would cost the earth. Chicago's so expensive."

"Not if you stay at the Y," Eloise said.

"What will Mrs. Kingsley think of Bold Millie?"

"What does it matter? You don't need her permission." This from Clovia, with Eloise echoing that their friend was right.

Millie felt a stab of panic. She'd always been the good girl of the family, never rebellious or defiant. Doing what she was told, even when she had to bite her tongue to hide her anger.

They sat down at the long table. Others were already at work fluffing crepe paper ribbons to be hung in the foyer. Clovia remarked that Millie was the opposite of Vi. "I remember how Vi went after Nat. She was so in love she didn't mind making a fool of herself for that man. *You* want to draw your skirts around you and not let life touch you. You seem to stand on the edge, as if you can't work up the courage to dip in even your big toe."

Was she really like that? Millie wondered. She explained. "It's just that I always felt my music should come first."

"Women do need something of their own," Clovia admitted. "I believe that passionately."

"So do I," Eloise echoed. "It's horrible to be totally dependent on a man. But that shouldn't mean we have to miss out on marriage"

"Not miss out, just wait for the right man," Millie asserted.

"Sometimes the right man doesn't come, and we must choose from those available." Clovia reached to her hair to reaffix pins.

"Look who's talking, Clovia. You waited until almost age thirty."

"I took a big risk and got lucky."

Their conversation was interrupted when Mrs. Durham came back. "I've put you on the program, Millicent," she said. "We'll have a sing at the opening session, and another to close the weekend. I'm so grateful you're willing to do it."

Millie dropped her ribbon onto the table. "If you'll all excuse me, I'll go practice."

She hurried home, ate a quick lunch, and brought out her song books, skimming through to look for the right songs. She did her finger-limbering exercises, and then learned new songs. Happy to be at her guitar again, she worked until late afternoon.

Bea came home, stood in the doorway, and harped on the familiar theme. "You need to go to Chicago, Millie. Keep that sailor boy happy. Alana agrees with me about it."

"I don't have the money for a trip like that." Millie knew she sounded peevish. She snapped out her words in annoyance.

"Don't be testy. I know Rob paid you well for that three-week stint at Macatawa."

"Severance pay. I can't spend that, there'll be no more where it came from."

Bea made a sour face. "For pity's sake, I give up! You're determined to be an old maid, and no one can stop you."

She flounced out of the room. Nettled, Millie turned the pages in her book, found a song, and worked out the tune.

> If we can't be the same old sweethearts
> Then we'll just be the same old friends.
> For I want someone like you
> Just to tell my troubles to,
> My happiness, on you it depends.
>
> I've known you too long to forget you,
> And my old dream of love never ends.
> Though I fear you can't be mine
> Let us meet from time to time
> And we'll just be the same old friends.

Tears sprang to Millie's eyes; her voice faltered. She couldn't be the same old friends with Charlie, nor with Harold who'd gone off to war. And certainly not with Rob. Since his marriage, her relationship to her brother had changed forever.

She decided she should visit Warren and make sure he remained the same old friend. If asked, her father would forbid the trip, so she wouldn't ask. Just go.

With sudden resolve, she hurried upstairs and wrote a note thanking Warren for his invitation and for sending boat schedules. She told him the trip sounded like fun, and she'd come right after the suffrage meetings ended. She admitted she looked forward to seeing him.

"Your mother and I will be leading the community sing," she added. "Piano and banjo. Too bad you can't be here for our great performance."

She tried to think of something light and funny to sign off with, the kind of thing he could always manage. She discarded several attempts before she came up with, "Yours till the roses bloom again."

It would have been so much simpler just to say, "Love, Millie," but she couldn't bring herself to do that. It sounded too forward.

❦   ❦   ❦

I find it awesome to think that Millie might have made the other decision, the decision not to go. Then Warren would have found another girl, Millie might never have married, and none of us would be here, not me, not Mom or Michael or Marla, not even Gran. I remark on all this to Gran when she arrives, saying how incredibly easy it would have been to change the timeline and put different people in our places, or no people at all. "I guess we should count ourselves lucky to be here."

She takes me off to lunch at Carrow's, which is her favorite restaurant after Denny's. Gran doesn't seem to know there are other restaurants, except for the Big Boy in Petoskey where she spends summers. Mom is always trying to get her to try something different.

Gran studies my multi-colored wrist. "Looks like you made your getaway just in time," she says.

"Not quite in time," I confess. "Kevin took my money. Not that I had much."

"What would you have done if I hadn't been nearby?"

"I don't know. Found a job, I suppose, and tried to earn enough for bus fare. Or cashed in my unused airline ticket." I add, "Sorry I dragged you away from your conference."

She shrugs. "No problem. I gave my speech yesterday."

"How'd it go?"

"Okay." She still eyes me curiously. "Would you like to tell me what happened? Why you seemed in such a hurry to leave Michigan? I heard the Michigan relatives were quite welcoming, and that you were doing interesting research."

"That's true—and I wasn't in a hurry to leave. I was just in a hurry to be with my Denzel Washington look-alike, my hearth-throb throughout high school. Mom and I used to fight about him because I never wanted to accept dates with other guys. Especially not Jonah. I kept hoping Kevin would ask me." Just like Vi with Nat, I realize now. The more things change, the more they stay the same.

"I remember. You never missed his ball game." She looked puzzled. "He can't be so bad, he's the spokesman for that black adoption agency."

"He's not bad, he's just not the man for me. I don't like being told what to do."

"Oh, another Jonah?"

"Not really. Kevin's more daring and adventuresome than Jonah. I think he just wanted to show off and play big shot."

"Not an unusual wish for a man."

"I guess I was as naïve as your Aunt Vi," I confess. "She fell for Natty Nat and I fell for Kevin. The women of our family don't seem to be great judges of guys. Well—except for Millie with Warren."

"Yes, Mother chose well," Gran concedes. "She and Dad had a good marriage. And your mother did all right, choosing your dad."

It's my opportunity to ask the question I've always wondered about. "Gran, didn't it bother you to have your daughter marry a black man?"

She jolts erect. "Ashley, I don't judge people by the color of their skin. Haven't I told you that?"

She had, of course—many times. I point out that other people judge that way. "I mean—didn't any of you think about *us*, what we would have to go through? How people would view us?"

"Someone has to be first, Ashley," she says. "Of course it's hard—but things have changed greatly. When I was young, intermarriage was illegal in many states. Now it's become commonplace. Why can't you just think of yourself as a pioneer? It should be exciting to be a pioneer."

"I'll try, I'll work on it—if my parents don't skin me alive when we get home."

"I'll make a deal with you," Gran said. "I'll put you on the plane for Michigan and not tell your parents about this caper with Kevin, if you'll agree to return to college."

"Ooh, you drive a hard bargain." I grimace.

"I feel you have so much potential, Ashley."

"With forebears like you and Millie, how can I refuse? My problem is, I can't come up with a major when I don't know what I want to do."

"Well, I can tell you one thing for sure. You won't ever find out by working at Taco Bell. If you stay in college, there's a chance you'll discover something to arouse your interest."

"You know what would be fun? To buy and restore Pennington House in Detroit. I can homestead it for a dollar, you know." I surprise myself by saying that; I hadn't really thought about it. I add, "It's a mess but it's basically beautiful."

"Expensive." Gran sips her iced tea. "To restore, I mean. However, there are colleges in Detroit. I'll settle for one of those. You'd have a couple of months to get a room or two livable before school starts."

"I'll look into it. Maybe Doug will help. He'll be in Ann Arbor—that's close, isn't it?"

"Only twenty miles away," she says. "He should like that sort of thing. I hear he plans to be an architect."

The restoration is something that, after initial doubts, I'm becoming enthusiastic about. "I'll have to hire a lot of the work done, but I can find a job."

Gran nods. "Perhaps you can stay with Carr Pennington while you look for work."

I take the diary out of my purse. "By the way, Gran, you'll want this. It's your mother's diary. I've finished reading it."

Gran's eyes light with pleasure. "I read it as a child and later thought it was lost. I'm so glad you brought it with you."

She doesn't know the half of it. I did more than bring it with me; I battled to rescue it. Twice. Once from Terri, once from Kevin. I decide not to boast of my heroics. I still feel an impulse, probably misguided, of loyalty toward my former heartthrob. I smile and nod. Gran reaches out to touch my hand.

"I dragged my feet about all that research," I confess. "Turned out I loved it." I ask her, "Did you know those people, Gran? Vi, Alana and all of them?"

"Of course I knew them," she says. "In my childhood, I spent summers at Stormland." She smiles reminiscently. "Sometime I'll tell you what happened to them."

"Tell me now," I urge.

"Well, Bea married a well-to-do Chicagoan. Rob and Laddie moved to Hollywood where the Royal Mandolin Orchestra performed in a movie. Alana and Menno inherited Stormland."

"And Vi and Don Dexter?"

"They carried on with the construction firm. Edgar was involved in high drama. I can't tell you about that in a few minutes over lunch. That will have to wait for another time."

"Oh, come on, Gran. You've got my curiosity up."

Gran shakes her head. "I need to do justice to that one, and our meal is served." The waitress comes with my hamburger and Gran's Senior Lunch Plate. I sigh. Gran talks about plane reservations, about getting a flight for that afternoon. I realize I'll see Doug again in a few hours. That will be good—I think. Good, anyway, if he isn't mad about my going off with Kevin.

But why should he be mad? He and I had no agreements or understandings; I didn't make any promises to him.

Who knows what the future will bring? Anything can happen if you're open to it.

After lunch we return to the Clairmont to get my bag and check out. To my astonishment, Kevin is in the room. He's standing over my suitcase on the bed and looking baffled. I stop in the doorway and stare. He glances up in surprise. On seeing him, I take a step backward, wanting to protect Gram, behind me. He doesn't seem angry; he looks long-faced and apologetic. He says, "Hey, Ash, where you been? I thought you walked out on me."

"I thought *you* walked out on me," I tell him. "And took my money."

"Nah, I just used your money to gas the car so we could go to Laughlin." He eyes Gran, behind me. His eyebrow quirks; his expression asks a question: who is she?

I introduce them. "Gran, this is Kevin. Kevin, my grandmother. She was in Victorville. I called her and she came for me."

"Hell, you didn't need anyone to come for you. I wouldn't walk out on a woman in the middle of the country. What do you take me for?"

"You disappeared. I didn't know where you went. I had no money. So I called Gran."

"I figured you'd know I went to service the car." He's looking abashed. I notice he isn't so brash in front of Gran.

"We need to hurry, Ashley; the plane goes in just over an hour," Gran reminds.

Kevin's expression grows anxious. He says, "Ash, you don't need to—. Hell, you should know I hadn't planned to—. I mean, what the hell, a lover's quarrel. No big deal, right?"

Just for a moment I'm tempted to step away from Gran and hurry over to hug and console him. I hesitate. I glance around at Gran waiting in the doorway, and glance back at Kevin looking as if he wants me to rush into his arms, as if he's readying his arms for that hug. Tempted, I decide: better not. I don't really trust him, and I'm sure Gran won't be up for a second rescue. Anyway, I gave her my promise.

"Kev, I really need to return to Michigan," I say. "My clothes are there and my hosts expect me. Why don't you use that tank of gas to go on home, and I'll see you in the fall." I go over to pick up my suitcase and try not to notice the forlorn look on his face.

Though uncertain, I follow Gran down the hall to the elevator. I worry that Kevin isn't used to having women walk out on him, and won't welcome me back with open arms.

Oh well, maybe I can find a way to make it right with him somehow. If I decide I want to, that is.

0-595-31735-9

Printed in the United States
20652LVS00005B/97-114

9 780595 317356